A Private and Her Foes

A Private and Her Foes

A Novel of the American Civil War

MARK GALLIK

Santa Fe

Sunstone books may be purchased for educational, business, or sales promotional use.
For information please write: Special Markets Department, Sunstone Press,
P.O. Box 2321, Santa Fe, New Mexico 87504-2321.

Design › R. Ahl

eBook 978-1-61139-626-3

Library of Congress Cataloging-in-Publication Data

Names: Gallik, Mark, 1955- author.
Title: A private and her foes : a novel of the American Civil War / Mark Gallik.
Description: Santa Fe : Sunstone Press, [2021] | Includes reader's guide. | Summary: "During the American Civil War, a young wife does everything in her power to keep close to her husband"-- Provided by publisher.
Identifiers: LCCN 2021048259 | ISBN 9781632933324 (paperback) | ISBN 9781611396263 (epub)
Subjects: LCGFT: Novels.
Classification: LCC PS3607.A4166 P75 2021 | DDC 813/.6--dc23

LC record available at https://lccn.loc.gov/2021048259

WWW.SUNSTONEPRESS.COM
SUNSTONE PRESS / POST OFFICE BOX 2321 / SANTA FE, NM 87504-2321 /USA
(505) 988-4418

Dedication

To my father, Leonard Stephen Gallik, the son of immigrants, who splashed ashore on D-Day plus one, and saw that war to its end.

CONTENTS

Preface

Once again, there arises a period of upheaval. Like so often before in so many other places, a section of a map is demanding its idea of justice, and in the process upsets the delicate balances. But instead of finding a middle ground, the factions continue to muster their forces in order to retain a new boundary, or erase it altogether. And so the bloodletting, with the wounds of 1861 and 1862 remaining open, the horrors of mass violence urged on by the irresistible cadences of blundering cannons.

As the current year approaches autumn, the nation continues to struggle, as do its communities, its families. On every scale, conflict is demanding dire adjustments, though with few assurances of what may come. Thus, as the events in their lives continue at their rapid paces, good people do their best to stumble through the darkness. These are the times.

1 ~ "All Fading Green and Yellow"

"Oh, this tiresome heat," sighs Henrietta Singleton. "Will a cool autumn ever arrive?"

Sitting beneath a small arbor, she fans herself with her straw hat, while the cascading roses about her blast free their pleasing scents. Unfortunately, the blossoms lack the strength and so are unable ease Henrietta's exhaustion, nor can the roses quell the anxieties of her damp brow.

But thankfully, there is more relief at hand—timely and thoughtful in its approach.

"Dear Henrietta, you must not wear yourself so," insists her sister, Georgina, while clasping two crystal tumblers of well water. "Find a better pace."

Caked with soil, a wooden hoe is propped against the bench, while the subject of its toil lies obscured beyond the wall of petals. Yet this can wait, as Georgina nestles beside Henrietta.

"Uh-h, what I long for most is ice," she comments. "If only a runner laden with ice could slink through that devilish blockade."

Clutching a tumbler, a flushed Henrietta forgets her mannered upbringing, instead opting for quenching gulps. "Yes," she gasps, her throat not quite clear for air. "Ice would do wonders."

And so, with their unsupported skirts drooping to the ground, the sisters take a much deserved rest. In spite of a difference of three years, they share an almost identical appearance, though the older Georgina is a tad more hardy. At one time inseparable, their combined charms and daintinesses had been the causes of confusion for many clumsy suitors. Luckily, two gentlemen have avoided the misstep, though the ensuing nuptials parted the McKie sisters by many miles. But even this is proving to be temporary, what with the recent circumstances having united the households of Georgina Shackelford and Henrietta Singleton.

"So much we have had to endure. So much change in so little time," laments Georgina. "If only things could return as they were. I would vow to never complain again."

"Oh, but how thoughtful to have kept up your roses." Henrietta closes her eyes, hoping the sensations will cease those powers of gloom. "Mmm. I do adore them so."

"Then perhaps we should pleasure amongst them more often. Cling to them if need be."

With that, the course of their conversation shifts toward the more agreeable: to Georgina's two small children, to the socials and weddings of previous years, and to the well-being of their near and dear. For all of a few moments the things which need to be forgotten are just that, and a genuine chatter takes hold.

Regardless, as so often before, Henrietta and her sister's diversion proves brief, the skulk of those accumulated concerns and fears being undeniable.

"How is John's day?" inquires Georgina of her brother-in-law.

It's a question which might be posed on an hourly basis. At least this is how Henrietta feels, as she turns to peek through the curtain of petals at the middle of the kitchen garden.

"Yes. My poor John," aches Henrietta. "It wounds me still to see my husband burdened with that horrible limp."

His back to the ladies and just out of earshot, the subject in question stands with the indispensable aid of a carved, orangewood cane.

"But he is getting along better," consoles Georgina with an optimistic dose of reality. "Especially when you recall the beginning of your stay."

"I suppose, Georgina. Though John's recovery has been slow. An agony of slow."

"But it is a recovery. Surely, you can see?"

With a rigid smile, Henrietta looks at her sister. "Yes," she murmurs, and then returns toward her husband. "He was much worse."

Stoically, John Singleton is attempting to put himself to good use. Dressed without a coat, his green linen vest is a bow to the broiling sun, as are the rolled up sleeves of his collared shirt. A brown, slouch hat covers John's head, adorned by an acorn-ended, yellow cord and a silver, Lone Star pin, thus giving hint to his current occupation. However, to don cavalry boots is too painful an exercise for a stiffened soldier on the mend, and so he wears a pair of brogans. Keeping with the trends, John's brown, blonde-streaked whiskers prosper upon his face and neck. And because of his recent travails, his tall frame of not quite 30 years has been thinned, his confinement giving him a pale tinge. Above all else, John longs to burst free, to be able to carry on as before and not be of any burden.

Even so, among Henrietta's neatly furrowed rows of Irish potatoes, he seems frozen as he stares into the distance. Whereas only minutes before John's concerns were for the mangled leaves of a nearby pepper plant, now his receptive eyes are focused upon a stark reminder of a far greater conflict.

Beneath the bluff and well beyond the Shackelford property snakes the Colorado River, John's view being of a vast valley of fertile alluvium and lucrative ends. The skies are blue, and the distant fields "all fading green and yellow," while specks of white cotton speak of a root cause to the nation's struggle. This is a truth never lost upon John, as he stands and gazes in disbelief. Had he had any clout, a more logical solution than that of war would have been cobbled. Instead, the courage and wisdom of peaceful compromise have given way to fanaticism. From both the North and the South, the hotheads of the day are having the loudest say, and John, like the many thousands of his comrades, is left with no choice but to defend his home. Now crippled, perhaps for life, he can only shake his head at what to him has become a shameless pity.

Be that as it may, the problem at hand does lie with that of one particular pepper plant. If indeed, it is endangered, then so are its varied neighbors, the end result being of less tasty meals to come. Resuming his steps, soon John spies the telltale signs of numerous droppings scattered about the fastly decimated plant. There can be only one explanation, and sure to form it is, as the sole culprit is spotted in the shade of the very leaf it is devouring. Content at its task is a tobacco hornworm, its size nearing three inches and growing rapidly. Beyond doubt, if the future crop of peppers is to be saved, John has but one course of action to take.

"You know, this morning he wrote a handful of letters," reveals Henrietta. "To department officials, though one for Colonel Parsons. He wants so much to return, even in his condition."

"How can that be?" asks Georgina. "For John to want to regain the saddle? So soon after Goodrich's?"

"Oh, I suppose one could always blame that manly dash. Though with John there is so much more." Henrietta takes the last gulp from her tumbler. "He may conceal it, but he suffers his guilt. His brothers, poor Frank and Simon. To have them left behind in that far country. Defending of a cornfield? And to be buried without ceremony? I could not suffer the loss of one to that. My John has had to do so for two."

"I cannot see them ever returning home," consoles Georgina. "Or that we can pay our proper respects."

The sentiments are heartfelt. However, Henrietta presses a more judicious case.

"My dear brothers are gone now, so I must insist upon my concerns for the living. You and yours, myself and mine." Bitterly, she shakes her head. "I wish the war would end tomorrow, whatever that may bring. Let the Lincolnites rule us all. I care nothing for this country. I only care for my John and all my kin."

In her own way, Henrietta's protest is an outburst, of which Georgina attempts to soothe. "Hush now, Henrietta. You cannot really mean that?"

"Oh yes, I do." Certainly, were it not directed at her sister, Henrietta's response would be angered. "To think that I came within a hair's breadth of becoming a widow. Before I could give that dear, charitable man a child of his own. He is the end of his line, of course."

"Oh, Henrietta."

"You know, Georgina. I ought to be thankful he was hurt so. For now, he is with me, safe at home," expresses a wistful Henrietta. "I should fear the day when he will be rid of that dreadful cane."

With a gentle, but firm stroke from his cane, John loosens the hornworm from its diminishing perch. It certainly is a striking creature—puffy fat within its brilliant green skin. Notwithstanding, being venomless, its profoundly titled appendage is useless, save to frighten away the uninitiated. Of course, behind the beauty of the worm's fierce look lurks its main weapon—a voracious and unrelenting appetite. And it's of this to which John must react, in spite of being impressed by the sheer volume of damage. Without toying, he examines briefly his captive at the tip of his cane. Then, with both a plunging and grinding motion, a calm and merciful John dispatches the offending insect.

For the five years of their marriage, Georgina and her husband William have resided in Bastrop, Texas. A reliable man who has served in many capacities, currently Captain Shackelford is away on frontier duty, thus leaving Georgina in charge of the couple's house and holdings. Pin neat, with its original coat of white paint still sheening beneath the sun, the Shackelford home is adorned with just the right touch of carved corners, sharp gables and cleverly fluted columns. And although cramped inside, especially with the activities of two inquisitive, little girls, its exterior is made spacious by a wide, lengthy porch to bear the withering summer. As for the grounds, it takes up half a city block, and along with nearby lots remaining vacant, there's ample room for a resident to roam.

A wealth of space is a fine description for Bastrop, itself. Situated on fertile land and bordered by a gangling forest of soft timber, with a river serving to ship cotton to eager mills both faraway and abroad, its continued prosperity should be certain.

Yet the times have been altered dramatically, as the misfortunes of war are sapping the fortunes of a region. Now, its issue must be hauled overland to neutral Mexico or entrusted into the hands of daring blockade runners—prolific profit cutters all.

Still, it remains remarkable how people will endure the physical shortages—the lack of niceties and necessities. A collective stubbornness with its endless assortments of adaptations can take hold of a community. If need be, ersatz coffee can be brewed from charred peanuts, newsprint fashioned from wallpaper and home panaceas substituted for manufactured medicines. Indeed, with scant sustenance the senses can be held at bay for years on end, so long as there is a reasonable promise of relief.

Unfortunately, a disastrous summer has dashed many a faith of convictions. Not only has the celebrated Army of Northern Virginia been thwarted, but with the dual collapses of the bastions at Vicksburg and Port Hudson, a country has been split apart. Now with the Mississippi River under Union control, Texas is but a nominal part of the Confederacy, the result being that a rural people are left to fend for themselves in an ever-expanding modern world.

Into this fray entered one Captain John Singleton of William Parsons' Cavalry Brigade. Goodrich's Landing isn't a memorable place, it being little more than a mound near the Mississippi in northern Louisiana. Nevertheless, the Union forces had placed there a weak fortification and their stranglehold around Vicksburg warranted some sort of diversionary move. Thus Goodrich's Landing is where John would meet a piece of his fate.

It wasn't much of a shot, one whistling over the heads of its intended and traversing another five hundred yards. At that instant, John was leading his dismounted company to take up its position on the line. Still, that one wayward Minie ball retained enough of its velocity and all of its weight, enabling it to tear a terrible wound into the upper thigh of John's right leg. Indeed, the severity was such that not only was John nearly deprived of his symmetry, he came very close to losing his life. For a long while he languished in a squalid hospital in Monroe, teetering between there and the netherworld. Then, almost by chance, some of the signs of recovery began to appear and the surgeons in charge decided to make room for the dying. Instead of being laid to rest, in early August John was sent to Texas so that he might find it.

Of course, time is the greatest healer of them all, and the passing of a few uneventful weeks allows the Shackelford household to continue its adjustments and establish more routines. Another Saturday evening approaches, and as is the case with their neighbors it promises not to be as sociable as it once was. Today's gatherings are more intimate, with their small conversations as opposed to assemblages of lively music, crowded tableaux and bountiful refreshments. Migrating to the porch in order to enjoy the breezes are Georgina and her charges, soon joined by her young servant Mairead, a former resident of Houston who also pitches in at two other Bastrop households.

As for John, bit by bit he is returning home, looking fitter from his loving care and consistent diet. With a fine Navarro County upbringing and a higher education from Rutersville and Transylvania Colleges, his background is of the teaching profession—at three institutions over the span of five years. And in spite of this calling being shortened by a law practice in San Antonio, untangling the morass of Spanish land grants and representing German merchants and Polish farmers, John still carries those academic urges.

Not quite two years in age, Martha perches on her uncle's useful lap, while older sister Mary, four, sits to his right, taking charge of his cane. Mairead, too, is eager to be taught as she holds Martha's left hand.

"Once more, girls. *Oikos,*" instructs the schoolmaster.

"*Oikos,*" comes the dutiful, although befuddled, reply.

And amused are mother and aunt while they tend to their knitting, their smiles justified as it's more than apparent that John is slipping into his old ways.

"Excellent, girls. Pardon me. La-a-dies."

The class responds with giggles.

But if John can revert to his former self, then it's incumbent upon Henrietta to do much of the same. "Dear. Do you suppose your pupils may wish to try their hand at English? Perhaps with the alphabet?"

"Hmm? My plans were to conduct some arithmetic. Followed by a little Homer. Although?" John turns to the girls. "Ladies?"

Having led a deprived life, Mairead may be confused at the offer of an unconditional choice. "I don't know, Captain Singleton," she replies with her gentle Munster accent.

As for little Martha, she gives a shrug and defers to her older sister.

With the aid of a lovely lilt, Mary is capable of reciting all twenty-six letters in their prescribed order. Nevertheless, said ditty is a delightful one and her pick is known to all. Soon, the lesson shifts to the alphabet—that is to say, the English one.

"A, B, C..."

To the enjoyment of everyone, Mary and Mairead perform splendidly, as does Martha, whose mumbles keep the rhythm. But as for John, he, too, fails to stray.

To be sure, such unwavering devotion deserves a reward, and for the moment Henrietta suggests to her husband a free hand. "Dear. Might you tell us a story?"

"A grand idea. Ladies? Would you like to hear a story?"

The "yeses" are resounding.

"Very well."

Scratching his chin, John searches through his repertoire, and in anticipation the girls nestle ever closer.

"Mary. Careful," reminds her mother.

The sun has given its all, and already Georgina has lit a candle lantern.

"I believe I may have something. A tale concerning honor and tragedy. Of keeping a promise-made in spite of the sufferings. All I am about to tell did happen, hundreds and hundreds of years ago, thousands and thousands of miles from here." John embellishes his expressions. "This was before there was an America. Before riverboats or potatoes, cigars and pipes. Chocolate! By thunder, before men even wore trousers!"

"Hoy, Captain Singleton! What did they wear?"

"Why a skirt. Much like yours, Mairead." John pauses for the snickers. "And the only manner ladies and gents could set themselves apart was that very few of the women had whiskers."

This time the pause is for Henrietta and Georgina, as they both roll their eyes.

"A long time ago, there was a king from France by the name of John. And another king from Mother England. Edward. Between their countries there had built over the ages a grand disgust, leading to a war that would rage on for a hundred years. You see, King Edward, with small cause, invaded France with his army of armored knights and archers. Bows and arrows. Why, you may well ask? This is a puzzle, though he seemed a most slippery character and his English were men steeped in perfidy and greed. Poor old France stood in their way. But there is no confusion that..."

Suddenly, a scuffling of leather soles to compacted clay is heard in the background, pricking the ears of all assembled. Before John's story can continue, the noise's shadow appears from the darkness of the street.

"Captain Singleton. Is that you?" it beckons. "Mrs. Singleton? Mrs. Shackelford?"

"Yes?"

"This is me. John Gaunt."

"Mr. Gaunt," replies Georgina. "What a pleasant surprise. Please come and cultivate amongst us."

Although by its nature the candle is weak, there's enough dim in it to show that the figure is, indeed, who it says. Doffing his hat, Gaunt steps onto the porch and reaches to shake John's outstretched hand.

"Pardon my intrusion upon your little soiree."

"Nonsense, Mr. Gaunt," insists the hostess. "Your company is always welcomed. Mairead was about to bring out a pitcher of lemonade."

"Ma'am, how can I resist your generous offer?"

"Wonderful. Girls, go help Mairead and allow Mr. Gaunt to have your seat."

"Thank you, Mrs. Shackelford. Mrs. Singleton. Captain, how have you been?"

"Much better, sir. What with the gentle concern of these fine ladies and the regard of your gracious town."

As the girls skip away, the guest takes his seat. A well-known figure in the county, though not from a large accumulation of wealth, John Gaunt is a man who seems to be everywhere, is seen with everyone, and is at once in on everything. Middle-aged and always neatly attired with a silk hat and frock coat, he's long been a kind of gathering house for rumor and news. Indeed, it wouldn't be inaccurate to say that sorting through said information and distributing it at his leisure is Gaunt's life's work.

"Glad to hear this. Such an honor, Captain, that you chose our humble town to make your recovery."

"Indeed, sir, it has been fortunate for me. Though I must

complain, at times I do feel lost. What with events fluttering by without my knowledge." John, of course, is well aware of Gaunt's reputation.

"Perhaps I might be of assistance," begins Mr. Gaunt with a chomp at the bit. "Captain. Ladies. I assume y'all have heard of the events at Sabine Pass?"

"Oh, yes," answers Georgina. "What a splendid victory."

"Perhaps that General Banks fellow will think twice before trespassing upon our soil again, Mrs. Shackelford. Yes, indeed." Gaunt pauses. "But it does sadden me to say, we have seen some failures."

"Oh, dear." Georgina's face turns sour. "Yet more failures?"

"Yes. Little Rock's fall being foremost."

"Little Rock? How could this have happened, Mr. Gaunt?"

"Well, ma'am. That might be hard to spell. Though it is certain its defenders were overwhelmed, but word has it two Arkansas generals fought a duel that came to a mortal wounding."

"Heavens!"

"Can you imagine how this affected the spine of our boys?"

"Of course, Mr. Gaunt," agrees Georgina, shaking her head. "What were those gentlemen thinking at such a dire time? Tsk, tsk. How thankful that our Texas generals would never attempt to assassinate one of their own."

John knows better than to agree wholeheartedly with his sister-in-law's assumption. As for Arkansas generals, since he's aware of only one or two who ever displayed any sort of competence, what's it to him if they want to reduce their numbers—the fewer the better? After all, his concerns press closer to his loyalties.

"Sir. By chance have you any word of Colonel Parsons? Of the Nineteenth?"

"Oh. Forgive me, Captain. Hmm? Not much, it seems. They remain in Louisiana. Though we must consider the possibility of they being sent north to meet the threat." At this point Gaunt remembers his setting. "Ladies, let me say that we are not in peril."

Although John's thoughts are being pushed elsewhere, he hears enough of Gaunt's reassurance to add some of his own. "Yes, Little Rock is leagues away."

"Mr. Gaunt, has there been news of merchandise coming in from the coast? Or the border?"

Up to now an inconspicuous Henrietta has been silent. The talk of war makes her jittery, to which usually she blocks out or at least deflects.

"Why yes, Mrs. Singleton. As we speak, goods are moving to Alleyton from Mexico. Bolts of English wool, not the shoddy. Even some Souchong tea, so I have heard. And there should be more from the other direction, what with a blockade runner sailing into Galveston on..."

Henrietta's attempt, however, is only partially successful, as it's her husband whose thoughts refuse to be redirected. As he gazes at his wife, John's reflections center on Arkansas, a place he knows firsthand is depleted of both food and forage. The questions arise as to how the 19th Texas and the rest of the brigade will survive? Can they be expected to hold their ground against overwhelming forces, and will they be supplied perhaps through Shreveport or Marshall? However, this has been a never-ending conflict of "perhaps," few of which have come to fruition. John knows that if Colonel Parsons' men are not to be furloughed home for the winter, then they are in for a miserable and dangerous time. Indeed, there's nothing he can do, this being a hideous notion sure to be repeating.

Suddenly, the front door comes ajar, with Georgina leaping to her feet and moving to the rescue. In spite of her "help," Mairead has completed her task, and is carrying a charger with its brimming pitcher and accompanying tumblers.

"My, that looks refreshing," proclaims Gaunt. "Such a delightful means to bid our week goodbye."

Sunday is the designated day of rest, and it's of this notion that John takes to heart, spending the after-breakfast hours within the tranquility of the porch. With an upbringing as an occasional Methodist, it's easy for him to lapse with his religion, especially since he holds the belief that God, Himself, has too much on His mind to worry over affiliation. Nevertheless, John does remain flexible, from time to time acting as his wife's sabbatical escort and renewing his promise that the children of their future will be brought up in her faith. Since June, however, he has been blessed with the ultimate of excuses, that being the need to regain his strength and equilibrium before facing the rigors of a sermon. Once again, and to his relief, John is to be left behind while the ladies do their worshiping.

As for Henrietta and Georgina, they love their Episcopal Church. Unfortunately, there is no such congregation in Bastrop, and the Presbyterian Church which makes for an intolerable substitute is a charred ruin—the result of a recent lightning bolt from the heavens. For this Sunday, and the many to come, Methodism will have to do.

This remains the only day for Henrietta and Georgina to shine at their best. There's much work involved, as their preparations began late Saturday, only to reconvene at dawn. In addition, there are two squirming, little girls who must be preened and dressed, this process complicated by the absence of Mairead and her duties spent elsewhere.

Be that as it may, what eventually emerges from the chaos inside is worth every ounce of the effort. It's the younger pair of sisters who lead the parade, their frilly petticoats providing much of the cover beneath their short dresses of vertical green stripes. In addition, to better show their sweet, beaming faces, both Mary and Martha have had their light brown hair bobbed and tucked, and their cheeks pinched into a blush. Inheriting the charms of their mother—even at such tender ages—it seems a response is mandatory from their audience of one.

"Will you take a gander at these pretty, little ladies."

Upon hearing the proclamation, Martha twirls on her toes, her skirt flaring outwardly.

"My, I do believe we have a dervish whirling about."

The procession continues, however, as the older pair of sisters begin to negotiate the threshold. The next to appear is Georgina, her crinoline-supported skirt and shapely bodice mimicking the striped pattern of her daughters'. Yet it's above her white collar which most dazzles, her all-around ringlets hanging like the bells of a heavenly carillon. No wonder there has been so much commotion throughout the previous 16 hours.

Still, this is only half of that fuss, for immediately Henrietta comes forth to reveal her tresses of the same style. So skillfully do her springing locks highlight her rounded cheeks of a natural blush, her lips practicing that wonderfully curvaceous allure. Then there's Henrietta's ensemble: an overturned tulip of a skirt in a rose-colored, watermark taffeta, matched with a Zouave jacket of the same cloth upon her white, silk shirt.

In spite of his discomfort, the last of the spectacle brings John to stand at attention, as his eyes stay fixed to the rear of the train and its special enticements.

"My dear Henrietta. As sweet as a dulcimer's notes." John extends his arm for his wife's hand. "Mary, might you fetch my coat and hat?"

The stroll to Calvary Church may have upset the healing process, as has the polite lingering and loitering. Then there was the never-ending service itself. Nonetheless, John has survived much worse ordeals, none of which was followed by the soothing hands of a loving wife.

It's late evening, and everyone has retired from the end of an active Sunday. A ritual of sorts is taking place, an indispensable remedy shielded by its privacy. In no way have the bone and muscles in John's thigh healed, a full recovery being perhaps a lost hope. In addition, the patch of skin suffers from a stitching gone awry, an infection taking its toll, although it is under control. The prescription has been the gentle application of a special salve, a soft rub to make sure the flesh absorbs every smudge of the medicine. Although John could do this himself, Henrietta has insisted, she considering his care to be her responsibility.

After giving his wife a sip of a small brandy and downing the rest, himself, John lies prone on their bed, while Henrietta locates the crock of salve.

"That was kind of Georgina to lend you the dress. I must say, dear, you have never been more handsome."

Her response is the special talent of her captivating smile. Kneeling at the bedside, Henrietta's ringlets jingle as she hikes up John's nightshirt, doing her tender best not to aggravate her husband's pain. Although it has been a full summer, the damage done by that errant Minie ball remains ghastly. Yet the sight of such a wound doesn't bring Henrietta to wax squeamishly, she long ago having forced aside her misgivings.

At first touch John winces, but the magic of Henrietta's fingers, as well as the concoction, alters the soreness and pain. Soon, the sensation becomes quite comforting.

"The healing seems to be advancing," she assesses.

"Mmm," as the feelings are furthered.

With one hand, John frolics his attentions to his wife's hair, fiddling his fingers into those ringlets of light brown. He moves to caress her rosy cheeks, as well as her lips, of which Henrietta uses to buss sweetly her husband's palm. And all the while, she continues to stroke away the horror of Goodrich's Landing from John's wound, distancing his memory from that near-tragedy.

It is a cure, indeed, as her husband's interest is very plain for Henrietta to see. She turns toward his eyes with her soft stare, her look being a beguiling one.

"John," Henrietta whispers. "Stay home. Away from the war."

Their gazes remain fixed, words being meaningless. At this point John's head may be muddled, whereas only hours before it was almost resolute. To be sure, in the middle of this confusion, he lies vulnerable.

On the other hand, Henrietta's mind is perfectly clear. She knows what she wants, and she knows what she must have.

A pleasant impasse takes hold, but then elapses, after which a cool Henrietta comes to her feet. Finding a handy cloth, she wipes away the medicine from her hand. Then, in tempting increments, just as she had done on the night of their wedding, Henrietta lifts free her chemise to reveal all.

The crack of dawn finds the couple in a tight embrace. As usual, Henrietta is the first to awaken, and so takes the opportunity for silent recollection. With tender scratches at John's beard, she tries to recall how he had looked so long ago without it, the day they first met when she was a girl of 12 years and he a college student at 19. Henrietta can smile at how she had become smitten of him and, of course, of how John was so oblivious. Thankfully, those intervening years gave her the chance to blossom, so that when their paths crossed again, after John had dispensed with the razor, her feelings were able to capture the heart of their intended. Has it been five years already since they were reacquainted, Henrietta wonders, since they formed their bond? Has it really been five years of mutual respect and utter devotion, without so much as a bitter word ever having been exchanged between John and herself?

Henrietta could go on like this for hours, especially as she's comforted by her persuasive abilities. With a dose of kind fortune, she knows that she and John will return to San Antonio or to some official post in another safe town. Regardless, all is well, or at the very least is moving toward that end.

But suddenly, Henrietta remembers one minor irritation which could upset her moment's tranquility. It seems that her nieces have the naughty habit of barging in when and where they please, the danger being that the bedroom door has no lock.

"John." Almost at a panic, Henrietta tries to rouse him. "Wake up. We need to don some clothes. John."

"Uh," responds her drowsy husband, who is not receiving the intended message. "Again, Henrietta? Umm. Very well, my dear."

2 ↝ A Twinkling of Stars and a Moon Full of Hearts

There's a serene flatness to this land, stretching into infinity. And because the views are interrupted by only a few, gentle undulations, the horizons, too, are immeasurable. Except for scattered tracts of woods along the streams, the land is dominated by the tall grasses and their weedy cohorts. Year upon year, upon thousands of years, this flora has paid homage to the endless cycles of growth and decay. The result is something of a wonder: incredibly rich soils, which by last measure are many feet deep. Thus the table has been set, and although the ground may be hard and compacted, it begs to be broken.

Indeed, it has, as central Iowa's settlement is more than a dozen years old. Although the scale is vast and the process incomplete, with the state capital having been relocated to nearby Des Moines, civilization's toehold is now knee-deep. As they exist, farms are strewn about in semi-sectional configurations, most adhering to the boundaries of right angles and straight lines. And within this patchwork lies a neat and tidy prosperity—a signature to the clever self-sufficiency of its inhabitants. Understandably so, that because there's ample elbow room, growth is an all-consuming passion.

In their varying degrees, communities are multiplying—gathering places for the offspring of the soil. Such is tiny Buena Vista, north of Polk City, its promises being a draw to those seeking a better life.

Anchored by a water wheel on Terra Bella Creek, a gristmill enables the gathered sheaves to become nurturing loaves. This in turn has helped to establish several other permanent dwellings. There's enough business for a blacksmith to have set up shop, the same being for Shiloh Church, an unembellished stalwart of Calvinism. In addition, small lots have been deeded to a handful of honest merchants, with few questions asked, but future close scrutiny implied. Truly, enough of the natural and man-made foundations have been laid, so that when viewed in the right sort of light, Buena Vista is a good place never to leave behind.

With the prospect of the early fall, one phase of farm life in Buena Vista is coming to a close, to be followed by others. The corn has been cribbed and the wheat garnered, wool flannel woven and woodpiles enlarged. Already, a few of the farmers have turned over their fields of stubble and have had the blacksmith repair their moldboard plows, hay mowers and reapers. Thus, with the long summer's toil at an end, there's the moment to catch one's breath and look forward to what lies ahead. Those ditch repairs and Osage orange hedges can wait, while that pivotal juncture for hog killing and its lard-related industries remains months away. Indeed, with these anticipations hovering over Buena Vista, the time may be as fitting as any for a young couple to exchange their vows and take a plunge into divine matrimony.

Suddenly, the door to Shiloh Church opens, freeing its sounds of shuffling feet and joyous voices. Just moments before, Elizabeth "Susha" Pye had taken Sylvetus Potter as her lawfully wedded spouse in a simple, but holy, ceremony. And so now the anxious newlyweds find themselves at the church's entrance, there to linger while the sanctuary empties and their witnesses migrate toward the table of refreshments.

Facing a bevy of congratulations and best wishes, at first glance the couple appear to be an odd match. Holding her posy of daisies, Susha is an inch taller than Sylvie and owns enough rough edges to reveal that this farm girl isn't afraid to take on some of those manly tasks. Still, although the bride may be a tad sturdy, she is worthy of a second look, now that she's being granted that blushing prerogative. Susha may have donned her familiar Sunday dress of a green satinet, but to mark this singular occasion she's topped her crown with a tasty coronet of silk flowers and an attached white veil flowing to the bottom of her bodice. Then there's that tangible radiance, which comes from being the center of attraction, positioned there by her proud escort, who is a year younger. There's little doubt, that on this day, Susha Potter can be described as a girl who is downright pretty.

As the bride emits her glow, she's joined by her sister, Emma. "Oh, Susha. Never have I been so happy," she whispers, sealing the sentiment with a kiss on the cheek.

From head to toe, Emma's dress and appearance are almost identical to that of her older sibling's—even down to the daisies. If it's true that one wedding is the making of another, then she's nothing if not a hopeful broadside.

"Emma, I cannot believe this is happening. That really is Sylvie?"

"Yes-s-s, Susha. Who else?"

"Then I can thank all those twinkling stars that I am now a Potter."

"Me too." Emma almost pines. There are, after all, several Potter cousins to be had.

It should be noted that Susha is not a shy bride, if only because she's known her husband for most of her life. For some time, the Potter and Pye families have been neighbors, even when they resided in Harrison County, Indiana. With such a close upbringing, perhaps it is a foregone conclusion that someday Susha and Sylvie should be married, that no other two could be more suitable for a pairing. Using all logic, this marriage has heaven's approval.

Susha turns to her husband, imparting the warmth of her smile.

"How are you feeling, Mrs. Potter?" he asks, with his own grinning face abutting her ear.

"I never have been better, husband. Never."

"Heh, heh. It all sounds peculiar. Does it not, Susha? Husband? Wife? Mrs. Potter?"

"Yes, it does. But I have a feeling we will get used to it. How proud I am of my new name."

"Susha Potter. A glorious name. Nothing will ever be so sweet."

By the very sound of it, it's a fact not worth debating.

What awaits the newlyweds is the result of Sylvie's search to assure marital bliss, of a dwelling far removed from the confines and complications of his parents' farm. Of course, a comfortable house is preferable, but even a simple cabin would make do for a nice beginning. In the end the choice has come down to a structure consisting of a single room, itself nestled atop a hole in the ground serving as an inadequate cellar. And on the same property there extends an open coal bank, of which is to figure prominently into the rent. As agreed, Sylvie is to excavate enough to fill 40 bins per month to make things square, with the profits taken for any additional coal split evenly with the landlord. Although it may seem grueling, for him the situation is ideal for the talents of his restless labors, with the chance to pitch in at the family farm when needed.

Only a few minutes of sunlight are left when the celebration decides it's had enough of a good time. An impromptu promenade forms, consisting, of course, of the wedding party and a few of the guests, though, quickly, the parents of the bride and groom show reserve and pivot homeward.

Fortunately, a candle lantern is produced to avoid those pits and falls of the rutted, two mile walk, this convenience making it certain that the assembled young people are able to concentrate on one another. Emma in particular shines in the light, her attire making her a very likely candidate. No doubt, she'll dream tonight with a slice of the wedding cake beneath her pillow.

And no doubt everyone is aware of what is about to occur, though propriety limits their mischievous comments to skillful subtlety. Carefully, the single males monitor the reactions of the single females, as this determines just how forward their actions may go. Yet at last, when the parade comes to a halt in front of the cabin, it's one of the married members, older brother Granger, who blurts out what all must be thinking.

"Come on, Sylvie. Give Susha a big kiss. It's what we have all been waiting for."

"Granger," nudges his wife, Eliza.

Emboldened by the dare, Sylvie grasps Susha around her waist and plants a lasting one on the side of her lips. The response from the entourage is one of immediate hoops and hollers, even from Eliza.

However, the surprise of the moment is that it's Susha's turn. Inspired by the accolades, she loops her arms around her husband's shoulders and gives him an even longer kiss square onto his mouth. When, finally, they part, it's Sylvie who lets out the first yell, while a funny-faced Susha ganders at her brother-in-law, protruding her tongue in the process.

"I am in for it now," proclaims Sylvie.

Displaying his manhood, he reaches down to Susha's legs and lifts her off the ground in a cradling hold.

Not to be outdone, Granger does the same to his relenting Eliza. And before any of the other young ladies can utter a protest, all find their feet dangling in the air. Especially so is Emma, who very nearly leaps into the arms a convenient beau.

But while soon the other young gents set free their captives, Sylvie maintains his grip. Swinging his bride with so much careless glee, he reveals a good portion of Susha's white, lisle stockings. Yet there's no undue notice of this accidental immodesty, particularly from the fellows who have received already plenty of thrills. Before long, things manage to calm themselves.

"I think we better leave these lovebirds alone," announces a timely Granger.

With that, the boisterous group begins their departure, as if they know that to linger would be intruding. Emma is the last to leave, giving her sister a peck on the cheek and a tender goodbye. Within minutes, the noise of the celebrants fades toward Buena Vista.

All the while Susha remains in her husband's cradle, for she's not a burden to Sylvie. Still, being left alone, the couple have little excuse to remain as they are.

"Maybe I should carry you across the threshold?" It's more of a request than a behest.

"Yes. We should go inside."

Fortunately, Sylvie remembers where he left a shallow dish of lard and twisted rag. After carefully placing Susha's feet to the floor, he feels about until he locates it.

With good reason there's an awkward silence as the room becomes dimly lit. Susha's quite familiar with the cabin, she having done her share to set it straight, especially in repairing the chinks. But also she has some idea concerning the rudiments of what's to come. Locating the bed, she walks to its side and begins to disrobe, this being a long, drawn-out process.

Enthralled, her husband stares in a frozen excitement.

"Sylvie," admonishes Susha. "Turn around."

"Oh. Yes. Sorry."

When she's down to her chemise and drawers, Susha slips into the wall-supported bed, removing the rest of her clothes beneath the safety of the covers. It's there that she's joined by a heedful Sylvie. No words are spoken, there being little reason. For this couple the night might last forever, its events happening more smoothly if taken at a snail's pace. With soft gazes, husband and wife lie stretched, facing each other in a nod to hesitancy. And though motionless, their bodies give weak trembles in ready for what each is about to relinquish. However, before the hands of the clock weaken, ever so slightly it's the man of the house who takes charge. At first he loosens and strokes Susha's flowing hair, after which the couple cuddle gently, advancing slowly to heavy kisses and embraces. Then, when all feels just right, when both are surer than sure, they finally...

"Ouch."

"Sorry."

"It's all right."

Like the multitudes of God's creatures abiding before them, Susha and Sylvie have taken that first step toward prosperity and creation. For the time being, passion's duty has run its course, and the couple lie side by side as they stare at the ceiling. The clay-plastered fireplace remains unlit and so the cabin is filled with a slight chill, forcing the two to huddle beneath the covers. Still, there's no sleep for Mr. and Mrs. Potter, their heads being flushed by the dizzying array of the day's affairs.

While Sylvie talks of the wedding, Susha's mind drifts to those apprehensions which are the privilege of every wife on her wedding night. Certainly, with all of their years together, she feels comfortable—more so than other brides. And should the notion of her husband's youth begin to bother, Susha can flay this with the knowledge that nearly all of her and Sylvie's kin are but a middling walk away. She's well aware of his industry, that she'll not be wanting, and that he would never make an important decision without first consulting her, an example being the cabin. Above all, however, is a genuine love forged over a long period of time, an undying desire for each to please the other. More than any one reason, this should be enough to quiet all disquietudes.

"Mmm," mutters Susha. "So this is what it's like to be a married woman."

She may never leave their bed, and demand that Sylvie do the same.

The placid air is soothing, as Sylvie reaches to give Susha a snuggle, of which she's receptive, returning with her share. Unfortunately, before the couple can retrace those steps taken earlier, a crashing commotion explodes from out of nowhere. It sounds as if all things tin and iron are clanging to a disruptive non-rhythm, an instigation coming from one source.

"Granger," growls Sylvie.

With a hand Susha hides her giggles.

And upon seeing her reaction, Sylvie alters his. Sliding out of bed, he crawls to the window.

"It's Granger, for certain. And both of my sisters. And Emma. And there's Robert and Jane." He looks over his shoulder to Susha. "Goodness, there must be ten."

"Brother, have you survived your ordeal!" Along with the cacophony of metal, Granger can be heard for miles. "How is my new sister doing!"

"I think he has had some of the bottle." Sylvie stands from his crouch, away from the window. "Pa would have a fit if he knew Granger was drinking in front of Narcissa and Lucretia. I better put a stop to this."

"Sylvie."

"What?"

"Put your clothes on."

"Oh. Yes."

He walks over to the chair, where hangs his trousers and shirt. With the last of the crude candle glowing from behind, Sylvie is a sight for Susha's attentive eyes. Actually, it's the first time she's seen him naked and his clumsy attempt to alleviate such makes for a comical scene. It can't be helped, as Susha lets out a laugh.

"You better get dressed, too, Susha. I think we are about to do some entertaining."

"But I don't have my nightgown."

"Oh, yes, you do. Granger's doing all his shouting from atop your chest."

The ensuing soiree lasts for more than two hours, during which a tactful Sylvie manages to confiscate the whiskey bottle from his brother's hand. And after reminding Granger that he should be returning home to his wife and child, and thanking everyone for bringing along Susha's chest, the hints are accepted. None too soon, the newlyweds with their arms around one another wave goodbye to their guests, whose lanterns flicker away into the darkness.

"Now what was that, you laughing at my nakedness?"

Susha giggles.

"Well, just wait 'til I start seeing you."

Her reply is a raised brow and a sly grin. Taking his hand, Susha leads her husband back to the cabin.

"Wait." Turning the bottle, Sylvie empties its contents onto the ground. "Now, to bed."

With much relief, the first month's rent is paid in full. Still, filling the five log bins eight times over is a more arduous chore than anticipated, especially since Sylvie is required to help load the wagon for its Polk City rounds. The reality is undeniably harsh, that there's not going to be much opportunity for other endeavors. Nevertheless, the couple has managed to construct a warm, roomy coop for Susha's chickens and also repair some worn furniture, thus making their cabin more livable. In addition, Sylvie is finding a little time to work at the family farm, in the process garnering some precious provisions for the winter ahead. Unfortunately, there's much more that the couple needs in order to maintain an independent household, be it so small. Although their families are willing to pitch in, the prideful gaps will have to be filled by Sylvie's coal money—one tedious, backbreaking cartful at a time.

Since it's too late in the year for Susha to begin a garden, she's had an overabundance of time. The result is a cabin turned immaculate—a stark improvement over the occupancy of the previous tenant/laborer, who one fine day had enough of mindless drudgery and volunteered for the Union Army. Meticulously cleansed, curtained, arranged and rearranged, the little home has attained a tidiness which before would have been deemed impossible. Indeed, Susha has every reason to be proud. Still, one room cabins can be enhanced only to the point of wasteful repetition, and the young Mrs. Potter is much too thrifty to allow this.

At least Susha can knit and sew—at any place and at any time. Certainly, she has plenty of material, all having been spun and loomed over the summer by her own adept hands. And since it makes little sense for her to spend the day confined within the cabin, as of late, Susha has taken her wool cloth and yarn to join her husband at the coal bank.

With the cloud cover, the sun's blaze is lessened, as Susha sits on a stool, concentrating on her stitching. In spite of the fact that she lacks the dainty fingers, each movement is swift and flawless, a perfection resulting from years of practice. And since it was Susha who clothed her younger brothers and father, the transition into doing the same for a husband is a cinch task. Soon, Sylvie will be the proud wearer of a splendid pullover shirt, fashioned from a red and white checked, homespun flannel.

For the moment, however, upper garments are strictly superfluous, as the heat generated by Sylvie's strenuous toil is forcing him to strip to the waste. Regardless, there is no immodesty, for he's in good and familiar company, and is free to carry on in exhausting comfort. Already, the pick axe has done its work and Sylvie is shoveling the black lumps into a two-wheeled cart.

"Well, Susha. What are we going to do with our coal money?" It's a much-posed question.

Without losing her train of thread, Susha gives her established reply. "You know I want to fill up the cellar, first thing. We are down to half a basket for the chickens."

"I know." Sylvie stops working and leans on his shovel. "But after we take care of that?"

"Hmm?"

"I was thinking. We should own a horse. We are the only couple in the county without one."

"Likely."

"With a horse I could buy you a sidesaddle. No more walking for your visits. And I could buy a few acres. Turn it over to be ready for spring planting." Sylvie's ambitions gain momentum.

"How much is all that going to cost?"

"Ugh. I suppose I need to dig as much I can." To which Sylvie returns to his shoveling.

The cart filled to just above a manageable level, Sylvie strains to haul it to the bins by the road, leaving behind Susha and her sewing. It's a grind to move the wheels and to keep the balance. Nonetheless, as always, Sylvie negotiates that first crucial incline, disappearing to the other side.

The struggle's not lost upon Susha, especially since her husband retires each day in a more and more exhausted state. Poor Sylvie, working himself into a frazzle so that she might have the comforts. Yet as far as Susha is concerned, already she's comfortable, this being the problem. Thus, with her conscience feeling gnawed, there's no consideration to put aside her needle and thread.

What a mighty weapon it is, the axe. Cautiously, Susha examines the business end, running her fingers along the fine curve of rigid iron. How solid and unforgiving it seems, including the long, hickory handle. Thus a tingle touches Susha, she considering the stamina to wield such an appendage, the forces reckoned.

Lifting the pick axe on high, she finds a target and allows the heavy tool to do the most of the work. Crunch! and a chunk of coal is loosened from its earthen grip. Amazed at her success, Susha takes another wack, and another and another, as a little pile forms. As much as the pick axe allows, soon she finds herself working into a steady frenzy, bellowing out the grunts and groans of exertion for those greater successes. Although she may be tiring and feels the blisters, Susha becomes excited at the pleasing results oozing forth.

"Susha," shouts her husband, he having returned from the bins. "Put that down."

"Sylvie," she replies with all innocence. "I just want to help."

"This is man's work, Susha. You ought not be doing that. Somebody might see you." Abandoning the cart, he hurries to her side. "What would they think?"

"Nobody can see."

"Come now, Susha. You know what I mean. It's just not right."

"Sylvie." From her sleeve she frees a handkerchief and wipes his wet brow, and then does the same to hers. "You know I always have been good at helping out. I cannot chop that coal as good as you. But when that axe is idle, why should I not swing it a few times?"

"Susha."

"And the quicker we get the coal, the sooner you can buy me a horse and sidesaddle. My feet sure are tender from all that walking." With her tongue she better moistens her handkerchief to remove the grime from Sylvie's chin.

"Susha."

"Or I could help you push that cart," she replies, as she continues her preening.

"No. Then somebody is sure to see you." Feeling pinched by his wife's logic, Sylvie has little choice but to pause and reconsider. "Well-l-l. I suppose there would be no harm. But don't you dare hurt yourself, Susha Potter. I mean that."

"You need not worry, Sylvie. I promise," she assures, surrendering his implement with a look of profound satisfaction.

As with nearly all parts of the country, central Iowa does its best to keep the Sabbath sacred. However, more so than most, the local economy compels its people to put every waking hour to good use. Sunday isn't for worshiping only, as also it's laid aside for the rejuvenation and socializing which the constraints of normal workdays won't allow. With this in mind, after the fire and brimstone has run its course, a multitude of Potters, including the newlyweds, are assembled at the home of Sylvie's parents.

Thanks to the chickens who sacrificed their lives for the greater good, Sunday's meal is bountiful. It also goes without saying that there never will be a shortage of the starchy dishes in this region, and that, indeed, the land does overflow with buttermilk and honey. Today's dessert is an apple pandowdy, baked with the remnants of last year's harvest. Still, in spite of the yearly surpluses of Winesaps, Russets and Ben Davis', there is no cider production at this farm. Mr. Potter doesn't look kindly upon alcohol, or for that matter, tobacco. In fact, he doesn't allow coffee or tea, or anything to do with stimulants. It goes without saying, that although the atmosphere around the Potter farm is healthful and wholesome, it's also rigid and austere.

This, too, is Susha's upbringing, the household of her childhood being like that of her husband's with only a different mix of siblings.

Since the dinner conversation consists only of mastication—a word can't squeeze itself in edgewise—it's the aftermath which must make up for the silence. Soon, the men migrate to the comfort of the sun, while the ladies return to their busy "day of rest." Thus there's plenty of opportunity for palaver, especially with Mr. Benjamin Pollard, mill operator and purveyor of strong opinions, and his wife being invited guests. As for the young children, they have dashed off to a far corner, to be less likely seen or heard.

Then there's Susha, who accepts the duty of wiping dry piles of rinsed dishes. As much as anything, the rubbing of cloth to ware allows her to roam about the kitchen, all the way to its open, rear door, where she positions herself almost midway between two disparate conversations:

"How does the government expect me to sell them my crops, when they're not willing to pay a fair price?" complains Mr. Potter. "I run no charity. I only sell to the best offer. Now that the Mississippi is open, our crops can be sent down there, like before."

"What with labor being short, you think the government would pay more," joins Ben Pollard. "Make it fair for our hardships."

"I could sow some acres of oats for them. But they would surely short change me if I did," adds Matthew Potter, Sylvie's uncle. "And do it with vouchers."

The men nod their sentiments in unison, as if rehearsed from previous Sunday confabulations.

"War sure has affected the price of horseflesh," furthers a strangely pensive Granger.

While Susha eavesdrops, her eyes stay fixed upon her husband.

As for Sylvie, he returns the favor, but with those subtle facial gestures that say he'd just as soon be elsewhere with his wife than be a party to this parley. However, the women have their place and the men have theirs, and for now all the young couple can do is exchange smirks.

"Did you hear what happened to the Taylor boy?" offers Mrs. Potter.

"Yes, the poor thing. Passed away at that St. Louis hospital," answers Mrs. Pollard.

"Oh dear. From what?" asks Sylvie's Aunt Mary.

"Came down with the flux." Mrs. Pollard is privy to everything coming through the mill. "He would not get better, so he was moved upriver from his camp. But the poor boy perished."

"Such a shame, with the war nearly done," continues Mrs. Potter. "Where was that camp?"

"Helena, Arkansas, I was told."

"Mercy. We hear so many terrible stories about that place. You remember, the Dinwiddie boys were sent there. Thank goodness the army moved them elsewhere before they got fluxed."

"At least the men will come home soon," speaks Narcissa. "Now that the war is playing out."

"Yes," adds Aunt Mary. "Thank goodness for that."

Continuing their playful duet, Susha and Sylvie all but ignore the proceedings around them.

"When I would not sell my corn to that agent, he started to threaten me. I told him my stock comes before him and to get off my farm."

"Why do they send our poor soldiers to that place, when they know about the sicknesses there?"

"So they want all my corn. But how do they suppose am I to winter my sows and fatten my shoats?"

"I think we have lost enough boys to this unholy war. Should we send any more?"

"Things sure would not get done if my sons were away."

"I just give thanks my sons have stayed out of it."

The young couple's silent signals persist, as do the mimicking impressions of their elders.

"Susha," beckons her mother-in-law. "Do you think that plate is dry enough?"

Compelled to abandon her post, a shrugging Susha smiles to her husband. Poor Sylvie, for he, too, has no choice but to listen to all the blither and carping, and do so with the look of interest.

By early evening the young Potters bid their goodbyes, affording them the chance to make a quick stop at the Pyes. Since it was only in the morning that Susha spent three grueling hours with her family at Shiloh Church, the visit proves brief. As it happens, the Potters stay long enough to pass along the Pollard tittle-tattle, this being a usable commodity. Still, by the time Susha and Sylvie step out of her parents' front door, the night has taken hold.

Graciously, a full moon lights the way to their cabin, and at the end of a long day they're together alone—arm in arm at a pace of their own making.

"What were the women really talking about?" asks Sylvie.

"Oh, mostly about the war and such."

"Hmm?"

"You mean the men were not?"

"Oh, I don't know. I was paying them little mind. Just thinking to myself, I suppose."

"About what, Sylvie?"

"Mostly about how grand it would be to have a farm to ourselves. Like our parents."

"Mmm." Susha places her cheek upon Sylvie's shoulder, their stroll missing not a step.

"And I suppose I was also thinking about the war. Someone had to."

Certainly, the ominous topic has been weighing on Susha's mind, and the manner her husband phrases his feeling triggers a smoldering fear. After all, she's all too aware that a restless man of his age is susceptible to all postures of pressure and persuasion. As Susha's feet stop in their tracks, so, too, do Sylvie's.

"Umm," she wisps. "So many empty chairs in these parts."

"I know what you mean, Susha. I heard of another one today."

"So mournful." As Susha continues, her eyes drift to the night sky. "Look at that sad moon, Sylvie. Emma thinks it's full of hearts. All broken." She loops her arms around her husband's neck. "What is it going to take to mend them?"

"Who can say?"

Returning to earth, Susha looks into her husband's face, lit as it is by the lunar glow. "Sylvie," she speaks solemnly. "Promise me to never leave my side. I could not bear being without you."

"Susha? Of course, I promise. Why, I would be lost without you. Leave you alone? You know I could never do that."

"Yes, I do." She clutches him ever surer. "Yes, I do."

Beyond doubt, Susha does, for what she's most certain about her Sylvie is that when cornered with a promise-made, he will keep it. The fact remains, as long as she has known him, Sylvetus Potter never has broken his word.

Sealed with a kiss and a tickled chin, the surest of bargains is struck, and with its details deemed unnecessary, the young couple is able to resume their walk. Indeed, how favorable for a restful day to end without challenge, enabling the new week to have an uncomplicated beginning.

The Potters' marriage begins another month, meaning that an additional quota of coal must be filled. Previously, there wasn't as much surplus as anticipated, nor were there enough spare days for those other concerns. Initially, Susha took up a portion of the slack by brandishing the unused pick axe, though this proved too little. However, leave it to Sylvie—at her prodding—to find a solution. With a few cents, and Susha's pledge never to tell a living soul, he's located a second serviceable pick axe. In addition, so that she might swing it more freely, she's donned a pair of Sylvie's trousers, as well as an overshirt. Thus for several days Susha has been working to her heart's content—at Sylvie's side and amidst the compounding coal dust.

As they take a break, the couple are a filthy, haggard sight. Such is the desire to make a profitable headway that, recklessly, they've abandoned a steady pace. Now, at mid-morning without having a breakfast, Susha and Sylvie are all but spent. To be sure, second thoughts are rearing their ugly selves, as the hardened miners find a seat on a patch of soft grass.

"Susha, I know I should not, but I feel too worn even to be hungry."

"Landsakes, look at our coal pile."

"I don't know. We have worked to the bone and have only just started. Susha, it's not that much coal."

"Ugh." She allows her back to settle to the ground, her face uncaring about the glaring sun.

"You know what we are, Susha?"

"What?"

"Just a pair of slaves. Owned by some Southern chivalry. Excepting, I wager they treat them better than Mr. Bland does us. Look at us, Susha. We could be taken for darkies, you know."

Normally, Susha would feel free to counter such hyperbole, but instead she replies with only a moan. Whether she's too exhausted or is unable to find the suitable logic matters little to her, resignation and indifference being sure signs of slavery.

"I cannot shake lose my doubts, Susha."

"We could always move in with one of our parents."

"No, Susha. And you would have none of that neither. But we need to find a better life. Keep our ears to the wind, so we can hear all the possibilities."

"Umm."

"I don't want us to live like this much longer. The idea of my wife all swarthy and covered in black."

"Sylvie. Sh-h. We can talk about this tonight."

"Umm."

Side by side the couple lie, their aching bones vying with their stretched muscles as to which is the sorest. It's a close contest, these assembled components wilting upon the ground, their energies sapped and awaiting a renewal. Regardless, Susha and Sylvie are able to find a mutual tranquility, undisturbed their comforting becomes from the outside world.

Indeed, the Potters do drift away for a blessed hour, never mind that said outside world is certain to return, and do so with a rush.

"Sylvie!" The faint, unexpected cry is distant. "Sylvie!"

"Somebody must be at the cabin," deduces Susha.

Quickly, Sylvie's attentions are sprung, and with some effort he comes to his feet. "Eliza?"

"What could it be?"

"Something must be wrong. She has little Ethan with her." A spark of tension shoves aside Sylvie's exhaustion. "Susha, wait here."

"Sylvie." Not being one to stay put, she, too, springs.

Almost simultaneously, the couple reach Eliza, finding her in a flustered state. She clutches her bawling Ethan, whose little head must be sensing the worst.

"Eliza! What is wrong!"

"It's Granger!"

"What! What!" Sylvie makes no attempt to calm. "What about Granger!"

"He's gone! What can I do!" As Eliza begins to sob, her pleading words falter, as if they're too afraid to reveal themselves. "Sylvie, he's run off. Granger has run off to enlist."

3 ↜ Three Hundred Dollars or Your Life

From the outset of the war and continuing into what is now its third year, the Union Army has been desperate for recruits. Enlistments haven't kept up with demand, while the Draft of '62 failed in that it placed too much responsibility upon the shoulders of state governors. There's no denying that conscription is a disagreeable enterprise, and that these politicians have sought ways to postpone their drafts, and, of course, play on favors.

There can be but one remedy to this logjam and that is to relieve the governors' burdens with a national conscription, as outlined by the Enrollment Act. Now each congressional district has been assigned an enlistment quota, to be filled before the prescribed hour, or else. No state wants to face the stigma of a draft—especially one with teeth—and so the pressures are being applied. Sub-districts and even communities are feeling the anxieties of conscription's ugly face, forcing them to seek avenues which would lure young men to volunteer three years of their lives. Given this atmosphere, almost anyone from anywhere will suffice.

Some men have the resolve to resist, devising excuses in order to justify their non-enlistments, while others are finding the courage to join the fight and defend their notions of honor and righteousness. Then there are those who have taken to fence-sitting, waiting, it seems, for the blunt impetuses to push them to one side or the other. In all likelihood, it's of this latter group which the Enrollment Act is targeting, setting its sights for a broad volley of enlistments or, if it comes down to it, conscription.

Within the comforts of their cabin, Susha and Sylvie try to soothe their sister-in-law. At least Ethan has ceased his crying, while his quivering mother strokes away his fears.

"Sh-h, Pumpkin. Sh-h," mutters Eliza, taking no notice of Susha's strange attire.

"Here, Eliza." Susha delivers a cup of water and then takes the empty chair at the table.

"When did Granger leave?" asks Sylvie.

"Early this morning. He slipped away without eating breakfast."

"Did he say anything about enlisting?"

"No."

"Then how do you know?"

"I just do, Sylvie." With her handkerchief Eliza blows her distressed nose. "What with all that has been about. Granger's been acting peculiarly."

"Where do you think he went?"

"I have no idea. I was hoping the two of you could help me find him."

Apparently, even in her panic, Eliza knows better than to seek her father-in-law when it concerns the headstrong attributes of her husband. Instead, she's willing to walk the distance and sacrifice a good wedge of valuable time. After all, better to have Granger's diplomatic brother apply the convincing arguments, than allow Mr. Potter to engage in a regrettable one.

"So you want me to bring him back?"

"Will you, Sylvie?" Almost in midstream, Eliza's tears cease.

It takes Sylvie five minutes to make himself presentable, and with the aid of Eliza's nervous hands, Susha is ready in only fifteen. Soon, it's off to the older brother's farm, to saddle one of his mounts and begin a harried search. Since Susha is asserting her right to accompany, the march is one of three abreast, with she supporting Eliza and a tired, sleepy Ethan grasped in the arms of his uncle. In spite of a hastened pace, it promises to be a long walk.

Retracing the foot prints she's laid down many times before offers Susha the chance to ponder silently. What could Granger be thinking, to leave his wife and child knowing that they would be reduced to such a state? Surely, he must realize that this may be the beginning of a sad, painful downfall, that he's heard of soldiers' families suffering the woes of threadbare poverty? Still, Susha knows full well that her brother-in-law is but one of many thousands, and so by the sheer numbers of it is almost blameless. For her, the greater fear is that there are still thousands more to go, the appetites of war having no sure ends.

Already, winter's frost has forced itself upon this October. However, today an Indian summer prevails, and by the time Eliza is escorted to her house, her drained strengths can give no more.

On the other hand, Susha's stamina is sure to be tested further.

"I should saddle up a grey." Sylvie wastes no time. "I suppose Granger took the other."

"Sylvie. I want to go too."

"No, Susha. You take Eliza and Ethan inside and look after them.

"Don't worry about us," insists Eliza. "We should be fine."

"Two of us have a better chance of finding Granger," reasons Susha.

"Put the sidesaddle on the roan," suggests Eliza. "She's gentle enough."

Feeling pressed, the best Sylvie can do is to force a compromise. "Very well, Susha. But we will both ride atop the grey, after you see to Eliza."

Minutes later, Sylvie helps Susha upon the grey, she securing her arms around his waist. Although not sure of what's expected of him, at least he has a clue concerning direction. As the couple turns south toward Polk City and Des Moines beyond, the promise of a frustrating day compels Sylvie to set a deliberate gait.

Several miles of silence follow before Susha airs her concerns. "Sylvie, do you know about this?"

He peers behind his tensed shoulders. "I suppose I now know it was coming to this. The things he said."

"Which was?"

"This and that. Mostly his friends that have gone. It all must have gotten to him."

"And poor Eliza was not able to stop it?" asks Susha.

"Maybe she never really caught wind of it. She might have been the first to know, but at the same time was the last. Things can slip passed between a man and his wife, sometimes." Sylvie turns to look forward.

As he does so, Susha constricts her grip, burying her face into the back of his neck. At least for the moment, she's not going to allow anything between them to "slip passed."

No Granger is found in Polk City, and even Des Moines proves empty, though the couple doesn't search the saloons. However, there is a military presence at these towns, ominously so in the form of recruiting details detached from their faraway and depleted regiments. With all her cunning Susha manages to steer Sylvie from these parties, diverting his attention to her, and, at one juncture when his feet stall, forces him to move with a push from her shoulder.

Fortunately, both escape unharmed and are well on their way to Buena Vista when dusk arrives. After passing through Polk City, however, the tired couple need a rest, and in spite of their desire to rush home, they take to the side of the road.

"Sylvie? What are we going to tell Eliza?"

"What we saw and what we did not see, I suppose."

"I wonder how fumed she will be at him?"

"Not half as much as me. We missed a day's work because of Granger. I hope he did enlist, so I don't have to see the sight of him." Sylvie rises to his feet. "Susha. We should move along."

Although the moon is dim, the lighted farmhouses are enough to show the way. Before long, though, even these fade away into a slumber, leaving Susha and Sylvie to grope in the dark.

Soon, however, one beacon does loom, its source being familiar, as Eliza must be awake.

Before Sylvie can dismount, Susha slides free from the grey and waits in front of her brother-in-law's house. With its brief, welcoming porch and exterior of white, board-and-batten siding, it's a tidy, admirable abode. Yet on this occasion she's prudent, and lets her husband do the knocking.

"Come on in, Sylvie." Unexpectedly, it's Granger's voice.

Although surprised, Sylvie's anger simmers as he enters the house, with Susha trailing.

The atmosphere inside is depressed, as Granger and Eliza sit at opposite ends of the dinner table. Twin candles reveal their silent, gloomy faces, while a pot of tea attests to the longevity of their evening.

Almost hidden behind, Susha places her hands on Sylvie's shoulders as he takes a deep breath.

"What has happened, Granger?" he exhales.

Usually, it's the older brother who dominates, but on this night Granger's at the disadvantage, outnumbered as he is. "Sylvie, we should care for the grey, first thing. Eliza, find something for Susha, while we see to it."

Without uttering another word, Granger rushes through the door, obliging Sylvie to follow.

"Susha, are you hungry?" asks Eliza of her diverted guest.

But how dare Granger take her husband away, excluding Susha in the process. "What did he tell you?" she poses, her empty stomach notwithstanding.

Eliza's tired eyes reveal, however, that she's not really in the mood to recite Granger's day.

"Never mind," resolves Susha, as she rushes to the front door to peek at her subjects.

"Susha. Go out the kitchen door to the back of the barn. You should be able to hear it all."

No time is wasted, and with her course thus laid before her, she's in position to eavesdrop.

"Look, little brother. I am sorry what I put you two through today."

"Don't apologize to me. Apologize to Susha." The sharpness of Sylvie's voice makes this term certain.

Susha's knees almost swoon, though her pride for Sylvie props them up all the same.

"Where were you? We went all the way to Des Moines, don't you know."

"I figured that," explains Granger. "No, I went the other way. To Nevada."

"I suppose I don't need to ask why."

"Well-l-l. Yes, I did enlist."

Susha's heart sinks at what already she knows is true.

There's a brief pause, ended by a huff from Sylvie. "I hope you know what you're doing. That you put some thought into this."

Granger gives the grey a pat on its neck, as he removes the saddle. "I knew I would be signing up for a long time coming. Just waiting for the right chance."

"Which was?"

"For a first-rate regiment to come along. When I heard the 5th Cavalry was sending up a recruiter, my mind was made up." Granger's face lights up. "You know what horseflesh means to me. Now I can sit upon a saddle, and not march on my feet."

Sylvie shakes his head. "Fool. You do know you will leave behind your family? What if you got killed?"

From Sylvie, it's a callous term, "killed," the sound sending a chill down Susha's spine.

"That is hardly likely," insists Granger. "The war's almost played out. You know what happened this summer. The Seceshes have little fight left. Besides, you would think twice calling me a fool, if you knew the bounty I signed for."

"Is it worth it?" poses Sylvie.

"Maybe it is, maybe not. Maybe a bounty makes no matter at all." With this recognition Granger becomes a bit more resigned. "I just grew tired of the quailing. How many men my age are still left here? All I know is I feel much better now that I enlisted. That I don't have to carry around a weight any longer."

"Damn."

For Susha, Sylvie's oath is a minor shock. Never before has she heard him use such a word.

"Fairly soon there will be none of your age. And when you turn twenty, Sylvie, the government will be able to draft you, all legal. At least I can say that nobody drafted me but myself. I can live with that."

Biting her knuckle, Susha cringes at the thoughts which have been forced into her head. Damn that Granger. Damn the war.

"Sylvie, we can saddle up the roan, so you and Susha can ride it home. And the two of you have dinner before you leave."

Enough has been heard—mountains upon mountains—

compelling a drooped Susha to sidle away and rejoin Eliza. By a quick bound she's learning exactly how her sister-in-law suffers, the feelings being shared.

Several days have passed since Granger left to join his regiment, this after making the necessary personal arrangements. Nevertheless, being optimistic, in no way has he settled his affairs, but instead created a verbal list to deal with most contingencies. Upon this, the onus for carrying out these functions falls upon Sylvie, for which Susha is thankful. Through it all she is standing up well, though her sister-in-law still sulks and an affronted Mr. Potter remains furious at his eldest son's audacity. As for Sylvie, for the most part he's maintaining a restless silence—contemplative and troubled in its nature.

Before dawn, Susha and Sylvie have breakfasted and are at the coal bank, for the days must be stretched if they're to help out at Granger's farm. Normally, she wouldn't fret over her brother-in-law's absence, he being a source of previous commotions. However, the state of things is unraveling in Granger's wake, the morning cold not tempering Susha's uneasiness.

"I feel worn out already," complains her husband of few complaints.

"Me too."

The sun has yet to warm the air, although its rays light up Sylvie's wistful expression. For him, it matters little that he's exhausted at such an early hour, but it is bothersome that so too is Susha. Hence, instead of grasping the pick axe for another try at the coal, Sylvie let's it slip free.

"Maybe it's time we leave behind this paradise. Move to the farm and take it over. Eliza will not mind, for sure. And I hardly care if Granger does. Susha. We should get cleaned."

With the tempting proposal thus proffered, Susha's axe loosens from her hands, it, too, falling harmlessly to the ground.

There's a certain relief coming from a decision made, and the greater the resolution the more comforting is its release. Susha and Sylvie can afford to spend the rest of the morning in front of their hospitable fireplace, the glowing flames working their warmth. Huddled together, they're drawn into the rapturing charms, the leaping tongues speaking out the wisdom of the ages. However, the fire's missives are brief, arising and retreating in the same instant, and never reappearing in an identical form, thus making for confusion. Still, it is soothing, as the couple chooses to while away the hours in silence.

The solutions come and go, and always the troubles will shadow as the fire begins to flicker away. Having freed himself, Sylvie steps outside in order to plunder a handy coal pile—the longer the morning, the better. However, as he grasps the bucket, his fleeting eyes catch the road to Buena Vista. Two figures on foot are approaching, and with a squint Sylvie discerns that they're both young ladies, ages fifteen and seventeen to be precise.

"Susha! Narcissa and Lucretia are coming!"

Between them they're swinging a large, willow basket, ever so slightly as it's fully loaded.

Sylvie drops the bucket as Susha joins his side, she stretching her waves to make up for the distance.

"What do you suppose is happening?" poses Susha, as she continues flapping.

"Probably Pa is happening," replies a frowning Sylvie. "We should meet them halfway."

Soon, there comes a merge, the result being hugs and kisses. "Are you two cold?"

Although bundled from head to toe, the sisters' exposed and blushed noses suggest a shiver.

"Oh, we're fine, Susha" responds the older Narcissa. "Look what we brought."

"Apple butter and honey," beams Lucretia. "And loaves of bread."

The basket teems with a sampling of the Potters' many specialties.

"Landsakes. We should go inside and have a bite. Sylvie's about to feed the fire."

There's no debate, and as the four walk toward the cabin, Narcissa expands the grocery list. "Sylvie. Pa wants you to come today and pick up some of potatoes and cabbages, and other things. He says you can use the wagon."

"Can it not wait for Saturday?"

"No, he wants to clear out some room today."

Knowing that something is afoot, Sylvie and even Susha give Narcissa a quizzical look.

"This is what he said."

To which Lucretia adds her nod.

After thawing out in front of the fire, as well as stoking their individual furnaces, the four take to the road. As if by tacit consent, or neglect, Susha and Sylvie fail to announce their impending move. Naturally, the talk steers toward Granger, though this proves to be passing as a letter from him has yet to be received. Soon enough, they arrive at the Potter farm.

As it happens, Mr. Potter is busying in full view. Wasting no time, he forces a wedge as if to divide.

"Girls, go in the house and help your mother. You, too, Susha."

To this they obey without breaking stride. Nevertheless, before she's compelled to shut the door behind her, Susha manages to maintain a fleeting contact with her husband. Her loud, gaping eyes give a warning to his that he's not to leap from his respectful bounds, that a son's place is to listen and absorb, rather than deflect and argue. Perhaps more than anyone, Susha understands that delicate situations need not heated words to decide their conclusions.

"Not the root cellar, Sylvie," directs Mr. Potter. "Under the house."

The words barely touch Susha's ears as she walks through the parlor toward the kitchen. However, the significance takes a firm grasp, she realizing that her husband and father-in-law will hold their meeting in the house cellar, lying beneath her very feet. Quickly, Susha improvises.

"Morning, dear," greets her mother-in-law, while tending the stove. "You came, as well. Perhaps you might lend a hand."

"Yes, ma'am. But would it be all right if I lie down for a few minutes. I feel so tired."

"Of course, Susha. Use the girl's bed."

In all truth there is no deceit on Susha's part, for she is exhausted and has been for some time. Yet her comfort will not be found on the soft accumulation of goose feathers. Instead, it'll come from the hard oak floor. After closing the door to insure privacy, Susha drops to her knees and presses her right ear, creating an unstopped vacuum to suck in all the sounds from below. At once, mumbles and shuffles are heard, becoming more discernible as they draw near.

"Move all this over here, Sylvie. But first we should tote out these baskets meant for you."

"Susha and me appreciate this, Pa."

Sensing that she may be in for a long stretch, Susha moves to make herself more comfortable. When father and son return to the cellar, she's flattened to the floor.

"You know they are raising the bounty tax for us property owners. Since Granger enrolled way off in Nevada, none of it will stay in the family."

Susha doesn't have to witness Mr. Potter's face to know that it's distinctly perturbed. As for her Sylvie, it's difficult to reason how he's taking his father's miserly moans.

"Paying to fight a war is one thing, but using my money to free the nagers is another. This is what Lincoln's war has come to."

"A lot of folks don't see it that way. I hear all kinds of arguments."

A tremble strikes Susha, from what may be perceived as a defiant statement.

"I hardly care what fools think. And now your brother's going to find himself in the middle of all that." There's a grunt as something heavy is being lifted. "Have you heard from him?"

"No."

"Well, he better be writing home. He's got your mother worried sick. And you know how Eliza is. Leaving her behind like that."

"She should make out. There's plenty of family to look after her and Ethan."

"We shall see. But I know Granger will be sorry someday. Rest assured."

Amen, as far as Susha is concerned. Odd it is, however, that she leans toward the logic of her father-in-law's and not her husband's. Up to now, this has never occurred.

"I think he feared the shame of getting drafted?"

"Granger? Huh. I know better. And even if he was drafted, he could have found the money for his commutation fee."

"This is what he told me."

"And you believed him?"

"Yessir, and I still do."

Poor Susha, lying helpless and unable to contain her husband's increasingly bold challenges.

"Granger would never lie to me," asserts Sylvie.

Silence follows, an ominous one speaking of rising tempers and a regrettable talk to follow. Susha holds her breath, afraid any slight whirring may drown out what is about to happen.

Suddenly, the bedroom door creeps open and she's caught exposed, with nothing to defend herself but a contrived look of innocence.

"Susha?" It's Narcissa, who has no trouble recognizing the position in which she finds her sister-in-law. "What are they saying?"

"Sh-h. Close the door."

With that, Narcissa spreads herself upon the empty space at Susha's side.

The terrible silence continues. It's apparent to the two interlopers that Mr. Potter is staring down his son, menacing him as much as he can with those cold, uncompromising eyes.

However, there's no relenting on Sylvie's part, no glint of second thoughts or, for that matter, restraint. "No one can say Granger is a Copperhead."

Upon hearing what amounts to an accusation, Susha's heart skips a beat. To be sure, her anxiety is heightened by the certain truth of Sylvie's outburst.

At this point piercing glares are of no further use, forcing Mr. Potter to resort to that paternal privilege which always has bound his younger son. "I know what you're thinking, Sylvie. And I forbid it." The message is terse.

But for Sylvie, the reality of the times speaks otherwise, as his tone begins to slacken. "That makes little difference, Pa. Soon there is to be a draft, with me part of it." He inhales a good portion of the cellar's dank air. "The law is the law."

With all due concern, Narcissa pulls a handkerchief from her sleeve to wipe a bead of Susha's trepidations. However, not a syllable from below is slighted, as the sisters-in-laws' ears remain fixed to the floor.

"That draft you're talking about is no cause for trouble," counters a barbed Mr. Potter. "I got the three hundred dollars that will buy your life."

Suddenly, the look on Susha's face hardens with anger, in effect shutting the spigot to her tear ducts. Not long ago requests for a loan to buy a small farm were answered by Mr. Potter's pleas of poverty. With his father being the source of Granger's financial backing, at the time Sylvie's petition wasn't unreasonable.

Now, out of nowhere, three hundred dollars have been placed upon the table, which itself seems to have been leveled by deceit. How could a man of the soil compel his son to ply a living from a miserable, dusty coal bank? Still, the worst of this, as far as Susha is concerned, is that if she under such preposterous circumstances can comprehend her father-in-law's knavery, then so, too, will her husband.

For the moment Sylvie is caught speechless, the sounds giving hint of one trying to compose himself.

"You have no business running off with the army. You have a wife, now. Why do you think I let you marry her, even though you're still a boy? It's so you would stay home."

To Sylvie, this should be taken as words of spite. Instead, they speed harmlessly passed his head, his mind busy with what already his careless father has revealed.

"You mean to tell me that instead of farming our own land, Susha and me have been living like slaves?"

"What are you saying?"

"The coal bank. That shack."

"Oh." Now, Mr. Potter must retrace. "Well, I wanted you and Susha to live here. This was my idea."

The cellar's thick atmosphere can be seen rising through the cracks in the floor, for mixed in with it is a little steam.

"Then it's goodbye." Sylvie has heard enough. "From now on, I do as I please."

"Sylvie. Don't you turn your back on me. Sylvie!"

The parting shout leaves a-gasp Susha and Narcissa. Still, with the aid of each other, both are able to come to their feet—weakened knees notwithstanding. Of course, Susha is the most affected, rendered without a voice and at a loss. About her, the bedroom and its cozy, girlish touches offer a harboring feeling, and so the nudge to remain with Narcissa at her side.

"Where's Susha?" Sylvie can be heard at the kitchen entry. Seconds later the bedroom door opens. Yet it's not a forceful entry, rather a contained one, as Sylvie isn't one to spread is ire. "Come, Susha. We should return home."

With a gentle grasp, he takes her hand to lead her away, one ordeal stepping aside for the next.

Throughout the rest of the day, and well into the next, little is spoken between the young couple. Occasionally, a monotonous inventory of their possessions takes place, by necessity dragging itself because of the small ledger. For the most part, however, Susha and Sylvie sit at their worn, empty table, attempting to collect the whirlwind of thoughts. As for the coal bank, it's been abandoned, the impending change of compass making further work senseless.

With needless hesitation, a hopeful Susha breaks the malaise. "Maybe I ought to tell Eliza."

"What?" It's as if Sylvie has been ensnared by a mind-sapping spell. "Oh. Maybe so."

"Then I should go?" Susha begins to leave her seat. "By myself?"

"Pardon? Yes."

As she inches toward the door, Susha grabs a quilt as an added wrap, and then turns to her husband. "I should be back quickly. To cook you something."

A weak nod and indifferent smile is Sylvie's reply, he wearing the look of one who needs to be alone.

Reluctantly, Susha lingers briefly at the door, though she knows she must push away. Yet she's determined not to be absent for long, and to shorten the distance to Buena Vista, her first step sets a brisk pace.

Not unexpectedly, Eliza is elated with the news that soon her household will expand. And with the arranging of the particulars surprisingly simple, the meeting between sisters-in-law proves short. Thus Susha is afforded the notion that the road back to the cabin can wait just a bit, that a little visit with her sister Emma might do her a world of good.

As she approaches her former home, Susha marvels at its roominess, its sturdiness standing with little compromise against time and nature. The trappings of a small, unadorned porch highlight the house's functional aspects, while the farm's numerous outbuildings speak of a thriving enterprise. Staunchly, the Pye dwelling's exterior is white, with the other structures blazed in red—an inalterable pattern. And although over the years its size has swelled to a second story, it remains an unpretentious house befitting its setting.

Too soon Susha is upon the Pyes' and all its comforts, her uneasiness showing little regard for a crawling rumination. How simple her life was before Sylvie whisked her away to the realities of a cramped cabin and a vast world. Still, before those collective harshnesses cause a stir, Susha recounts the stern leanings of her father and the demands of her bothersome brothers. Thank God they're away on a hog drive and shouldn't return until, at the earliest, this evening. For Susha, the fact remains that the day she married Sylvie was the day she was freed.

In spite of the harmonies of barnyard sounds, the farm feels empty to Susha, a sense accented by the delayed reaction to her knocks.

Finally, it's Emma who answers the door. "Susha." Quickly, she recovers from her surprise and delivers a warm embrace. "What are you doing here? Is something wrong?"

"Where is Mamma?"

"She took Addie and Lucy to visit the Claytons."

How convenient, for now Susha has her closest sibling all to herself.

It's also convenient for one who more and more has been bestowed the charge of the household, Emma's teenage years notwithstanding. Currently, she's piecing together a flannel shirt, and after divvying up part of this labor, the stitching commences.

Luckily, Susha's needle is threaded already. Under normal circumstances, there would flow a free and easy chatter. Susha's fears, however, have erected a reluctance of the tongue, as if to air her troubles would insure their certainty. Although her fingers become busy, her mouth is shut and her eyes become downcast.

Because of Susha's state of mind, it's up to Emma to strum up the first words. Unfortunately, the mood is catching, resulting in an unwanted silence. Only the needles to flannel speak, sewing up the folded frays which otherwise would unravel with disastrous results. Slowly, each stitch in time makes the shirt more durable, viable and wearable.

"How is Sylvie?" It's only when a sleeve is completed that Emma manages to drip forth, her innocent query falling upon the crux of the matter.

At once Susha's French seam comes to a halt, she posing a weak smile. Her lips falter and her cheeks quiver, revealing the true weight of her sister's feathery question.

"Susha. What is wrong with Sylvie?"

"Ah-h." Susha releases her held breath. "He's not hurt or sick. We are fine. Excepting." She's stopped short by her fears.

"Excepting you think he might be up to the same foolish notion that Granger had. And most of the other boys around here."

"Yes."

"But I would have thought Sylvie not like that. Granger, I can see. But Sylvie?"

"He is now."

"Oh, Susha." Emma nestles her sister in her arms. "Sylvie is much too sensible."

"I don't think good sense matters anymore. Sylvie is being pushed into a corner. It's all moving so fast."

"What do you mean, Susha?"

Clarifying with what she knows, Susha recounts the father/son confrontation of the previous day. "And I thought it was going to turn into a more terrible quarrel. But Sylvie charged out of the cellar just in time."

"And you heard everything that was said?"

"Nearly every word."

"Still, all that you say does not amount to Sylvie enlisting. Has he told you such?"

"No."

"Do you not think he would, that you would be the first to know? He might be a little flustered, but Sylvie will calm down."

"I suppose. Sylvie was never one to hold secrets."

"And the two of you are still newlyweds. Sylvie would not dare part from you, Susha."

These are sound, comforting words from a previously fickle Emma, whose recently added responsibilities may have forced her to exercise her thinking.

Susha takes a few moments to search through her past and sanction her sister's views. The most fitting point is that ever since she and Sylvie were young children, they have spent no more than a day or two apart. Why should there be any cause for change? If anything, it should be lessened, for now they are married, permanently united. Although Sylvie may be experiencing a disturbed, unsettled period, this will pass. Cooler heads will outlast.

"Yes. Sylvie would never part from me. He did promise." A beam of hope plants itself upon Susha's face, compelling the urge to continue as before. "Here. Hand me that collar."

It's passed noon, and already Susha has bid Emma farewell. Because of a purposeful sun, she's rolled and tucked her quilt as she treads upon the perfectly straight road. All about her is the faded decay of light browns and yellows, brought on by the prospects of a cold, cruel winter—in spite of the current, pleasant air. More than anyone else, Susha knows the rhythms of the land, that this will be the last tolerable weather for the year, with no hope for renewal until the bitter season runs its course. Undeniably so, it's a dreaded reminder of what's to come, that as with many times before, she'll have to endure without a whimper. On the other hand, for the first time in her life, Susha feels that a decision of her own making is approaching, and that she might take steps in order to shorten winter's duration.

Upon entering the cabin, Susha's surprised by an unfed

fireplace. With hardly a blink of response, Sylvie sits folded at the table. Along with an absence of murmuring flames, an awful silence persists, thus compelling Susha to fidget about the cabin in a needless chore of rearranging the tin ware.

"Susha." Understandably, it's not long before Sylvie can take no more. "Please sit down."

Her blood seizes, as bravely she takes her chair at the small table, her head bowed just above her outstretched arms.

"Susha." Softly, Sylvie reaches to cup his hands over hers. "I can take it no more. My mind is made up. I have decided to enlist."

In a jolt Susha raises her head. With her wide eyes and slackened jaw, she shouts her silent objection.

"Please, forgive me, Susha."

Without knowing, Sylvie's regrets are squelching any forthcoming arguments. After all, he is asserting his rights as a husband. More so, Sylvie's manner speaks of intransigence, the events building to this.

Susha's face falls upon Sylvie's hands, one of which he frees so that he might comfort her bunned hair—tender strokes of unavoidable sorrows. As for the other, tears cascade across its form, it being trapped beneath the weight of her collapse.

At last, Susha's smothered fear is coming true—Emma's reassurances notwithstanding. Numbed by the blunt reality, her head is clouded into inaction.

"Sh-h. Susha. Everything will be all right," comforts Sylvie, trying to add a little warmth. "I will return soon enough. The war is almost played out."

Susha's bleary eyes gaze down the short, horizontal length of the table, as if it's a vast, empty plain. A long silence coincides, although even the interminable cannot last forever.

"I don't want to be alone," moans Susha, her hurt having the time to build.

"Don't be afraid. There should be none of the sort."

Sylvie's lenitive may be brief in words, but for Susha its implications are broad. Her face turns to his with her testy response. "I don't want to be away from you. Don't you see?"

"Susha." Abandoning his seat, Sylvie eases to her side and places his arms around her.

"Don't touch me, Sylvie," she mutters.

"Susha. Please."

"Don't touch me." Susha sits erect and then leans away.

But Sylvie is persistent.

"No!" Susha comes to her feet and pushes away her husband's approach. "You promised! You broke your promise, Sylvie!" Now, her voice is indignant, and she makes for the door.

"Susha," eases Sylvie. "What could I do?"

His weak plea, however, angers her further. "You promised you would never leave me, Sylvetus Potter!"

Rapidly expanding, Susha's ire threatens its confinement. Indeed, with this pressure rising within its box, she needs to be free from the four corners of the stuffy cabin.

Never before has Sylvie seen Susha rise to such a rancor, and so, wisely, he offers little resistance when she rushes away.

Indeed, it is a rush, conceived on the fly and briskly attended. Yet as Susha becomes blanketed by the fresh, open air, she lacks a pure direction. Guided by her feet, she hastens away, taking her chances upon a random choice.

"Susha! Please, stay!"

To which she ignores.

As it happens, Susha doesn't wander far, though her wonderings do take her miles away, as she rests against the gnarled remains of a once mighty bur oak. Although the season has demanded the loss of its leaves, most of its branches are, in fact, lifeless. Long ago one side of the tree's trunk rotted away into a hollow, unique covey hole, which harbored the playful antics of a younger Susha and Sylvie. Nevertheless, it remains as good a place as any for a long, brooding pause. After all, some of the venerable oak's more memorable moments were shared with Susha, and it may have yet a few more years to bear witness.

For three hours Susha has planted herself beside the oak, the time spent with its ages tempering her hurt and clearing her head. She knows that Sylvie means no harm, that his broken vow in no way belittles his devotion to her. Indeed, the fault belongs to an uncaring world shifting its woes upon her innocent husband. Poor Sylvie, what is he supposed to do? How should he carry on? Are not his tumults any less severe than her own?

The answers to Susha's dilemma are faint, whizzing passed her thwarted thoughts as flawed fragments and unusable measures. Certainly, her return to the cabin will be all the more difficult, as the day nears its end.

Nevertheless, when Susha comes to her feet, a glance toward the heavens transforms into an inspired gaze. With the sun nearing the horizon, the clear sky becomes a rainbow of blue: a light kersey in the west fading eastward into a deep, shadowy navy. It's as if the far above is marching by, demonstrating its colors in parade order. Then suddenly, an idea strikes Susha, as so vividly painted before her in the form of a genuine solution. Suffice to say, that if Sylvie is to make good on his promise never to leave her behind, he's going to need some assistance.

Still caught wide-eyed, Susha races home toward that darker edge of the sky. The path she pounds is flat and smooth, allowing her dazzled eyes to remain fixed on high. In a brief span Susha's atmosphere alters into an exhilarating one, her spreading arms feeling the air. Such is her captivation, that soon she may speed by her cabin without realizing it.

"Susha!" Of course, it's Sylvie in a search for his wife. Strangled by guilt, he's a pitiable sight—vulnerable and receptive.

But standing at the end of that bluish spectrum, Sylvie's adorned for Susha's appreciation. Although stopped by his unexpected appearance, she doesn't hesitate and sprints toward him. In no time, the couple is in an unpriable embrace.

"Sylvie?" whispers Susha.

"What?" He's confused by her change in demeanor.

"Tell me all you know about the army."

"Why?"

"I want to go with you. That's why."

"Huh?"

What should be a late night, in fact, turns into an early one, the couple taking to their bed. Still, Susha and Sylvie are not falling into a quiet sleep. Although their muscles and bones beg otherwise, their thoughts and hearts are in a state of flux, with Susha presenting her case and Sylvie weakening his.

"Your bounty and mine together would make six hundred dollars."

"Yes, Susha. I know."

"And there are the Iowa bounties. We could own a nice farm when the war's done."

"Susha, you seem to be forgetting that war is all about fighting. You wanting to be a soldier means you would be doing just that. Don't forget, the Seceshes shoot back."

"But Sylvie, you said there's not much left in them. That the war will be over soon."

"Well, you never know."

"They probably cannot make it through the winter. When spring comes the Seceshes will all be played out, and we can go down there and make them surrender."

Susha's point taps a familiarity into Sylvie, it being one of several he's used to justify his decisions. Still, his deeper recesses surface in order to voice their protests over silly, girlish initiatives.

"Susha, bringing up money is well and good. But you're talking about living in an army, with a crowd of men. How are you supposed to get along with that? You might not know that the army draws its men from all kinds of circles. The tottery and unscrupled ones at that."

"Well, I am sure we would stay clear of them and fall in with the God-fearers. Besides, I have you to protect me." Susha's voice softens. "There would be no one here. No one as sure as my husband."

"But Susha, it would be rough living."

"What have we been doing, Sylvie?"

"Much rougher than this, Susha." In the darkness, Sylvie may have difficulty seeing her face, though he has no problem sensing its expression. "Ugh-h-h."

"Sylvie?" Susha prods for more objections, to which she could counter.

She certainly has her reasoning in order. Although she mentions nothing of her strengths, Sylvie deems it not questionable enough for him to bother. Almost helpless, all he can do for the moment is lie at her side and mull over the confusion tussling within his impoverished head.

"Let me think about it."

Doing her best to muffle her excitement, Susha snuggles her arm around her husband and tickles his neck with the cushion of her lips. Whether Sylvie knows it or not, the question of his wife's enlistment has been settled. As to how the two of them will go about it is the only true remaining doubt.

4 ↝ Champions of Folly

What a day it has been for the young couple. Then there happens the night in all its silent overtures and muted protests. Susha's mind roams through the sundry situations she believes are likely to occur. However, being prudent, she dares not go beyond these. Thus, when her anticipations begin repeating themselves, it's a cinch to slip into a restive sleep.

On the other hand, Sylvie cannot catch a wink, worried by the haze of the immediate future. For him, the notion of Susha's becoming a soldier is nonsense, if not disturbing. Determined to enlist, he possesses enough apprehensions for himself, which would double if she has her way.

Nevertheless, before dawn, Sylvie does manage to calm his distress, he realizing that in no way does he wish to join the conflict companionless. After all, never in his life has he been without friends or family, both roles of which Susha is best qualified. Soldiering as a pair just might work, considers Sylvie, as already it's been established she can look quite fetching in a pair of trousers. But what he finds most soothing concerns her safety, that if events were to become too harsh, or even dangerous, a woman in disguise could forgo her obligations by revealing the truth. For him, the gains are accepted and the risks set aside.

Under the guise of moving in with Eliza, the couple can set about with their enlistment scheme. At least this is how Susha sees it, she darting about the cabin in a flurry of packing. As for Sylvie, he's not certain all has been settled, though he manages to lend a hand as directed.

"Sylvie. Maybe you ought to go tell Eliza we are coming. Hitch Granger's wagon, so we can haul this."

"Umm."

"By the time you get back, I should be ready."

Almost without thought, Sylvie grabs his hat and coat, and moves for the door.

"Do you want me to cook something for you, Sylvie?"

"Pardon? Oh. No need to bother." His motions are like that of some droning machine.

"Sylvie." Susha steps to her husband's side. "All will be fine. I can feel it inside."

He gives a half-smile. "I know it will. I believe you, Susha."

A tiny pause is broken when a meticulous Susha begins to map Sylvie's face with her kisses. As far as she's concerned, Eliza can wait, for her intent is to have one comforting thing lead to a passionate other.

Unfortunately, Sylvie's powers to concentrate are depleted. "I need to be off."

It's Susha who'll have to do the waiting. Standing at the door, she sighs and watches her husband trudge toward the horizon. Poor Sylvie, for shouldering the burdens of two are beginning to tell. Indeed, realizes Susha, if he's to maintain his status as head of the household, then it's going to be up to her to carry more of the load.

Although a cold gust stings Susha's face, she keeps her distant gaze as she leans against the doorway. That Granger was a sly fellow, carrying on as usual, all the while plotting and planning his enlistment as if it were a business venture. Certainly, he seemed happy with the deal he made, and so, believes Susha, why shouldn't she and Sylvie? Why not search for a veteran regiment of jovial spirits and Christian virtue, and avoid the newly-forming ones of unknown fabrics?

Of course, this is foremost on Susha's mind, but then there is the material, the need to accumulate for a secure future. Granger, the horse trader, sought the best bargain available—from a community more desperate than most to sign up young men. In addition to the federal bounty, Susha is aware of the local ones, coming in the form of both money and land, and varying widely from sub-district to sub-district, township to township. It would be wise to repeat her brother-in-law's process and, as well, keep a close eye on Sylvie, who might be inclined to enlist with the first friendly voice. But above all, because of Susha's questionable status, a secrecy must be cultivated. Only those who can be trusted should know, and the fewer people she and Sylvie do confide in, the better.

The wind whirls through the dingy, threadbare cabin, flickering away the last of the fireplace's coals. It's just as well, for never again will Susha light a fire there, her promises being the convenience of cast iron, not to mention the warmth and vastness of prosperity.

When Sylvie returns with the team and wagon, it takes only a few, silent minutes to load it full. As it happens, the chicken coop and its occupants use most of the space, as the couple sees fit to move them intact.

Already, Sylvie has the reins in hand when Susha takes it upon herself to make the final gesture. It remains a stubborn door which could never be put to right, and now more so than ever it refuses to slam shut. Not being one who would want to expose a house's interior to the elements, Susha runs through the gamut of combinations—lift and pull, pull and lift, gentle and forceful—all to no avail.

"Leave it be, Susha."

She peeks inside and sees nothing but a dark bleakness. In spite of the cabin being the scene of the Potters' beginning, there is no sentiment from her. Instead, she loosens her grip on the knob and allows the door to flap as it may. With a hand from Sylvie, Susha climbs onto the wagon and sits by his side, clutching his arm for good measure. There's no looking back now, not even a fleeting glance, as Sylvie guides the team toward Buena Vista.

The clops of horse hooves, the clucks of nervous hens and the squeaks of turning wheels are entrancing sounds indeed. Susha is silent as she huddles against Sylvie. Because the wagon's load is not balanced to his satisfaction, the pace is safe and lumbering. Thus with the added time the words have ample opportunity to seep forth, especially from Susha with her head being crowded by so many.

"Sylvie, I have been thinking..." And so, Susha begins to unveil her design—tentative at first, and then to a rapid succession.

To his credit, Sylvie listens attentively. That is until he feels a bump in the road. "Susha?"

"What is it, Sylvie?"

"You need to take hold for yourself for a while."

"How do you mean?"

"You're forgetting about Eliza. I think she expects me to enlist. But not the pair of us. Surely, Eliza is figuring on you to help out at the farm."

"Oh."

"How are you going to sneak passed her? Or any of our kin? It would take only one to put a stop to your enlisting, you know. To tell some official of our plans." It's not Sylvie's fault if he feels a little self-satisfied.

Then again, Susha's not of a mind to be stumped. "We will think of something, the two of us." Though now, she feels the remorse of abandoning Eliza.

After settling into their new home, it takes only a few days for Susha and Sylvie to establish their routines. Indeed, moving in with their sister-in-law is proving to be a nice fit.

"I hear of a recruiter coming to Polk City," mentions Eliza, as she and Susha perform some tidying. "Do you think Sylvie may pay him a call?"

"Enlist in Polk City? So near? That would be unwise for us." It seems Susha's comfort has loosened her guard.

"Us?"

"Uh-h-h." Her slip too obvious, Susha can see no point in keeping a secret from one so sharp as Eliza. "I suppose you should know. I may be enlisting with Sylvie."

"What? Susha!" A blissful morning ends abruptly. "Do you mean what you're saying?"

"Yes. I do," asserts Susha, with Ethan gathered upon her hip.

"But how can you?" Eliza's face makes a tight contortion. "You're not a man."

"I can look like one if need be. Sylvie is teaching me."

"Sylvie is allowing this?"

"He hardly minds at all."

It's obvious that, in spite of Susha's candid expression, her sudden and outrageous announcement is hard for Eliza to consume.

"This is no joke. I mean what I say. Sylvie is about to get himself conscripted, so we decided to enlist together. We don't want to be apart. We are still newly married. And besides, we will have two bounties."

In an instant, Eliza's bearing changes from the incredulous to the disapproving.

"Promise me not to tell a soul, Eliza."

As if aiding his aunt's cause, Ethan pouts his lips.

"Susha. You know I was counting on at least one of you lending me a hand."

"Sylvie and me can find help. And we will not leave here until we do."

"Goodness gracious."

A moment of silence ensues, enabling Eliza to consider her sister-in-law's weak inventions. But like any person with a little worldliness, she probably doubts Susha's capacity to withstand the crude realities coming with the company of men—not to mention those rigid deprivations, the stamp of army life. But in addition, Eliza may not even need to question the merits, if she believes a woman wouldn't last long in a uniform and that Susha will make a fast return to Buena Vista. Indeed, why should Eliza risk a friendship over a matter of no genuine concern?

"No need to worry. Your secret is safe," she assures, grudgingly. "Uh-h. For heaven's sake."

Susha's beam is a wide one, as the scale she holds, once again, balances in her favor.

But although a portion of the picture may be coated, Eliza's cooperative silence in no way helps Susha with her next quandary, that of explaining her absence from Buena Vista. In this she envies Sylvie, who as a man can do as he pleases with no apologies. As for Susha, she can't allow herself even to be contrite. Thus a story must be concocted, one to fool the fools and convince the clever all. Yet Susha realizes this may be too daunting a task for her alone, that she needs a contriving mind, who not only would carry on dutifully, but savor the role.

Fortunately, Susha's wait for another accomplice may not be

long in coming. A Sunday dinner at the Pye home has entered upon its noisiest stage, dividing itself into factions of roving children, deliberating men and fussying women. In the midst of all this by the sunny side of the house are two sisters, plying their labors at two wooden tubs, one filled with a clear rinse and the other soapy water and dirty dishes. At last, in spite of the activity about them, Susha and Emma are isolated and unnoticed.

"Is Sylvie really enlisting?"

The news has traveled fast and freely, disconcerting for Susha. "Yes. But we are not sure as to when?"

"Is Mr. Potter going to talk some sense into Sylvie?" asks Emma.

"I don't want him to. Besides, Sylvie already has plenty enough sense."

"Susha, you sure are taking this coolly." Emma seems puzzled. "I would be all torn if my new husband was about to march away."

Looking about for eavesdroppers, Susha lowers her voice. "Can you keep a secret?"

"Susha! Yes, of course."

"Sh-h. Are you sure? You promise?"

"Yes," assures Emma in an anxious whisper.

Hesitantly, Susha continues. "Sylvie and me are enlisting together."

Her secret is met by an amazed silence and a stunned, open face.

"Emma."

A nudge from Susha's elbow breaks the shock. "You're running off to join the army!"

"Emma hush!"

"You mean you're running off to join the army?"

"Yes."

Grabbing a plate, a flushed Emma rubs it clean, also compelling Susha to contribute to the spotless parade of dinnerware. But the warmth which has been the tub is merging into the chilly air, making a change of venue all the more receivable

"We should go inside for a spell," declares Susha after a moment of silence.

Her shock lessening, Emma drops the next plate back into the soapy water and gives her sister an agreeable grin. "How about our bedroom?"

Arm in arm the sisters proceed, ignored by the ignorers who are far too engaged to voice their supervisions. Soon, even as the door slams shut, both are plopping onto their bed.

"Oh, this feels so good." Susha has forgotten just how.

"I wonder if they have beds this big and soft in the army?" comes a dose of sarcasm.

"Emma, I do mean it. Sylvie and me are joining together. We just have to sort through a few things."

"Like how are you going to get Mamma and Pappa to let you go?"

"That hardly matters. You forget, I am a married woman. I go where my husband tells me."

Emma's frown obliges Susha to recite her motives and excuses in a rapid and repetitive order. The figures fly loosely and the suppositions are presented as hard facts, as the soldier-to-be does her best to persuade her most prized recruit.

All the while Emma lovingly strokes her most prized relative, fingering through her strands of hair so as to position them just right. "I don't want you to leave, Susha. I should miss you so."

"The war is not long to last. Not after spring. And I will write and tell you all that happens."

"You better."

"And Sylvie will look over me. We should have a grand adventure of it, and earn enough for a nice farm."

"Oh, I wish I could go with you, Susha. If only for a few weeks."

"Me too. But Sylvie and me will have enough on our minds keeping up with my pretending."

"I think you can do it. You are strong and tall. And even if you lack whiskers, there are plenty of young men who are the same." With the back of her hand, a giggling Emma caresses Susha's smooth face. "Some with fairly high voices."

"And already I like wearing trousers."

But the snickering fades away when Emma comes up with a potential snag. "Susha. Have you thought of what to tell Mamma and Pappa? About you being away?"

For Susha, this has been a nagging question, which now compels her to sit up and sigh.

But as it happens, Emma may be of help. After all, a young lady with ambitious dreams must harbor a scheme of her own, one to put her in the company of handsome and unattached men. Still, such a design is likely beyond Emma's capabilities, though that's not to say a portion of it can't be put to good use.

"You can tell them you are going to St. Louis to work for the Sanitary Commission."

"What?"

"To become a nurse and take care of the soldiers. They have many hospitals there. The Benton Hospital, the City Hospital to name a few."

Susha is surprised at what is probably the scratched surface of her sister's clandestine facts.

"You could tell Mamma and Pappa you will be nearer to Sylvie. Because your husband wants you there."

"Really? What else do you know?"

"About St. Louis?"

With that, an eager Emma bursts free with all she has learned and accumulated. For many reasons there's a shortage of nurses: meager pay, petty prejudices and the overwhelming number of patients standing apart.

"You remember Clara Snow? She's there. Became a nurse after her baby died. And her husband too. I think he was killed in Mississippi." Emma speaks almost matter-of-factly, as one should when they have so much to present. "Oh, and Julia McCrory from Polk City went to St. Louis to visit her husband, and stayed when his regiment was sent away."

Emma may be on to something, for the situation in St. Louis sounds very confusing, a perfect place to lose a name. Still, although her sister may be excited by the promise of a proxy intrigue, Susha can't help but feel disturbed by the deception of it. Never before has she told a lie to her parents—or anyone, for that matter --the same being true for her husband, who would be forced to follow her path of fibbery.

"I don't think I have ever told Mamma and Pappa a story, Emma."

“Oh, come now, Susha. It will be nothing of the sort. Not if you tell them what happened when you and Sylvie return home and all is right. Or-r-r.”

“What?”

“Or you could never tell them a thing. What is the harm if they never know? Either way they should be proud of you for serving the country.”

How typical of Emma to be this bold, recovering so resoundingly from her initial shock and loss of words. She certainly seems to comprehend what she’s talking about, impressing her older sister into a decision.

“Maybe what they don’t know cannot hurt them,” considers Susha. “I could get Sylvie to tell me to become a nurse, while the pair of us enlist. But can I trust you to help me, and to keep this between us?”

“Yes, yes,” agrees an elated Emma. “Just tell me what to do.”

“I can hardly say as yet. We don’t even know when or where to enlist. But you will be the first to hear.”

“Ooh, yes, Susha. I do so want to know.”

For nearly a week, Sylvie scours the neighboring townships for pertaining news. Returning each day to his co-cartographer, together they sort through the confusing array of bounties and enticements. This jumble, however, is made worse when matched with the availability of appropriate regiments and their recruiting parties. At some locales these low-ranking officers and high-ranking enlisted men promise to be thicker than thieves, while at others are as sparse as Quakers. However, with both Susha and Sylvie eager to get on with their lives, there’s little tolerance for tarrying. Thus an imperfect compromise is settled upon—reluctantly at first, acceptable in the end.

Just south of Des Moines, in Warren County, lies Indianola. Neither Susha or Sylvie have ever set foot there, a round trip requiring all of a long day. Yet this is a definite advantage, for it’s likely that no citizen of Indianola is well-acquainted with the Potters or the Pyes.

What has been learned from two unconnected sources is that as far as local bounties are concerned, Indianola is fairly common.

Apparently, it's not a wealthy town, its inhabitants apportioning only $36.50 for each of its enlistees, to be paid upon their mustering out of the army. But what really has captured the attention of Sylvie, and, hence, Susha, is the lure of titled land—40 acres of flat, fertile soil. In addition, there will be a small, but expansible, pen of livestock, enough to have sealed the couple's interest. To be sure, their excitement swells each time they sum the total, which including the federal bounty comes to 80 acres, $673, four ewes, six swine, 10 hens and two milk cows, not to mention a still-to-be determined amount of milled lumber. Beyond doubt, the prizes of bordering Illinois and the kings' ransoms of distant Massachusetts are meant for those recruits of lesser castes.

It takes every fiber of Susha's muscles to push Sylvie out of bed. Although the week has given its share of fascinations, it's been a draining one as well, thus explaining Sylvie's reluctance to abandon his comfort.

"Sylvie, you need to be on your way."

"I know."

The idea is that while Susha remains behind, Sylvie will ride to Indianola, investigate things, and if all pans out, enroll both himself and his "cousin." Hopefully, a grace period will be included, so that like Granger, Susha and Sylvie will not be compelled to muster in for several days, or weeks.

Dawn is still two hours away when Susha dishes out a hardy breakfast. Already the couple have talked over their plans to a point just shy of a cadence. Nevertheless, a jittery Susha can't help but feel that large, vital chunks of their story are being excluded, ones which could weaken seriously the whole of their scheme.

"I keep thinking we just might have forgotten something."

"We probably have," shrugs Sylvie, as he gulps down some warm milk. "Not much we can do for now."

"I suppose. But Sylvie, when you get to Indianola, ask if we can take ducks or geese instead of hens. We have enough as is."

Earlier, Sylvie had saddled one of Granger's greys, so that when Susha ceases stuffing his face, his departure is a simple one. Even as he mounts the horse, he's still chewing through a mouthful of eggs and ham. Yet there's more, for as Susha places her hand upon her husband's leg, she passes up to him a small sack crammed with bread, sausage and cheese.

"Susha, you don't have to feed the whole army."

"I don't want you to go hungry. So you be sure to eat all this. It is going to be a long day."

"Hmm? I do believe I will be the best looked after soldier of them all."

"Be-e-e careful."

"I will." But although Sylvie may be ready to urge the grey onward, he stops short. "I just thought of something. What do you want me to call you?"

"What?"

"Your army name. Susha, you need the name of a man."

Perhaps this is that item which has pestered Susha's mind. Indeed, it is a fierce quandary—and an important one, as well. Unfortunately, for the moment Susha is at a loss, unable to give herself a sweet and clever moniker. Then it comes to her, a recent name she has chosen to bestow upon her first son, when and wherever he may arrive.

"How about Robert. Robert Potter. Bob for short."

Although he knows nothing concerning the name, Sylvie is delighted. "Well then, I shall see you soon, Bob Potter," he muses as he nudges his mount. "Private Potter."

With the approach of a long, hard winter, there never can be enough firewood. With this in mind, later in the day after seeing to the livestock, Susha takes it upon herself to increase Eliza's cordage, and as well, spend her nerves.

The sky is clear and the sun bright and blinding when Eliza forgoes her kitchen chores in order to join her sister-in-law, who struggles with the cross saw, sectioning the logs for splitting. Without a word, and with Ethan on her hip, Eliza grasps the opposite handle and puts some muscle into it. However, owing to the unbalance of the moment, it is a feeble attempt.

"Oh Susha. We should stop, so I can put Ethan down."

Little Ethan is much the crawler—an explorer by nature. As the young ladies resume the rude rasp, under watchful eyes he's shooed around the potential dangers of serrated tools and falling objects. Making the wide arc with many diversions along the way, eventually Ethan finds himself at his aunt's feet. For him, Susha's skirt and supporting crinoline are but movable curtains, through which he enters without hesitation. Soon, he's between his aunt's legs, tugging at her stockings to her ticklish amusement.

"You will not be able to hide there much longer, Pumpkin. Your Aunt Susha will be taking to trousers. Just like Pappa."

Ceasing her sawing, Susha takes a peek at her nephew, happy he is in his cozy hideaway.

"Have you put much thought into it, Susha?"

"Quite a bit. Let me assure you."

"What I mean is, have you thought about how you are to conduct your private business? Especially with all those men around you. It might be difficult."

"Well. Sylvie and me figure that each time the two of us can go off together, away from everyone else. That way he can watch over me. I don't think that would appear to be too queer. Sylvie and me should never leave each other's sight, we being cousins."

"No. That should arouse little suspicion. Sylvie has always struck me as a private person, anyhow." Then Eliza offers a smirk. "Not like his brother."

"No." Susha smiles at the blessed understatement. "Not at all."

Holding up dinner as long as they may, the sisters-in-law's hopes are that Sylvie's journey will be shorter than expected. As it happens, it may be much longer.

While Susha clears the dirty dishes, her worries begin to surface. "I don't like this."

"Try not to be fretful, Susha. Sylvie can take care of himself," notes Eliza at the table with Ethan on her lap. "He has a good head on his shoulders."

"Yes."

"But you don't suppose?" ponders Eliza, as she strokes her son's soft, blonde hair.

"What?"

"That Sylvie had a change of heart, and enlisted by himself?"

Stopping in mid-step, Susha's response is immediate and firm. "Oh, no, Eliza. Sylvie would never do such a thing. Never." She takes her seat, her wounded eyes pointing toward her sister-in-law's.

Apparently, realizing her error, Eliza concurs. "No, he really would not, would he?"

"No."

"Sweet Sylvie." Eliza gives a kiss to Ethan's crown. "You know, I envy you."

For Susha, the words seem strange as spoken by a comely woman amidst her many comforts.

"I think you ended up with the better of the brothers."

Silence ensues, enough for both to fathom what is spoken and what is heard.

"Susha," offers Eliza. "We should have some apple pie. See what my Pumpkin can do with his tooth."

Finally, after having succumbed to the late hour, Ethan has been cribbed and tucked. But while his mother readies herself for bed, his aunt is prepared to stay up all night.

"Susha, if your fingers get fidgety, there is yarn in that basket. You can never have enough stockings."

"Of course."

"And if Sylvie seems a bit chilled, you might give him a sip of Granger's spirits."

"Thanks. But, I don't think Sylvie would take to that."

"I shall leave you to it." Eliza struggles to contain her yawn. "Good night, Susha."

"'Night."

Soon, Eliza's withdrawal leaves an immediate void to the sounds of the house. Indeed, the silence is such that even the flickering candles can be heard, the gloominess putting Susha in no mood to knit—whatever the stocking shortage.

But eventually, something does stir—faint and barely traceable—a sound emanating from outside. Susha shifts to peer through the window, but owing to the blackness of the night she sees only her own reflection. Frustrated, she rushes to the door, without bothering to bundle herself against the cold.

"Sylvie. Is that you?"

Through the dark a tired voice returns, "Susha." And into the dim light Sylvie walks, leading Granger's grey, which apparently has thrown a shoe.

Immediately, Susha leaves the doorway and runs to him, grasping her husband around his waist and planting her face into his neck.

"There now, Susha. Was I gone that long?" Sylvie matches her embrace.

"I just missed you."

Quickly, the couple see to the grey, and so, shortly, Susha is able to see to Sylvie. But although he's exhausted from his arduous march, he remains talkative.

"So you mean neither one of us signed up, Sylvie?"

"No, you have to do your own signing. And it bothered me too much to enlist without you."

Susha's heart rises, for no one knows her Sylvie like she. "Who did you talk with?"

"A sergeant from the 42nd Infantry. They sent him here to sign up people like us. Is there more milk?" Sylvie's head follows Susha as she locates the pitcher. "He seemed an honorable man. First-rate and trustworthy. Talkative too. I could have listened to him for hours. Soon, you will. Tomorrow."

"Tomorrow?"

"Yes. To Indianola, for us both to enlist. Rise up early and..."

Although Susha has been waiting for this moment, its arrival evokes a certain dread, that in less than a day she'll be signing away her life. However, there's no chance for retreat, as Susha couldn't bear for her persistency to go to waste. Instantly, she smothers her second thoughts.

"Tell me more what he said."

"Well, it sounds like that Forty-second is a regiment, first-rate. They have come through all sorts of scrapes and are still full of fight."

"Where are they, now?"

"Down in Arkansas." Sylvie gives a shrug to the exact locale, his geographical ignorance not staying his enthusiasm. "That sergeant says Arkansas is nearly all captured, and going on into Texas is not worth the trouble. Only Mobile, Alabama on the Gulf is left. The Forty-second should be going there in March or so. And then the war will be over, quickly."

"Was he sure about that?"

A slight squeak in Susha's voice tells Sylvie that he needs to reassure.

"He was. He said that the rebels are all but played out. They're now down to militia. Old men and boys who run away at the first sign of a fight. 'Well versed in the art of skedaddling' is what he said of them. I tell you, Susha, we are on to something. We will hardly have to serve three years to get our bonus. In a few months we could muster out, and be building a house on our new eighty-acre farm. And..."

With no uncertainty, the visit to Indianola has heightened Sylvie's expectations, airing themselves well into the covers. As it turns out, so much are the rantings that there is little call for any "pleasant dreams" from either side of the bed. In the end, the evening's affair is forced to wane away into a reluctant sleep.

With the morning, the couple set about in a deliberate preparation, especially Susha, who must don a disguise. In regards to this, without knowing and with Eliza's previous insistence, Granger is of an invaluable aid. It is, after all, he who's providing the coat and oversized shirt to hide Susha's feminine qualities. In addition, Granger has left behind a grey, wide-brimmed hat. It's into this topping that Susha carefully tucks her flows of hair, with the warning that the hat is to stay put, whatever circumstance arises. Bottomed with a pair of Sylvie's Sunday brogans, Susha is as ready as she'll ever be.

Taking her by the hand for a look under the kitchen lantern, Sylvie offers an approving nod. "I think we might make a man of you yet." He gives Susha a kiss on her cheek, where the sweet, girlish rose for some time has been covered by the sun's light brown. "We ought to be careful, or people might think us peculiar."

Before leaving the house, Susha scribbles a note. It seems that a soon-to-be disappointed Eliza will have to wait to hear the entire story. On the other hand, Susha is in for a nice surprise, for as the couple enter the barn, Sylvie grabs not one but two saddles. Having learned his lesson from his first trip to Indianola, this time around there will be a pair of mounts.

"Sylvie," interrupts Susha. "I don't think that might look right."

"What?"

"Eliza's sidesaddle?"

"Oh."

If the trip is to be a long one, at least it'll afford Susha and Sylvie the opportunity for a prolonged rehearsal. There are, after all, many "does and don'ts" to being a man. Although she is familiar with most of these, it wouldn't hurt to add a few more tidbits to her routine.

"Susha," advises Sylvie, shortly after they take to the road. "Remember that when a man walks, he swaggers his shoulders and not his hips."

"You don't swagger your shoulders."

"If so, it's because I don't naturally move my hips. Swagger above and it ought to keep your bottom still."

"I will try."

"Be sure to take big steps, not tiny ones."

"I don't take tiny steps."

"Well. Take bigger ones to be sure. And remind me some time to teach you how to shave."

"Shave?"

"Yes. Just so the other soldiers won't think you are too different."

"Oh."

"And for pity's sake, Susha. It will be proper to belch and fart out loud, and not make apologies for it."

"Goodness. What you fellows do."

To be sure, the sergeant is a sharp one. Upon seeing Sylvie entering the courthouse's main hall, he spouts out the recruit's first and last names, and slides right into conversation. It's here that the sergeant has set up a table and chair, as well as an assortment of official-looking papers. Impressive, with his crisp, machine-made uniform of fine wool and polished brass, his face is dominated by proud and skillfully-crafted muttonchops. In fact, the only thing amiss with this sergeant is the gap of a missing tooth, which his affable nature displays continuously.

Quickly, Sylvie introduces his "cousin." But a forgotten portion of her repertoire leads to a flimsy, unmanly handshake. Now, this is all Susha can think about, as her husband and the sergeant engage in a rigorous discussion. Harmlessly, their words pass her head, even as a pen is put to the blank spaces of some of the papers. Fortunately, Sylvie is able to do all the talking, for at this moment, Susha is unable to offer more than a stare.

But upon feeling a sudden nudge from Sylvie's elbow, her spell becomes broken.

"Go ahead and sign your name."

Already, the sergeant has dipped the pen, and points to where her mark should be made.

Grasping the implement with her nervous hand, Susha stops short of the paper, as if something is askew. She leans over to her husband's ear.

"I forgot my name."

But leave it to Sylvie to be quick on his feet. "No, Bob," he says aloud. "You should sign it Robert."

Though Susha is compelled to write her *nom de guerre* on several official papers, for her, enlisting into the army becomes a surprisingly, uncomplicated process.

"Congratulations, Robert," gives the sergeant, as he takes back the pen.

This time Susha's handshake is robust.

"Sylvie did tell you about the regiment and what is expected of you?"

"Yessir. It all sounds agreeable."

"Is there more you wish to know? You should not have it rough. War's nearly done."

Be that as it may, Susha would do well to ask about regular rations, the sicknesses of the South and the dangers of campaigning there. In addition, there is the question of how much in bonuses does the sergeant earn for every recruit he signs.

"I don't think so."

"None from me," adds Sylvie.

"Good. Then I will give these papers to the clerk here and send these to the regiment. Just be sure, Sylvetus and Robert, to show up in six days at the capitol grounds in Des Moines. That will be on a Thursday, before two o'clock. Understand?"

"Yessir."

"There will be a surgeon there to look you over."

Surgeon? Although she's able to maintain an even face, a shock rushes into Susha. Things have gone so well, and now this, the most insurmountable of complications.

"You two look like fit fellows, so there should not be any worry. Be seeing you in Arkansas."

So goes the friendly sendoff.

Soon, the door of the courthouse shuts behind the couple, and Susha is able to let free her panic. "Did you hear that?" she vents, while tugging at Sylvie's coat.

"Yes, I did. What?"

"A surgeon is going to be looking us over. A surgeon is going to be looking at me!"

Sylvie stops his descent upon the steps to peruse Susha from top to bottom. "You think that a problem?"

"Sylvie! How can you say that!" With that, Susha's tugs alter into a hard jerk. "A surgeon, Sylvie! Landsakes, a surgeon!"

5 ↝ The Weary Landscape

Since Bastrop's beginning, its people have relished their autumns. Although usually brief, the season can concentrate a year of accomplished hopes, making winter little more than a tolerable nuisance. However, war is having its way, with the changes squelching this time of open festivity and serious accounting.

Nevertheless, things could be worse, as they are with the other states of the Confederacy. Because Union politicians and generals are of too many minds, faraway Texas endures only half-hearted invasions along its edges. Then there is the border with neutral and opportunistic Mexico, which remains porous in spite of a confusion of Union encroachers, French imperialists and Juarista nationalists. Most importantly, Texas is a vast, seemingly unconquerable land, with many climates and their independent attitudes to match. And regardless of the belligerent rantings from the outside world, the soils remain fertile, the same of which can be said for their progenies.

There's less of a strain to John Singleton's stretch as he goes about filling cane baskets with a portion of the fall harvest. Turnips, carrots, cabbages and Irish potatoes will make for many a noteworthy pot, to go along with the added crunches of white radishes and pale green lettuce. In spite of a chilly night, the garden remains alive with color and growth. So, too, does John, he having regained all of his weight and a good deal of his mettle. Although he retains his orangewood cane to help ward off those sharp winces of activity, all is well with John and his satisfaction for the surrounding bounty.

The midday finds Henrietta and Georgina on the front porch,

busy with their needles and thread. In fact, they're so occupied that they've exiled Mary and Martha to the inner confines under Mairead's watch. Whereas only days before they were piecing together uniforms for John, as well as articles for the Ladies Soldier Aid Society, at his selfless insistence their industry has shifted to infant's clothes. With Henrietta's announcement being only a week old, the atmosphere about her remains cheerful and airy, notwithstanding her husband's nonsensical edict.

"This becomes sillier by the moment," complains Henrietta without a pout.

"Yes, I know," agrees Georgina. "But I do enjoy it so."

"As do I. Still, I think the time has come for us to set right that husband of mine."

Georgina smiles at what promises to be an amusing, little episode.

And as if on cue, from around the corner, the sound of John's limp precedes him.

"Do be merciful," whispers Georgina.

"John, I do wish you would join us for a while, and provide some entertainment."

"Of course, dear." He's never one to turn down such an invitation.

"Tell us how the garden is doing," asks Georgina, while her brother-in-law negotiates the porch steps.

As John eases into the chair next to his wife, he places his cane across his lap. "Things are looking perky on that front. Just harvested six, prideful basketfuls. Washed and sitting at the kitchen door. Quite a spectacle." But then he pauses at what to him seems amiss. "Where are the girls? I was just conjuring a twisted tale for them."

"Oh, we had to send them away, so that we could better concentrate on our assigned tasks," explains Henrietta. "We felt duty bound."

"Yes. Our honors are at stake," assists Georgina

The fact that the sisters speak with contained smiles while they stitch, perplexes John.

"This all seems rather superfluous. Do you not agree, Georgina?"

"Yes, indeed, Henrietta. Very superfluous when you consider that the baby could wear Mary and Martha's clothes. Perfectly fit and threadful they are. And so accessible."

As he props a cheek upon an open hand, John recognizes the conspiracy.

"I think, Georgina, that even the poorest of intellects could see that our present talents are being put to waste. And against their wills."

"Oh, how we take pride at being resourceful, in spite of the shortages, Henrietta. This empty exercise runs against our very natures."

"Our dear parents did teach us better, Georgina. Tsk, tsk."

John holds his grin as best he can.

"I am almost ashamed by this luxury, dear Georgina," continues his wife. "Especially when you consider the hardships endured by those less fortunate."

"Such an awful feeling I share, dear Henrietta."

"The fact that we should be piecing warm coats and trousers for the cruel winter is lost on some." With that, Henrietta redirects her attention away from her sister. "Tell me, John. What sort of husband would want his expectant wife to grieve over his deprivations? Hmm? Shame on you, John Singleton. Shame."

"Henrietta." John straightens himself upon his seat.

"Forgive me. But on this occasion, it is I who must take the logical pursuit. After all, you have so much else to contend."

"I have that appreciation, dear." Now, John's mouth smiles fully.

"Then if you are to march off to Shreveport, it is my place to see you properly attired."

"I have more spare blankets to suit the cause," notes Georgina, doing her best to smother her giggles.

"There. So you may see there is no lack of material. And certainly none of resolve."

"Yes, my dear," responds John.

"Regardless of what the world may say, I am going to finish sewing the finest of frock coats. A lined one that will drive the winter away."

Surrendering to her sagacity, John takes Henrietta's firm, but gentle hand and applies a proud and grateful kiss. "The winter will not stand a chance. Of this, I am certain, Mrs. Singleton."

That Henrietta would piece together uniforms so willingly for her husband may appear to be an about-face. It seems like only a few days ago the prospect of John galloping off to distant fields of battle would have caused her heart to falter. However, the circumstances of late have been altered to a rapid cadence.

Judging that he may be of some assistance, Captain Singleton is being summoned to the northwestern Louisiana city of Shreveport. It's here that the commander of the Confederate Army's Department of the Trans-Mississippi, Edmund Kirby Smith, has centered his fiefdom. John is to become an unspecified underling to the general's expanding coterie of thinkers and planners. However, aware of the rumors casting doubts upon the abilities of this group, he's had a few misgivings with his considerably flexible orders.

Henrietta's ticklish mood comes because she's convinced John of Shreveport's merits—an ideal setting to spend the remainder of the war. Knowing that the city is far removed from those arenas of conflict, and that even a lowly member within the department has little reason to enter the fray, Henrietta's mind is at rest. Thus, with her husband's safe future arranged, Henrietta is better able to prepare herself for motherhood.

As to how John is to travel to Shreveport, he does carry a concern. But later in the day, thanks to John Gaunt's openhanded reputation, this matter is being put to rest.

"I took him, myself, for a gallop and found him to be gentle." In front of the Shackelford's, Gaunt holds a grey gelding, while John gives a walk around scrutiny. "But with a surprising stamina."

Although there's no shortage of horseflesh in Texas, John's needs are delicate ones, requiring a more thoughtful search. "Yes, indeed. He does seem a fit fellow."

"I trust you will be happy with the price I negotiated."

From the gallery of the porch, there's another voice of approval. "A handsome specimen!"

John looks to his wife. "I feel the same, Henrietta!" And then returns to Gaunt. "Sir, once again I am in your debt."

"Nonsense, Captain. I feel compelled to contribute when I can."

"As well you do." John offers his appreciative hand.

"Of course, Captain, you will come again to me at first need. Regardless of the request."

"Certainly, Mr. Gaunt. To you and your dependability."

"It is a shame I failed to finish a deal for one of those swords. That their sentimental masters were unwilling to part with them."

Although John has managed to keep his '51 Navy Colt, somewhere between Bastrop and Goodrich's Landing, he's lost his fine Thomas, Griswold sword. To most captains of cavalry, this would be a tragedy.

"Oh, I can understand, Mr. Gaunt. But as I will not lead troops into battle, is a sword worth the fuss? Then again, should the need arise, this blunt edge could point the way." In rapid repetition, a grinning John taps his cane.

Although looking somewhat surprised, Gaunt seems to accept John's unperturbed loss of what is an officer's proud plume. "Of course. The blood of battle will flow regardless of ceremony." A brief pause ensues to honor this flutter of sapience. "Very well, Captain. For now, I think I will deposit your grey at the livery and send someone to fetch your saddle and bridle."

"That would be splendid, sir."

"May I ask if you have determined your date of departure?"

"I haven't as yet. But there is no hurry. My advice has been to set an easy pace for the journey." John's eyes motion toward Henrietta's direction.

"Sage counsel from a lady whose wisdom is beyond her years."

"Indeed, sir. Thank you."

With a little help from Georgina and Mairead, the skills of Henrietta prove remarkable. This is especially so when the end results come not from the routine of practiced fingers, but rather, dogged persistence. Through trial and error, countless mistakes and the corrections thereof, Henrietta has fitted her husband to a proud, practical degree. Not only has she fashioned a handsome frock coat from the quality wool cloth of a dark grey, but also has matched it with a collared vest. Even for the larger garment's single row, Henrietta has located some brass buttons of a Lone Star motif, lent to her under specific conditions. As for Georgina's other spare blanket, John's personal depot now includes two pairs of black trousers, one of which is lined. Yet after such a prolific production, Henrietta's ambitions weren't contained, for the remnants of the red and black checked, table linen is now a new shirt. Finally, a green, oil cloth, also once covering the table, has been transformed into a roomy raincoat.

And because John's patient frame has been available during all phases of Henrietta's work, the fit of his uniform is a special one, each piece of which could force a jealous thread through the best of New Orleans' tailors. For her, the finger pocks and calluses are but meager sacrifices.

But if the clothes stitched by Henrietta are for wearing, then they're also for viewing. What could be a better venue than Bastrop, to stroll about after each article is issued? Now that Henrietta has met her goals, John treads upon its streets several times a day, usually escorting the seamstress in question.

The Saturday mid-afternoon is a blustery one, but the conditions are made perfect by the simple adornment of Georgina's black satin cape. Meanwhile, the mud of Pecan Street has hardened into a passable mire, as the loop of Captain Singleton's left arm entertains the squeeze of Mrs. Singleton's right.

"It matters little, a son or daughter. Though I confess, I own a fondness for feminine names."

"Then a daughter I shall bear."

As far as size and color are concerned, it's surprising that John Gaunt's house is a modest one. Covered in a failing white, its single story is dominated above by a fronted, octagonal cupola. The rest of the box-like house trails behind, almost unnoticeable because it consists of only five rooms. However, Gaunt does have a fancy for ornamentation, with decorative brackets supporting the wide eaves and a dramatic finial of three feet perched atop the cupola. Then there's the enveloping, lace-like tracery atop the long portico—delicate and airy in its frosting. It's no wonder that John Gaunt's is known to the locals as the "Wedding Cake House." A lifelong bachelor, he shares his home with his sixteen year-old niece, Lucie, she being a refugee from the ongoing travails of Baton Rouge.

No sooner than John and Henrietta walk passed the front gate, then a barefooted Gaunt bolts through his front entry.

"Captain Singleton. Mrs. Singleton," he bellows through his quid of tobacco. "What a happy coincidence. I was just thinking of you."

"Mr. Gaunt."

He rushes to the gate. "May I impose upon the two of you for the pleasure of your company?"

"Certainly, Mr. Gaunt," accepts Henrietta. "We would love to divert our saunter."

Ushered into the parlor, the Singletons are greeted by a beaming Lucie, who closes her well-worn copy of *The Widow Bidott Papers.*

"How are you, Lucie?"

"Splendid, Mrs. Singleton."

"It is always such a delight, Miss Lucie," addresses John.

"I should say the same, Captain."

At first the fickleness of weather dominates the conversation, followed by talk of even smaller varieties. However, when Gaunt returns after having excused himself, the Singletons' visit appears ready to evolve.

"Mrs. Singleton. Might I offer you and the captain a cordial. I have a very tasty, blackberry one." With his cheek flattened, it's obvious that Gaunt performed a full expectoration during his quick absence.

"Mr. Gaunt, that would be so agreeable."

"Then a cordial it is," affirms Gaunt. He turns toward the kitchen and, hopefully, his servant. "Echo!"

Almost like a ghost, Echo appears at the parlor's edge. Short and plump, her waste is adorned in a white apron, with her hair wrapped in a similar cloth. Like her master, Echo wears no shoes.

"There you are. In the pantry is a tall, green bottle, filled with a dark liquid. Bring it here."

Her eyes to the ground, Echo answers in a barely audible whisper, "Yes, Massa Gann."

"It is on the top shelf. So you will need to use the stool."

"Yes, Massa Gann." To which Echo slips away.

"The poor thing," speaks Lucie. "She is so terribly shy."

"Echo has been with us for only a month," explains Gaunt. "First time she has been away from home. But Lucie has accomplished wonders with her."

"She seems to be a sweet dear," notes Henrietta. "But she must miss her family so."

"Yes. Though I may allow her visit them from time to time. In Webberville."

"Oh, Mr. Gaunt, you must. Do you not think so, John?" Henrietta knows all too well her husband's sentiments on the subject, of which he maintains a judicious privacy.

"How can I not take the advice from the wisdom of compassion, Mrs. Singleton. Of course, in due time Echo shall visit her family."

In the corner of the parlor stands a mahogany secretary, topped by glass encased shelves. It's from here that Gaunt gathers four cordial glasses, while from a drawer he locates a rosewood case. After distributing the glasses, Gaunt takes his seat and lifts free an Allen and Thurber six-barreled, pepperbox pistol.

"Captain. What is your opinion of this?"

John takes the weapon in hand, stroking its ivory handle as well as the leafy engraving of all the metal parts, including the five-inch barrels.

"It certainly is a token to beauty."

"I knew you would appreciate it. And I was thinking, since you possess only a Navy pistol, perhaps a reserve would make you feel more secure."

"Mr. Gaunt, I cannot. It is much too fine. Besides, how could I leave you and Miss Lucie defenseless?"

"Captain, that is hardly a bother in Bastrop. And I do have my father's Mexican musket. But you, yourself, can never be too careful. If it is charity that makes you squeamish, well then, we can call it a loan."

"Oh, John. Do accept it. Mr. Gaunt is correct."

"Yes, dear. Thank you, sir. Thank you, for all you've done."

With all the pounce of a wayward leaf, Echo reenters the parlor, holding a cathedral bottle.

Unstopping it, Gaunt does the pouring. "Shall we toast to a swift and just conclusion?"

"Yes, we may, Mr. Gaunt," insists Henrietta. "Yes, we may."

From the clear sky, many rays of hope gleam down to Bastrop. They also fall upon John's gelding, which is hitched to the post in front of the Shackelford home. Although Captain Singleton prefers to travel light, his mount is burdened with a Grimsley saddle, carpetbags and haversacks, a roll of blankets, a dangling assortment of cookware and a precious supply of stationery. Thus the captain's preparations and restorations are coming to a close, with only a sweet and sorrowful parting awaiting.

Already, John has scattered his goodbyes among the citizens of Bastrop, so that this final assemblage is a concentration of his near and dear. With his escorts tugging and clinging, John is led to his mount. Georgina is the first to apply her farewell kiss, supplanted by a slobbery Martha. Mairead follows, shyly as she's not quite sure of her place. However, an unflinching John takes her by the shoulders, leading to a heartfelt embrace and a tear-stained collar. Then there's Mary, wearing the cavalryman's hat of which she's festooned with pink, silk flowers.

Still, the kiss of all kisses is the right of Henrietta. Without reserve, she reaches up to her husband to render a deep and time-consuming buss. As she does so, Henrietta strokes the nape of John's neck, her other hand entangled into the flow of his beard.

All the while the girls giggle and Mairead swoons, and Georgina pines for the return of her William.

"Promise me, you will look after yourself." John is the first to come up for air. "For the baby's sake."

"I will."

"Georgina. Mairead. Take care of Henrietta. You, too, girls."

Retrieving his hat from its smiling perch, John prepares to mount, backing his gelding away from the post. As he takes to the saddle, Henrietta maintains a grip on his left hand, while John leans over and attempts to lift her off her feet. Unfortunately, the strain is too much on his thigh.

"Perhaps I should leave before I create a calamity."

"Yes. Perhaps," sighs Henrietta, who then convenes a stoic self-promise. "Remember, I will send you a light jacket for the spring. If need be a butternut Osnaburg. But I hope to do better."

"That would be splendid."

"Do go through Nashville. The Blakes are very hospitable. And do set a comfortable pace. There is no need to hurry." Once again, Henrietta reviews the roster of cautions. "Oh, John. Go now," she finishes with a pleading smile.

Pulling away by dawdling increments, the inches stretch into feet, which themselves become yards. John's eyes never leave his farewell party, as he allows his mount to find its way through the streets of Bastrop. Too soon, however, does the gelding take the proper turn, and John loses sight of the waving handkerchiefs and flapping palms. Thus compelled to face forward, it's now up to him to steer the course.

As for Henrietta, she's managing to quell her emotions, made all the more noteworthy when contrasted by Mairead's tears.

"I do admire your coolness, Henrietta," notes Georgina. "I would have thought you might have broken into pieces."

Henrietta smiles. "No. My mind is at peace. Yes, I will miss the touch of his manly hands and the humor coming off his brow. But at least I know he will be safely occupied. And will return to me." She takes a gasp. "Soon, we will be together. Never to be separated. Never."

The name of the route John takes, The Old San Antonio Road, reveals only one of its two directions. Its original intent still holds true in that it connects John's adopted city to Louisiana, the compass of which he follows, though with the likelihood that he'll vary his path. Be that as it may, as mandated on at least two higher levels, John doesn't rush himself, the slower gait of his gelding being less aggravating to his thigh.

Although Caldwell is reachable within a day, for John the town will have to wait. It's been a couple of years since last he was able to enjoy unhindered the countryside of Central Texas. Thus, when the pleasant hills surrounding Yegua Creek offer an invitation, John is too polite to decline. For this night, his sleep will come beneath the umbrella of a massive live oak shadowing over an ungrazed sea of grasses.

The darkness isn't quite full, as the light of a brilliant moon rises to replace that of the sun's. As well, added to the heavens' illumination is the earthly glow of a well-fed fire. John is fortunate that his variety of edibles allows him a choice of fare. The sweet potatoes, bacon, beans, turnips, etc. require cooking, while the cornbread and oranges are ready to be consumed. Not in the mood, John chooses the latter group, and as he's finished crushing enough roasted peanuts for his coffee, he's ready for the evening.

Already the wind has died, and with the croaking creatures beaten into submission by the latest chill, there's an absence of sound. His mount tethered well away to a stake, John lies prone in comfort, devoid of any agony that would muddle his thinking. He remains struck by the changes in the land through which he's traveling. By all appearances it's underutilized, the very soil un-ceding or not being pressed upon to give. It's as if the landscape has become weary of the conflict and is lying dormant for better times. Even the cattle are gone, and what now will be driven into the camps of Louisiana and Arkansas are beeves from the far-flung corners of Texas—stringy and poor. For John, the feeling is that after departing the full friendliness of Bastrop, he's entering an increasingly vast and empty world.

Still, the land about him is wondrous, especially since sleeping in the open draws an indisputable end to his recent confinement. Even without Henrietta at his side, John knows he'll sleep soundly under the open sky. Inevitably, beneath the edge of the live oak's canopy, the question arises as to why he should leave this region in trade for the constrictions of Shreveport.

Staring at nothing but the vastness in front of him, suddenly, John's miraculous eyes catch sight of two pointed ears, seemingly lifted above the gentle waves of grass. He realizes that he's under a stealthy vigil barely fifty feet from beyond his toes. Aside from cautious puffs on his pipe, John dares not flinch.

For what seems to be an eternity, so, too, do the pointed ears stay motionless. Apparently, the attached snout is having difficulty with its perspective, for the dainty whiffs of air are coming from the wrong direction. Added to this are the combined glints of moonlight and campfire, making for confusing shadows. The ears can stand it no more, to which they float to another spot in perfect silence.

Before long, much to the amusement of their focus, they flit from point to point along a crude arc.

However, a surprise occurs when soon the ears' orbit crosses a wallow of compacted grass, created hours earlier by John's gelding. His suspicions are confirmed when a grey fox is caught frozen in full view. The lights plunge through the animal, giving it a feathery, almost ethereal, appearance. It's as if the fox doesn't exist, except for some trick of the eye. But John knows otherwise, and wonders what could compel the vulpine to behave so recklessly. Of course, the grey fox must be captivated by the uproar invading its realm. Yet to carry this curiosity to the brink of exposing its vulnerable slabs is an unthinking at its utmost. Indeed, John reaches the point of denouncing the sly reputations of all foxes.

But then a strange kinship emerges, unspoken between John and his bold Reynard. It would be a cinch for him to make a slow move to his Colt and dispatch the fox. Nevertheless, John will have none of this, no sharp blasts to curtail this stimulating skirmish. The fox's eyes gleam in the lights: one being from the madness of the moon, the other from the wise creation of fire. And somewhere within that stare is John's reflection, its vulnerable self caught in the open.

"Go home. Go home before it's too late."

The fox hesitates at the suggestion.

"Shoo, now." John speaks more forcefully and gestures with a wave. "Shoo!"

This time the fox heeds the advice and seeks the safety of the taller grass. Once again, the creature alters into little more than pointed ears, and then, quickly, disappears into the darkness.

The following noon, at Caldwell's red-bricked courthouse, John trades stories with some paroled soldiers of the 2nd Texas Infantry, who had been captured at Vicksburg. Officially exchanged in October, the men are now in a state of confused limbo, as they await word on what's to become of their dwindled regiment. With his limited information, John can offer little to the mill, and as there is no drink on hand, reminiscing over a shared campaign gone bad lacks the stamina. Before long, he leaves the Old San Antonio Road to head north toward Nashville and another night on the prairie.

Situated on the Brazos, Nashville's decline predates the war, what with the size of its port limited by how much water flows down the river. All too often, there's not enough of a trickle for even the shallowest-drafted steamboats, while the schemes to improve the channel with locks and dams are just that—schemes. As for Mr. and Mrs. P. Putnam Blake, who own scattered acreages and nearly thirty slaves, they're longtime friends of Henrietta and Georgina's family, as well as of the Shackelfords. John had met them on two occasions—his wedding and someone else's funeral—meaning he has kin-like obligations. Coupled with Henrietta's encouragement, he expects a stay with the Blakes will last at least two days.

It's early afternoon when John locates the Blake home in the middle of tiny Nashville, it being a sizable, two story house with a Greek-inspired portico. Yet as he applies his knocks to its door and waits for the response, he's met with nothing more than indifference.

"Is anyone home!"

It seems that Captain Singleton will have to employ some patience, which suits him as he needs a break from any sitting posture. At least John has the opportunity to scrutinize the house's features: a solid and true structure, though with little ornamentation. The two wooden capitals are Ionic, they being the only real signatures to the house's exterior. Strangely, they don't stand out as they're painted the same dull grey as the rest of the facade, which by the looks of it was done recently—an extravagant expense for the times.

Giving it one last try, John re-approaches the door. This time, instead of applying a polite rap with his cane, he delivers a fistful of clamor. Soon, faint noises from within tells John that his drastic action is successful. The door creeps open, revealing a tall, jittery man of about fifty years.

"Mr. Blake? I don't know if you remember..."

"John Singleton?" He corrects himself. "Captain Singleton. Please, come in."

John's impressed by the man's capacity to recall, especially since his own abilities to caption faces from the past are rather random.

"To what do I owe this pleasant surprise?" So elated is Mr.

Blake, that he shakes John's hand as if to rid its sleeve of dust.

As he's led into the parlor, John attempts to explain his circumstances. However, the heavy, closed curtains spread their gloom, and negotiating the dark interior requires all of his concentration. A window is freed, and through it a sharp ray of sunlight forms a corridor across the room. Within the span of half a moment, John's poor eyes are being abused by the extremes. Regardless, they follow the guide of light all the way to the far end of the room. There, placed upon a table and cascading to the floor, flows a current of ambrotypes, tintypes and portraits, festooned with bouquets of everlasting flowers. Instantly, John recognizes this corner for what it is—a memorial to the dead.

"Captain. Why don't you take that seat, while I inform Mrs. Blake. She has taken to bed, but your presence just might hasten a cure." Mr. Blake rushes away, and as his feet are heard ascending the stairway, he shouts his announcement. "Mother. It's Henrietta McKie's husband. He's paying us a call and..."

It doesn't take long before John familiarizes himself with the flowing of likenesses. Somehow, Henrietta hasn't been informed over the Blakes' loss of their two sons—both young privates. However, before John can reconvene his own share of mourning, the creaking stairway shouts the return of his host.

"Ahh," gasps Mr. Blake, as he re-enters the parlor. "Mrs. Blake should be down soon. She is utterly delighted. In the meantime, my servant is bringing a refreshment."

Thus an interval to reacquaint. But while Mr. Blake banters, John's adjusted eyes wander about the parlor. What a clutter of accumulation, he observes, gilded with the qualities of silver, mahogany, satin and silk, although somewhat negated by the dankness of the air.

Then out of nowhere, a filled decanter appears—along with two stemmed glasses and their presenter, a white-haired septuagenarian.

"Set it there, Uncle Hux," speaks Mr. Blake, who turns to his guest as he pours, "I hope you find this wine not too foxy."

While John's tongue shrivels at the thought, his smiling lips keep tactful. "Oh, but that is how I prefer it."

"Captain Singleton, I must say you look the same as when you married Henrietta. How is the dear girl, and how is Georgina?" Mr. Blake notices the cane sitting across John's lap. "Oh. Forgive me. I had not realized or I would have offered another chair."

"This is no bother, Mr. Blake. I am fine, and so is Henrietta. In fact, she is expecting."

Upon hearing the announcement, Mr. Blake's face fumbles with nervous excitement. "Oh, my. Such wonderful news. Dear little Henrietta to become a mother. Just like Georgina."

"Oh, yes. My sister-in-law and nieces are all doing well. As is William."

"But to think both those girls being mothers, themselves. Mrs. Blake and I have known them since they were infants. She will be so excited." Mr. Blake turns in his chair toward the parlor entry. "Mother," he shouts, while realizing the futility. "Will you excuse me, Captain?" Not waiting for a reply, Mr. Blake bolts for the stairway, stumbling several times in his haste.

Meanwhile, John is not one to waste such a golden opportunity, as he returns the foxy contents of his stemmed glass into the decanter.

With his tongue in its right order, John sits loosely for what he knows will be a long wait. Perhaps it's unavoidable that the Blake boys' memorial would bring up the subject of his own loss, too easy to transfer its intents upon his brothers. While his eyes fix in a gaze, John is reminded that never again will he be the target of Frank and Simon's practical conspiracies, and no more will they torment their older brother for having been born in Kentucky instead of Texas. Nevertheless, John is able to relish through his vengeances, such as his clandestine rewriting of their school assignments: confusing Virgil with Homer, Scott with Thackery and turning the sacred sequences of algebra asunder. And, of course, there was no stopping when adulthood arose, the complexities of courtships providing many scenarios for fraternal atrocities.

With all the time, John loses his mind to the past, thumbing through the memories destined to fade, and mourning over the unfulfilled hopes and dreams. Somewhat numbed, his trance wanders beyond the Blakes' memorial, to the years which have occurred and to the years never to be.

Clump! Clump! Once again, the clamorous stairway tells of a re-emergence, thus breaking John's stare.

"Mrs. Blake will be down quickly," declares Mr. Blake, who scrambles up again, likely to provide aide.

In anticipation, John comes to his feet, taking the caution of leaning against his cane. Eventually, the first to enter the parlor is Mrs. Blake, her black taffeta dress and cotton cap highlighted by the ghostly pale of her face. John is shocked by how much the woman has aged. Indeed, the reason Mr. Blake refers to her as "Mother" is that she may very well be his.

Upon seeing John, Mrs. Blake perks up, although under her condition the face of any young man may do.

"Mother, you remember John Singleton."

"How is Henrietta?" asks Mrs. Blake, as she finds her seat.

"Fine, thank you. I am on my way to Shreveport and Henrietta insisted that I pay a call."

"Oh, that is sweet of her. Uh-h-h-h." Suddenly, Mrs. Blake is overcome by an uncontrollable wheeze. "Papa, I need my medicine."

Mr. Blake springs into action. "Uncle Hux!" However, realizing the urgency, he runs the gauntlet of stairs himself and in an instant returns with a bottle and tea cup in hand.

Without hesitation, Mrs. Blake downs a generous portion. The result is a brief sequence of coughs, followed by a look of satisfaction.

"A compound bitter for her ailments," explains Mr. Blake.

John knows better, that the potency of the concoction comes not from native roots and sour herbs, but from the still. "I understand completely." As John rubs his thigh, he extends his other arm, holding steady his begging glass for a full measure. After all, strong drink may be the only way through this ordeal.

Truly, John's visit to the Blakes' becomes a tribulation or even a punishment for previous misdeeds. As the afternoon wears on, Mrs. Blake's conversation and reminiscences become ever the more addled. All the while a fidgety Mr. Blake is there to help drench her sorrows. It doesn't take long before John's visit bears witness to the sickening display of parents having outlived their offspring, the miseries of the conflict having reaped far more victims than battlefield casualties. For John, there's a small thanks that God spared his mother and father from such a travesty.

And thank God for the knock on the door which just might

upset Mrs. Blake's liquored tears. Unfortunately, Mr. Blake is far too occupied to pull away, while Uncle Hux's hearing isn't what it used to be.

The knocks continue in stubborn succession, forcing John to volunteer his services. As fast as he can work his cane, he makes for the door, and upon opening it comes face to face with the sediment of the South.

"Mr. Blake in?" The visitor's voice is gruff, aided in its ill-manner by a protruding, well-worn cigar. His face is both scrabbled and weathered, with an apparent aversion for soap. As for his apparel, its sources are disparate: a once-proud silk coat above cheap jeancloth trousers, along with an open, homespun shirt and a brand new, black slouch hat.

"I am afraid Mr. Blake is occupied." John feels obliged to defend the sepulchral house. "Sir, you should return some other time."

However, the man is insistent. "Just tell Mr. Blake it's Butler. He'll come."

"Very well. Wait here." John pushes the door until it's just ajar and returns to the parlor.

The very mention of the name "Butler" alters the look on Mr. Blake's face. He leaves his wife under John's care and rushes to the door.

Meanwhile, John positions himself with one foot in the parlor and the other in the front hall.

"Butler." Mr. Blake's voice is angered. "I told you to never come to the front entry." Then he shuts the door behind him, putting the conversation out of earshot.

"Was that the kind Mr. Butler, Captain McKie?"

"Yes, it is, ma'am." It's at this point that John can't resist making a suggestion. "Might it be wise to apportion your medicine more sporadically, Mrs. Blake?"

"Oh, no, Captain McKie. Papa and I have already tried, but to no use."

Minutes later Mr. Blake returns, swinging his mood as he enters the parlor. "That was my new overseer, Captain Singleton." He looks to his wife. "Mother. Have you asked how many days Captain Singleton will be staying with us?"

"Oh, Mr. Blake." Although the question may seem shocking, John is prepared. "I am unable. Thank you for your kind hospitality, but there is an urgency to my travels. My apologies, as Shreveport beckons."

With the sudden news the Blakes' faces draw long and sad, the pathos of which could melt rocks.

Under such withering fire most mortals would buckle their resolve. On the other hand, John has stood against worse, those experiences having taught him the tactics of guile. Indeed, if a liar's fate is to be found in Hell, then he'll gladly strut that path. Anything to extract him from this mournful situation.

"I would like to stay. But I am afraid the offices of the department demand my presence."

It takes an hour before John is able to pull away. In his parting, however, the captain is asked to perform a simple chore. It seems that Mr. Blake forgot to inform Butler about a change concerning the division of labor. For some time, Uncle Hux's advanced age has demanded some assistance, and it's been decided that a boy named Rascal should fit the bill. He's to come to the house straight away, and to make things perfectly clear, Mr. Blake has written a note.

There remains at least three hours of daylight and one more of tolerable darkness. Since John sees fit to put all four to use, he makes his goodbyes to the Blakes sweet, but brief. With the sun being pleasantly warm, he strips himself of his frock coat and removes his Colt, looping it and its belt upon his saddle. Thus John is comfortably on his way, and after only a half mile or so he comes upon a meadow being fenced in by Butler's charges. It's because of the split rails that he's forced to tether his mount and walk a short distance to the overseer.

"Butler. I have a message from Mr. Blake."

His shoulders carry a distinctive lurch, while the rest of his body seems lean and full of bile. In one hand Butler holds a willow switch, with the other resting upon a sheathed Bowie knife.

"What is it?"

"Here." John hands him the paper with Mr. Blake's instructions. "He wants you to send him a boy, Rascal, to be the house servant."

"What? Now?"

"Yes."

"Well ain't that kind of him." Butler looks to a group of field slaves, busy at work. "Rascal! Get over here!" He snaps the switch against his boot.

Apparently, knowing better than to loiter, the boy runs.

"Rascal. What d'ya know about Mr. Blake making a house boy out of you?"

"Nuttin', Massa." Perhaps 11 years of age, it's clear that Rascal is terrified of his overseer.

Staring down to Rascal, Butler works the spell of his intimidation. "Hmm. Well don't just stand there. Can't you see I'm thirsty. Fetch me a dipperful from my bucket."

With his source of water only a few feet away, such a command seems ludicrous. There is, of course, no difficulty in seeing through Butler's real intent.

A nervous Rascal hands the dipper to Butler, but in the process spills a few drops on the overseer's mud-caked boots.

Swatting the dipper aside, Butler flies into a rage, whipping the boy with two sharp swats from his switch.

"Butler," intervenes John. "Enough of that."

However, the overseer is obstinate, as he reaches back for another swing with his willow.

"I said enough!"

Wisely, Butler heeds the warning.

As for John, he turns to the wincing boy. "Rascal. Go to the house. Mr. Blake wants you." But as Rascal rushes away, John looks toward Butler. "Be sure to go to the front of the house! Knock on the door!"

With those insulting words, Butler bites his lower lip.

For a few seconds nothing is spoken. Yet John has more provocation in mind, the beliefs he's penned over the years finding their release. He picks up the dipper and fills it with water, and, in front of Butler, raises it to his mouth. Yet instead of taking a swallow, John dribbles the entire contents onto the overseer's boots.

A minute of silence ensues, as the sudden adversaries swap their hostile stares.

Butler's hand grasps the hilt of his Bowie knife, as if waiting for the decision. Nevertheless, although his head seethes, it also wears the look of one wanting to back down.

As for John, his eyes issue the invitation. They also mete out an indictment, the crux of which is understood by every able-bodied man who has yet to don the uniform. However, because he lacks the patience for a time-consuming impasse, cautiously John begins to step away.

"I knew you would have no fight in you," he sneers. "But I had my hopes." And upon reaching his gelding, John shouts a final warning. "If I hear of you abusing these people, or taking advantage of the Blakes, mark my words, Butler, I will return and drag you up to the fighting. Hog-tied if need be."

With that, it's off to Wheelock Prairie in order to regain the Old San Antonio Road, to ride to said town where its young men have suffered in the same regiment as those of Caldwell.

Mile after mile and the journey accumulates three more days, with John nearing William's Ferry on the Neches River. It's here that the heretofore friendly sky alters its mood, declaring such with thundering illuminations and large, chilling raindrops. John is forced to seek refuge at a friendly dogtrot cabin, this being a lucky happenstance. And because the weather evolves quickly into a gloomy drizzle, there remains for him little reason to budge.

It's a crowded affair, what with the Anglins having seven children and only two rooms, this amidst a hardscrabble existence of planting corn and notching the ears of free-roaming, bottomland swine.

And there's not much time for John to get to know the family before nightfall. William does reveal he's on furlough from the 12th Texas Infantry, claiming that his papers stating such are misplaced. Yet John suspects otherwise, and as a commissioned officer it's his duty to follow these doubts. However, the day has been long and tiring, with the captain realizing that seven hungry children need their father and a much beleaguered wife her husband. Placated, he spends the night under the cold, but dry breezeway.

Morning finds John relinquishing his edibles for the common

good. As for himself, he soon discovers a use. Their ages between one and twelve years, the children are at varying degrees of illiteracy. Undaunted, John begins with the basics, soon enthralling his students with the sounds and rhythms of the alphabet. With little choice, he unwraps his writing paper and puts to practice the Anglin children's introductory penmanship, soon accumulating enough material to keep the class in study for months to come. Before long, evening arrives, but with no dismissal, as teacher and pupils bed down together before the kitchen fireplace.

The next dawn brushes aside the clouds, thus signaling an end to John's stay. With a mix of handshakes and pinched cheeks, he bids farewell to his students, each of whom clutches a silk flower as a laurel for lessons well done.

But before Captain Singleton mounts his rested gelding, he takes William Anglin aside for a bit of sage advice. "Private. Be sure to get your corn planted as early as you can, so that you can rejoin your regiment."

"Yessir, Captain."

"There's sure to be an amnesty for those who return voluntarily."

William seems taken aback by the turn of John's calm candor.

"You understand? Do not let them apprehend you. Make sure your captain knows you are returning on your own."

"Yessir."

"If you have any problems, send for me. I should be with the Shreveport provost. Or one of the bureaus."

"I duly appreciate that, sir."

John extends his hand. "Good luck, Private. Perhaps we will meet again." He turns to Mrs. Anglin. "Thank you, ma'am, for your kind hospitality."

With that, the captain mounts his gelding and dons his flowerless hat.

Nacogdoches is remembered by John as a bustling place—a gathering point for men, equipment and cotton. But riding into town he encounters none of this, that is until he enters the town's center. Assembling there is a haphazard company of mounted

Home Guards, and although they number at least thirty men, John collects not a single salute. To him, these "Heel Flies" are a curious blend, with none of their ages being in the twenties or thirties, but representing those years above and below. Still, some of them are armed—with shotguns, squirrel rifles and a few revolvers—and all are adorned with proud Bowie knives. However, with their rough and individualistic ideas of what is a uniform, it would be difficult to described these men as belonging to any category of soldier.

"Howdy, Captain," greets their lieutenant, whose face would be pressed to coax a whisker.

"Son. You boys enforcing the conscription laws?"

"You betcha. 'Bout to head up north."

"Good luck."

With no reason to linger, John leaves Nacogdoches behind, soon taking the more easterly route at the Trite Flat P.O. fork. So far, he's surprised that his leg has held up, but the weather is putting a scratch to his throat, the symptoms worsening with each mile of exposure. Upon reaching Buena Vista, the condition spreads to his lungs, thus producing an irritable hack not to be ignored.

There's little activity in this tiny town. Hemmed by pine forests and stubble fields, Buena Vista suffers from the dreariness of war's neglect. John doesn't expect this place to be any great source of medicine, especially with the shortages. So it's astounding when his brief inquiry to a citizen is answered with directions, be they given with a shrug.

Although John's path takes him away from town, the information proves to be true when he locates the building as described. It's a small, one room structure, feebly erected and left unpainted. Peering through the window, John notes a stark interior of crude benches, empty shelves and no activity. Nevertheless, somebody may be at home, for behind the building there does stand a house—an impressive one at that.

Stepping onto the porch, John knocks on the door.

"May I help you?" A man of John's age, he seems startled at having opened his door to an army captain.

"Perhaps you can. Is that establishment an apothecary, and are you its proprietor?"

The man seems reluctant. “Y-y-yes-s.”

“I was hoping to find some medicine.” For good measure, John lets out a cough.

“Oh. I see. Then I suppose we should step into my, uh, apothecary.”

It doesn’t take much for John to sense that something may be amiss. He follows the proprietor, who opens his door without the aid of a key. Wasting not a moment, John begins his subtle probing.

“My name is Captain Singleton.”

“Oh. Pleased to meet you. I am the Reverend Falder.”

“So you have dual occupations. A service to your community in these trying times.”

“That I am.” Seemingly touched by the flattery, Falder reveals more. “I have other occupations, as well.”

“Really. Do tell.”

“Well, as you might see, I am the teacher for my neighbors’ children.”

Judging by the size of things, the number of Falder’s students couldn’t add up to a handful. Besides, with no slate or textbooks in evidence—or for that matter, pupils—the building isn’t much of a classroom.

“I also serve as an assistant to the county clerk.”

This, in spite of the fact that the county seat is too many miles away.

“And I am also the postmaster.”

Owing to the lack of officianalia, John assumes that Falder may have purchased the title, without accepting its responsibilities. “Reverend, how do you find the time?”

“Well, I am a bachelor. So there is...”

“Now about that medicine?” interrupts John. “Perhaps a remedy containing brimstone?”

“Pardon?”

“Brimstone. That is to say, sulphur. They are the same element.”

“Oh? Yes. Yes, I know.”

But John feels that Falder doesn’t, it being odd for a man of both the Bible and chemistry not to make the connection?

Hesitantly, Falder steps to a corner shelf—feeble in its contents.

Could it be that a dozen bottles of pills and potions entitles one to refer to himself as an apothecary?

"I believe there is no sulphur in any of these medicines."

"Then perhaps I should not trouble you any further, Reverend. But I thank you for your time. Good day."

"Pardon? Oh. Yes. Good day, sir."

As he mounts his gelding, John's mind runs through Falder's curious choice of occupations. Certainly, he's no apothecary, nor a clerk, teacher and postmaster. As for being a man of the cloth, this only requires referring to one's self as such, without the pains of announcing a denomination or gathering a congregation. John knows that Falder's real occupation is one of avoiding conscription. And without shame, he's hedging his bets by stacking those positions exempting him from military service. Still, if the captain's parting seems to be abrupt, then he may have in mind a cure for his sudden vexation. Indeed, John needs only to wait for dark, and all will be made right.

Only the stars light his way, as John retraces his path from a few hours previous. Falder's lair is hidden well enough during the day, so that finding it by night is a slow, cautious task. Eventually John does, and after securing his mount at a safe distance, he approaches his target. Every creature in the world lies fast asleep, especially those which would betray him. Thus John finds no trouble as he creaks open the door and slips into the "apothecary." Taking a knee, he pulls from one pocket a candle and matches and from all the others an assortment of dry kindling. Soon, a flicker builds into a small flame and, along with the fuel of the offending benches and shelves, transforms into a warm, soothing fire. Indeed, the smoke of burning resin has a curative effect on John's lungs, this giving him cause to savor the moment. When, finally, he decides to retreat, a full conflagration lights the way to his gelding.

"I pity the regiment that has to stomach him," utters John, as he bids goodbye to the arsoned exemption.

To be sure, it's a job well done, with the only factor to finish the plot being a likely encounter with a detail of those Nacogdoches "Heel Flies," and to file a much-edited report. Smugly satisfied, John's sole regret is that he will be unable to witness the look on Falder's faltering face.

It's a fair distance to Bethany, beyond which lies Louisiana. As for the sandy road John has chosen, it traverses through a land of lonely farms, occasional pastures and thick, hilly forests. Certainly, were it not for the year-round verdancy of pines, the land would seem desolate. The trees, themselves, prevent far-reaching thoughts of bleak horizons, their density hemming in its few inhabitants and the odd traveler or two. Still, John is not alone, or at least he's not without accompaniment. Swaying with the breezes, the pines whistle their tunes, constant whisps to lull a man asleep. Several times John finds himself nodding off in the saddle and several times he has to pinch himself in order to stay awake, within a land repeating itself all the way to the Red River Valley.

But then there emerges a strange sight around another bend. At first, it seems to be another dogtrot, but as John draws closer he discerns its true dimensions. The cabin is three times the size as all the others, large enough to be sectioned into several rooms. In addition, John spots a neat row of shanties—the surest sign of slavery's proximity. What sort of rough-hewn dogtrot owner—regardless of his home's girth—could afford the expense of slaves? Because this makes little sense, John has no option but to pleasure his curiosity.

Although no one is about, there is a presence, so attest the staccato sounds of working axes. As best he can afoot, John follows the sharp echoes, negotiating the tangled ground, while his ears point the way. Before he ventures too far, however, he deems it polite to announce himself.

Cocking his head, John melds that ancestry of the Scots with the current Comanche. "E-e-e-e y-a-a-a-h!"

The axes fall idle.

"E-e-e y-a-a-h!"

A moment of silence is followed by hesitant wedges of iron, culminated by the crashing report of a falling tree. There's little John can see, his view barred by a morass of greenbriar, buttonbush and beautyberry. Regardless, there must be a way through, for suddenly, a wide-eyed head emerges from within the thicket.

"Yeow. Is them Yankees a-coming?" He's a boy of about ten years.

"Not as yet," smiles John. "Is your master nearby?"

"Massa Simmons done told me to fetch them that's making the hollering."

"Then show the way."

The wall of vegetation proves surprisingly thin as John emerges into the acreage being cleared. In the near-distance he sees a gang of seven male slaves, while the man in charge sits on a stump. Immediately, John senses that it'll be up to him to close the gap.

"That be Massa Simmons."

Certainly, he's no hired overseer. A man in his early fifties, Simmons has all the hallmarks of a gentleman planter, his dress being one of fine tailored tastes and his bearing erect. Yet the air about him is one of lassitude, as if he's inflicted by a troubled dispassion instead of simple boredom. Although Simmons may be in his element, also he seems out of place.

"Good morning to you, sir."

"Captain, I see. What can I do for you?" He comes to his feet and offers his hand. "Francis Simmons."

"John Singleton. I happen to be traveling to Shreveport and was hoping you would allow my mount to rest on your property."

"Certainly, sir. You may be my guest as long as you please." Simmons' invitation comes through his stylish Van Dyke. "And if I rediscover my cook, we should have a meal." He turns to the boy. "Octave. See to the gentlemen's horse. Water it and give it some corn." Then Simmons looks to a slave who is splitting rails. "Herod. Thirty more trees split, and the boys can go to their cabins for a meal. Understand?"

"Yes, Massa."

"Come, Captain. Let us retire to my house and get acquainted."

"Most gracious, sir."

With the walk the conversation continues. "I suppose you might have already ascertained my position. We refugees seem to pervade a distinctive aura."

Thus Simmons unburdens himself with his story. So far his

two sons have survived unscathed with their Mississippi regiment of the Army of Tennessee, while his wife and daughters have taken up a more comfortable residence in Marshall, Texas. Simmons is attempting to re-establish a portion of his life before the war, of a prosperous Louisiana plantation worked by more than a hundred slaves. However, the forlorn hope is that, someday, he'll be able to return to Carroll Parish.

It's with the mention of Simmons' origins that runs a jolt through John. "The Bayou Macon country?"

"Why, yes," replies Simmons. "I take it you are familiar with the land."

"Very much so." John directs his eyes to the point of entry on his thigh.

"I see. Providence?" reckons Simmons.

"Goodrich's," reveals John.

"Umm. A very coarse affair."

"Indeed. As was the entire campaign. Very disagreeable."

John speaks with no hyperbole on that episode of his life when he was forced into barbarity. The strategy behind that campaign involved more than creating a diversion for beleaguered Vicksburg. Many of the plantations west of the Mississippi were being run by agents of the North for the prize of cotton. While most of this land had been acquired through coercion or by simple abandonment, some of the planters cooperated, becoming in effect opportunistic traitors. For too many days, John and his regiment's orders were to play the role of the Vandal, to destroy fields of cotton and burn whatever could be of use to the enemy. Regardless, what became more distasteful was the order positioning them too close to being that of a lowly slave trader. The runaways, the contrabands and those who had been left behind to fend for themselves had to be gathered forcibly and sent west, away from Unionist influences and exploitations. Indeed, a hard campaign against lead and starvation would have been preferred over what had occurred in northeastern Louisiana.

"I trust your home still stands."

"Yes. But the last I had seen, it had been looted and was in a deplorable state."

Suddenly, some voices are heard, chatter coming from around the slaves' quarters.

"Eugenia. Is that you?" shouts Simmons. "Captain, I believe we may be in for a hot meal."

"Sounds wonderful."

As the men step onto the porch, a short, plump-faced, young woman approaches them from the opposite end of the dogtrot.

"Eugenia. My guest and I wish to dine. Prepare some ham and white potatoes."

"Yes, Massa Simmons." But as Eugenia turns to open the door to the kitchen, she sees fit to air a suggestion. "They just brung in a mess of buffaloes and perches from the river. And catfish. Won't you be better off liking them fresh fish, instead of that old, nasty ham?"

Simmons looks to his guest.

"Mmm," chooses John.

"And some pones? Some turnips?"

"Very well, Eugenia. We will have the fish, pones and turnips. And did you gather any nuts?"

"Massa Simmons, we done got basketfuls of hickories and beeches from them woods. And it puts me wanting to make some cakes."

"Do you have enough flour and molasses?"

"You know I do, Massa Simmons. We done talked about that. But we done did nearly run out of eggs."

"Can you still bake a cake?"

"Why you know I can, Massa Simmons."

"Very well, Eugenia." At this point Simmons is ready to give in well short of any compromise. "Why don't you prepare what you think we might like. And I promise there will be no complaints."

"That's what I be wanting all along, Massa Simmons," continues Eugenia, as she retreats to her kitchen.

With a sigh of relief, Simmons turns to John. "During normal times, Mrs. Simmons would have instructed our eldest daughters to handle Eugenia. Come. Let us avoid her stage for the time being and step over to what poses as my parlor. Where I keep my whiskey. The taste may be somewhat harsh, but it settles well. Perhaps your leg could use some doses."

"My leg and all that is attached."

With the men unwilling to budge, Eugenia is forced to bring the plates of fried yellow bass and goggle-eye into the parlor. The room is a crowded affair, more like a repository for those belongings which accompanied Simmons in his flight. And although the furniture may be comfortable, its owner cares not a whit if it's polluted by tobacco smoke or stained by careless drops of whiskey.

"How does your leg feel, Captain?"

"Less troubled and becoming more sure. Which is more than I can say for the workings of my head."

"I am afraid that has become a chronic malady for many of us."

Even with the door left wide open, the parlor's air has a thick pall of smoke.

"Captain. Might you join me to see how my negroes are doing. Then we can retire to the open porch with our discussions and whiskey."

"Delighted."

Upon reaching the clearing, Simmons seems satisfied with his count of stumps and instructs Herod to create five more. He relates to John his original plan of planting cotton in the spring and rafting his harvest down the Sabine to Orange County. Yet the realities are conspiring against this ambition, so that the best Simmons can hope for is to plant enough corn and sweet potatoes to feed his slaves and livestock.

For the rest of the day, the slaves are given permission to better the conditions of their quarters. As for their master and his guest, they have it in mind to improve not a thing, only to smoke and drink without fear upon the comforts of rocking chairs.

"I must say. And Captain, I steer no insults toward your direction. That upon first stepping onto the soil of your state, I had feelings that I was entering a country in some distant corner of the world. Dare I say, your Texas has become an unabashed nurturer of many of my pet aversions."

John experiences no affront. In fact, he's amused. "Tell me, sir, about these aversions."

"Well, Captain. Can you explain to me what compels an

otherwise proud and hardened soldier to adorn his uniform and hat with all makes of ribbons and flowers? Is this done to possibly confuse the enemy, or to incapacitate him with laughter? Thus far you are the only Texas cavalryman I have seen who has yet to desecrate his uniform."

"I, too, have noticed this upon occasion. And no, I cannot relate as to why."

"And women, who dress elegantly, although out of fashion as Mrs. Simmons informs me. Dress elegantly, but strut about in their bare feet, while expectorating tobacco and emitting foul language. And teaching their children to do the same!"

"Let me assure you that my wife is not of that number." John, however, fails to mention his aunts and cousins, their habits being indefensible.

"Nor would I suspect that she is, Captain, from what I know of your character. But there are enough of those women to besmudge all the good names."

"Indeed, there are."

"Still. It is a beautiful country, I must admit. It cannot allow me to forget of my home, but I do, somehow, find it appealing."

"That it is. Throughout."

As if to affirm, Simmons points to a simple fact on his own property. "See that sweet gum. All of those colors in one. Red above, golden in the middle, green at the bottom. I would say nature has become a jovial confectioner to appeal to the child within us. To help us deny our troubles, if for only moments of time."

John nods in agreement, for he knows that all is not lost when in the midst of all his sorrows, a man like Simmons retains an eye for beauty.

With evening's approach, the two men build a fire in front of the porch, recruiting Octave to keep it fed. John's intent had been to stay briefly, but now the lure of melancholy truths causes him to remain. It's not often that he's able to speak his mind without fear of repercussions, and it's even rarer when he can listen to much of the same.

"So Captain. Do you see the Sabine as a formidable barrier?"

"I trust this is not the only reason you selected this site."

"The circumstances were many. Not the least were the difficulties I had in keeping my negroes together."

So far John has seen evidence of less than twenty slaves, and his confused look is easy to read.

"I have hired out some in Tyler and Marshall. But I cannot account for the rest."

"Where did you lose them? Bayou Macon?"

"Yes. They began running away when word came of the approaching Yankees. Scampering off at night in pairs and threes. I was forced to begin exiling those I deemed likely to run. But even the others became unpredictable. There was no sense in staying. I had to abandon my plantation with what I could carry. My only hope being that none of my runaways allowed themselves to be tricked into joining Lincoln's army."

John knows firsthand that this is likely, that at least a few of Simmons' slaves would have enlisted into one of the designated negro regiments. His near-mortal wound had been inflicted by one of those soldiers, almost certainly the Minie ball coming from the rifle of a former Louisiana slave. Still, what good would it do to air this, to add to Simmons' burdens the pains of guilt?

"Captain. What is your opinion of the negro soldier?"

"They can fight like demons. But it is likely that your runaways are being used as contraband labor. Working the confiscated plantations."

"Yes. Of course."

By now, the fire has become the only source of light, its flaring coals intoxicating to the senses. Laughter is drifting from the slaves' quarters, the buffalo and catfish making their contributions. However, for the most part there's silence, as no longer the pines whisper, while the rocking chairs cease their motions.

Simmons' tongue has tasted too much whiskey, and so it deplores the quietude. "My wishes had been to become an Episcopal minister. But I accepted other responsibilities early on." And then his mood becomes even more downcast. "I shall never forget. The saddest day of my life. The day Wallace left home."

John knows better than to interrupt and ask the obvious.

Instead, he waits for Simmons, who himself stares intensely at the fire.

"Wallace was my house servant. My house servant. Had been with me since I was nine years-old. So you see, we grew up together. I know Wallace better than anyone else. Trusted him more than any." Simmons pauses to pour a little more sustenance from the demijohn. "When I found out Wallace had run away, everything affirmed to me, and everything I had convinced unto myself, had been disavowed. What I am saying may be difficult for you to understand, Captain. You having never held a man under bond."

"I believe I can grasp it."

"Yes. My apologies." Simmons takes another sip of whiskey. "I always took my responsibilities seriously. My negroes are my children. My patronage has always been paternal and Christian. But now I have come to believe it has always been wrongly applied."

It's John's turn to brace himself with the fortitude. "Those, too, are my thoughts."

"Yes. But what to do? What to do? Perhaps, soon enough the decision will be made for me."

"In spite of my feeble efforts," grins John, as he tugs at the collar.

"The inevitable." Simmons returns the smile. "I say let us be done with it, and perhaps my family will have a better chance of getting into Heaven." Then he looks at Octave, possibly searching for a resemblance. "But I do wish Wallace would return. Some day. I would forgive him. Forgive him without thought."

With that, the night has little choice but to linger on.

In spite of an aching head, John makes it an early morning. By the time Simmons awakens, the gelding is saddled and the soldier is ready to travel.

"Good luck, Captain."

"I am in your debt, sir. I trust that your prosperity will return."

As he finds the road, John's suspicions are that Simmons is not an altogether unusual phenomenon. Having had his eyes forced wide open by upheaval, the refugee planter has cast himself upon the wilderness. Trapped in some dark corner, full of doubts, Francis Simmons has no option but to flounder and flail.

Before long, John crosses the Sabine, pushing his gelding toward Bethany. The ride is an uneventful one, the landscape going unnoticed by the weary captain. When by early evening he approaches Bethany, John chooses to continue on, ignoring the protests of aching bones and empty stomachs. In spite of his rapidly slowing pace, it's not long after that he breeches the boundary and lumbers into Louisiana. Thus, while the sky to his back remains lit, the road ahead for John is dark, its course heading into an uncertainty of an unknown duration.

6 ↝ No More the Swirl of Her Long, Brown Hair

Across the country, parents are bewildered over the decisions of their wayward children, Buena Vista being no exception to this nation of divisions. The Pyes remain astounded by the course of their eldest daughter, although they are accepting the close supervision of a St. Louis "hospital." As for Mr. Potter, now that both of his sons have removed themselves far from his narrow sphere, he most likely will take his bitterness to his grave.

But then there are the offspring's attitudes and motives. Sylvie is free of regrets. Aside from his marriage to Susha, standing up to his father is now that segment of his life he most cherishes, and every day spent in the army will be another relish upon this heap. On the other hand, there is Susha, whose adventure begins with a tincture of guilt. Not only is she deceiving her mother and father, also she's abandoning both sister and sister-in-law.

The final afternoon before Des Moines arrives. Joining the Potters' send-off is Emma, doing her all to add more chatter to the confusion. Still, everyone understands what the morrow will bring, so that although a festive atmosphere is maintained, the gaeity is taut.

At the last possible moment, part-time farmhands have been found in the form of two "Dutch" boys and their sister, who, although speak little English, are brimming with all sorts of German. As for all else, the delicate and intricate web is woven, along with words of caution concerning the ease of an unraveling. Nevertheless, there does remain one final, crucial preparation, the act of which Sylvie cannot bear to witness.

With scissors in hand, Emma does the bidding, while Eliza hovers with her advice, and a stoic Susha sits as still as she can. It's a pose for her sisters' combined artistry, made necessary if she's to carry on as a soldier. Unfortunately, Emma is at a loss as to where to start, there being so many possibilities.

"Cut here," points Eliza.

The scissors move nearer to Susha's lavishly hirsute head. In spite of the slight trembles from each of the trio, Emma manages a respectable snip, and a swirl of Susha's long, brown falls to the floor. A brief hush ensues, as if a heresy is being committed.

"Emma," chides Eliza. "Did you have to cut so much?"

"You should have told me."

An argument is brewing, of which its subject cannot tolerate. "Will you two please keep cutting, or I will do it myself." Looking down over her shoulder, Susha sees her innocent sprig sprawled upon the floor. "It will take more than that to make me look like Sylvie."

"Susha!" responds Eliza.

"Come now. You need to cut here for me to become a soldier." She levels her hand to the top of her neck.

Still, the hesitancy to molest Susha's lovely locks.

"It will grow back," she reassures. "No matter how short you cut it."

"Well, if you say so." Upon managing a shrug, Emma grasps a finger full.

For most of an hour the transformation continues. With this in mind, it would seem a shame to allow Susha's hair to go to waste. Thus, while Emma finishes her handiwork, so, too, does Eliza. Skillfully, she's taken a severed lock and braids it into a pocket-size loop, intertwined and bound by a section of red ribbon—all in all, a graceful little keepsake.

"Here, Susha. Take this with you."

"Tell your soldier comrades it's from your betrothed," joins Emma. "They will be so jealous."

The door to the kitchen inches open, and into the house creeps

Sylvie with Ethan in his arms. Reluctant to view the damage to his wife's head, his downcast eyes happen upon the scattered piles of hair. The horrible sight proves shocking, and as Sylvie forces himself to look up, he very nearly drops Ethan.

"Susha, have you seen what they have done to you?"

She turns around in her seat to greet Sylvie's agitated face, giving him a frown.

And perhaps believing that a strange man is invading his happiness, Ethan lets loose a cry.

"There now, Pumpkin. This is your Aunt Susha." Eliza rushes to cradle her child. "Sh-h-h."

"You mean Uncle Robert," reminds Emma, as she snips the last lengthy strand.

"Sylvie, you knew I was getting it cut to look like yours."

Understanding that he's as much to blame for Susha's change as anyone else, Sylvie's demeanor alters to one of resignation. "It will take some getting used to." He moves closer to Susha's side to take in several angles. "I don't think I like it. Look at all that hair on the floor. All of your prettiness."

"Sylvie. How can you talk to Susha like that?" admonishes Eliza. "Goodness."

"I don't mean that, Susha. You are still pretty. But without your hair you look too much like a boy."

"Is that not how it's suppose to be?"

"Well. Yes."

"Don't you worry. My hair will come back."

"It had better. When we are mustered out, I want you never to cut it again. Never."

"Sylvie, I promise."

Continuing the scrutiny of his bride's alteration, Sylvie ignores the surrounding silence, allowing himself to compose what he hopes is a face-saving thought.

"If you really want to look like a man, you ought to comb your hair from the left side. Like me. Parting it in the middle will likely draw suspicions."

"We are aware of that, Sylvie," counters Eliza.

"Umm."

"Susha. Show Sylvie what Eliza made for you."

"Look." She displays her small treasure.

"Susha is going to tell your soldier comrades that it's from her sweetheart," explains Emma.

"What?" Sylvie replies.

"So I might be more convincing."

"No, Susha. You cannot have a sweetheart. That loop of hair belongs to me. From my sweetheart." Sylvie snatches the keepsake from his Susha's hand. "I think I should tend to the horses," he declares proudly, turning to leave behind three bemused, though bewildered, ladies.

A brief hush follows, broken, of course, by Emma. "See," she muses. "I told you your comrades would be jealous."

It's Ethan who serves as the early morning roust, his balling complaints besting even the roosters' crows.

As for Susha, the end of her sleep is greeted by a strange, uneasy feeling—one of a knotted stomach and an unsure head. Already well-practiced, she dons her manly apparel before Sylvie awakens, and unwilling to wait in the chilly bedroom, she seeks the warmer refuge of the kitchen.

Upon entering the room, Susha sees Eliza comforting her child, rubbing his agitated gums with her tenderly curative finger. Staring silently at her husband's blood, she's touched by the sight, and of how Ethan could very well be her own. At this affectionate juncture, it's no great shock that second thoughts are blossoming, late as they are. Yet Susha's doubts aren't whether she could endure the hardships, rather should she even be giving them a try? After all, wouldn't it be better if she were to stay and raise her Robert, and be more demanding that Sylvie remain as well? Instead, here she stands, dressed as a man, with her hair bobbed and parted for the same. Was there really a compelling reason why she and her husband are to wander off to some dark and distant land—Arkansas, was it?

Suddenly, there's a voice from behind.

"We need to be leaving within the hour." An awakened Sylvie nestles up to Susha, engulfing her in his arms. "Are you happy as me?"

"Huh? Yes. Happy."

Even after Emma awakens, Susha remains aloof. Instead of filling her stomach for the journey ahead, she leaves the table to take a ponderous tour of the house she will miss for many months. In spite of limited funds, the parlor is a wonderment: the maple settee where Emma had slept, a rosewood sewing table, an inlaid sideboard bedecked with Eliza's own lace doilies. Around the room Susha's head spins, and through the tasseled, taffeta curtains she parts, pressing her face to the window. But the sun's rays remain hidden, revealing only the blackness of the neighboring landscape. Regardless, Susha is well aware of what is out there, her fervent hope being that it all stays the same for her return.

Since most of what Susha and Silvie will need is to be issued to them, the recruiting sergeant's recommendation has been for the couple to travel light, with but a few personal items to keep. As Sylvie brings the mare to the front of the house, Susha meets him holding the small bundle meant for the both of them. Everything else, including the clothes they're wearing, will be posted to Eliza for safe-keeping.

"I will write often. With those letters for Mamma and Pappa's eyes. As a nurse."

"Yes, Susha," responds Emma. "And we shall write too."

Eliza has one last instruction. "Just leave the mare at the stable and Adolphus will fetch her."

Climbing upon the saddle, Sylvie waits for his wife to bid her goodbyes. Indeed, that dreaded moment of truth has arrived, as the moisture of warm tears merges with the fog of chilled breaths.

"Susha, I will miss you so."

"So will I. And so will Ethan."

"We should not be away long." Sylvie's eager to move on. "You hardly will miss us before we return." But his anxiousness arouses little sympathy. "I look forward to getting away. See what the country is like." Again, his subtle plea fails. "Susha. We need to be going."

Annoyed, Susha turns to deliver a sharp note. "You shush now, Sylvetus Potter."

Eventually, the parting hastens when Susha gets a boost from

Sylvie. Darkness prevents any harmful, lasting views, there being only the fading sounds of sundering voices to remember. Not unexpectedly, after the mare carries its load for a mile or two, Susha manages a full recovery.

"Susha, there is no bawling when we become soldiers. Do that and the officers will be on to us."

"I know. But since we will leave home no more, there is no reason to cry."

Before long, sunlight touches the horizon. Still, it'll be a while before there's any warmth in the air, compelling the couple to remain in a tight huddle.

"Sylvie?"

"What?"

"Have you figured out how we are going get passed that army doctor?" asks Susha.

"No. We may have to play it by ear."

"Or maybe catch a little luck."

"I can always go for that."

To Susha's amazement, the enrollment process is proving to be an indifferent affair, so far treating her as if she is a man. However, her womanly traits take no offense, she accepting the atmosphere of impartiality as a tribute to her burgeoning feminine guile.

As for Sylvie, his wide eyes have yet to blink, dazzled by the events surrounding Iowa's modest capitol. Although relatively new, but in obvious need of an expansion, the crowded, brick building itself is more agitated than a stepped-upon ant mound. Already, Susha and Sylvie's names have been entered officially, and because of limited space they've been given the order to wait outside. Surprisingly, the officer in charge is a mere first lieutenant, assisted by a lowly corporal and his private, with all three being quite young.

Susha had expected there to be a horde of hundreds, but as best as she can tally there may be less than fifty enlistees. And it all seems unmilitary in its lack of order or even concern. Especially so is the lieutenant, who more than once has disappeared into the unofficial part of Des Moines, only to re-emerge at his leisure.

"Sylvie, look at him," alerts Susha. "He's nipping at a flask."

"Well, it is cold."

"Do we need a nip, Sylvie?"

"Hmm? He really does look paltry. Not very manly, and not at all spit and polished."

"Sylvie, I hardly think he has any room under that greatcoat for a sword. I thought officers were obliged to wear one. Sure hope he keeps handy a pistol."

"I suppose all the real officers are needed down south. But you think they could have sent someone to make a better impression. I was hoping for a general."

There is the chance among the enlistees that Susha and Sylvie might happen upon an acquaintance. So far, however, they've been fortunate to find themselves amidst the comfort of strangers. With no fires allowed, the enlistees must rely upon their internal systems for heat. Indeed, misery may very well love company, if only to share its warmth. But at least on this occasion, there's also a generous exchange of words.

"So, where are you two from?"

"Buena Vista. My name is Sylvie Potter, and this is my cousin, Bob."

"Haven't run into anybody from there. We come in all the way from Jefferson. Cyrus Nye," he shakes. "This is Issie Trowbridge, and that would be Enoch Snyder."

Sooner or later it was bound to happen, that Susha would be forced not only to listen, but participate in an all-male conversation. Her only choices may be to blush silently at the talk not meant for her feminine head or pretend that she's enjoying herself with even a few words of her own. Determined to see this through, Susha opts for the former, and if need be, flood her ears with a hum to counter coarse lips.

"Who did you two signed up with?" asks Cyrus. Tall and all-knowing, he seems to be a leader amongst men, that is to say of at least two.

"The Forty-second."

"There's a few of you here. We're with the Twenty-third. Signed up three weeks ago. Had thought about the cavalry, but decided that the infantry is nobler work."

All nod in agreement, Susha included.

"Yes, I think the Twenty-third will suit us fine. Been a first-rate regiment down Vicksburg way. Picked up a mountain of glory when they captured those Seceshes on the Black. Colors are brimming with honors."

To Susha, Cyrus' proxy boasts seem a stretch. By the temper of his enthusiasm, it's as if he's led the regiment himself, when, in fact, he's had no influence over his beloved 23rd, whatsoever. Still, Susha knows it's not her place to take issue. Besides, Cyrus is full of information, some of which may be useful.

"What do you know about the Forty-second?" he asks of Sylvie.

"They're down in Arkansas. I believe spread out on picket duty against the partisans." The battle record isn't much to dwell. "Judging by all the fellows here, I would say there's nothing but first-rate volunteers."

"I have to agree," responds Cyrus. "The Twenty-third would have nothing to do with poltroons."

"Neither the Forty-second," matches Sylvie.

"You think they would make room for us inside," interrupts a shivering Enoch. "Look at the chimneys spewing out that heat."

"For certain," adds Cyrus. "Say, Sylvie? What do you think of that lieutenant?"

"Well-l-l."

"I know what you mean. Hell, looks too much like a damn, snotty fool."

With such rough language being offered at close proximity, Susha's ears petrify. And it's likely that more will transpire, for Sylvie is powerless to come to her defense.

"I hardly think that son-of-a-bitch knows what he's doing. While he's warm inside, we're a-freezing."

Apparently, rattling off oaths comes natural to Cyrus, which forces Susha to fill her head with a low hum.

"Brrrh, this wind," complains Cyrus. "Issie, how about another from your bottle?"

All too happy to comply, Issie locates a nine-inch, green bottle from inside his coat.

Immediately, Susha recognizes it as Old Dr. Townsend's

Sarsaparilla, a medicine favored by many a mother. However, the color of this liquid seems to be of a much lighter shade.

Issie is the first to sample the contents, the result being a satisfied, but pinched, face. Next is Enoch's turn, who does much of the same before passing the bottle. With his little finger posed delicately, Cyrus turns the bottle and flushes down a significant portion.

"Yeow. I think it found my spot. Have a touch, Sylvie. This ought to fend off the cold."

Unknowing, Sylvie takes a fair sip. The result is a wheeze and a cough, followed by open gasps for air.

"Easy now. You didn't think this is sarsaparilla, did you? It's first-rate whiskey from Issie's uncle."

Sylvie smiles away the effect.

"Your turn, Bob," continues Cyrus. "Have a good swallow, now. It ought to put some hair on your chest."

Not thinking, Sylvie delivers the bottle to Susha's open hand. And because the center of attraction is in her possession, all eyes turn to her as she brings the bottle to her nose. How could any person drink this evil poison, Susha wonders? Certainly, it smells as such, although Sylvie is recovering, as are the others. Realizing she has few options if she's to continue as a soldier, Susha decides to confront her first enemy. Placing the lip to her mouth, she tilts the bottom of the bottle to the sky, keeping it there for several seconds. Thus satisfied, Susha rights it and responds to her onlookers.

"Tastes fine," declares the conqueror, who displays no ill effects.

"Well, this soldier knows his whiskey," congratulates Cyrus. "Boys, we have an officer in the making."

"Here, here."

The cold wind does little to hush the camaraderie, as a tight circle forms around not only the issues of Lincoln's re-election and an imminent Confederate downfall, but also the contents of Susha's bundle—cheese, sausage, soft bread and ginger snaps. Indeed, between the five there's enough to arrange for a nice soiree, especially if Susha were to learn how to dance.

But if all good things have something in common, it's that they cannot have no end. Something is brewing as the lieutenant descends the steps of the capitol, his sword strapped and his underlings close behind. Wading through the sea of mud and passing by the islands of enlistees, the young officer positions himself to the front of his disassembled company.

"Attention, everyone." The lieutenant speaks tersely. "Attention!" He waits for a moment in silence, carefully observing his recruits. "My name is Lieutenant Warner and I have been appointed to lead you through the mustering process. The corporal here will read off your names. As he does so, you will form a single rank beginning on this mark." Again, he pauses. "Corporal, begin."

"Abbot, Joshua C! Akers, Elijah! Straight line! Brunnen, Augustus Z!"

At last, now things are sounding military, moving the enlistees to comply.

As the line forms, Lieutenant Warner paces its increasing length. "Straight line. Arms at your side."

Before long, the alphabet touches Susha and Sylvie's group, which becomes separated by a Parish and a Pitts, as well as two Rosenheims and a Swaim, the comfort being that nothing can split the name Potter.

Regardless, Sylvie's curiosity begs, as he leans forward to catch his wife's ear. "How could you drink all that whiskey?"

She turns with her own whisper. "I corked the bottle with my tongue and pretended."

"Oh. Wished I had thought of that."

"All present, sir!"

"Good. Corporal, show them the right face."

"Yessir! Company! On the command of right face, you will pivot to your right side!" The corporal demonstrates the move. "Company! Right face!"

Although not in sharp unison, all of the enlistees manage the turn.

"Dress right!" shouts the corporal. "Straighten your ranks to the man on your right! Touching elbows! Every man should touch elbows with the soldier on each side!"

It's a little close for Susha's comfort, the man at her left elbow being a stranger.

"Have them count off."

"Company! On the command, beginning at that end, you will count off! Alternating one, two, one, two! Remember your number!" The corporal looks for those not paying attention. "Company! Count off!"

The "one/twos" are shouted twenty-four times.

"Corporal. See if they can form two files and march them to the surgeon. Use Private Simms to demonstrate. But keep it simple."

The word "surgeon" re-invokes a certain fear.

"Company!" The corporal motions for the private to stand at his side. "When I give the command to form two files, right face, the "ones" will pivot and stand on their mark, while the "twos" will move to his side! Like this!" The corporal turns his back to the enlistees, as does the private at his left. "Company! In files of two, right face!" The corporal pivots and Private Simms steps forward into the space to the right. "Company! Front!" The two return to their original positions, which leads to a moment of truth. "Company! In files of two! Right face!"

With all due precision, Sylvie pivots, while Susha scrambles to take the space at his right. Remarkably, most of the others are just as admirable in their steps.

"Company! With the left foot! Forward! March!"

Thus begins the first of many drills, most of which should drag into eternity.

However, this march is to be only a mile or so, to the outskirts of town. Although the paired files are kept, the left/right cadence is abandoned for the "route step," marching in a manner most comfortable to each individual. Along the way, murmurs are traded between the ranks: of bonuses, uniforms and weapons, the mustering ceremony and, of course, dinner.

As for Susha, her sharp concerns point toward that surgeon, a doctor of physique whose expertise should allow him to detect a female's presence. Even Sylvie's concerted tutorship as to the ways of manhood hasn't accounted for this. And so with the pressure approaching, Susha fears are of her crumbling facade, and that Sylvie alone will be swept away to parts unknown.

"Company! Halt!"

With little to do, Susha discovers quickly that her nervous legs function better when they're marching.

"Company! Front!" There's a bit of confusion. "Line up as you were when you counted off!"

The enlistees have marched to the front of a porched building, situated in the middle of a military facility. It's plain to see that the entire grounds are of a shrinking importance, the original purpose for having erected this outpost running its course. Since the porched edifice seems to be the best maintained, and that to its side is parked a buggy and one, then indeed, it must be what remains as the hospital.

Lieutenant Warner slips inside, and minutes later re-emerges, accompanied by two white-frocked men—the surgeon and his orderly. From the porch, they look over the latest batch of Lincoln's volunteers, the two officers muttering comments to one another. All in all, when considering that the pool is now at its shallowest, they're not a bad-looking group, molded by the clean, rugged demands of Iowa's farms. In fact, isolated as they are from the purges and impurities of the cities, there's not a sickly enlistee among them.

However, at least one of their number conceals the feelings of being ill. Susha's stomach churns and her head lightens as she stares at the surgeon. Like an overmatched duelist facing her challenger, a sense of doom prevails. Filled with the perception of isolation, her hat soaking with nervous sweat, Susha has no alternative but to look to her husband.

"Sylvie," she murmurs, nervously. "What is to become of us?"

"Don't worry. Just do your best to behave like a man," he reassures in a mumble.

Meanwhile, leaving his orderly, the surgeon disappears inside.

"Company. Attention," shouts the corporal.

"Company." Lieutenant Warner addresses his charges. "You are to be examined five at a time. When the orderly calls out your name, follow him to the surgeon."

Soon, Abbot through Cunningham are whisked away.

"Sylvie." Susha's lowered voice cannot hide her near-panic.

"Settle down, Bob." Sylvie puts his arm around her shoulders and speaks aloud. "That surgeon's not to do a thing." He adds a little explanation for his fellow recruits. "My cousin's never seen a doctor."

"Won't be a bother," is a comment from nearby.

"See, I told you, Bob."

Nonetheless, the longer "Abbot through Cunningham" remain inside, the less valid become those reassurances. When the examined do emerge with their coats unbuttoned, Susha becomes resigned to the point of giving Sylvie a goodbye kiss.

But suddenly, as the orderly summons the next group, from nowhere the clamor of hooves draws attention.

It's a soldier, clinging to the back of a racing mule, which he manages to bring to a frantic stop. Handing the reins to an enlistee, he rushes inside without saluting the lieutenant, who, himself, follows. Once again, within the rank there's murmur and speculation, especially after the second five are ordered to rejoin the line.

"Company! Attention!"

Lieutenant Warner leads the way to the porch. "Company. Listen to the surgeon's instructions."

As the surgeon speaks, the soldier with the message remounts his mule and speeds away.

"Company. Hold your arms forward, with your fingers spread apart. Like this."

The surgeon scans the rank to see if all the important fingers are present and accounted.

"Company. You will bend your knees in an 'up and down' fashion. Continue repeating this." Satisfied, the surgeon gives his next command. "As I walk passed your file, you will open wide your mouths."

About three seconds are allotted per enlistee, so that the surgeon can discern if each has enough teeth to tear open a paper cartridge.

Susha's in luck, for her mouth is quite pearly.

Finally, after Ziegler reveals his yellow tusks, the surgeon turns to Lieutenant Warner. "Lieutenant. They look healthy to me. Orderly, you can finish the paperwork later."

Wasting no time, the medical pair scamper to their buggy and speed away, presumably to practice their professions elsewhere.

As for Susha, she lets free a long sigh of relief. "Sylvie." Elated, it's all she can do to keep from giving her husband that kiss.

“I told you, Bob,” he responds, his cool facade concealing his own share of nerves.

The schedule calls for a week of drilling at Fort Des Moines. However, the orders from across the country are to expedite. In addition, the recruits’ uniforms are to be issued in Keokuk, where their mustering officer awaits to administer the oath. Then there’s a rendezvous with an assigned steamboat. Regretfully, Des Moines is an isolated capital, the scheme to connect it to the rest of the world by rail having been disrupted by other matters. As for the town’s namesake river, its shallow waters would rather freeze solid than float anything larger than a raft. The fact of the matter exists, that if these young Iowans have it in their minds to join the war, they’re going to have to do some marching.

For the night, the recruits’ numbers are divided in half, so that they can be accommodated into two, coal-heated barracks. By clinging to Sylvie’s side, Susha makes sure that she will sleep with him, albeit in separate bunks. Still, in spite of the warmth, and the relief of eluding the scrutiny of the surgeon, she cannot find a restive slumber. If for no other reason, it’s because of the company Susha keeps—twenty-odd men of unknown virtues. They and their motives have her awake all night, what with their whispers and snores and midnight dashes upon the creaking floor.

As for the state of mind of Bob Potter’s husband, he sleeps through it like a baby.

Breakfast is before dawn, consisting of boiled beef and soft bread. To wash this down is nothing but strong coffee, and upon first scent its consumption becomes a source of discussion between Susha and Sylvie. Since they survived whiskey, the consensus is that the hot brew shouldn’t be a source of harm. Indeed, although the taste is bitter, it does brace the Potters’ insides against the 20-degree temperature and the long road to come.

The day progresses and the recruits find themselves nearing Indianola, as the temperature toasts to just above freezing. Though Lieutenant Warner keeps his charges in good order, the march’s pace is set by a team of horses and driver, along with a wagon loaded with company essentials. Even if the occasional wheel bogs in the mud, pressing the recruits into service, the time made is suitable.

Marching side by side, Susha and Sylvie are able to keep a discreet conversation.

"Do you think when we get our uniforms, they will also give us our bounties?"

"I don't know, Bob." Sylvie glances behind. "You know something about that, Cyrus?"

"Not 'til we get mustered out. Don't tell me you're thinking of spending it already. Hiring a carriage?"

The respect from the ranks for the lieutenant increases wildly when a hot meal awaits them at Indianola. After all, it is a remarkable feat to have juggled the arrangements. On the other hand, performing his duty is the corporal, who pushes the repast into a mad dash. Still, the recruits are able to stoke their furnaces for their march across the steppes of Iowa, and can be thankful that there is no enemy at their heels.

Regardless, back on the road midway between Indianola and Knoxville, a few of the feet become sullen and flat, with the disruption of straggling emerging. Lieutenant Warner, however, is quick to the task, ordering the three severest cases atop the wagon. Among the recruits, pride prevents resentment at these tokens of infirmity, who display their leisured shame in full view of the company. Without their realizing, good soldiering is being instilled upon the raw Iowans.

"Company halt!"

A desolate dusk of flat prairie surrounds the road. Yet nearby is a winding ribbon of leafless trees and its stream, allowing for a suitable bivouac. Wasting no time, the details are formed: one to remain with Lieutenant Warner and the private, and another to follow the unhitched team to the creek. Then there is the corporal's.

"You, and you! And you, Ziegler! You three, and you Potters! Take those two axes and follow me!"

Anxious to make a good impression, Sylvie grabs both. "We know how to chop wood, Bob."

And chop so they do. Quickly enough, the blankets which have been spread are loaded and the detail grabs the corners in order to take the firewood to camp. Until they return, Susha and Sylvie are left to wield the axes on their own.

"Susha. What do you think?"

"About what, Sylvie?"

"What do you think about soldiering, so far?"

"I think I might be liking it."

"This is a company first-rate."

"Yes, it is, Sylvie."

For a moment, they continue with their axes. But even stalwart soldiers must have their rest. With only the dull flicker of a candle lantern, Susha deems it prudent to lessen their enthusiasm.

"Sylvie. We should slow down. These axes are sharp."

His response is to stop swinging altogether, and come to his wife's side. "Susha. You know what you forgot to do last night?" Sylvie embraces her.

"What was that?" giggles Susha.

"You forgot to give me a kiss. Like you always do."

"How could I with all those men watching?"

"Nobody is watching us now." With his lips, Sylvie explores her neck. "Give me a big kiss."

"Sylvie, if I started kissing you, then you should want more. I hardly think we can have that." Susha is being playful, happy that her disguise hasn't harmed her appeal.

"I need a kiss. I'm a lonely soldier, don't you know." Sylvie continues to tickle his wife's weaknesses.

"I know, Sylvie," murmurs Susha. "I'm a lonely soldier too." She plunges her lips onto her husband's, wrapping her arms about his shoulders and pulling tightly.

In a flash, the passion is left to fly, their embrace so firm that there's scarcely any room to breathe. Sylvie's hands find themselves around Susha's curved bottom, rubbing and feeling their way. Rest assured, they know what to do, to slip free the galluses and unbutton the trousers.

"Susha."

"What, Sylvie?" she gasps.

"We had better stop."

"Yes."

"And we need to figure some way to do this good and proper."

"Yes, Sylvie. Soon."

Upon returning with the wood detail, the Potters marvel at the orderliness of what has become the company bivouac. Five fires and accompanying piles of fuel have been built in a neat row, their combined glow falling upon three miraculous Sibley tents of large, bell-like configurations.

But while the eyes wonder, the more dominant sense detects a rich odor, sending several stomachs into a fury of growls.

From the darkness Lieutenant Warner is heard. "Corporal. Your detail's rations are on the canvas."

"Sir! Detail! Line up in front of those rations!"

As luck would have it, Susha is pushed to the front. Beneath her feet are nine, carefully arranged rows, each consisting of a small slab of salt pork and five hardtack crackers. As for cooking implements, there's no need to ask as sticks of green wood have already been fashioned.

"Take your hardtack and sowbelly! Find a fire! Help yourselves to a cup and coffee!"

Securing their rations, quickly Susha and Sylvie find two empty spaces next to a familiar face.

"You two look worn out," remarks Cyrus, as he chews on his pork.

The future private of the 23rd is learning his lessons well. As often is the case, the army's salt pork is so poor that the only way to make it edible is to cook it to a char—excessive brininess notwithstanding. As for the hardtack, it having been produced in Des Moines may help explain its fresh taste and lack of infestation, a luxury sure to become rarer the further from home.

Still, it's been a rousing day for most and more so for Susha. The doubts she's held within herself are being flailed. Not only has Susha kept up during their day-long march, she's also become an inconspicuous part of the company. Exhausted, but growing in confidence, she'll have no trouble sleeping on this night.

Following their meal, like wedges in a pie, the recruits arrange themselves inside the Sibleys. As there are no stoves to heat the interiors, the crowded conditions become their own sources of warmth. Indeed, the recruits have been encouraged to share blankets and body heat with a partner. And it's of this suggestion that two "cousins" eagerly accept—with restraint—covering themselves in a head to toe fashion under a quilt of Susha's making.

Two more days are spent on the prairie, when at dusk the company reaches Eddyville. Already the townsfolk have retired to their homes, taking with them the hustle and bustle of daylight. Along with the expanding darkness, the impression Eddyville evokes is that it's much less of a burgh when compared to the gleam of Des Moines, or even Indianola and Knoxville. Be that as it may, none of those towns can boast of a railroad, which brings to a close the company's long trudge through the Iowa countryside.

It's deep into the night when the recruits line up at the depot, and it's during the wee hours when they board a train of the Des Moines Valley R.R. At first there is some trepidation about the timing of this departure. It seems the environs of Eddyville have a reputation for Copperheadism, the concern being of sabotage under the cover of darkness. Skillfully, Lieutenant Warner calms these fears, relating how pro-Southern sentiment in Iowa has been put down roughly and that any remaining Copperheads will have chosen to keep their attitudes and train-wrecking ways to themselves. From Eddyville all the way to Keokuk, the company should have nothing to do but sit back and enjoy the ride.

"Sylvie," whispers Susha. "Are you asleep?"

While Sylvie's head uses her shoulder as a cushion, Susha marvels at how anyone can sleep amidst the excitement of a train fare, although a quick scan reveals that her husband is part of a majority. Certainly, the plush seats are comfortable enough for slumber. But Susha will have none of it, choosing instead to enjoy the passenger coach. For her taste, with stoves at each end, kerosene lamps, curtained windows and brass fittings, it could make for a wonderful home.

However, the lamps may be too strong, as they prevent a look of the passing countryside. Instead, all Susha can see is her own reflection, her smooth face floating above the bumps and grinds of the tracks. What a funny looking fellow, she thinks, not enough of a man, but too little of a woman. Could it be that she really is in this situation, that she has gotten this far, so swiftly? And to what distance will she be able to go? Knowing that the answers depend on the events lying beyond view, for now, all Susha can see is that doubtful reflection in the window.

"Potter." Even with the locomotive's din the voice is distinct.

Immediately, Susha's attention is diverted to the front of the coach.

There, next to a barrel, sits the corporal. In his hand is a bitten apple and in one cheek the juicy contents. It seems that now, he and Susha are the only two who remain awake.

"Want one?"

Susha musters a response in the form of a nod.

Reaching into the barrel, the corporal locates an apple and pitches it halfway across the coach.

Alerted, Susha's catch is expert, with Sylvie's sleep paying no heed. "Thanks, Corporal."

Responding with a nod of his own, the corporal takes no undue notice and returns to his apple.

As for Susha, she, too, takes a bite, only to resume her gaze at that man in the window.

A sudden jolt awakens Susha. The train slows considerably, with the fireman applying his hand brake. Taking a groggy look outside, Susha is met by the first glimmer of dawn, as well as a depot and its adjoining town. However, a sign speaks of Bentonsport and not Keokuk, hence, some confusion.

What Susha doesn't realize is that the Des Moines Valley is a working railroad, commerce being its chief concern. In between the two passenger coaches are seven boxcars, some of which are loaded with barrels of lard and cider, sacks of feed grain, and wool in the grease. However, two of the cars are empty, begging to be filled with much of the same.

The train comes to a complete stop and Susha tries to nudge Sylvie out of his sleep. All about them are rousing men, stretched upon the floor space or having taken the Potters' example of propping in pairs.

From the front platform the conductor enters the coach and exchanges a few words with the lieutenant.

"Company!" alerts the corporal.

"Company. Listen closely." Lieutenant Warner waits as his charges gather themselves. "The train's conductor has told me we have 30 minutes before we depart. Each of you is free to leave the train to take care of business. Do not leave the depot. Do not leave the depot or go into town. The train will blow its whistle when it is ready to depart. Any questions? Very well. Corporal."

"Company! Dismissed!"

"What did he say?" asks Sylvie, as he opens his eyes. "We in Keokuk?"

Although the speed of the train isn't blinding, it does move faster than a man on horseback, and emits much more smoke. Along with the beautiful countryside and its views of the river, Susha's fare proves to be a pleasant goodbye to Iowa.

Yet finally, the train pulls into the last depot, that being of Keokuk. There's a clamor of excitement, the talk being thick of this destination. Lieutenant Warner wastes no time and has his company exit the coach, lining up in two ranks. After taking roll, hastily, he departs for town.

Breaking ranks, the company is allowed to loiter in full view. As it happens, each recruit is learning the dilatory ways of the army, that their wait for the lieutenant's return is liable to be a long one. Normally, this might be of no concern, for a soldier gets paid whether he does little or nothing. However, the company's apple barrel has been bottomed, the train's route being marked by a trail of bare cores. Coupled with the cold wind, any delay is sure to be made longer.

"I sure could use some coffee and hardtack."

"Me too, Sylvie."

Lieutenant Warner, however, is proving his efficiency, he keeping his absence to barely two hours. Night arrives, as he re-assembles the company.

"Men." The lieutenant smiles as he addresses the recruits. "As our boat to St. Louis will not be here for another day, we will bide our time at Camp Halleck. You will dine there and sleep in the barracks. But in the morning, the company will see the quartermaster to be issued uniforms."

A round of babble and backslaps interrupts Lieutenant Warner, which he allows to die on its own.

"In addition, I have located the mustering officer, who will swear you in."

Suddenly, there's an outburst from of all people, Cyrus. "Three cheers for the lieutenant!"

"Hurrah! Hurrah! Hurrah!"

Boiled beef and potatoes never tasted so good, nor has coffee ever been as invigorating. Even when the same meal is prepared for the following morning, the recruits partake with a hearty zeal. Still, nothing can better the day than the anticipated appointment with the quartermaster. After all, what best defines a soldier than his uniform? In short order, what was once a ragged group of every color and pattern known to man is transformed into a smart company of navy blue, sack coats and sky blue trousers.

And to make certain that Susha and her comrades won't be confused as to the purpose behind this uniformity, Lieutenant Warner puts them through the drill. As it occurs, hours are stomped upon the parade ground at Camp Halleck. Not only is the company familiarized with the various formations and maneuvers, but also the lieutenant and corporal introduce the recruits to the manual of arms, substituting pieces of lumber for the genuine article. Nevertheless, the high point of the day is undeniable, taking place in the early afternoon with the mustering officer in attendance. The oath is administered and, as the major makes a bow to the graces of God, solemnly accepted.

Officially, Robert and Sylvetus Potter are subject to all the regulations and punishments of the army, to which they've pledged themselves with no allowances for regrets. Along with the camaraderie and experiences of a lifetime, in every sense of the word Susha and Sylvie are soldiers, even if they are at a loss as to nearly all of the procedures.

Its schedule still in a shambles, the steamboat isn't ready to take on passengers. Therefore, it's another cold morning spent on the parade ground. Regardless, the intricacies of the drill must be sinking into some, for murmuring complaints of monotony are emerging from the ranks.

Susha's attention to detail doesn't waver, however, and neither does Sylvie's, for they both realize that lagging and shirking will bring notice upon themselves.

"Left wheel! March!" commands the lieutenant. "Guide on the private! Keep your elbows touching! Guide! Forward, march!"

Before the next maneuver can be determined, however, the corporal appears with a message.

"Company, halt!"

There's a lively trade of whispers within the ranks, which Lieutenant Warner puts down with his facts. "Company. Gather around. Listen closely." He pauses. "In two hours' time, we leave Camp Halleck to embark on the steamboat *Duchess of Brownsville*. Bound for St. Louis."

"Company!" hushes the corporal of the garrulous response.

"Thank you, Corporal. You will return to the barracks to make your preparations. Dispose of your civilian clothing as you see fit. If you wish to bundle them home, we will be marching passed a post office. As for your other personal possessions, keep as few as possible. Is there more to add, Corporal?"

"Yessir! If you can, write a letter home!"

"Yes. Stow it in your bundle. Corporal, form two ranks and I will see you there in one hour."

Soon, the company's barrack becomes a mad scene of frantic joviality. Fortunately, Susha has Sylvie to pack away their clothes, enabling her to locate a secluded corner. It seems the female in her has been dying to speak its natural tongue. What now may be Susha's most important personal possession is a writing pen left over from her school days, along with a bottle of Stuart Ink given to her by Eliza, and 24 sheets of stationery purchased from the camp sutler.

Dear Emma and Eliza,

All is good for Sylvie and me have kept our health in good order while we did our marching across the state. We are in Keokuk at Camp Halleck and soon will be on the Mississippi on a boat named Duchess of Brownsville bound for Saint Louis. I said we did march across the state but that is not all truthful for we did catch a train in Eddyville and what a beautiful train coach it was. Our Company is one of fine fellows but I did not think this to begin with. Sylvie and me are making fine friends even if this is for just a short while for some will be going to different Regiments than our own when our training is done. Our officer is named Lieutenant Warner and he is firstrate and knows all the Army rules to heart. He is young and also very handsome. Emma you would like Lieutenant Warner because I think he would be a perfect match for you. And would you know that he told Sylvie and me that he is an officer in our Regiment so that we should get to know him realy good. May be after the war is done we can invite him for a visit. He lives in Indianola and Eliza you would like him to. We got our uniforms yesterday from the Quarter Master. We stood in lines and he and his Privates just looked at us to size us just right. Sylvie and me did our own hemming. He did fine but I pretended not to. We get thirteen dollars for our regular pay but what Sylvie and me did not know was that we also get three and one half dollars a month for a clothing allowunce. If we take care of our uniforms then the extra money is ours to keep but if we dont then the Army will draw the allowunce from our regular pay. Sylvie and me will be ultra careful. The shirts they issued are awful rough so Sylvie thinks we should keep our civilian shirts. We also will keep our drawers and the Corporal said that would be fine. The blouse they issued is fine it being unlined and costing $2.40. But the Great Coat is firstrate it costing $9.25 and being the color of sky blue the same as the trousers. Our shoes are firstrate they being sewn taut and costing $2.55 but the stockings are poor and not worth drawing. We got good blankets so I am sending back my quilt and also our hats. We drew caps but were told we should buy black slouch hats when we get to Saint Louis. This we will do. Sylvie and me got to dress privately as he always finds a place to do this and there are others in the Company who behave the same. May be I am not the only woman here. Sylvie is a good protector but I must say that living with all these men is no different than if I had become a nurse or better since I do not have to bath or dress them. We will be issued our muskets in Saint Louis and I am not afraid at all for Sylvie has let me shoot his rabbit gun. Yesterday we got sworn in by a Mustering Major and it was a ceremony in every regard. It reminded me of my wedding some of the words being the same. I even said I do and almost gave Sylvie a kiss but I did not. I suppose I have two husbands but Sylvie does not mind. Our Regiment is in Arkansas so after Saint Louis we will be going there. I hope it is not Helena. When we get there then you will know the address to write to and when Mamma starts writing be sure you get the letter to mail and put the right address on it or else some hospital in Saint Louis might be getting confused. Soon I will write a letter that Mamma and Pappa can read about me being a nurse. Put away our bundle of clothes and give Ethan a kiss from me and Sylvie too and say a prayer for us. I almost forgot to say that first thing Sylvie wants us to have our likeness taken so that when we tell our story after the war people will have to believe us. So far Sylvie and me like soldiering. It sure is better than digging dirty coal.

Your effectionate Sister
Susha.

Intended to ply the trade of the Ohio and Monongahela Rivers, the commerce of war has shifted the *Duchess of Brownsville's* compass westward. Built in '59, she seems much older, too busy steaming upon the Mississippi to lay over for even a fresh coat of paint. Yet to the eyes of dry-landers, the *Duchess* is an elegant and powerful lady, belying her workhorse stock. Her main deck is jammed with mortarless walls of crates and barrels, as the twin-chimneyed, 156-feet sternwheeler glides through the churlish waters. And above this, the need to transport more material has carried its weight to the boiler deck, where half of the twenty cabins house freight instead of passengers.

In spite of a blustery tail wind funneling down the Mississippi Valley, Susha and Sylvie abandon their assigned cabin, it being too crowded and smoke-filled. Nevertheless, their perch upon a cord of wood suits them just fine, it providing an unclouded view. With its constancy and swirling flows, the nation's river is a sedative, acting to calm all frets and shivers. The stoker opens the door in order to feed a firebox, sending heated wafts across Susha and Sylvie's huddled laps. This shared touch of warmth is much appreciated by the couple, and the comfort gained allows for some reminiscing of their common pasts.

"Susha? You recall the other time we saw the Mississippi?"

"I thought we would never get across. But this time I am not in the least afraid. Truth to tell, I feel safe out here in its middle."

"I know what you mean. As safe as home."

Through the night, the *Duchess* makes a cautious crawl down the Mississippi, the pilot doing his best to steer clear of snags and bars. Sleeping soundly in spite of the stoker's busy chore, Susha and Sylvie are not awakened by a pre-dawn whistle, but instead are roused because of a much greater alarm. The boat's toilets are at the stern, a pair of privies each housing a bottomless seat above the paddlewheel. Thus it's up the stairs leading to the far end of the boiler deck, the groggy Potters hoping for the privacy of the early hour.

However, at least one of them is in for a rude greeting, as they round the corner and step onto the long gallery. It's here, onto where each cabin door opens, that none other than Cyrus Nye is relieving himself upon the Mississippi—fifteen feet below. Because there's enough light to reveal the obvious, Susha's feet stall.

"Is that you, Potters? Come and make water with me."

Yet Sylvie refuses to stumble. "No thanks. To the back of the boat for us. Come on, Bob." He takes a petrified Susha by the arm and gives her a whisper. "Don't look down."

Complying as best she can, Susha's steps grow even more timid, her heart almost freezing when, as she walks passed Cyrus, she receives a gentle poke from his free elbow.

"What do you think about my waterfall, Bob?"

Minutes later, the first to complete his round, Sylvie takes it upon himself to post sentry over the other toilet. "Susha, understand that it was all sudden. Cyrus didn't mean a thing. He has no notion that you're not a man." Because of the noise of the paddlewheel, Sylvie must shout. "You have to get used to some of the boys not being bashful."

The door flings open, narrowly missing Sylvie's bothered head.

"It was just unexpected, Sylvie. But I have gotten over it."

Relieved, Sylvie lets out a sigh.

"I think now if I have to, I can watch men pee."

Unbound in both size and growth, St. Louis' capacities are a blur to the untried imaginations of Iowa farm boys. It's mid-afternoon and the *Duchess* has managed to insert its bow onto the swarming levee. Said landmark is a 200-feet wide berm, affording not only protection from flood waters, but also serving as docking space for the shallow-drafted steamboats. Because of this, the levee is an active hive of on-loading and off-loading, and of horse-drawn, delivery wagons making their circuits. As for the city, its crowded mark rises where the aforementioned slope eases, continuing its commercial and residential runs for miles.

Already, the company has been assembled on both sides of the boiler deck, waiting for barrels of salt pork to be moved before they can disembark. Meanwhile, those imaginations are trying to sort themselves, the recruits gawking in awe at what is almost at their very feet.

No one is more enthralled than Susha, she staring through the hazy smoke of a hundred steamboats and thousands of fireplaces and stoves. How could one city be so vast, she ponders to herself, so congested with all makes of structures: buildings up to six stories, smokestacks towering higher, and looming church steeples with even greater reaches? Notwithstanding, how is the company supposed to find its way to the Benton Barracks on St. Louis' other outskirts? Could it be that there's enough room in this packed city for streets? When combined with the levee, where it seems every kind of person in the world is mingling with their assigned degrees of commerce, St. Louis is a frightening spectacle.

"Bob, can you believe all the darkies," notes Cyrus. "There's more on this one levee than our entire state."

"That could be true," adds Sylvie. "I wonder if they're slaves, Bob?"

Indeed, could they be slaves? Certainly, they're hard at toil, rolling barrels and shouldering heavy sacks. However, having never seen a bondsman, let alone anyone of that race, Susha can't avail an opinion.

"They can hardly all be slaves," concludes Cyrus. "Look there. Dressed too fine."

By some miracle and much more facility, soon, Lieutenant Warner guides his company through the streets of the city. The Benton Barracks is one of several installations scattered about St. Louis, and is something of a sizable town all its own. Several framed buildings comprise the headquarters, while the soldiers' housing is strung along the parade grounds, itself being a half-mile in area. Behind these buildings are located the kitchens as well as numerous outhouses, all serviced by underground pipes to carry their assorted flows. In addition, further to the rear are several stables.

The impression on the recruits is that the Benton Barracks is a military post of the first order, its facilities maintained to a high degree. Fort Des Moines and Camp Halleck were nearly deserted, while this place is a hum of human activity. Although the numbers of gathering recruits are relatively small, forming only a weak battalion, the calendar is forcing several veteran regiments to make their winter quarters here. And to add a little more fervor to their daily diets, some of the recruits catch word that there may be Confederate prisoners present, huddled in the stockade to await their processing.

It all makes for a crowded situation, the same conditions which always seem to foment winter sicknesses. But the Barracks is blessed with a fine hospital, large enough to accept the issues of a bloody campaign or a seasonal epidemic. In fact, first thing the company is sent there to receive their smallpox inoculations, where Sylvie's scar exempts both the Potters.

Still, Susha manages to get something out of her wait at the hospital, an idea she conveys to Sylvie at a corner within the company quarters.

"Sylvie, I think I might tell Mamma and Pappa that I am a nurse at the hospital here. That way I can better describe my nursing in my letters."

"It's a good notion," he grins. "But can you believe there are Seceshes about. I tell you they had better not cross paths with this company."

"What would we do, Sylvie? We are not even armed, yet."

"Hmm. I hope they issue our muskets soon. I would sure feel less naked."

The morning is spent drilling as a battalion with the other companies, as commanded by a captain. Recruited from several parts of Iowa, as well as Illinois and Missouri, it becomes evident that these men have received no instructions, whatsoever. Deservedly, Lieutenant Warner's hardened company is given the "A" designation, to be called upon when the captain needs to have a command demonstrated. For the boys from central Iowa, the shifting of formations, the mock firing by files and even the movements of the left and right wheels have become etched already into their second natures.

As a matter of fact, Company A is so well ahead in learning the drill, that by afternoon, they need to be excused so that the rest of the battalion might catch up. Regardless, Lieutenant Warner, isn't about to offer his charges a break from the cold rigors of the drill. Indeed, for his company, the young officer and the captain may have in mind a greater reward.

"Company! Halt!" snaps the corporal.

Housing those most vital implements of a soldier's life, the Barracks' armory stirs an excitement, even if it's not an impressive building. As with everything done by the army, issuing arms comes in a well-ordered fashion: four recruits at a time enter the building and four soldiers emerge to retake their places in their files. Each has hanging from a shoulder a leather sling and cartridge box, while grasping a small cap box and a bayonet with scabbard. But as for their other hand, it cradles a bright-barreled firearm of long proportions and solid, modern manufacture.

With her fears and timidity dissolving by the hour, Susha's

anticipations build. Before she knows it, she's standing in front of the ordnance sergeant, and is being handed her weapon and accoutrements. The immediate sensation is one of cold grease, for the barrel is caked with it. As well, there is the oiled stock, and, of course, the unexpected weightiness of the weapon. To say the least, this isn't Sylvie's half-stock, rabbit rifle, the reality that she clutches a deadly implement of war not lost.

After the clerk enters the serial number with Susha's name and regiment, her group rejoins the ranks.

"Bob, have you ever seen anything as sure as this?

"It is first-rate, Sylvie."

"Feel the balance. I bet it could almost shoot by itself."

"Fine piece of furniture," agrees Susha.

"You got that right, Bob," joins Cyrus, his eyes not leaving his weapon. "Nothing in my parents' parlor could better this."

When the last group falls in, the corporal, armed in his own right, barks for attention. "Company!"

"Company," speaks Lieutenant Warner. "Each of you will place your cap box in your pocket and hold your bayonet and scabbard in your left hand. Make sure your cartridge box is on your right side." The lieutenant waits a moment for his men to straighten themselves. "Company. Order, arms. Company. Shoulder, arms."

Susha snaps through the commands. Surprisingly, it's much easier with the genuine article than with a substitute stick.

"Thumbs on top of the trigger guard. Forefinger below," reminds the lieutenant.

As he does so, the corporal and the private are in among the ranks, personally helping out with the adjustments.

"Company. Right face. Forward, march." The lieutenant leads his charges a few feet into a more open area. "Company. Halt. Front. Order, arms. In place, rest. Place your bayonet on the ground in front of you. Corporal, take command."

This he does, in a series of demonstrations and lectures concerning the functions and forms of the Pattern 1853 Enfield Rifle-Musket. A full stock weapon 55 inches in length, it's been imported from the mother country in massive numbers—not only for the Union cause, but for Richmond's as well. In repeated detail the corporal goes through the procedures: of loading in nine distinct movements, of maintaining the correct stance, and of the safety protocols. All of these the company imitates—dozens and dozens of times in cartridgeless, pantomime fashion. Then there are the concerns of maintenance and cleaning—the daily applications of steel wool and grease. However, the most complicated of the corporal's subjects involves the stacking of arms, entangling the fixed bayonets to form a pyramid of rifle-muskets. Simultaneously by fours, the company practices this command many times over, and many times it falls into confusion. Only after the soldiers appear to grasp the concept is the matter allowed to rest.

After a lengthy visit to the quartermaster, Company A becomes fully accoutred with the proper array of belts and belt plates, haversacks and knapsacks, canteens and cups. In addition to that of the wool variety already in their possession, each soldier is issued a gum blanket—a canvas rubberized on one side—and half of a shelter tent designed to be matched with a partner's. Along with a few smaller items, as well as the myriad of personal possessions, Lieutenant Warner's company is equipped to the fullest. When they rejoin the rest of the battalion, the boys from Iowa evince all the smartness and luster of veteran solders, save for the fact that they have yet to fire a shot. So continues the endless drudgery of the drill.

For ten days Susha and her comrades have stomped upon the parade ground, learning the complicated art of soldiering. And it's on an early dawn that they bid their goodbyes to the Benton Barracks. But although the officers have been diligent with their instructions, they could use double the time. Regardless, the generals have their motives, the thinking being that recruits everywhere need to get acquainted with their regiments before the campaigns begin.

The march upon the cold, slippery streets of St. Louis belies the city's rank as the heaviest populated in the west. In no way is Company A's short trek alone, for the entire battalion is making its way to the levee in an impressive demonstration, played before a crowd of none.

For most of the Iowans and their brethren, there's been a minor change in the uniform. After visiting a sutler, Susha and Sylvie have purchased full-brimmed, low-rounded crown, black slouch hats, together costing the sensible sum of $4.30.

What awaits on the levee is a true spectacle upon the water. Massive by design and all-powerful in performance, the sidewheeler *Empress of the South* is a sight to dazzle, with its scrolled trim and turned columns painted to a glistening white. Even the roof of the wheelhouse has been edged with a row of delicate, ribbon-like tracery. Indeed, it's a unique pleasure to walk across the gangplank onto such luxury. Unfortunately, the battalion learns quickly that the main deck is occupied by the soldiers of an artillery battery, as well their six 12-pound Napoleans, limbers and caissons, and one third of their 150 horses. Thus it's to the rear of the boiler deck that the officers and their newly designated 192 privates must go.

As it happens, the cabins near the stern are too few to accommodate all. Lieutenant Warner, however, isn't one to negotiate an unresolvable outcome, and so has his company seek the sanctuary upon the empty hurricane deck—the topmost of the *Empress'* three. In front of the pilot's wheelhouse sits an open area, where by using the boat's support wires, Company A can pitch its shelters. Warmed by the twin chimneys, the touch being hot enough to brew coffee, it'll be an ideal bivouac, made all the more so by the breathtaking views. With the odors of trampled manure wafting from below, the boys of Iowa should be comforted by those reminders of home.

And so the *Empress* departs, the second boat to leave St. Louis in the morning. Down the Mississippi she steams with her assortment of passengers and freight. Before the first bend is encountered, however, the company passes the town of Carondelet and its construction yard of ironclad gunboats. It's a bit of a shock, the fever at which these monsters are being built, what with the war nearly over. Regardless, such troubling discoveries are easily forgotten in the brisk air. Especially so for a certain Iowa couple, who after overcoming their fear of heights, sit upon the deck with their playful feet dangling over the side.

7 ↭ To the War's Edge

With the Mississippi and its upper tributaries serving as watery pikes, Union forces can move to converging points in a matter of days. Further to the south, the mighty river's other arteries plunge deep into the Confederacy, partitioning these lands rather than nurturing them. At its own choosing the Union Army can conquer any of these sections—and then the next, and the next—until all is devoured. Indeed, the blood of the vanquishers flows through the Mississippi, and if led competently, the war should end within months.

While the *Empress* stops for a load of wood fuel at Belmont, Missouri, the captain takes an excursion ashore, returning with a bundle as the boat is about to depart.

And just after the side-wheeler gets under way, the corporal hurries onto the hurricane deck with a message from below.

Receiving such, the lieutenant wastes no time. "Company! Gather arms and accoutrements! Fall in at the private's mark by the stairs! Musket, cartridge box, bayonet and cap box!"

The men react with a rush to arms and, after a cursory inspection, are led to the rounded stern of the boiler deck. Formed into two ranks and facing away from the curved wall, their murmurs run amuck when the captain walks onto the space between Company A and the stern's rail.

"Company. To be better acquainted with your rifle, each of you will be firing a live ball. Front rank, when the lieutenant walks by, take a cartridge and place it into a tin in your cartridge box. The corporal will follow with a cap for your cap box. Lieutenant."

Susha and Sylvie are in the center of the front rank and so must wait a few moments before the upended hats reach them.

"Corporal," speaks Lieutenant Warner, as he dons his hat. "Take them through it."

"Front rank! Shoulder arms! Forward! March! Halt!" The corporal has them a step away from the rail. "Front rank! Order arms! Prepare to load! Load in nine times!"

Although Susha knows the routine, she keeps an eye on a surer Sylvie, mimicking his moves. With the muzzle of her Enfield held away from her face, she fishes out the cartridge with her right hand. Her heart beats faster as she tears open the paper with her teeth and pours the powder down the barrel. Subsequently, the greased Minie ball finds the muzzle and is seated, whereupon Susha forces it the down to the breech with her metal ramrod. Thus, with the powder and conical bullet loaded, she twirls around the ramrod in her fingers and returns it to its position within the gunstock's bottom. Upon bringing the lock area to her hip with the muzzle tilted upward, Susha locates the cap and primes her weapon. It's now safely at the half cock, as she freezes at her position.

"Potter, come to the shoulder!"

It takes a few more seconds for the slower privates to load, but in time all are standing at the shoulder. A brief pause ensues, only to be broken by Lieutenant Warner, who flings a large, cobalt bottle into the Mississippi.

"Company. That is your target."

The corporal hesitates in order to give the bottle a fighting chance, and then he renders the command. "Front rank! Come to the ready! Form a 'T' with your feet!"

Susha returns her weapon to her hip, and takes a large gasp of air.

"Ready! A-a-aim!"

She levels her Enfield, securing its buttplate against her shoulder and cocking the hammer to full.

"Fire!"

Boom! The noise is sharp and ear-splitting, with the sparks short-lived and the acrid smoke lasting. Though it may not be severe, the recoil does kick into Susha's shoulder, making its introduction a memorable one. Nevertheless, a stoic Private Potter keeps her eye on the target, eager to see its demise. Within this instant the water around the bottle becomes dotted with the splashes of 24 Minie balls. Indeed, the volley is a devastating one, its remarkably tight pattern giving a deadly impression.

"Sylvie." Immediately, Susha notices that something is amiss. "That bottle is still floating."

"How can that be?"

Before the men can beseech their lieutenant for another try, however, the corporal carries out his orders. "Front rank! Shoulder arms! Left face! Forward march!"

And so it remains for the rear rank to finish the job, leaving the other half of the company bewildered as to how that bottle could have escaped their collected ire.

Memphis, Tennessee is a place of much anticipation, as well as the cause for a dose of sadness. There'll be more room on the *Empress*, as the artillery battery disembarks to points of no real concern. However, Company A is learning that the realities of army life care little for sentiment, for it's at Memphis where some of its members are to join their assigned regiment. Along with the corporal, twelve men follow the battery into town, this group including Cyrus and his friends.

"Potters. Perhaps we might see you in Mobile," he yells, as he walks across the gangplank. "We should meet in Des Moines after the war. Trade stories."

"You can count on us, Cyrus," shouts Sylvie from the main deck. Wearing a grin that could stretch for miles, he turns to Susha. "The look on his face, when he hears our story."

Since space is made available, Company A no longer needs to reside atop the hurricane deck. First things are first, however, and that is to clean up the mess left by the artillery battery, even as the *Empress* departs.

Regardless, there'll be no complaints from any Potter. Sweeping manure into the greatest of rivers is an unusual twist to a familiar chore, but also, Sylvie manages to finagle sublime accommodations. To be sure, it may be the Mississippi's tiniest cabin with room for only a single bunk. Yet the space belongs to Susha and Sylvie alone, it coming with the uproar of sidewheel machinery, able to mask any suspicious sound.

The hard raps to the cabin doors grow louder as they near Susha and Sylvie's. But as these "wake-ups" are slowed by undecipherable instructions, the couple is afforded enough time to rouse themselves, and at least don their socks and drawers.

Thump! Thump! "To the main deck with accoutrements and trappings! Ten minutes! Home at last!"

It's a shocking bit of news, that the Potters have reached their destination.

"I can hardly believe it," confesses Sylvie.

"Neither can I."

Before long, thirty-eight privates form two ranks in front of the boiler on the main deck, including ten from the original Des Moines recruits. With them are the captain of the battalion and Lieutenant Warner, as well as acting corporal Simms and a Lieutenant McNeath.

"Soldiers. Break ranks and gather 'round." The captain opts for the less formal. "Good morning, men."

"Morning, sir."

"Shortly, you will leave the battalion, as we are bound for Vicksburg. Lieutenants Warner and McNeath will lead you to your regiments. This is the third group of recruits I have commanded, and should I say the most noteworthy. In spite of time constraints, my confidence is that each of you will make a gallant soldier."

The captain's clear sincerity inspires spontaneity. "Three cheers for the captain!"

"Hurrah! Hurrah! Hurrah!"

"Men. Break out your cups and let us make a proper cheer."

Several bottles of different shapes and colors appear, and when each cup is given its share, the captain raises his. "Men of Iowa and Missouri. Here's to the Union. God bless President Lincoln."

As Susha's reluctant tongue samples the contents of her cup, she discovers a small surprise. Instead of the vulgarities of charcoaled alcohol, the taste is one of bitter potions balanced by the sweetness of sugar. When all the other privates down their good cheers, Susha does the same without a whimper.

"Much better than whiskey, Bob."

"Sure is, Sylvie."

It's curious that the captain should choose to anoint his toast with something other than whiskey. Of course, the bitters he's distributed is laced with a goodly amount of alcohol. However, for the most part it's considered to be good medicine, prescribed for a host of ailments and as a preventative.

The company of Iowans and Missourians remains on the main deck, as the captain bids goodbye to two of his lieutenants. Shortly thereafter, a line of hills looms in the distance, emanating from the shore and stretching deep into the heart of Arkansas. A town emerges, nestled at the foot of the ridge, it becoming apparent that the *Empress* is steering toward the river port's wharves.

The anticipation runs rampant through Susha's stomach, that in a matter of minutes she'll be stepping upon the land of the enemy—the Confederacy itself. As much as any one thing, it promises to be a foreign country, with its strange people and their strange ways, along with their confusing abuses of the English language. Memphis was but a taste, seen from afar and filtered through the multitudes of bluecoats gathered about its riverside. This place is much smaller and so, should be less purified by the refined practices having steamed down the Mississippi.

"Sylvie. Have you heard the name of that town?"

"I think it's Helena, Arkansas."

Overhearing Sylvie's conclusion, the acting corporal renders a more precise place name. "No, not Helena, Arkansas. Rather, Hell-in-Arkansas. You shall see."

A flood of mud greets the disembarked company. As best he can, Lieutenant Warner leads his charges through a maze of lesser streets, seeking a more passable path. Nevertheless, there's no avoiding the mires, for Helena is full of them, the greatest ambition being that no one loses their brogans to the tentacles of ooze. The town seems to mimic the afflicted grey of the thick sky, while the stench is one of decay and illness—one could wonder what the heat of summer will bring. It's obvious that Helena is a much abused place, the will to keep it habitable having faded with its forlorn occupation. The fact of the matter exists, that although only six months ago this was a contested place, more men have died from sicknesses here than from the bloody battle on Crowley's Ridge. The less time spent in Helena, the better chance a soldier will have.

A couple of blocks behind the old Nash and Cleburne Drugstore, the company comes to a halt in front of a modest house. It's here that Lieutenant McNeath splits from the company, leaving behind those soldiers of the 42nd.

"Do you think this is where Colonel Burness lives?" asks Susha.

"Could be," replies Sylvie. "But you think he would have found a grander house."

With papers in hand, Lieutenant Warner knocks on the door and enters. When he emerges moments later, he accompanies two officers of high rank.

The acting corporal whips the remnants of the company into shape. "Detail. Guide right. Order arms. Fix bayonets." Quickly, his charges comply, and he salutes Lieutenant Warner. "Detail ready for inspection, sir."

"Present arms," the lieutenant commands. "Colonel. Ready for inspection."

"Very well, Lieutenant."

One by one, the colonel checks the uniform, accoutrements and weapon of each soldier.

As for Susha, she might very well slip into the shallow mud beneath her feet were it not that her towering colonel seems to be a man with genuine concerns.

"Where are you from?" he asks of each private. "What is your calling?"

Yet when he returns Susha's Enfield to her hands, he issues a small item of advice. "Be sure to put more grease to your barrel, soldier."

To Susha's relief, her commanding officer refers to her as a soldier, with no apparent clue as to how wrong he really is.

"Lieutenant," speaks Colonel Burness, as he scrutinizes the weapon of the last private. "I believe your men have not used their muskets."

"Sir. We only managed one shot each from the stern of the boat."

"Nothing at St. Louis?"

"No, sir."

"Then their companies will have to see to it. I trust they have not been issued cartridges. Nor rations."

"No, sir."

"Major Slough, write an order. Lieutenant, you should have time to visit the commissary and the ordnance captain, and then catch the supply train. Good luck."

"Thank you, sir."

Upon hearing the colonel's words, muted sighs of relief are released from among the detail, happy they are to be free of the gates of "Hell-in-Arkansas."

The supply train in question consists of eleven wagons and provides sustenance for parts of Colonel Burness's scattered regiment. Only his Company A resides in Helena, with Company F detached as far west as Little Rock, performing wharf duties. A battalion consisting of "E," "G" and "I" is part of a force picketing the Memphis and Little Rock Railroad, a line serving the capital city east to Devall's Bluff, while "H" does garrison duty at said terminus town on the White River. Companies D and K picket the road several miles west of Helena, while "B" and "C" stand watch where this artery enters the Cache country, near Clarendon. It's of Company C to which Lieutenant Warner belongs, and it's to that battalion that he is to divide his detail.

Thus is situated the 42nd Iowa Infantry Regiment, not so much a cohesive fighting unit, but rather an umbrella organization for dispersed wintering and picketing groups. Still, even though the Confederates have abandoned Pine Bluff to the south, the 42nd's duties are important. There remains the threat of partisan bands, who probe and prick, and carry on the struggle to survive. And then there are the regular units of the Confederacy, veterans on horseback who by piecemeal have been assigned their own versions of picket duty—beyond the edges of their territory.

After traversing Crowley's Ridge, Susha and her comrades overtake the supply train and its detail of 12 soldiers from Company B under the command of a sergeant. His salute to Lieutenant Warner is formal, while their handshake reveals the amity of two friends. As it happens, the men of Company B seem happy to see their safety increased by numbers, and for having the added muscle to free mud-stuck wagons. In this country of woodland patches and ramshackle farms, the route taken by these Iowans is a miserable excuse for a road.

"Don't see any people stirring about," observes one of the privates, as the detail trudges behind the train.

"Those staying behind usually keep to themselves," explains the acting corporal, pointing to a nearby, billowing chimney. "From time to time we purchase food from them. That is about it."

In some ways it's a repeat of their trek from Des Moines to Eddyville, that is with the exception of uniforms and loaded rifle-muskets. But leave it to Sylvie to air the most notable difference to his Iowa.

"One thing is for certain. These people are not too clever at farming. Can you imagine what we could do to this backward land?"

"Turn it all into first-rate farms, don't you know," agrees Susha.

As for the others, they give their expert assents.

Dusk finds the train well short of Companies D and K, and so camp is made along the roadside. The shelters are pitched and the fires lit, and as his charges slurp their coffee and chew their salt pork, Lieutenant Warner renders an informal state of affairs.

"The next three pickets will be ours and then Company B will relieve us. Firstly, will be you Potters and Ziegler. Grove, Howell and Schmidt will relieve them and then the corporal will bring up the rest. Do your business in those trees. Use a shovel so no one will step in it. And don't go beyond there. Password for tonight is 'Duchess'. Any questions?"

"Lieutenant, how long..."

"Two hours, Howell. There has been no trouble from partisans. Should be uneventful. Excepting the cold. But that is no bother to us. Am I correct?"

"Yessir."

"Good. Cameron, Hastings, Clarke, Grove and Howell. When we get to the battalion, follow the corporal to Company B. Captain

Parmeter will be your commander. You others—Potters, Julg, Ziegler, Schmidt—accompany me to Company C and Captain Pillow. When you get to your company, you will join a mess, to eat and bunk with. Swap picket duties, tend chores. They will teach you most of what you need to know."

Suddenly, an uneasy thought enters Susha's head, that she and Sylvie might be split apart.

"Don't worry, Potters. You will stay in the same mess. And you three, we have a few Dutch, err-uhh, German-speakers in the company. For you others, the corporal will see to you." The lieutenant reaches into his haversack and liberates an amber, scrolled flask. "Pass this around. Remember. It is important that you listen to your messmates. Follow their counsel. The 42nd may not have seen much fighting, but it has spent much time getting sick. Your messmates are the ones who got through it, so they can help you keep your health." He pauses. "One thing is in your favor. We sure got out of Helena in a hurry."

Fed by rivers and bayous, the Cache country is a flat, hardwood land interspersed by open fields. Although not ideal, it does suit the tastes of some Confederates, and so draws the interests of the Union Army. After all, communications must be kept, a vulnerable flank guarded and contact with the enemy maintained.

Minus the four wagons marked for Companies D and K, Lieutenant Warner's detail arrives at the battalion camp. More precisely, it's a winter quarters, with its perfectly aligned streets bordered by small, log shanties of imaginative specifications. Some have canvas roofs, while others are shingled, the pieces held in place by split rails or weighted tin cans. Most have a functional clay-covered chimney, while a few sport covered porches and makeshift furniture. And though a portion of the brief, main thoroughfare is planked, the remainder is a whip of configured mud, traversed at various intervals by floating lumber for the sake of pedestrians. Camp Parmeter it's called, after the commander of both the small battalion and Company B, and for 119 soldiers of the 42nd Iowa Infantry Regiment, soon to be 129, it's a home away from home.

However, the first impression upon Susha is an opaque one.

Not that her head is overwhelmed to the brink of confusion, but because of the haze which literally is the atmosphere. The stubborn smoke wafts from many sources—cooking, heating, incinerating—with the resulting pall blanketing the ground. More than anything, what Susha wishes upon Camp Parmeter is a sweeping, Iowa wind.

With their destination at hand, the drivers pull their wagons and teams away from the escort detail, the battalion commissary being their last stop.

"Sergeant, let's part here," orders Lieutenant Warner. "Tell the captain I will report to him after I settle my men."

"Yessir. Company B detail. Fall in on this mark."

With the sergeant's men marching away, Lieutenant Warner's original 48 recruits are now down to a paltry five. "Very well. We will report to Captain Pillow and then to your messes. Follow me." As they do so, the lieutenant continues to offer some advice. "Anyone who knows how to cook will have a feather in his cap. Your messmates will relieve you from some duties."

This is welcomed news for Susha. Modest as she may be, she knows her ability to prepare tasty meals would better most.

After Lieutenant Warner leads the replacements into a clearing, they come upon a fair-sized, clapboarded house, speckled white by neglect and rickety by abuse.

"You see the cistern," points the lieutenant. "This is your best source of water. Form a single rank." Lieutenant Warner gives his men a few seconds. "Touch elbows. Good. Order arms. In place, rest." Wasting no time, he steps to the front door of the house, knocking only once before helping himself to an invitation.

Just as quickly, Sylvie takes advantage of the interval. "Susha," he whispers. "Don't let anyone know you are a good cook. They might get suspicious."

"What?"

"Yes, Bob." Sylvie's firm brow squelches Susha's objection.

Almost immediately, a peeved lieutenant exits the house. "Not that it matters, but the captain will be out. Order arms."

As he emerges, with one hand adjusting the slouch hat atop his head and the other clutching his smoking cap, Captain Pillow and his attire seem to be in a period of transition. His collar is unbuttoned, as are both his vest and coat, while from his mouth protrudes a briar pipe. Because his feet are protected by leather slippers, it's certain he won't be leaving the porch.

"Replacement detail reporting for duty, sir," barks Lieutenant Warner.

"Is this it? Five?"

"Yes." Clearly, it's an affront to the lieutenant that he must explain himself. "I began with forty-eight in Iowa. Most were for other regiments. Ten recruits for ours, five for Company C. But they are full of fervor."

"Is that so, Lieutenant?"

"Captain. Would you care to inspect the troops?"

"I do not think it necessary. Just have the orderly sergeant enter their names and put each in a different mess. Make sure the first sergeant sees them."

"Captain. As these two are close cousins, would they not be better off in the same mess?"

"Very well, Lieutenant. You see to it. I am busy."

As the captain begins to turn away, Lieutenant Warner decides to force a parting piece of protocol. "Sir!" He snaps a salute. "Detail! Present, arms!"

In response, the company commander manages to touch his brow.

As whimsical and revealing this episode might seem to the other privates, for Susha it's another close call, to have been separated from her husband by a thoughtless edict. Once again, it's left to Lieutenant Warner to look after the welfare of his privates.

On the other hand, it's the first sergeant who really runs the company, it being appropriate that he's not at his shanty—the smokehouse behind the captain's. However, there is a stroke of luck, for as Lieutenant Warner leads his charges to their messes, he spies a familiar gait.

"Sergeant Wilkins," he yells. "Over here."

The sergeant marches to the lieutenant, his arms swinging back and forth as if to keep his balance. A robust build more than compensates for his short stature, his barrel chest threatening to punch through his greatcoat. And in the middle of his Van Dyke rests a small, clay pipe, while a forage cap covers his head.

"Sir," he salutes. "Welcome back."

"Thank you, Sergeant Wilkins. Nice to be back. Brought with me your newest privates."

While the lieutenant goes through the introductions, the sergeant listens and, more closely, measures.

But as far as Susha is concerned, she's the center of the sergeant's attentions, his piercing eyes giving the others only a scant notice.

"Bob Potter, huh? My you look young. How old are you?"

"Twenty, First Sergeant," she answers from her dry mouth.

"Hmm? Hold out your hands."

This Susha does, but with the trepidation that at last she's being found out. Slipping passed hordes of soldiers and officers, and even a surgeon may be one thing. Yet, at this end, she realizes suddenly that few can deceive an unrelenting first sergeant.

He grabs her hands, thus pushing Susha to point of confession, if only to make things easier on Sylvie.

"You're a farmer. Correct, Private Potter?"

"Yes, First Sergeant."

"The sergeant has a gift for divining occupations," explains Lieutenant Warner. "Excepting the time he mistook that sanitary commission woman for a madam. Remember?"

"Yes, Lieutenant. It was her manner that fooled me."

Soon, Susha and Sylvie's names are entered into the company books. Yet nothing makes them more a part of the 42nd than when they join a mess. The scrupulous matchmaker he is, Lieutenant Warner finds suitable homes for Ziegler, Julg and Schmidt, so that now it's down to the Potters.

"Your mess is at the end of the street. The last two shanties."

The structures in question are both porched, clay-chinked and chimneyed, and connected by a canvas overhang. Beneath said cover a pot is suspended over a campfire, marking this space as a makeshift kitchen. Detecting some movement, Susha spies three residents, one sitting on a rocker and two on a bench, and all puffing their pipes.

"Lord, the prodigal's son has come home," quips the man on the rocker. "How you been, George?"

"Fine, Paps. You?"

Immediately, Susha is struck by the unusual. Not so much from the informal greeting between officer and private, but by Paps' uncanny resemblance to Sylvie's Uncle Matthew, and of how a man whose age hovers around forty years would have the same rank as herself.

The lieutenant looks to the other soldiers, neither of whom budge from their bench. "How about you, Bill? Leo?"

"No complaints," responds Leo.

"Not much good if we did," adds William Stewart. "But congratulations, you becoming first lieutenant."

"Thanks. Where are Proctor and Ben?" asks Lieutenant Warner.

"Foraging at the farms," replies Leo.

"Then I take it Lorenzo got his discharge."

"Two weeks ago. That fester on his leg never did heel," replies Paps. "Sure do miss his clever cooking."

"Mess has been in a turmoil, what with the loss," agrees Bill.

"Perhaps some fresh fish might oblige. This is Sylvie and Bob Potter. Cousins from Buena Vista."

Susha's nervous smile compels her to defer to her husband.

"Nice to meet you, gentlemen."

Lieutenant Warner completes the introduction. "Potters, this is Flavius Hutchinson. Call him Paps. Bill Stewart. And that is Leonidas Garrett. Leo? Gentlemen? Do you have room?"

For Susha, it's an odd moment, as if she and Sylvie are on display.

"Oh, we got room, all right," informs Bill. "Modest as our little resort is."

"George, you're not putting them on the block, are you?" asks Paps.

"Of course not."

"Just leave them here. We can take care of them." Paps looks at Susha. "Ever done any cooking, Bob?"

Such an unnerving question to be asked. Susha's beginning to wonder if she's overlooked a marked, feminine attribute that points her out to those who are otherwise unaware. However, Sylvie's instructions remain fresh on her mind, making her reaction a prompt one.

"No. Not really. But Sylvie has."

Dear Emma and Eliza,

We are with our Regiment Sylvie and me down here near the Cache Swamp in Arkansas. We are near Helena. So write to us to the 42nd Iowa Infantry Company C Helena Arkansas and you should find us. Please put some stamps there being a shortage. Sylvie and me have five Mess Mates who we eat and sleep with and who we spend our time. One of them is the very likeness of Sylvies Uncle Matt and is a soldier of the Mexican War with strange tales about that race. The other Mess Mates are of their 20s but are all older than me. We live in two shantys with chimneys Sylvie and me sleeping in different bunks for we share the shanty with two others. The Mess Mates are good at keeping hunky and they spend most of their time outdoors even if it is cold as they say there is a miasma in the shantys during winter. Our floor is made from a white picket fence. Captain Pillow is the Company Commander and I do not think much of him. Lieutenant Warner is in our Company and I have seen him every day since Des Moines. His first name is George and he is well liked. Our 5 Mess Mates are fine fellows so I am protected even if they do not know if I am a girl. Only two are married. Today we shot our muskets 7 times and are getting used to them. We have no tattoos in camp for there are no musicians they being with the other Companys. The Regiment is spread over Arkansas so the Companys are mostly apart. We get woken up by the Sergeants and Corporals. So far we have not seen any rebels and I do not want to for they must be a pestulent and savage people. We only see farmers here and what poor farms they have. I would almost have pity for them if they had not started the rebellion but I suppose I do feel sorry for some of them even the darkeys. I cannot write much more but to say that they have no privys but open toilets they call sinks. Sylvie has found a place in the woods where we go so I can keep my secrecy. I wrote a letter to Mamma and Pappa as a nurse but do not let them read this one. Keep us in your prayers.

Your effectionate Sister
Susha

Although it's been only two days, the Potters are adjusting nicely to their new setting. But so are their accomodating messmates, even to the point of muffling any complaints over Sylvie's cooking. Aside from the odd sentry duty, there's a lull in the mess' activities, allowing for an easier meld.

While Sylvie gathers firewood, Proctor, Bill, Leo and Ben occupy themselves with a leaden game of bluff.

And from his rocker, Paps cleans his brogans, with his momentary companion doing the same.

"How's your feet, Bob?" Owing to his pipe, he speaks through gripped teeth.

"Fine. I think."

"Better let me have a look."

In spite being a life-long bachelor, Paps' demeanor seems benignly fatherly. Without reserve, Susha slips off her socks.

"My, you have dainty feet." Pap's poor sight impedes, so he leans over for a closer inspection. "They look fine to me. You keep them nice and dry," he notes. "How many pairs of socks you own?"

"Three good ones."

"Better get another pair. Two to wear and two for when the others get wet. Too bad you don't knit, what with no sutler about."

Artfully, Susha plays silent to this wrong assumption.

"I rub dry soap on the insides. Keeps my feet from getting blistered. And I never wash my feet at night. Always in the morning. Keeps them from cracking."

Susha nods at what to a soldier is vital advice. All the while she thinks of how much more of a man Flavius Hutchinson is when compared to Uncle Matthew, which brings to mind another dubious subject.

"Tell me, Paps," she speaks, as she dons her socks. "Why does no one like Captain Pillow?"

"Well I suppose he gives them little cause," he chuckles. "Valentine Pillow. You see him about. Not a man to inspire. Is he?"

"Not from me."

"You know he is a politician. And politicians are mostly liars and thieves. You can bet, he was happy to sit out the war with such an honorable exemption. But then he got voted out of office. Heh, heh. Begged the governor for a commission, so now he is our burden. Though it could be, if you went to the trouble, you might find some who don't dislike Captain Pillow."

The game of bluff enlivens. No doubt a small amount of money is exchanging hands, with Proctor Keedy favoring the loss. Walking passed Susha and Paps in order to pour a cup of coffee, he appears primed for another diversion.

"What are you two babbling about?"

"The captain."

"Him! He can kiss my ass!"

"Oh? Do tell us more of your notions, Proctor?" It's obvious that Paps is looking to be entertained.

"Pillow and his paltroonery. His word doesn't carry the weight of a feather with me. Why, I would hardly put him in charge of an empty room, never mind a company of good men."

"What have you done to set him straight, Private Keedy?"

"You know very well, Private Hutchinson." Proctor looks to Susha. "You may notice an inside bulge on the left breast of his frock coat. Where that he keeps his ready copy of *Casey's Infantry Tactics*, for the man does not know the drill. Does he, Private Hutchinson?"

"He does not."

"During one of our bivouacs on Crowley's Ridge, I managed to slip into his shelter, my flanks being covered by his uproarious act of snoring, and liberated that mentioned piece of literature. And fine kindling it did make. Did it not, Private Hutchinson?"

"First-rate."

"But, oh, my thwartations. For would you know that on the very next day, with me keeping a close scout on the enemy, I spied him thumbing through a copy of the same book. He must be keeping a trunkful!"

"What must we do, Private Keedy?"

"Private Hutchinson, I believe we must take it upon ourselves a grand strategy of attrition. So that, with God's help, we can wear down the captain's arsenal."

"Amen to that," agrees Paps with a cheerful grin.

"Amen," adds Susha, whose content for her setting grows by the hour.

For the Potters, their days at Camp Parmeter flow uneventfully. Yet as noted, the 42nd's task is to keep a watch on the hinterlands, those regions with little strategic value save that they may harbor an enemy. On a rotating basis, members of the battalion man several outposts, positions which would respond to a threat with the alarm of Enfields. The most remote of these is Outpost B, situated two miles from camp, and requiring the services of eight privates and a corporal.

Rising to prepare breakfast, Sylvie is the first to feel the morning's freeze. Soon, Sergeant Wilkins appears and enters Paps, Proctor and Bill's shanty, unusual in that his practice is to delegate the verbal reveille.

As he feeds the fire, a diverted Sylvie is joined by Susha. "What is happening?"

"Sergeant Wilkins is in there."

Before Susha poses another question, however, the topic of Sylvie's words emerges from the shanty, accompanied by its inhabitants.

"Sometime this evening, Lieutenant Warner will join you. The password is 'cracker.'"

"Again?" reacts Bill.

"Bob," speaks Paps. "You're to join us on outpost duty for three days. Be ready at 11 o'clock. Sylvie. The rest will still do sentry while we are gone."

Although Susha has come to expect this, the realization that she and Sylvie will be apart forces some trepidation. Still, she manages a brave front, made all the more difficult by the glare of doubting eyes.

"Do you think him able?" asks Sergeant Wilkins.

"Bob?" answers Paps. "He should do fine. Right, Bob?"

"For sure."

"We'll make certain he knows what to do."

"Very well. Assemble with Corporal Davison and Farrell's mess. They have your rations."

As Sergeant Wilkins departs, both Susha and Sylvie cast their fears upon one another, each biting their lips in order to mute their protests.

But leave it to Paps to pick up on this. "Don't worry, Sylvie. Your cousin will be fine. Outpost B is a dry place, and there is a spring nearby. And any Seceshes we might see up there are not bad fellows." Paps reassures Susha with a kind pat on the back. "Remember. We are there just to keep an eye on them. And they on us. Nobody is going to make war. That sort of deviltry is just not done on winter picket."

It's a comforting thought, accepted as intended by a nodding Susha.

Then again, to soothe and allay is Sylvie's obligation. He steps to Susha, removing her hat with one hand and patting her head with the other. "Sounds like a grand time. Wish I didn't have my chores."

"Soon as you boil some coffee, see that Bob's traps are in order," suggests Paps. "No hurry."

With Sylvie's help, in time Susha is ready for outpost duty, even convincing herself that she's eager to go.

"We should walk to Farrell's mess," announces Paps.

However, Sylvie isn't finished with his fuss. "One thing more." For the sake of privacy, he leads her inside the shanty. "Are you all right with this?" Sylvie puts his arms around Susha.

"I think I am. I will be with friends and not too far away. Paps says there is nothing to fear. Maybe I will chance to see a Secesh."

"Stay away from them, Susha. They're not God-fearing like us. Not trustworthy."

"I know."

"Do as Paps tells you."

"I will."

"Hmm? I suppose we ought to be going. Why not give me a kiss?"

This Susha does with some enthusiasm.

"Mmm. You keep that up and I might not let you go."

When Susha and Sylvie exit the shanty, they have to rush to catch Paps and the others. Farrell's mess is nearby, where their chosen four, as well as Corporal Davison, is ready to depart.

"Your rations are divvied up," directs the corporal, when Susha and her messmates approach.

Upon a canvas rests four neat rows of small piles: raw coffee beans, dried peaches, hardtack and salt pork.

"'Coutre up, Bob," offers Sylvie. "While I fill up your haversack."

Into Susha's poke bags he keeps the rations separated, while she dons her knapsack.

"Detail. Form one rank," instructs Corporal Davison.

A brief inspection of weapons and equipment ensues.

"Detail. Order arms. Shoulder, arms. Right face. Forward, march. Left, left..."

With that, Susha marches off to face the enemy of her country, of whom she's been assured is in no mood for a fight.

"Right shoulder shift. Arms." Yet immediately, the corporal alters to the more practical. "To the route step. March."

As Susha slings her Enfield around her shoulder, she looks back to Sylvie.

"See you in three days, Bob," he bids.

To which Susha's reply is a short wave and a long smile, given in spite of her wobbly cheeks.

Passed the sentry at the edge of camp the detail proceeds, and through open woods and neglected farmlands it continues. As the soldiers near Outpost B, the trees grow thicker and the height of the land gains a few, precious feet. Before long, a lazy plume of thin smoke marks the site from the near-distance.

Susha is the first to spot the outpost through the barren black oaks. "There they are."

Indeed, a milling of sky blue greatcoats tells Corporal Davison's detail they have arrived.

What strikes Susha as odd is that Outpost B consists of nothing but a campfire and a primitive lean-to—no shelter tents or cooking implements. Fully accoutred, it's apparent that Corporal Massie's men of Company B are anxious to leave.

As for Susha's comrades, without any encouragement, they break ranks and begin to make themselves at home. There's to be no formality in this exchange, as the deal is a tacit one between two well-acquainted corporals. Then there are the privates, who are inclined always to dispense with any unnecessary movement.

"How has it been, John?" inquires Corporal Davison, as he offers his hand.

"No problems, Ezra. Excepting the weather. The Seceshes seem content with their misery."

"Like us," quips Proctor, as he frees his shelter half from his knapsack.

"You should have no trouble," continues Corporal Massie.

"Then I suppose we will relieve you."

"Fine. Let me escort your first pair to the sentry, and then we can be on our way."

Corporal Davison is brief in making his choices. "Nelling and Roy. Leave behind your cups and some beans, and I will bring you your coffee."

After propping up their knapsacks against a tree, and fixing their bayonets, Nelling and Roy follow Corporal Massie up a meandering and vanishing trail.

"In two hours' time, Keedy, you and Potter will relieve them," decides Corporal Davison. "Put up the shelters. Potter. Roast those beans and boil them up."

Moments later Corporal Massie returns with his sentries, and along with the rest of his detail takes the route back to Camp Parmeter.

If safety lies in numbers, then also peril must loom with the lack thereof. However, none of Susha's comrades seem to pay any heed of their isolation from the rest of the battalion. Therefore, if they go about their business, then so must she, to shake the coffee beans in her tin pan over the hot coals.

Time winds slowly when there's waiting to be done. Her chores completed, Susha has little to do. Since her feet feel a damp, she decides to remove the two pair of socks in favor of her dry spare. But to her surprise, instead of locating the remaining two in her knapsack, Susha finds four. Sitting barefooted upon her stump, she scratches her head over the additional pair, posing to herself the question of her miscount. As it happens, the truth is not a difficult puzzle, there being but one possible conclusion.

"Sylvie," mutters a smiling Susha. Although he can't be present, at least his thoughtfulness is, as Susha's feet can attest. "That Sylvie."

So far, army life hasn't been too rigorous. Even those episodes when she feared discovery were unnecessarily daunting, as things are playing out so favorably. In addition, Susha's dread of Outpost B is short-lived, the site being both dry and peaceful. Aside from the light camp chatter, the only sounds she hears are the winds winnowing through the leafless trees and the occasional caws from curious crows. It's into nature's hum that Susha loses herself, dreaming of those prosperities to come. Indeed, she can picture herself, clutching little Robert in her arms as she stands by her house, gazing at a field of Sylvie's corn. When this minor diversion to Arkansas will have run its course, a wonderful life will be waiting in Iowa, and Susha will be able to look back and laugh of those times when she "fought" for the cause of union.

Notwithstanding, the tranquilities born from Buena Vista's ample soil are brought to a jarring cessation when Susha's ears pick up a troubling noise. It can be only shouting from not too far away, originating from the direction of the recently posted sentries, of whom Susha will relieve.

"Paps. What is it?"

The veteran private motions for silence, while the others try to make sense of the strange shouts.

Yet it seems stranger to Susha that none of her comrades are alarmed. In fact, they seem amused.

"I know him," declares Proctor. "He's..."

"The one missing all those teeth?" interrupts Bill. "Bites with his tongue and gums?"

"That's him, all right," agrees Paps.

For Susha, Outpost B is becoming a confusing place. "Are you talking about a rebel?"

To which her comrades respond with a round of laughter.

"You soon shall see. At what an original specimen is their Snaggle Tooth."

Soon enough it is. With the corporal up front, Susha and Proctor are led to what she believes is the very heart of Secessia. Her weapon carries heavier than usual and her heart beats faster, and the view from Susha's eyes becomes a little boxed. Be that as it may, after only a few yards outside of camp, she does manage to spot a figure cloaked in blue.

Corporal Davison shouts to gain his attention. "Private."

Standing by a small fire is Nelling, who waves his relief onward.

At least things appear to be safe to Susha, she forcing herself to keep up with Proctor.

"Everything going fine?" asks the corporal of Nelling.

"No problems as yet."

"We could hear you talking to Snaggle Tooth."

"That was him. He's gone, now. Got one standing over there and another behind that tree."

It's a moment of truth as Susha focuses toward the pointed direction, spotting a crude footbridge over a creek. And only a few feet beyond is the subject of Nelling's mark. Greater than his duty, this Confederate appears to covet the warmth from his flickering fire. Draped in a raggedy, old quilt, he hardly looks the part of a soldier. Yet this shivering soul must belong to someone's cavalry, as his plaid trousers are tucked into his tall boots, while his short-barreled shotgun leans against a tree. Even for Susha, this enemy isn't much from which to draw fear, she knowing how easy a victim he would be to the longer range of her Enfield.

"This way, Potter."

Roy is thirty yards from what is Proctor's right, and it's to this position that Susha is guided.

"You know what you are to do."

"Yes, Corporal.

"Just follow Keedy. Boil up a cup and I should see you in two hours."

Thus, Susha is left on her own to guard a section of the Union's flank, her nearest help being a stone's throw away. Nevertheless, the enemy appears to be in no shape to take an initiative, it's present representatives having no fight in them. At once, Susha suspects she's in for an uneventful two hours.

Still, there is a little life in the Confederacy, as the butternut sentry who has been sitting against a mossy tree begins to stir. The subject of his concern is a willow rod, to which is attached a string and baited hook.

“Arkansas,” shouts Proctor, he being in his element. “You catch anything?”

And so begins the parley, which after its initial introductions evolves into a bellowing palaver of camp gossip, ration bashing and general braggadocio.

“So Joshua! How about a wager!” enlivens Proctor.

“How’s that!” responds the friendly foe.

“A challenge in marksmanship!”

“Go on!”

“I will lay down a month’s wages, I can shoot that hat from off your head, without drawing blood or parting any hair!”

The quilted one reacts with all undue calm. “That sounds like a losing proposition to me! Best be thinking of another wager!”

“We got plenty time for that, Josh!” continues Proctor, who might babble forever.

But eventually, a pause follows, only to be broken by the fisherman. “Say, you boys got any war news! We don’t hear nothing ‘round here!”

“Let me see! Lee got licked in Virginia! Bragg in Chattanooga! And Grant’s moving on Georgia!”

“Ain’t heard none of that!” replies the quilted one.

“You heard of Gettysburg!” persists Proctor.

“Can’t say I have!”

“Vicksburg! The Fourth of July!”

“Caught wind of that some weeks ago!” Because of the astonished look on Proctor, the quilted one must feel the need to repeat himself. “Like I said, we don’t get no news!”

Up to now Susha has been satisfied with her status as a bemused observer.

“Hey, Iowa!” yells the fisherman. “What’s your friend’s name!”

“Bob!”

“Bob! How come you ain’t talking none!”

Susha shrugs her shoulders.

“You got yourself a sweetheart, Bob!” Obviously, the fisherman is searching for a topic to trigger Susha’s tongue.

“No!” she replies.

“How come!”

"Bob doesn't have a duck 'cause he is a little shy!" interrupts Proctor. "But I plan on making him into a lady-killer of the first order! After I introduce him to the mysterious ways of the cherry kind!" He turns to Susha. "Yessir, Bob! You and your cousin will hold me to an eternal gratitude when I take you to this particular establishment of fancy Memphis Cyprians!"

Susha does her best to appear interested, and at the same instant conceal her giggles.

"What's the name of that there establishment!" asks the quilted one.

"Mrs. LeFlore's Wayward Hotel, in the tenderloin!"

"Mrs. LeFlore's! Ain't you heard!"

"Heard what!" Proctor seems worried.

"The Yankee provost shut her down two days ago! Turned her business over to them temperance women!"

Suddenly, Proctor's mood turns. "Damn that son-of-a-bitch! I don't believe it! Why I have a mind to declare war on that rascalite!"

"You can count on us, Iowa!"

"Much obliged, Josh!"

The exchange of friendly words continues at a lazy pace. What only hours ago would have been an unconscionable act now is acceptable, though Susha remains confused as to how a soldier is to behave. On the one hand her comrades seem to be proficient at their profession, while on the other have a difficult time figuring out just who is their enemy. Should Proctor Keedy have his way, he'd be warring against Captain Pillow and that Memphis provost marshal, recruiting at least two Arkansas cavalrymen to assist him. One thing is certain, however, this being that Susha can't wait to send home another letter.

"Proctor!" The call comes from the direction of camp.

Susha turns around to see Lieutenant Warner. Laden with knapsack, revolver, and a paper-wrapped bundle, he approaches Proctor and stops for a brief talk, acknowledging her with a wave.

"Hey, Joshua!" shouts Lieutenant Warner to the quilted one. "Is Lieutenant Likens in camp!"

"He just might be!"

"Might you fetch the chap for me! By honor of a truce!"

The quilted one looks to the fisherman, shrugs and picks up his shotgun. "I suppose I might!"

At first, it seems odd to Susha that the lieutenant might inquire about someone from the other side. Then again, if privates can exchange friendly words, why not officers?

As he continues to talk with Proctor, Lieutenant Warner looks toward Susha. "Potter! Everything going fine!"

"Yessir!"

Within a few minutes the quilted one returns with another butternut of similar shabby dress and no apparent rank.

"George Warner! Is that you!"

"Certainly is, Sam Likens!"

"Come on over!"

To Susha's shock, not only does Lieutenant Warner accept the offer and cross the footbridge, also he's greeted with a jovial handshake and slap on the back. Under the influence of their combined buoyancies, the two waste no time and disappear to what must be the Confederate's camp.

Although it seems untoward, this consorting with the enemy, Susha decides to accept what already her comrades take for granted. Indeed, friendships are capable of leaping across boundaries. If two like-minded foes wish to suspend hostilities from time to time, then what's the harm? After all, with it situated somewhere on the war's edge, the 42nd Iowa isn't a real part of the great conflict.

It's not long afterward when Susha and Proctor are relieved from the picket. And as they return to camp, she poses the obvious.

"What is Lieutenant Warner doing?"

"He's gotten friendly with that Secesh lieutenant. The two will probably play bluff all night."

Dusk is coming and the soldiers in camp prepare to make a short evening of it. Susha and Proctor are cooking their salt pork, while the others sit back with their coffee and tobacco.

As for Paps, he's serenading the camp with his reminiscences of the Mexican War, and of his comrades of a different era. "Yessir. I got a good look at Jeff Davis. What with his Mississippians forming alongside my own regiment. We sure put that Santie Annie to flight."

Suddenly, a distant holler echoes into the camp. It's a singular signal, one originating from a pair of raspy lungs and shooting out of a mostly barren mouth.

"I do believe that is Snaggle Tooth," announces Bill.

"By God," joins Proctor, holding his ramrodded salt pork over the fire. "I have to agree."

"I might be of a mind to see what he's up to," speaks Bill. "Proctor?"

For Private Keedy, the invitation is irresistible. "Bob. Watch my sowbelly." He hands over his ramrod, leaving behind his unbuttoned greatcoat.

By all rights, Corporal Davison could raise his objections, but instead, enforces his authority. "Take your muskets. It is getting dark."

Hurriedly, the two grab their weapons and hustle toward the pickets.

"You boys be careful," advises Paps.

As to whether Pvts. Stewart and Keedy will take any heed, Susha isn't sure. For that matter, is caution even required, for she has seen her foes firsthand and a fierce impression they do not make. There is within Susha a spark of curiosity, to leave the fire and see for herself just who or what this Snaggle Tooth is. However, Paps is a sober-minded man, whose every word has some meaning. As he did air a slight caution, perhaps it would be better for Susha to leave Snaggle Tooth to the company of his "friends."

Soon, she's chewing the fat with her comrades—and of her salt pork—as she bundles herself against the increasing cold. Certainly, Susha has found herself in interesting company, men who have been places and done things. If one can omit their slips in language, her fellow soldiers are even polite, as they possess that gentlemanly deference toward their comrades. Indeed, as far as Susha is concerned, with the exception of Sylvie and possibly Granger, her Potter and Pye male kin are decidedly inferior to her present coterie.

"Old Abe is a clever general," declares Nelling. "I hardly care for darkies, and when he started recruiting them I was well against it. But from all I have gathered, some of them are beginning to behave like soldiers. Full of fight and fortitude. Give them time and they ought to better those damn New England Yankees. Old Abe had it right all along."

In between the mumblings of agreement, Susha's ears begin to pick up a different sort of noise. At first it's only a faint, unreadable sound. Quickly, however, she makes out the cadence of rushing feet, accompanied by the familiar clangs of brass, iron and tin. Did someone forget an item which demands a mad dash? Since there's nothing of importance around this camp, Susha's heart decides to hasten its pace. As for her head, it, too, would like to take some sort of course, that is if it had the time.

"They're a-coming! They're a-coming!" It's Bill, frantic and panic-driven, and not caring to linger with an explanation, as he races through the camp.

Then there's Susha, sitting on her stump with hardtack crumbs trickling from her gaping mouth. In an instant, her body becomes as frozen as a wintry Iowa pond, although her mind is able to move. And oh, how it scurries with thoughts of impending disaster, of plans going awry and of separation from her beloved Sylvie. What's to become of Sylvie?

Though the campfire provides an ideal beacon for this invasion, it also serves to highlight the invaders. And then he appears, one of their number barging into camp as if he owns the place.

Such is her shock, that Susha feels like a detached observer and not a participant. Even as the Secesh heads straight toward her, she summons a denial that she is the apparent blunt of attack.

A wild-eyed, savage beast—the perfect opposite of a civilized Iowan—stops short with his cavalry carbine held to port. His brown slouch hat is well-aerated from wear, while his butternut shell jacket is bone-buttoned and of a shoddy weave. Yet in contrast, he wears sky blue trousers—quality produced and no doubt stolen. The oddities of his uniform aside, this Confederate holds his prey at a decided disadvantage, her fate being his whim.

Still, in spite of the overwhelming odds, Susha can't compel herself to do the obvious. Perhaps it's part of that Pye stubbornness which always seems to surface when faced with a crisis. Although, Susha's arms may be limp from fear, they do not rise to strength in order to offer her surrender.

"Hey, Bob," shouts the Secesh. "It's me. What do you think of my new uniform?"

To Susha's amazement, and even greater relief, the face looking down upon her belongs to Proctor Keedy. An uproar of laughter intercedes, with some of her comrades rolling uncontrollably on the ground. Since none of them had reached for their Enfields, the purpose behind Proctor's galvanizing is plain for Susha to see. It's all a joke, one big joke played upon the newest member of Company C.

"You sure swallowed that one, Bob," declares Bill, who stands hidden behind a tree. He walks up to Susha to give her a slap on the back. "But you never turned Quakerly. What do you say, boys? Our Bob was not about to surrender."

An anger which Susha may be able to conjure quickly is allayed.

"Bob's a soldier, first-rate," adds Paps. "You can bet. How about your opinion, Pleasent?"

Pleasent? An unusual name, thinks Susha, one she's never heard in camp.

"Looks like you all picked a fierce-looking fella. Yessiree. Ready to stand up to all parcels of fightin'."

Immediately, Susha directs her attention to the soldier in question. A man of short stature, his blonde hair dangles over the shoulders of his ill-fitted sack coat, as well as down the chest. As for his trousers, they're of a tighter butternut, patched many times over and tucked into well-worn boots. However, more revealing to Susha is not what Pleasent is wearing, but rather the high-pitched, nasally words funneling through the great gaps of his grinning mouth. Snaggle Tooth! Who else could it be! Standing there wearing the Union blue, he seems proud of the role which his hat, jacket and weapon have played in the farce.

"Still fierce as a plague, even after he'd done gone coon."

Before she can realize, not only is Susha introduced to one Private Pleasent Hill, but also she shakes his receptive hand. Soon, along with the other members of the detail, she's breaking bread with her sworn enemy. The campfire burns crisply, making a good source for congenial warmth. It also serves to cook, as with the tin cups of coffee, boiled three times over as regulation suggests. While all assembled drink their thick brews, Susha can't keep her curious eyes off Pleasent. Never before has she seen such a character, what with his dirty, unkempt appearance and his threadbare mouth. Yet Pleasent seems perfectly suited to his destitution, happy to be alive. As well he should, for as he sips his coffee in one instant and expectorates tobacco juices in another, Susha understands that "Snaggle Tooth" is swimming in his luxury.

"Yessiree. I felt like Jonah when that bear wrapped his paws 'round my scraggly carcass. 'Bout to send me to my accounts, 'til I got hold of his manly parts and give 'em a good yank. Put him to a high yelpin' and turned him fugitive, you can believe. Yessiree..."

Try as she might, Susha could never regard Pleasent as a foe, nor can she see how he could be the intended of an angry rifle. That's too cruel a sentiment for such a content, guiltless creature. In the end, the pity is that he belongs to the Seceshes. As far as Susha is concerned, Pleasent Hill would make a fine Iowan.

Soon, the three days of outpost duty expire, with the members of the detail having packed their knapsacks. As it occurs, Susha and Proctor are the last on the picket, and to her surprise, she sees that they're being relieved by two of their messmates, Leo Garrett and Ben Goad.

"That cousin of yours sure has gotten gloomy," informs Leo.

Following Proctor and Corporal Davison back to camp, a tincture of guilt builds within Susha. Mired in the dreariness of Camp Parmeter sits Sylvie, while she experiences the world. The worst of it is that Susha's woes of separation have been less painful, thus the want to make amends for her poor, pining husband.

As the detail marches through the Cache Country, it's Sylvie who dominates the recesses of Susha's thoughts. And it's just short of Camp Parmeter when she realizes that with Leo and Ben having taken their snores and rumblings to Outpost B, she and Sylvie will have the shanty all to themselves. Soon, there will be three days of wedded bliss surrounded by a battalion of soldiers, none of whom should be any the wiser.

Awaiting anxiously at the edge of Camp Parmeter is Sylvie, himself.

"Detail. Shoulder. Arms," commands Corporal Davison. "Left, left..."

Susha waves to Sylvie, who rushes to join his wife's side as the detail continues its march.

"How was it, Bob?" Although he wants to burst free, Sylvie maintains the pose.

"It all went fine. But I am glad to be back. I want to hear what happened, while I was gone."

"Detail. Halt." The corporal hesitates, as if considering a parting thought. Fortunately, he thinks the better of it. "Dismissed."

Immediately, Sylvie relieves Susha of her Enfield. "Bob, I got something in the shanty."

As soon as they light a candle and shut the door, the couple begins to smother one another with their pented hugs and kisses. At first, Susha's traps make for only a trifle barrier, their sparks rekindling where they stand. However, after their initial reintroduction, they do manage to settle down and make things cozy.

"Susha." Reaching into a small box, a beaming Sylvie locates an object. "Merry Christmas." It's a lace handkerchief—frilly and delicate, and all things feminine. "I got it for just a handful of coffee beans. From that Prudhum woman. You would have thought by her I handed over a treasure."

"Sylvie. It's wonderful." She rubs its dainty softness against her cheek, closing her eyes to help perk her imaginations. "Eliza will love to see this."

"She says it's from Belgium. One of those places."

"Sylvie, I have a present for you too." She looks into her knapsack and pulls out a poke bag. "I also traded coffee. Look inside."

The bag bulges with tobacco, upon which rests a small clay pipe.

"Susha? How did you come by this?"

"From the Seceshes on picket."

"Susha? Did you talk to any of them?"

"Not really. But Proctor and Bill sure did. They got me this."

"Oh?" Although it sounds reasonable enough, Sylvie still has his doubts. After all, it is tobacco. "You think I ought to try some?"

"Just a little cannot hurt."

Indeed, it doesn't. In fact, the few puffs Sylvie dares take are almost enjoyable, even tempering. This could be handy when the time comes for Susha to relate her stories on the picket. However, first things first, and that is to get better reacquainted—all fitting and proper—with the door barred for good measure.

As January gains several days, so too do the Potters acquire experience. Not only have they learned the ways of Company C, but by a short reach also of the 42nd. Most importantly, however, is that the couple is getting along famously with their messmates, and with Susha's surreptitious advice, Sylvie is making progress with his cooking.

It's just after dusk, and the mess huddles around their fire. A small flask of whiskey is passed around in aid to a celebration. At long last, Sylvie has attained that draftable age, and aside from political participation, he can claim that he's as full-fledged a man as any, Susha included.

"So tell me, Sylvie," asks Proctor. "Now that you are a man of high degree, when do you think you will settle down and get married?"

"Well-l-l." He's at a loss.

"When do you plan on getting married?" Susha can't resist.

Encouraged by his wife's gentle poke, Sylvie manages the words. "The same day as you, Bob. We can get married at the same ceremony. Find us a couple of rich, fat, spinster sisters and wed them quick."

"Sounds like you been thinking about this for a while. But if that makes you happy, Sylvie, I am for it."

"I know just such sisters," declares Bill. "In Des Moines. I should introduce you two."

"Thank you. Sylvie and me will look forward to courting them."

At this point, Paps makes short his conspicuous absence, returning to his chair by the fire.

"Did you get any news out of Wilkins?" asks Ben.

"Something." Paps puts the flickering end of a stick to his unlit pipe. "Not much in the manner of direct report. But this I did learn." He takes a few puffs. "Captain Parmenter is moving Outpost A closer to camp. And the colonel has found a new sutler."

As far as Susha is concerned, this is good tidings, for she needs desperately several items. Nevertheless, around the campfire she notices that her comrades' moods are altering from the jovial to the serious.

"I don't like the sound of that," speaks Proctor.

"This is not the worst of it," continues Paps. "In a day or two we are to start drilling. As a battalion."

"Damn," airs Leo. "It's not even February."

Except from Susha and Sylvie, there's a collective moan, for beyond its boredom and exertion, resuming the drill carries a significant portent. Indeed, what would be the point of re-schooling the ranks if they're not to put their skills to a martial use at a very near date?

"No. I don't like the sound of that at all."

8 ↝ Bureau of Posterior Legal Affairs

Winter has yet to find its stride. Although the leaves and temperatures have fallen, the season's harshest core hasn't reached northwestern Louisiana. However, there are fewer promises of celebration concerning the approaching eves, three years of attrition have seen to this. Perhaps the only hope is for a short winter, though even this wish has a pitfall. For the influential few, an early spring would provide a profitable opportunity for the year's first campaign.

This is the reason why the addresses for some are tenuous at best. However, there are those who seek some sort of permanency, that is for the duration. Although many of the days may prove to be trying—slowly can the clocks unwind—at least residing in the same place enables a man to give solace to his blossoming family. This is possible regardless of the distance:

> My Dearest Henrietta,
>
> As you can see, I am able to compose a proper letter, now that I have become better settled. Shreveport is a dreary place, with the already established in a desperate need of repair, while much of the rest is makeshift and unhealthful. It seems my adopted home is inhabited largely by refugees and those who despise them, with the remainder surmounted by government officials and politicians. Of course, Henrietta, you are well aware of what an unsavory mob that latter species can be, their influences ruinous to communities of honest men and women. I do not doubt the citizens here were once a pleasant and

hopeful people before the War Between the Sophists altered their temperaments. Who could blame the poor wretches when one witnesses the struggles of their everyday lives, the existence of every commodity being scarce, while the prices abundant? But never mind, for with the cheery thoughts of my Henrietta and the impending birth of our beautiful child, Shreveport cannot be a bother.

As for my purpose in this setting, I have yet to discover. This much I do know: as this is the Land of Bureaus, General Smith is very proud of them, one has been created for me. The Bureau of Posterior Legal Affairs it has been designated. Dear Henrietta, you may ask of the functions of this bureau and my reply would be one of confusion. I might pose the same question to you and have every confidence that your answer would better that of your of your poor, confounded husband's. As for the staff of the B.P.L.A., my sweet Henrietta, your husband is it! Not only do I command the Bureau, I am the Bureau! To date, my duties demand little of my efforts and all of my patience. Thus I spend little time at its dank and windowless setting, opting to exercise my cane and familiarizing myself with my sad posting.

Henrietta, you must be nurturing a curiosity concerning my lately secured quarters. Home for me is a section of a garret in a large dwelling serving as a boarding house. I shall not detail the fee for fear of shock. However, in future years when our returning prosperity allows for many moments of light diversions, you may ask. The room itself, consists of nothing more than a tiny bed and mattress, its contents being a speculation, a severely warped writing desk, and a loplegged chair. But a luxury of luxuries exists in that my room owns a small stove and is lighted by one of Sig. Palladio's windows. Stark as it may be, my room is free of filth, it being myself who keeps it clean.

Perhaps I should relate to you my landlady, a Miss Ariadne Smallbones of all things. Older than myself, she is a spinster, with justifiable cause. Sometimes, after my eyes fail to avert themselves from her frightening image, I stand stunned at how she and the beautiful McKie sisters could be of the same sex!

I think it impossible and that Miss Smallbones must be of her own category. But war has been kind to her, for not only does she profit from it, playing a cagey hand she might procure a husband. You see, Henrietta, the boarding house where I find myself is brimming with young, unwily officers. This is by no accident, for I have observed Miss Smallbones turn away inquiries from several potential boarders, but never from those of bachelors. The War Between the Sophists may be her last chance, and she means to take advantage. You may well speculate that the only reason I find myself under her care is that at first sight she thought me a single man! I can only believe she misread my forlorned and homesick face as being one that was lovestarved. But Miss Smallbones' disposition soon changed after she realized my true status. Now my requests for such things as a cup of tea, a bar of soap or a candle, or even the time of day, are met with disdain. Still, I harbor no ill will for Miss Smallbones, for I understand her time is short and she cannot afford to waste any portion of it on me!

As to how I will spend my moments is an entirely different matter. Although I have reflected deeply upon this subject, my strategy is incomplete, accounting for only a few hours of each day. Indeed, I have come upon the conclusion that the day contains far too many hours. Why use 24 when 20 will suffice? Believe me, Henrietta, in what I say, for I have figured the balances and consider myself a scholar on the subject. For the seeable future I am be to confronted with idleness. As for reading, the begged for and the borrowed will constitute my library, books not of my choosing and not likely of my taste. Alas, your husband should have paid your concerns a better heed when you advised me to hitch my plow to a mixed team of ox and mule. I am left with few options, but as I have penetrated its walls, perhaps at the first chance I should lay a fiery waste to the city so that I may return home.

Speaking of journeys, I should say that mine proved to be uneventful, yet entertaining, and healthful, it being a restorative to have toured the countryside. There was, however, a high degree of sadness concerning the Blakes. Their sons have been lost, and Mrs. Blake in particular has been unable to reconcile herself with the tragedy. I must confess I could not summon the courage to remain to their company for more than a few hours, so declining was the pall. Henrietta, you and Georgina must compose a letter of condolence to the poor, wounded couple and offer them the kindnesses of your hearts, for mine proved too weak for the cause.

I encountered a few refugees in East Texas, whom it seems are being accorded the same reception as people of their status everywhere. It fails me to figure why this is so, especially when I was charitably received by one of their number, a Mr. Simmons of Carroll Parish. As you know, to abuse those who have met misfortune is chief among my pet aversions, and I find its expanding practice both shameless and telling.

The meals that nourished me during my journey were savory and healthful, beginning with the tasty plunder as was prepared by my talented wife. About the countryside, the foodstuffs are available, but Louisiana's estimable capital is a different matter. As my connections have yet to be exploited my meals are left to the discretion of Miss Smallbones and her negro cook, beef and hominy being the standard fare. As you may have guessed, Henrietta, there is a ready stream of Texas beeves being driven into Shreveport. Pork is absent from this region, and any hog able to meet its appointed fate will have its parts sold at unattainable premiums. As for fowl, although Miss Smallbones keeps a roomy coop, she guards its issue with her life. It is no wonder I have yet to be served so much as a solitary egg, for the rumored price of just one caused my stomach to churn sour. Only once have I pleasured on poultry fare, a stringy captive of Admiral Noah that surely lost its ability to contribute to Miss Smallbones' enterprise. Henrietta, I must confess that the devil in me introduced the temptation of a midnight foray into poultry manumission. Could my guilt outweigh my honor? I doubt it. Miss Smallbones must find a husband, and I being a judge of what is becoming understand better than most her necessity to acquire every cent. Such is the sacrifice of the scrupulous, even if said mischief remains a consideration.

I do miss the harvests of Georgina's garden. But I have an eye on a small footage of ground belonging to my landlady. Perhaps she will allow me to till it for spring vegetables, or more likely I will have to negotiate for the privilege, with Miss Smallbones at the advantage. Still, it would be worth her tithe. At this point I must say that whiskey and similar drink are effortless to procure in Shreveport, in spite of threats of official proscription. In fact, I was told by one resident that after the town was designated the capital, the availability of the ardent increased. This, of course, confirms to me a long held suspicion. Gambling is also near to rampant. As you know, with the exception of horses, this holds for me no interest. But at the one race I did attend, worn out nags were passed as thoroughbreds, thus ruining a harmless diversion.

As for the concern of the care of my mount, there is none. Henrietta, since a number of my junior officer acquaintances are without horses, they have agreed to share my saddle with the provision that they see to the expenses. With myself needing only the occasional ride to insure that I maintain my balance, my mount will still receive ample activity for its own sake, while not costing me a penny.

Because of the nature of my sinecure, I am considering a return to teaching. There are a number of institutes and seminaries scattered about, of which are in desperate need for pro tempore lecturers and instructors. Or perhaps I should do some tutoring or even found my own cozy academy, teaching Singletonian Philosophy! On the other hand, I may practice a bit of law and take on a client or two. I also realize I should better my weak German, in preparation for our return to San Antonio. I have yet to encounter a practitioner of that tongue, though there are nearby communities. Inquiries will be made. Or perhaps I will forgo any ambitions and bide my time writing to my Dearest Henrietta, as such would bring me great pleasure. And I do have the means, for I am a part of the bureaucracy, privy to its inner workings, with access to its reams of writing paper. Bully for the neverending flow of paper! And I will send my dispatches to Austin. There a friend will post them to Bastrop by civilian mail. It should require my letters a week to complete each trek, which I find remarkable. As for yours, Henrietta, they will take another course. Address your letters to: Maj. Robert Spates, The District of Texas, New Mexico and Arizona, Houston. Include a brief instruction so that he will know to send them by dispatch to me, and the Bureau of Posterior Legal Affairs. Before I became your suitor, I had represented his brother in a breach of promise, so Maj. Spates should oblige us.

So far, 1863 has not been kind to our country, and there is too little remaining to be hopeful. Yesterday I had my first encounter with Shreveport coffee, that is a hot beverage made from roasted okra seeds. The flavor is foul, but the citizens have convinced themselves to refer this brew as a favorite. To accomplish this feat must have required an unrelenting delusion. These three years have seen plague after plague of such behavior, a draining accumulation unto itself. Here in Shreveport, and I assume in hundreds of other placenames, I have detected fewer hearts still kindled for war. The comfort would be to allow the war to continue elsewhere, so that the populace might consume the ill tidings of faraway places with less passion and more resignation. There being little left in Louisiana, for the enemy an adventure of further conquest seems foolish. As for Texas, sustained efforts to capture the Rio Grande are not out of the question, what with the want to put an end to the cotton trade. And I fear those who live on the coast are also fair game. Yet being far inland, Bastrop is as safe from attack as fortress Washington. I doubt that Austin holds any interest for Lincoln's generals, and for this I commend their sagacity.

Then there are my keepers. The Trans-Mississippi Department is a perfect machine of organization and bureaucracy, the translation being that it can also be a quagmire of inaction. Henrietta, being in charge of the B.P.L.A. evokes a lofty title, but let me assure that with the ever expanding list of like offices, this is no such thing. The truth of it is, a sausage stuffer in San Antonio enjoys a greater status than many gentlemen officers who possess a bureau. How I long to learn the degrees of making sausage, a captivating ritual for me to bide the remainder of the war.

But it seems that the B.P.L.A. is my destiny, and so be it. Though separated, Captain and Mrs. Singleton are safely tucked, far from harm's path. This suits me, for it assures that we have a future as one. Being apart from my lovely wife may be a miserable circumstance, but it is endurable. Henrietta, it is no small boast to say that my life is owed to your care. You mothered me with skillful and loving devotion, and soon you shall mother again. It may be many months until my return, with the chance that when I next see home you will be cradling our child. What a splendid mother you shall be, for never have I known a more pondering and caring person. Such pleasures I will have to gaze in awe, to watch as your inspirations are bestowed upon another. Forgive me if this is all I do for the years to come. Death has been my acquaintance on too many occasions, and now that I have bid it farewell, life's simplicities are becoming my raison d'etre.

The war is running its course, and with this the threats to Texas diminished. You and Georgina, and your neighbors, are as safe as any cursed New England Yankee, and perhaps better situated, for most Texans have been schooled in the lessons of honest ingenuity, rather than greed and duplicity. Any fear you may have concealed, Henrietta, I feel is unfounded, for I see the war's end as an opportunity for rebirth. As Texas has avoided the destruction of other regions, there is little need to rebuild. We can return to San Antonio with little effort and resume a prosperous life.

As for myself and the epoch in which I will spend in Shreveport? Henrietta, you know that I will not idle away my time, that I will put it to a fitful use. My fettle is sound and I am well clothed. Truth to tell, the uniform you skillfully fashioned is the envy of the company I am beginning to keep. As long as I know my Henrietta is safe and happy, and our child is taking its natural course, then I can endure every and all. Indeed, I could crush the Gates of Hell should the cause arise.

Henrietta, for my sake make certain you and Georgina give our nieces a happy Christmas. To assure that our year's end will be pleasant, some of my fellow officers and myself are assembling an assault on that which is gloom, to see that the side of mirth and glee will carry the day! The rumors are of festive food and libations, of music and frills, all in hopes of attracting the young damsels. Henrietta, I must confess this old man looks forward to viewing the dancing and revelry, for it should recall those special memories of our courtship. And that is where my head lies, with you instead of the dearthful duties. With you when I take my aimless wanderings through town. With you when I feel the sun and stare at the stars. And when at night I lie awake, I lie with you. Christmas will not be bleak, if only because of the ones that were and the ones that are to come.

Henrietta, I write these words with love and adoration, and with the comfort of our eternal bond. We shall never be apart. Not by conflict, not by hundreds of miles, not by oceans of muddied roads nor valleys in flood. Within days I shall write anew and I look forward to your words with trembling anticipation. Do give the girls a kiss from me. Georgina, too. And do not neglect Mairead. Give my regards to all of our kind friends and neighbors. But most importantly, Henrietta, look after yourself. Be selfish if need be, for my sake and that of our baby's. As for now, I must bid a gentle farewell from the deepest flames of my heart.

Your affectionate husband,
John

John's spirits are rising. What he feels is a contentment derived by private amusement and its sure measure of retribution. Then there is the Christmas soiree: days in planning, hours in passing and years in future reminiscing, and certain to extend John's momentary happiness.

The venue for the affair is a large, clapboarded dogtrot on the edge of town. Requisitioned by the officers who inhabit one side of the structure, both halves are clear of most furnishings, while its breezeway is covered at its open ends. Thus the entire house has been transformed into a roomy hall, albeit one sectioned by parallel walls and having some unheated corners.

Thanks to Lieutenant Hall and his committee of two others, there are no stark spaces for the occasion. Managing with their assemblage of four arms and five legs, the house is festooned with all varieties of holiday decorations: ribbons, bunting and candles, as well as lace tablecloths, silverware and china. In addition, hanging about are the final touches of ubiquitous display, they being the symbolisms of holly and the opportunisms of mistletoe. To be sure, what was once simple and dismal is now a marvel for the eyes.

Yet to keep the air merry requires that also it should be kept proper, so that parents would have no reservations about sending their daughters to a dance sponsored by young officers. Cleverly, Captain Ellerton, organizer of invitations, has sent a liberal number to respectable couples, bestowing upon each the status of chaperone. With this news that local deportment is to be maintained, the soiree has been deemed an innocent one. Hence, the original intent to attract the young ladies of Shreveport is achieving a resounding success. To the captains and lieutenants' joy, the reconfigured dogtrot is overflowing with handsome and delicate damsels.

That is with one notable exception. Somehow, Ariadne Smallbones has managed an invitation, a feat John finds galling. It's he who is in charge of procuring the edibles, a difficult task which had him scouring the countryside. Using all of the trickery of bureaucracy's privilege, not only has he found wheat flour, sugar and flavorings for the cakes, but by chance and miracle five smoked hams, insuring the glorious absence of stringy beef. In addition, there are Irish potatoes, apples and pears, grape wine, sardines, candies, lemonade, and much more. And to supplement the hams there is displayed roast chicken, as well as hard-boiled eggs.

However, it's of the poultry which still stirs John's rancor, for when, with all diplomacy, he approached Miss Smallbones to contribute her connections for the common good, he was spurned. Even his suggestion of a discount was denied, and when John asked for the services of her cook, again he was rejected. Now Miss

Smallbones has the audacity to show her face at the party she's refused to support.

Still, this is only a passing annoyance for John. After all, the soiree is proceeding splendidly, the rooms being thick with happy feet and gay faces. Already John has fielded many compliments for his efforts, and because he's new to Shreveport and has yet to tarnish his reputation—rumor has it, he's to be promoted – he's a center of attraction for the ladies. Indeed, his gallant name has been entered on a number of dance cards. And why shouldn't it? Within the breezeway, the musicians are at the mandola, clarinet, flute and triangle, producing some lively tunes which even set John's cane to tapping. Because some wine has joined the rhythm, his leg feels little discomfort.

The dogtrot shudders as dozens of feet stomp to a spirited reel. But while a prudent John sits out this round, he's approached by the father of Miss Sally Hey. A young lady of 16, it's her parents who are supervising the selections for her dance card. With Captain Singleton being a respectable married man, his name appears twice, as well as onto that of the elder Hey daughter.

"Major. I believe your name has once again appeared on my daughter's card."

"Miss Sally. How delightful."

Indeed, she is, as John is led to the opposite end of the room, where Sally awaits with her mother. Dressed in a red, silk-wool skirt and bodice with a black waist, she comes to her feet to show her dainty stature. Around her neck Sally wears a gold chain and as well, has donned a pair of golden earrings, no doubt jewelry borrowed from her proud mother.

"Mrs. Hey," greets John. "Miss Sally. I believe the next dance is my pleasure."

"Yes, Major."

"I see Miss Rebecca is enjoying the reel. Once again, I must apologize if I cannot indulge you on the livelier tunes."

"Father has arranged another waltz."

John turns to Mr. Hey. "I commend you on your thoughtfulness, sir."

"But as this is my first dance, I, too, need the slower tunes," explains Sally.

"Miss Sally, had you not informed me previously, I would have never guessed. Mrs. Hey, of all my partners on this evening, your daughter's feet have been the lightest."

"Thank you, Major."

With that, the reel comes to an abrupt end and John offers his escorting hand. "Miss Sally. Sir. Ma'am. With your permission."

To the middle of the room they meander, and it's there that John clasps the small of Sally's back. Perhaps he draws her too near for two who are barely acquainted. However, Sally seems to care not a whit, knowing she's in safe hands. Soon, in a sharp contrast to the resounding reel, the waltz begins with a purr, and the pair gently whirls to the slow one-two-three.

"I trust you and Miss Rebecca have enjoyed yourselves."

"Yes, Major," smiles Sally. "I think I shall always treasure this evening."

She feels familiar in John's arms, her light brown ringlets jingling to her dainty, springing steps.

"Then if that be the case, all of my fellow officers' efforts have proven their worth." With that, John, too, lightens his feet.

The waltz itself lingers into a lengthy set—much to the appreciation of it patrons.

"Major. Please, tell me something of your wife. I would love to know about her."

"Of course. She is awfully pretty, such as yourself. In fact, the two of you share a resemblance."

"Do tell, Major."

"And Henrietta is very kind and charitable, with a clever mind. Attributes I most admire of her. And she is expecting, with our first child."

"Oh, how wonderful, Major. You must be so happy. But how cruel to be apart."

"Yes, but there are many who share my predicament. I really cannot complain."

"But I do hope you write to her often. That you tell her all."

In time, the waltz fades away, with John and Sally rejoining her parents. Mr. Hey is also an attorney, who has promised to cast some work to John. In addition, there is the Heys' open invitation to all the Sunday dinners to come.

"Mother. Major Singleton was telling me about his wife. She is a very charming person. The sort I would love to meet. And she is expecting."

"Oh. Congratulations, Major."

"Thank you, Mrs. Hey."

"We do look forward to the possibility of making her acquaintance. If only she could be with us now. But do tell us more about her."

To be sure, John knows full well that this is the type of affair at which Henrietta's sparkle would prosper. "Well. Where shall I start?"

The evening flies, although a good portion of it remains when John decides to bid his farewell to the Heys. But as he taps his way toward the door, he happens upon a prominent feature in the landscape, its crooked and gangly traits being easy to recognize. When the person in question turns around to reveal her great hook of a nose and piano key teeth, John realizes that he's in for an inescapable diversion.

"Why, Miss Smallbones. So pleasant to see you. How glad I am you harbored no ill feelings and decided to attend our party."

"Captain. I have little idea to what you are referring. But thank you all the same." She diverts her eyes to the dancers on the floor.

"I trust you have enjoyed yourself."

"Yes." But Miss Smallbones seems reluctant in surrendering her reply. "Yes, I have."

"And that the evening has proved profitable."

John notices that the dance card she clutches has remarkably few blemishes. Overwhelmed by the competition, Miss Smallbones hasn't had much of a sporting chance.

"Such a lovely array of lasses. Were I a bachelor, my head would be dizzy and confused."

The smirk on Miss Smallbones's face shows that she, too, has come to this conclusion. "Where did they come from?"

"Hard to say. Captain Ellerton was in charge of the invitations."

"Yes. Captain Ellerton." Miss Smallbones grinds her teeth as she utters his name, perhaps considering some retribution for one of her boarders.

"Well, Miss Smallbones, I must be retiring now. So I will leave you to the revelry."

"Captain."

"By the way. Have you recovered all of your hens?"

"Not as yet."

"A terrible crime to have set loose your poultry. I hope the Police Jury apprehends and punishes the scoundrel."

"I doubt that they will. But that won't stop me."

"Then should you require the services of an attorney, I am available."

"Thank you, Captain. I shall keep that under consideration."

The cold wind greets John as he exits the dogtrot, following him all the way to the boarding house. Whereas on previous years Shreveport may have been sprinkled with holiday regalia, tonight the streets are black and reserve. Once again, John is alone.

After negotiating the dark stairs to his room, he strikes a match to his candle lantern, which throws off a good light. In fact, it illuminates much more for a person who is readying himself for sleep. When John spoke of retiring, he in no way meant that he was taking to his bed. He stirs the embers in his stove, feeding it fist size chunks of wood. It's to his desk where John does retire, to several blank sheets of paper and a bottle of ink. For now, and what should be several hours to come, he'll cease being alone and the company he keeps will be the closest to his heart:

My Dearest Henrietta,

I have just returned from what in my estimation is the social event of the year...

9 ~ Beggars, Thieves and Vandals

Military campaigns are complicated endeavors. Before an enemy is confronted, the sheer volume of soldiery dictates cautious planning. Troops must be assembled, their cartridge boxes kept full, and the horses shod and fed. But just as vital, generals must devise their brilliant strategies, as well as concoct the justifications for these profligacies. And equal to all this are favorable conditions, which may explain why spring is referred to as the "campaign season."

On the other hand, any competent commander should be able to summon his forces and gather the needed supplies on short notice, and were the situation to arise, improvise and experiment. Indeed, although winter's hold remains firm, given such boldness, what harm could come by pushing up the calendar a good measure or two?

The streets of Helena have never been muddier, sure to ripen into a *noxious effluvia* when the weather warms. Because of an outbreak of mumps, the battalion consisting of Companies E, G and I has returned with slightly fewer in number than before. In addition, Company A has been susceptible to the lingering diarrhea for which the town is notorious. As for Captain Parmeter's Battalion and Susha's comrades of Company C, the random fortune of their stops and movements has allowed them to avoid the outbreaks. Regardless, although for now Helena may be sickness free, it would be imprudent to extend one's stay.

This is exactly what Colonel Burness is being forced to do. It seems that Company F in faraway Little Rock isn't rushing its return to Helena, meaning that the 42nd Iowa is able to convene only nine of its ten companies. Colonel Burness is determined not to embark toward the yet to be disclosed destination without the regiment's full compliment. Hence, the wait accompanied with its frustrations and hardships.

As it happens, Helena is a converging point for several other regiments, their numbers far outstretching all accommodations. It's hoped that the hours of the soldiers' arrivals and partings would be approximate to one another. However, if hopes have one thing in common, it's that they are open to abuse. Colonel Burness has no option but to spread his companies upon the open environs surrounding Helena, where the men fend for themselves against the hostile winter.

A small canopy of branches and twigs leaks rain upon the very campfire it is designed to protect. The weather is thick, its wet chill drizzling down the back of Proctor Keedy's neck, while a relentless cold besieges his sodden feet.

"Goddam that Captain Adams," he grumbles. "Goddam Fish Adams and his Company F. I would sooner fight alongside a pew of Quakers than those poltroons."

"Wager they're too busy gathering fucks from the fast tricks of Little Rock," reasons Bill.

"Then I hope the scoundrels come down with a clap to confound our loose bowel of a surgeon. Hmmph."

In spite of her seat being adjacent to Bill's, Susha's response is one of fleeting amusement. Certainly, she feels no insult, nor are her delicate ears being set aflame.

As for her husband, with whom Susha shares the cover of a gum blanket, he's more interested in stuffing the bowl of his pipe than his wife's honor. This being the last of his tobacco, Sylvie's cautious to waste not a strand. Upon lighting his pipe, he seizes a soothing draft, after which he positions the mouthpiece in front of Susha's face.

She takes a couple of puffs, the taste and sensation of which she's learning to enjoy.

"You boys always talking of women," speaks Sylvie. "Why, Bob and me know more than you two will ever understand."

"Is that so, Private Potter?"

"Yes it is, Private Keedy. One day I will tell you all about it, and an earful you shall have." Sylvie looks at his comrades with a self-satisfied grin. After all, between friends such things as "honor" have little cause.

With no wind to push it aside, the cold drizzle has little reason to relent, and the soldiers of the 42nd can do nothing but complain of their miseries. Then again, perhaps the well-being of one of its messes is about to improve, by what may be a generous increment. Paps and Leo are returning from a forage, reclaiming their stumps around the diminishing fire. As for their success, the bulges of their greatcoats speak volumes.

"Tell me you two will make our sad lives more agreeable."

"Very well, Ben," replies Paps, as he covers himself with his gum blanket.

Reaching into his pockets, he liberates a can of brandied peaches, followed by two more. And as if by magic, three bottles of pickled gherkins follow suit.

Then it's Leo's turn, who awes his audience with four loaves of soft bread, a tin of China tea and a coffin bottle of gin. "You show me a temperance man and I can show you a coward too afraid to confront his weaknesses."

"How in God's name did you find this?" marvels Proctor.

"Shall we say that Company A took pity upon us," explains Paps.

"Or that their hearts turned charitable under the threat of Colonel Burness catching wind of that commissary pillage of theirs," furthers Leo. "Besides, they have no need for this. Their roster coming up shorter."

"Color company, the asses," sneers Ben.

In spite of the present gloomy climate, at least the 42nd Iowa is back in the business of being a regiment. Within a couple of hours, the boys are scheduled to slosh through yet another full regimental drill, minus a wayward Company F. The proud colors will be unfurled, the musicians will play a cadence, and every battlefield maneuver yet conceived will be performed in anticipation of glorious returns.

As for Susha, she has all the confidence that she'll be able to maintain her steps and react flawlessly at the barks of command. Be it the stacking of arms, the deploying as skirmishers, the rallying as sections, etc., she's adopted the soldiering movements as a reactive part of her nature.

"Did the two of you come upon that new sutler of ours?" asks Sylvie.

"No," replies Paps. "The canard has him moving to our next posting. Wherever that might be."

Dear Emma and Eliza,

Vicksburg Miss. is where our Rgt. is. The same place where there was the great battle. We landed here from Helena by steamboat a few days ago and our camp is in the pretty sandy hills that are outside the city. Our Rgt. is all together now that Company F joined us. We have been into Vicksburg twice all ready it being a city of magnificent houses and palaces and also of shanties and dug outs. It is a queer place as the ravages of war has taken a toll what with the damages from the artillery and mortars that happened during the notable siege. There is much repairing and building going on now that there is peace and there is much commerce. The citizens of Vicksburg do not mind us much and I think they are happy that the war is over for them. Our camp is a fine one with good water and the hills protect us from the cold winds but we do have to walk far for our wood. Since we have been here we got our pay that has been owed to us in Ark. The Rgts. Sutler is here and we have purchased items of comfort from him even if his prices are shameful. Our Rgt now belongs to Gen. A.J. Smiths 3rd Division in 16th Corps in Gen. William Tecumseh Shermans Army Of The Tennessee. All of my comrades consider this to be blessed for his reputation is esteemible. We were to join a Brigade with New Yorkers which did not sit well. But now we are with other Iowa Rgts. and one Missouri Rgt which suits us fine. Our commander is Colonel William Shaw from Iowa so we are in good hands. We have inspections to see that our muskets are in working order. I keep the rust off my barrel with steel wool and rub it with lard to keep away the water. This I do every day. We are certain to be going on an expedition into Alabama to conquer Mobile on the gulf of Mexico and after we finish every one thinks that we will move on Georgia. When we finish this the rebellion will be played out. Sylvie is exited about the expedition saying he wants to capture a rebel and bring him back home as a pet. As for me I prefer other animals the rebels being too queer to keep. We were ordered by Captain Pillow to shine our brass which we did with wood ash. But we have been told by soldiers in other Rgts that Uncle Billy which is what we call Gen. Sherman does not care much for pomp and is more caring of victories. We can have a victory when we choose because the rebels are terribly scarse One strange site we have seen was of darkeys in uniforms. Negro troops they are called and from what I heard they caused a fuss when their Rgts were formed but now the soldiers seem to pay them no mind. We sleep in dog tents on top of planks Sylvie and my self having our own. But to his disgrace Captain Pillow sleeps in a house and does not share our ordeals. Lieutenant Warner would make a much better Captain Pillow even hired a runaway which we call contrabands to look after him. This darkey must have been a house servant for he comes as being hauty. I do not think he will be with us long because no body likes him. Never would I think I should see so many contrabands they having run away from their masters to come to our camps. Some have found work but most can only sit and wait and beg. They get nothing from us for we have become beggers our selves always looking for better food and luxurys for our little homes. If it sounds rough then it is. But Sylvie and me are able and hunky and together we can with stand the hardships that will not last much longer. Our comrades are our close friends now and we look out for each other. But I think it is a wonder to see these thousands of soldiers and me a female all the while. No one has any notion or if they do they are too embarrassed to say. I believe our First Sergeant is like this because he is always giving me strange looks but it is no bother. I am out of paper but if you two wish to send me some I can write much more. It would also be nice to send us some cookies and sweets and both Sylvie and me will be needing shirts and drawers for when the warm weather comes. I must go now and I will write a Saint Louis letter the next time.

Your effectionate Sister
Susha

"Bob. You finished with that?" interrupts Private Goad.

"Yes, Ben."

"Why don't you fill the canteens, while the rest of us go on our wood detail? Sylvie will stay here and watch over camp."

"As good as done."

In spite of water wells dotting the hills, most of the messes of the 42nd Iowa, as well as others of 3rd Division, use a nearby spring. Protected by split rails, the only such fencing remaining for miles around, rather than gushing, its issue seeps from the bottom of a tiny pool. And although the spring's popularity is at a steady increase, on this morning Susha experiences no wait. When her last canteen takes its dip, she finds herself alone.

"You look done, soldier."

He's a big bear of a man, laden with four times the number of canteens as Susha. Beneath his forage cap, his wild, stringy black hair dangles to his shoulders, while his uniform is decidedly sloven. Unkempt appearance set aside, oddly enough, the private is clean shaven.

"Where you from, fella?" he asks, as he loosens his canteens.

"Iowa," answers Susha. "The Forty-second."

"A fine state and a fine regiment. Me, I'm from the One Hundred Nineteeth Illinois. Been guarding railroads around Memphis, 'til they sent us down here."

Although at first glance this private may seem frightful, his open demeanor invites a second look—even from one as watchful as Susha.

"Here. Let me help you."

"Well, that's mighty kind of you, uh-h-h."

"Bob. Bob Potter."

"Zeke Ellenburgh."

After shaking his greasy hand, Susha relieves Zeke of several canteens and together, the two proceed.

A talk of immeasurable unimportance helps to pass the time. In spite of his fierce look, Zeke proves to be quite amiable. Still, there's something about his manner which seems amiss, an oddity Susha's senses suspect, but as yet are unable to pinpoint. With this, a curiosity develops as the canteens are filled.

"I can help you carry these back to your company," offers Susha.

"Appreciate that, missy."

It's a sobriquet which brings no comfort to Susha's ears. To the contrary its sound is menacing, evincing a stillness to her tongue and a pale blank to her face. For the first time her true gender is forced to the surface, with Susha finding no clever retort or stalling defense.

"You are a woman, aren't you?" But in no way are Zeke's words threatening.

"Y-y-yes."

"Heh, heh," grins Zeke. "Then that makes two of us."

Susha's chin drops at the outlandish confession.

"I thought it was so when I first saw you walk passed my bivouac. What do you know, Bob? I finally have run into another."

At that moment two other soldiers, presumably male, negotiate their way down the gully, limiting the springside palaver.

"Come on, Bob. Let's go," urges Zeke, as she helps Susha don the canteens.

It's an ear-opening walk to the 119th Illinois, one in which Susha listens, while Zeke discreetly prattles the story she must be dying to tell.

"I don't know. I just didn't want to be left out. So that's when I went to Athens and enrolled in the Eighteenth O.V.I., back in August of sixty-one. Sure was a cracker of a regiment. But I got found out while we were in Bowling Green." Zeke puts a pipe to her mouth. "February of sixty-two. Someone peeked at me while I was taking a bath, so they sent me home. Never catch me doing that again. Smoke?"

"Thanks." Susha takes a couple of puffs.

"Wasn't long after that I moved to Zanesville and enrolled in the Hundred Twenty-second O.V.I. But I got found out right away when the surgeon took a close look. Too bad, 'cause those fellas are in Virginia and I sure did want to go there. Mmm. Good tobacco. And since I was fearing that people were hearing about my exploits, I left for Wabash, Indiana and joined the 101st. Saw some fighting with those boys. Chased Bragg out of Kentucky. Morgan too. Marched down to Murfreesboro, where I got sick and was found out again. That was February of '63. So I moved on. This time to the Hundred Nineteeth. A good bunch of boys. Not one of them a conscript. I got no tolerance for poltroons."

It's at this point that Susha pries a few words of her own. "We are all volunteers too."

"We did have some substitutes. One got mustered out when the colonel caught word he got hired out of a Chicago lunatic asylum by some devil of a crimp."

"Landsakes."

"Sure to tell, there's a lot of that foolery going around."

"For shame."

"So tell me, Bob. You alone?"

"No. I have my husband. This is why I enlisted, so I would not be left behind."

"It's good that you got someone to watch over you. And to share your shelter with."

"Yes. My Sylvie is a good husband."

"Me. I got my secret to keep. But I am glad I ran into you, Bob. So now there's two of us who know."

"Likewise, Zeke."

With the canteens thus delivered, it's time for Susha to return to her company. "So tell me, Zeke. How did you know about me?"

"It must have been your manner. The way you were walking. But I wouldn't put any fear to it, 'cause I think it's too slight for a man to catch notice. Much less say anything."

Soon, it's a tittering Susha who tells of her discovery of having been discovered.

Sylvie's initial reaction is one of shock, but upon rumination he becomes displeased. "Damn it. Somebody else has come up with our idea. I thought we had it all to ourselves."

"Oh Sylvie. Chances are of even more female soldiers out there."

"You might be right. But it makes our story not so unrivaled, anymore. Uhh."

As far as the men of the 42nd Iowa are concerned, February 3, 1864 is a date to be remembered as one of decamping the battlefields of others so that they might create those of their own. Their march cuts through the web of rumors which would have them taking all opposites of directions. But as confirmed, they're to make war on Meridian and, after rendezvousing with General Sooey Smith's cavalry coming down from Tennessee, the factories and foundries of Selma 116 miles further east.

Planned and supervised by General Sherman before spring returns to northern Georgia, the Selma Expedition is to have a distinctly punitive nature. The people of Mississippi and Alabama are to pay for providing succor to the enemies of the Army of the Tennessee. As is being played out already, this campaign isn't about occupation, but rather to insure that the territory invaded becomes of no further use to anyone. Timetables are crucial, meaning the sluggish supply trains upon the muddy roads have been reduced in size. For Company C, there's no room for baggage, the blankets carried by the men being their only protection from the elements. As for their rations, when their haversacks become depleted, the men may not be able to rely upon the army to fill them.

Although General Leonidas Polk's Confederates put up a fight at Jackson, they abandon their hopeless stand well before the 42nd Iowa can come up the line. Still, the rest of 2nd Brigade has made a good account of itself, capturing several prisoners and even a twelve-pounder. This is the second time for poor Jackson to be occupied, its bones offering little through which to pick. However, beyond the capital city lies what to an invader is a virgin land of comestibles and fodder. Yet with this lure lurks a peril in the form of General Stephen Lee's vengeful-minded Confederate cavalry. With this in mind, General Sherman's greatest struggle may be in keeping his columns bunched, his regiments ready to assist one another should trouble arise.

The previous day's march exceeded twenty miles, lasting to midnight. Small as they are, the trains are a hindrance, all too often requiring the aid of cold and hungry infantrymen pushing them through the endless quagmires. It's for this reason that the men of the 42nd Iowa spent their brief night strewn along the Hillsboro Road. Only Companies A and C have managed to make it into the regiment's bivouac, where they must spend their early morning waiting for the others to close up. But at least this gives the men a chance to huddle around the fires and dry themselves, and to form foraging details under explicit orders not to stray.

The Potters' mess, along with members of another, are discovering a promising thicket-lined path intersecting the Hillsboro Road. As Proctor and Bill take the lead, the others follow in scattered formation.

"Not only did Pillow put a trunk on a wagon," grumbles Proctor. "He's got Thomaston loaded with traps."

"I do believe Pillow is working him like a true massa," adds Bill. "Damn, he would make a fine Secesh. A chivalry one at that."

"Don't I know. But what a sight was our glorious captain trying to keep from straggling. Sure was satisfying that Colonel Burness pushed us to keep up with Company A. Just to see Pillow suffer."

"A spectacle first-rate."

"I tell you, before this is done, I will do something about that goddam trunk." But as Proctor finishes his latest vow, his eyes catch view of a more pressing interest. "Look, over there. Is that an old cornfield?"

"I believe it is," confirms Bill, who looks back. "Corporal. Got a farm."

Corporal Davison rushes to the front.

"There looks to be a cabin over there," points Proctor. "Seems deserted."

"Potters, up front," commands Corporal Davison. "Go with Keedy and Stewart."

Said cabin lies in the middle of a field, more or less bordered by woods—a perfect setting for the bushwacking trade. With their rifle-muskets held to port and their eyes scanning the surroundings, Susha and Sylvie are ready for the worst.

On the other hand, Proctor and Bill seem perfectly at ease, while they approach the cabin.

"You two inspect the cabin, while we see to the smokehouse and shed," outlines Proctor, as he and Bill split away.

If silence is a precursor for danger, then Susha and Sylvie are sure to be in peril. There's a notable lack of activity on this farm—nothing of human or even of livestock. Nevertheless, the stoic Potters perform their duty, forcing their way through a blanket of stillness to the cabin door.

"Should we knock?" asks Sylvie.

"Yes."

He delivers a careful rap, but to no response.

"Hello!"

"Hello! Is anybody home!"

Still nothing, to which Sylvie applies a harder blow. This time, however, answering to the greater force the door swings inward. With all due caution, Susha and Sylvie enter the tiny, one-room affair, which appears to be half-empty of its furnishings and possessions.

"Seems familiar, Susha."

"Very familiar."

In spite of the cabin's abandonment, it's interior lacks both filth and cobwebs, no doubt its inhabitants becoming refugees only a short time ago.

"We could have slept here last night," notes Sylvie.

"Warm and dry," agrees Susha.

Quicker than expected, Proctor approaches. "Is there anything?"

"Not much, it seems," answers Sylvie.

"Smokehouse is empty," informs Proctor, as he scans the interior. "These folks skeddadled with what they could carry." His nose continues the search. "You certain there's nothing?"

Meanwhile, Bill rejoins the party. "Not much to the corncrib."

Ignoring the report, Proctor continues to follow the divine of his nose. Suddenly, he stops at the corner bed, and after producing a pocket knife slits open the mattress. At first there's nothing more than corn husks, until Proctor comes upon the source of his nasal distraction. Then, with all the aplomb of a showman, he liberates a slab of bacon, waving his trophy in the air.

"Is there a mattress in the loft?" asks Bill of the obvious.

No further words are needed for Sylvie to scramble up the ladder, disappearing above. "It's not a mattress. All sacks of corn, covered over."

"Hallelujah."

Soon enough, the rest of the detail is called forth, so that they might bulge their haversacks with bacon and burden their shoulders with the sacks of corn.

As she watches the divvying of spoils, Susha's stomach raises no objections, so that it's up to her heart to bear the guilt. In spite of the circumstances, for her there's no mistake that this is thievery. What worsens the deed is that the plunder comes from a poor family as opposed to a wealthy planter. Absent as they may be, however, these people are the enemy, and so, it is their sad fortune to provide sustenance.

As for Susha's comrades, they regale at their shared fortune, absolved of sin by the etiquettes of war. Perhaps she, too, should put to rest this harsh reality, for there are sure to be far greater ones as the expedition pushes further into the core of the Confederacy.

The remainder of the road to Hillsboro is a short one. Now that the 42nd Iowa and its brigade have closed-up, the urgency to forage increases. Not much living has remained in Hillsboro, making the duty of the invader all the less complicated. For the soldiers who swarm over this town, there's little to keep them from the paths of excess.

The courthouse is the first building to be searched, and as it's a symbol of Confederate officialdom, the first to be ransacked. For some, the strewn papers of the county records become an irresistible kindling, and in no time the warmth and exuberance provided by the engulfed courthouse inspires more of the same.

Compared to its neighbors, the portico where Susha and her messmates find themselves is fairly small. Already, Proctor and Bill have begun a search, breaking open the double door in response to their unanswered knocks. As for the others, they've chosen to remain with the frenzy of the smoke-wafted air.

"Sure is an estimable house," admires Susha.

It's hipped roof and boxed dimensions have limited the structure to a reasonable size. Yet the details of its facade reveal a careful construction of red-bricked walls and finely carved brackets. Along with a glimpse at the darkened front hall, Susha's swelling appreciation sets her apart.

There's not much of a clamor from within, but in time, Bill does emerge with a bewildered, if not troubled, crease to his grin. "Full of furnishings, and its people are huddled in a bedroom."

Thus the invitation to the rest of the detail. While the others only peer inside for a few moments, Paps and the Potters follow Bill.

Her eyes adjusting, Susha marvels at the family's accumulations: colored and framed ambrotypes, a cushioned, rosewood settee, porcelain vases covering the surface of an occasional table and an inlaid, Connecticut shelf clock. Although not of fabulous wealth, the household is appreciated by her as being one of gracious composition. Nervous, as she and the others enter the bedroom in question, Susha's not surprised to see Proctor engaging in a casual conversation, comforting himself by propping against his weapon.

"Oh." Thus Proctor proceeds with the formalities. "Mrs. Thacher, these are three of my friends from Iowa. Private Potter and his cousin, also a Potter. And Private Hutchinson."

The soldiers tip their hats, with Susha's manners lagging somewhat.

"Gentlemen. Allow me to introduce Mrs. William Thacher, wife of Dr. Thacher, who has been called upon to practice in Virginia."

Seated in a chair next to a canopy bed, Mrs. Thacher receives her guests with the calm defiance of her cordiality, her clever smile concealing what must be a shaky foundation. On the other hand, clustered to her right are her two teenage daughters, both striving to break free of their trembles. And with them, tucked in bed, is Mrs. Thacher's young son, his consumptive face revealing as to why the family is unable to flee.

"This is Miss Lizzie and Miss Jeannie. And young Earl," continues Proctor. "Mrs. Thacher was telling me how her two servants abandoned her two days ago. Headed west, she believes."

"Likely, we passed by them this morning, ma'am," speaks Paps.

And so in all its fits and starts the conversation continues.

Guards are allowed to drop, the latest news tossed around, and even a few sympathies exchanged. To be sure, it's a curious array, the conquered and their conquerors doing their best to level the mountain of tension. Unfortunately, before things are allowed to become pleasant, the harsh sounds of a commotion startle the faces of the house's rightful inhabitants.

"Bill. Could you tell the boys outside to settle down?" asks a testy Proctor. "And behave like gentlemen."

"Thank you, Private Keedy," acknowledges Mrs. Thacher.

"Never mind, Bill. I should see to it, myself."

Proctor is able only to step through the doorway when he's met by Corporal Davison, who himself has been busy elsewhere. As the mumblings of a discussion erupt, each of the Iowans peels away from the bedroom.

"What do you mean we should set fire to everything?" protests Proctor.

"It's what Pillow said. The whole town. Everything we cannot use."

"Where is that son-of-a-bitch?"

"East of town. With the trains."

"Damn it," joins Bill. "How can we do that?"

Realizing that their hubbub might disturb the Thachers, Paps attempts to calm things. "Simmer down. Let me go and find George."

Standing in the doorway, Susha's view is of both sides. It's plain for her to see that, while her comrades argue over the house's fate, the Thachers' are sensing the peril. For the family, what had been building toward the hopeful, precipitously has turned sullen.

"They're going to bring our lieutenant here," assures Susha. "He is a fair man."

Before long, Lieutenant Warner approaches the house with a look of both fire and disgust in his eyes. "Just tell me what Pillow said," he demands, as he steps onto the portico.

"To burn everything we are unable to carry. Houses, mills, stores," relates Corporal Davison. "That the orders came down from Colonel Shaw."

"That is Pillow's interpretation. Corporal, you should know better than to take orders from a man who prefers the company of teamsters. And their mules."

There's an appreciative chorus of chuckles from the men.

"Corporal. I want you to remain here with a detail to watch over the house. Paps you stay. You too, Sylvie. Where is Bob?"

"Inside."

"He too." Lieutenant Warner catches sight of the damage done. "Mend the door while you're here."

"Maybe you should talk to the family, George. Calm their fears."

"Of course. Show the way."

This time it's Susha's conversation which is interrupted, she using her weapon also as a prop.

"Mrs. Thacher? My name is Lieutenant Warner."

"Lieutenant."

"I want to apologize for the inconvenience done to your family. While our brigade remains in town, I shall leave a detail here to guard against intruders. And to do your bidding. Ma'am, you may want to answer the door when it is again knocked. And please keep your fireplaces lit."

"I will do that. And I am grateful for your consideration."

"Very well. Bob, stay here with the detail. Ma'am." With that, Lieutenant Warner rushes away.

"Our lieutenant is awfully clever in settling things," notes Susha, her head bobbing with pride.

As well, she's elated with her agreeable assignment. Considering the circumstances, Mrs. Thacher has given some warmth, and even Earl, between coughs, has shown his charms. Yet what Susha treasures most is the chance to converse with someone near to her age and exactly her gender—Lizzie and Jeannie. It's been months since Susha last wore a dress. Now, such fine examples stand before her, adeptly displayed by two comely, young ladies. There's a touch of envy as Susha casts her eyes upon their crisp dresses of checked fabrics, each highlighted by dark, satin belts and partially covered with solid capes.

Unfortunately, with the calmness of the moment, Susha forgets her ruse, allowing herself to slip over her words. "I sure like what you two are wearing. Perfectly fitted."

The read on the faces of the Thacher women is one of reproach, offended as they must be by one whose comment is far too forward.

"Oh. My apologies." But Susha feels too clumsy to remedy her misstep. "Uhh. Maybe I should fetch some firewood. Excuse me."

Hillsboro may never be the same. As for the next town, Decatur, its fate is similar, except that the Newton County records have been evacuated, securing at least a foundation for rebuilding, or even providing the inspiration to exact revenge.

To his credit, Colonel Burness keeps the gaps between his companies as narrow as possible. While the rest of the brigade experiences difficulties, from van to rear the 42nd Iowa's spread is less than a mile.

"I wish we could stop to boil some coffee," sighs Susha, as she marches.

"I doubt a fitful rest is short in coming," replies Sylvie

"Just suck on a bean," suggests Proctor, upon which he spits one into his palm.

Before Susha can accept the offer, however, a sharp clamor erupts from up the road, its source hidden by nearby woods.

"Company, halt," shouts Captain Pillow.

Wasting no time, Lieutenant Warner runs to his side, just feet away from Susha. "Captain, what do you see?"

"Nothing, Lieutenant. Company A is out of view and I believe Company D still marches."

Again, the cracking sounds pierce the air. With the ears thus alerted, they can pick up the tune of a volley.

"Captain, the enemy must be attacking the train ahead of us."

A heavy thud of truth strikes Susha, and as she looks at Sylvie, she sees that he, too, has been impacted.

"I believe you are correct, Lieutenant. We should march on the double quick."

"Sir, they may be far off and I fear straggling. I suggest quick time, until we receive orders?"

"Uhh, I agree." Upon looking back at his company, Pillow prepares to bark his command. That is until his attention strays to an entirely different matter. "Thomaston! Come back!

It seems that Captain Pillow's frantic and frightened servant is seeking his freedom elsewhere, and is forgetting to drop his master's load.

Incredulous, Lieutenant Warner's presses his concerns to the east. "Captain! Give the command!"

The distant musketry is now brisk and at will.

Urged by this harsh nudge, the captain detaches himself from his loss and draws his sword. "Company! Forward, on the quick time! March!"

As Sergeant Wilkins sets the prescribed and well-practiced pace, the soldiers should be thankful for Lieutenant Warner's intervention. The step for quick time is the same as common time—28 inches, heel to heel. Only its pace is hastened, from that of 90 steps per minute to 110. On the other hand, not only would the step of the double quick be increased to 33 inches, so, too, would its number to a tiring 165 per minute.

The company nears the bend of the road, keeping its formation tight. It's at this point that Major Slough is encountered, he skidding his horse passed Captain Pillow and then turning it around to match the pace.

"Captain, there's rebel cavalry in the woods firing at the train! Form up with Company D! On the double quick!"

Abruptly, the major gallops away toward the other companies, kicking up a wake of mud in the process.

"Company! Forward, on the double quick! March!"

Unlike Thomaston, the soldiers of Company C haven't the freedom to choose a direction. Slipping and sloshing with their weapons positioned high upon their right shoulders, their hearts race from both exertion and trepidation. There's a battle being waged down the road, and to what degree none of them know. Regardless, each soldier refuses to falter, the powers of camaraderie proving to be the greater force.

At the brink of exhaustion, but not of breaking, Susha is able only to catch glimpses of her surroundings. The woods are opening up into the fallow fields of several farms or perhaps one large plantation. She recognizes Company D, lined up in formation in the middle of the road, ahead of them being the train of wagons and its panicked mules. Yet there's also the serious business of death in the air, as Susha's appalled eyes spot the figures of those animals having collapsed from their wounds: some struggling, others having surrendered their last gasps. As for the drivers, wisely they've flattened themselves behind available stumps or into a shallow ditch.

Through the chaos of clamor, a distant trumpet blares its pleas. Yet countering this confusion rides Colonel Burness, darting back and forth in order to consolidate what forces are at hand.

"Company. Halt." cries Captain Pillow.

High on his mount and oblivious to any danger, Colonel Burness comes up to Company C. "Captain! Have your company fire by ranks!"

"Where, sir?"

"At that treeline, damn it!"

Looking to her left at a good 300 yards away, Susha spots the tiny puffs of white smoke.

"Company! Front!"

In one unfailing swoop Company C alters from a vulnerable column of fours into two battle-readied ranks.

As she turns to face her distant foes, the gap forming to Susha's left is filled instantly by Sylvie. The feeling is reassuring, that with her husband to bolster her side, she's certain not to fail in her duty.

By the looks of it, Lieutenant Warner, too, is inspired. With sword in hand, he dashes to a spot in front of the two ranks and delivers a last, practical instruction.

"Find your targets in the treeline!" he directs. "Right oblique!"

Yet just as quickly, the lieutenant abandons the line of fire.

"Front rank!" commands Captain Pillow. "Ready!"

Her feet forming a "T," Susha comes to the ready with her Enfield. In spite of the chilled air, beads of sweat stream down toward her eyes, uncontrolled as she cannot wipe her brow.

"On the right oblique! Aim!"

With her weapon leveled and its hammer cocked, Susha's open eye searches for a target through the Enfield's sights. At this instant it doesn't occur to her that she may be about to maim a stranger. Rather, like an efficient machine, her thoughts focus upon performing each of the procedures to their precise forms.

"Fire!"

Boom! The noise and smoke of more than 30 rifle-muskets dominate the air. From the butt of her weapon, Susha receives a hard kick. However, there's no time to speculate on the success of her Minie ball, for even as it remains spinning through the air, another command is bellowed.

"Load!"

Once again, a fearless Lieutenant Warner rushes to the front. "Rear rank! Steady your aim!"

Already, Susha's fingers are pouring powder down her barrel. By the sounds of it, some of the other companies are active as well, not to mention those of the 14th Iowa. It's a wild confusion of blasts and shouts as Susha finishes loading by flicking off the spent cap, replacing it with a fresh one. Taking a glance at Sylvie, she sees that he, too, has readied his weapon.

"Rear rank! Ready! On the right oblique! Aim!"

As Proctor reaches over, the middle of his barrel is at Susha's right ear.

"Fire!"

Boom! With no flinching on Susha's part, another tier of rifle-muskets seethes its anger.

"Load!"

"Bully, men," cheers Lieutenant Warner. "A volley, first-rate."

As the men of the front rank wait for the rear to reload, they can see other companies marching up the road. Somewhat less than a coincidence, the fire from the Confederate treeline becomes more sporadic.

"Front rank! Ready! On the right oblique! Aim! Fire!"

Boom!

"Load!"

The interval between volleys shrinks, as soon the rear rank lets loose its second. And although the company is ready to deliver more, to their disappointment Captain Pillow seems to delay the command.

"Sir!" The captain's attention is abducted by a returning Colonel Burness.

"Captain! Cease fire!"

"Yessir! Company! Order! Arms!"

"Come to order!" repeats Lieutenant Warner.

There can be little doubt that the Confederates are withdrawing, they having succeeded their goal of injuring the train. And with the timely arrival of a squadron of Illinois cavalry to give chase, Company C's portion of the skirmish is done. For them, the fear and exhilaration of battle has lasted less than two minutes.

"We showed that Secesh horse what good infantry can do!" boasts Bill.

"I don't know if they're afraid of us, but they sure have no fear of flight!" Paps, too, feels the glory.

Regardless, leave it to Susha to air a comment of a more practical nature. "Do you think we really shot any of them?" She poses her question as if worried she may have.

"Damn, I hope so!" joins Proctor. "We tore the hell out of them!"

Susha and Sylvie look at one another with shrugged shoulders. Certainly, she has her doubts, for during the skirmish not only did she fail to aim at an individual Confederate, she can't lay the claim of actually seeing one. The fact remains, for either of Susha's Minie balls to have struck a foe would defy even the wildest of possibilities.

The expedition continues its trudge toward its objectives. Meridian, Mississippi exists for its junction of railroads: the Mobile & Ohio running north to south, the Southern Mississippi from the west and the Alabama & Mississippi the east. But for Susha and her hungry comrades, tiny Meridian and its stockpiles become a table set, with one of its railroads being a conduit to the rich interior of Alabama, itself.

Notwithstanding, where is Sooey Smith? The ultimate goal of the Selma Expedition depends upon linking with his cavalry brigades, and little has been heard of his progress. Larger than rumor, the speculation is that Smith has shared the same fate as many before him. That his superior force has turned tail after being confronted by the devil himself, a cunning fighter otherwise known as Nathan Forrest.

Regardless, William Sherman is not a patient man, and to have his divisions wait at their bivouacs for an unreliable force will not suffice. This is especially so when one of the reasons behind the Selma Expedition is to keep the men busy, instead of idling away in winter camps. With this in mind, General Sherman's soldiers are being employed, working at an industry of which they've been developing a proficient talent.

Slowly, the A&M Railroad is being reduced to a disconnected line of pyres, fueled by uprooted ties and crowned with iron rails. In addition, it's rolling stock consists of the occasional wrecked beast of locomotion and the unburnable iron wheels of its cars. Their arms stacked, the soldiers of the 42nd Iowa are divided into gangs of systematic destruction. The fires making the winter more bearable also alter cold, hard iron into drooping, red hot metal. Clasping the ends with confiscated and borrowed smithy tools, the men leave these rails to cool into loops, twisted around the nearest available trees.

Certainly, this is a monotonous route in which to reach Selma. A.J. Smith's division has been plying this trade for nearly three days, managing less than twelve miles. As for Susha and her comrades, already this singular duty has lost its fascination.

Prying loose another spike, Proctor airs a growing concern. "I fear we may be mangling track for the rest of the war."

Before his complaint can go any further, however, he's stopped by an approaching Sergeant Wilkins.

"Private. Soon as you can, light up this pile and have the detail 'coutre up. Assemble with the company."

"Any news, Sergeant?" asks Sylvie.

"Lieutenant Warner has the details. But this much I know. We are quitting the railroad business."

"Damn," interrupts Proctor with a mock protest. "Just as I was learning to love it."

It's a ceremonial fire of sorts, a pyre to mark the occasion that it is, indeed, the final one. Still volatile as they're barely over a year old, the pine ties feed the upwardly-licking flames. The soldiers of the 42nd have become quite adept at building these infernos, finding ways to ignite them under a host of conditions. Upon the intense heat, the rails are destined to sag from their middles—another assault upon a limited resource.

Having assembled Company C, Lieutenant Warner has the men standing at rest. Already he's addressed them on the confirmation of Sooey Smith's failure and the report of Polk's Confederates digging in at Demopolis, and that to continue further into Alabama would be too risky even for General Sherman.

"The brigade is to form up with the division at Marion Station and return to Vicksburg. By way of Union and Canton."

Instantly, Susha grasps that the idea behind a different route is to spread the destruction.

"The company will continue to forage and destroy property useful to the enemy." Then Lieutenant Warner stresses the most important part of his instructions. "We will sleep with our arms. The dangers are sure to increase, so we will keep vigilant. Remember, Forrest is free to come south. After we rest in Vicksburg, I think you can assume that we will be moving on to Georgia by boat and rail. That will be all." He pauses. "Sergeant. Lead us out."

As Company C marches away, Susha glances at the pyre. While the weakening rails wait in vain to be further disfigured, she can't help but think of the shame of not having completed the task at hand, that Selma will not be achieved. Even as a lowly private, Susha understands that the wasted opportunity to end the war in one place only serves to extend the rebellion in another.

Thus, with the expectations having been expended, the campaign reaches its zenith. And with this comes a change in name, for no longer does "Selma" seem appropriate. Henceforth, "The Meridian Expedition" will have to suffice.

Perhaps convinced that Selma is no longer threatened, General Polk has set loose Stephen Lee's cavalry. However, this Confederate force is too weak for a head on confrontation, able only to peck at the Army of the Tennessee and gobble up some of its strays. Regardless, at the very least they should hasten the exit of the Union soldiers and so, disturb their crusade of depredations.

While Company C carries out its orders in the town of Union, a foraging party from Company F stumbles into an ambush. The result is two killed, one wounded and five missing including their third sergeant.

For the most part, the haversacks, as well as the wagons, are kept full with sweet potatoes, pork, peanuts, corn and the like. However, since the hostile contacts between the foragers and their enemy are at an increase, the corps commander, General S.A. Hurlbutt, has been forced toward a more stringent discipline. As directed, foraging in the countryside is to cease, and the officers are to take all precautions against straggling, even to the point where the colonels will follow instead of lead their regiments. Needless to say, without resupply those haversacks won't stay full forever. More than Confederate cavalry nipping at their heels, the concerns over empty stomachs should keep the troops moving.

"Landsakes. There's more of them, Sylvie."

"Must be coming in from all over, Bob. Leaked through the Seceshes' pickets last night."

It's early morning, with Susha and her messmates resting alongside the road west of Union. With no more coffee available, Sylvie is trying his hand at roasting peanuts for an ersatz variety. Carefully, he shuffles his pan over the fire.

"Smells fine," judges Susha

"Here, Bob."

After Sylvie spills some peanuts into Susha's tin cup, she takes the blunt end of her bayonet and smashes the contents, affecting a sort of grind. Upon filling the cup with water, she settles it at the edge of the fire.

"I would wager we have five thousand contrabands tailing our army," estimates Sylvie.

"And a perfect nuisance they are," figures Ben. "They just catch a whiff of our army's approach and, presto, here comes a flood."

Slowly, the waves of runaways pass, tired and worn from a night spent avoiding Confederate patrols. Grouped by family and association, or by mere convenience, they carry and drag with them every last possession of their lives, trudging toward an unsure future and away from a much too certain past.

"Miserable crowd of darkies," smirks Ben. "Why would they want to leave their homes to go hungry in the wet and cold?"

"Why would anyone want to do so, I suppose?" winks Paps. "Crazy, is it not?"

There's a pause among the messmates, only to be broken by a sharp-eyed Bill.

"Look there. Is that one smoking a pipe? What do you say, Private Keedy?"

"That we might be able to purchase some tobacco?"

Since Proctor is the first to his feet, the deal is his to make. He rushes off to stop the man in question.

"Look at him," admires Bill of the negotiation. "You think Proctor was dealing horses."

"Sure is a lot of head-shaking," notes Susha.

"I don't think our Private Keedy's dickering is going too well," grins Paps.

After a few more moments, Proctor can be seen throwing his arms into the air. Empty-handed, he returns to the mess with a look of disgust.

"What went wrong?" asks Bill.

"Can you believe it? He refused to take my money. Only wanted Confederate paper."

"Devil you say?"

"You saw me trying to reason with him," shrugs Proctor.

"Should have taken his tobacco," urges Ben. "As those Illinois boys do. Rough him up, if he got saucy."

"Or we could follow the New Yorkers' manner," offers Leo. "Have the folks back home send us that counterfeit Confederate money."

"What?" questions Ben.

"Costs only five cents on the dollar, so I have heard. Better than the original. Hell, I give odds their sutlers sell it. Our government surely is unbothered."

"Well, how do you like that," marvels Proctor. "There just might be a cleverness to all that Yankee perfidy. God help me, but I am beginning to admire those people."

The bland, peanut brew provides some sips of thought as Susha sits upon her root. Paps' shrewd comparison takes a ponderous trek through her head, bringing up the subject of slavery. Although the 42nd Iowa may be nominally Republican—one of the reasons Sylvie chose it was as an additional act of defiance—it isn't a regiment dominated by political sentiment. As is with Susha's own private views, there has been little concern among her comrades over abolition. Yet there it lives, and in a few moments she'll be joining its procession, marching to the same direction in a roughly side-by-side fashion. After gazing at more ragged clothing and bare feet than she could ever have imagined, Susha is beginning to lose her indifference. After all, she, too, is taking desperate measures.

The roads to Canton wind through a country of increasingly stark contrasts. The destruction which once had a purpose is becoming in its exuberance a bit more wanton and vandalistic. Any building left unoccupied is subject to be set upon by those regiments less troubled. Even some of the churches have been targeted, the reasoning being that because their parishioners donated their bells to the metal-starved cause many months prior, they also sacrificed any respect of sanctuary. Thus there are fewer knells to toll the deaths of these once propitious communities, many of which may never recover.

Still, surrounding the upheaval are the sure signs of renewal, of a spring descending upon the land. As delicate green buds begin to fill the trees, the cruel, grey clouds give way to friendly, azure skies. Although they still slosh through and around mud, the men of Company C have folded away their greatcoats.

And accompanying the soldiers are the chaotic throngs of runaways, drawn to the blue-clad formations of their reluctant Moses. Together they leave a land of plagues, a country built by a portion of its number and pleasured by others. And while the campaign draws to its conclusion, the smoke of ruin streams upward, continuing to stain the otherwise clean air.

"I sure hope the quartermaster is ready for us in Vicksburg." Marching with his comrades, Proctor sees fit to air the obvious. "There's not enough left of my trousers to patch."

"Should have been issued trousers and blouses at Helena," figures Paps. "I hardly would count on Vicksburg."

"Be that so, then I believe we might become the first naked regiment." Proctor pauses his thoughts for a few seconds. "The sun is warm. I say we strip ourselves of our clothes as we march. Heh.

Would that not put a fear to the Seceshes, to come up against a naked army?"

"I doubt it," answers Bill. "Any other army but theirs."

Ordered to march through Canton, the 42nd deploys as the van west of town. It's just before sunset, and having thrown out its pickets and dug its sinks, the regiment is ready to settle for the night.

After locating their bivouac and fashioning their bed pallets out of pine needles, Susha and her messmates build a fire from the cordage of a nearby split rail fence. And deciding that dinner will be the last of the sweet potatoes, they ring the campfire with the tubers. Coupled with a sassafras brew, to be followed by tobacco procured from the 179th New York, dinner should be satisfying.

In keeping with their discreet custom, Susha and Sylvie beg away to see to their personal functions, avoiding the public sinks for a wooded tangle. Soon, all but done, with the last of their soap they wash themselves and their toilet cloths in an intermittent creek. Meanwhile, the couple is being entertained, for in the distance the lively music of some brigade's band is sparking "Johnny Fill Up the Bowl."

"Hear that, Susha?"

"It sounds sweet."

"Some colonel let their musicians bring their brass. Nice to have had that serenade for our wedding."

"I don't think there would have been a wedding had there been music, Sylvie"

"A shame we cannot get married all over again, Susha. With that band playing and with our messmates attending. Paps could give you away and all the boys could be my best man."

Sylvie places his arm around Susha, as she nestles her head upon his shoulder. It's a perfectly tranquil moment, what with the faint, melodic elixir and the relative privacy prevailing. Thus the mood is struck as their lips press in unison, their hands beginning their tender searches for the familiar. Since it's been awhile, Sylvie wastes no time in laying Susha upon her back. Deftly, half of his fingers loosen the four buttons of her sack coat, while the other set caresses her feminine face.

But suddenly, the purrs of lilting music and satisfying itches are parted by a sharp gasp of shock.

"Jumping Joshua!" Alone stands Leo, who has stumbled upon the surprise of his life. "What are you two doing?" But he appears to think better of the question, and scampers away.

"Leo," pleas Sylvie, as he sits up. "It's not what you think."

Numbed, Susha and Sylvie stare at the back of Leo, as he vanishes into the thick growth and fading sun. There's hardly the need to air the gravity of the situation, that their accumulated efforts to remain together are coming to a spoil—all for the want of a little restraint.

"What are we to do, Sylvie?"

He pauses a moment, as if there exists any choice in the matter. "Return to camp."

With "Johnny Fill Up the Bowl" losing its charm, their walk to the bivouac is both shaky and quiet. At this moment Susha and Sylvie's fears are far greater than those experienced two weeks prior, facing the flashing muzzles of Confederate cavalry. At least then they were a part of something large—comrades to several dozens and to many hundreds. Now the feeling is that they are but two, with the added dread that even this will end abruptly with a disgraceful separation.

When the Potters reach camp, they find their messmates sitting around the fire, just as they had left them. Even with the dimming light, the looks on their faces reveal that Leo has told all. And although no one utters a word, the glares from their comrades are both raucous and confusing.

Boldly, Sylvie wastes no time. "Bob is not my cousin. Her real name is Elizabeth. Susha for short. And she is my wife."

"We figured as much," replies Paps.

"I guess some of it makes sense now," adds Ben. "Still, you had us fooled."

Bolstered by at least two additional cornets, as well as a drum, that brigade band sees fit to change tunes to the ever-popular "The Girl I Left Behind Me."

Smiling at the coincidence, Paps makes an offer, "Sit down, you two. Your tea is ready."

Thus it begins, an inquisition of dismay concerning the motives of a female soldier. For the most part, it's Sylvie who tenders the explanations, while Susha assists with affirmatives. Nevertheless, the session remains friendly and, because Paps urges decorum so that the neighboring messes won't catch wind, hopeful.

Regardless, it is strange that Proctor has been silent, he keeping to himself. Before long, however, what can't be contained must be vented.

"I got to ask. If you're Sylvie's wife, why did he cook? We suffered much back in Arkansas."

"We are sorry for that," explains Sylvie. "But we thought she cooking might bring suspicion."

"But you can cook?"

Unaffronted, Sylvie continues with enthusiasm. "Nobody can fix meals like Susha. She is a cook first-rate. And there are many who would attest."

"Hmm?"

It's Paps who returns to the more serious. "The problem is, what are we to do?"

A dead silence ensues as each around the fire considers the possibilities.

"Does anything need to be done?" Once again, Sylvie breaks the hush. "Can we not carry on like we have?" He presses his bid. "There was no trouble when you thought Susha a man. She has been a soldier first-rate. Knows the drill, with no straggling or shirking."

It's difficult to tell, but some of the messmates may be warming to Susha's side.

"I give her that," agrees Ben. "But what I am afraid is we will have to change our ways, now that we have the company of a woman."

"That may not be so bad," counters Paps. "I should hate to think we might take our foul habits back to Iowa. They ought to be left here in Secessia, where we found them."

"Nobody should mind me." At last, the peculiar feeling of being haggled over evokes a response from Susha. "Never I have found offense from any of you. Truth to tell, I am fond of your foul habits. But mostly, I just want to stay with Sylvie."

"It is certain that if the colonel found out, he would send Bob, uhh, Susha, home," speaks Leo. "And punish Sylvie. Hard."

"How hard, do you think?" asks Bill.

"Who can say?"

"You boys know me," interrupts Proctor. "I always enjoy sneaking one passed Valentine Pillow, that mail boy. How about you, Private Stewart?"

"Does have its appeal."

Though he may be unconvinced, Ben seems to be losing patience. "Why don't we see how this plays out? The rebellion will be done by summer and we are sure to be mustered out."

"What do you say, boys?" polls Proctor.

In spite of it consisting of nods and shrugs, the vote is an undeniable landslide.

Nonetheless, there is an additional consideration which needs to be resolved. "What do you want us to call you?" asks Leo.

Sylvie is quick with his preference. "I think we better keep with 'Bob.'"

"Yes. Call me 'Bob.'"

"Then that tops it there," declares Proctor. "Gentlemen, we are in proud possession of a female comrade, which makes us the rarest of all the messes in the entire Army of the Tennessee. I would say this calls for a toast of the finest libation. But as we lack even a lowly skull-knock, this poor root tea will have to suffice."

Understanding that it would do little to aid their cause, Susha and Sylvie fail to mention what they know about the 119th Illinois. Instead, they raise their cups with the others, sealing the agreement of loose terms and *status quos,* and lessening their burdens by the addition of five closer than ever friends.

The Meridian Expedition nears its end, with Vicksburg being only a three-day march. However, hunger is a sharp thorn, and with the promises of the commissary, not to mention the quartermaster's, the inspirations are enough for the soldiers to complete their return in two. Because Stephen Lee's harassment has all but fizzled away, other than the promptness of the paymaster and the stocks of the sutler, the men of the 42nd have little over which to fret.

Besides the obvious, much has been learned by Susha's

messmates during their month-long expedition. Along with others, they've gained the confidence that their ranks will not unravel when confronted, that they can deliver a greater measure than they would receive. Perhaps just as impressive, especially to the generals, is that the soldiers can withstand the miseries of the open climate with barely a blanket per man, and that even a sizable army can live off the land so long as it keeps on the move. These are valuable lessons for that final campaign of the war, be it in Georgia or elsewhere. However, none are so priceless as the knowledge that decent, law-abiding men, when backed by a just cause, will take so kindly to systematic destruction. When it comes down to it, only God can have pity on the next land these soldiers invade.

10 ↭ A World Turned Asunder

There comes a sure serenity with an early spring. Indeed, the dismal greys of the country are slipping passed, giving way to the season's inculcations of more promising colors. With this, the efforts to keep warm and to stave off hunger are easing—for man and creatures all. Fields are more pliable and the emerging, tender vegetation is a salvation of forage. Even the roads are becoming passable and the streams fordable, thus creating the chances for more frequent communications.

"Jewhillikens, Major," declares Private Francis L. Peevy, his eyes wandering from *Life and Death of David Copperfield.* "Do you think any folks know about us?"

From Waxahachie, Texas, Private Peevy is a new addition to the Bureau of Posterior Legal Affairs, his mere presence doubling its size. With his right arm lost in Arkansas and he only recently recovered, it's been decided that clerking for the B.P.L.A. will be an ideal situation for the private to learn the ways of the left hand. Because of the relative inactivity, however, schooling for this twenty year-old should be gradual.

"Not likely, Frank," answers John, who himself is preparing a paper for Mr. Hey. "We have to account for our own entertainment."

With the continuing expansion of officialdom, John's bureau has been evicted from its covey, forcing him to take his "business" elsewhere. The back room of a back street cottage is now the home of the B.P.L.A., with the lack of furniture in this humbling "office" forcing John to share the side of his desk with Frank.

"That's not good, Major. I am a sure reader, and'll be whizzing through them books quick as a wink."

"We can think of something, Frank. In fact, I should offer a bargain. Show me what you are made of and I might allow you to read the law."

"Jewhillikens, Major. I sure could take to that."

Unfortunately, an unexpected knock interrupts any attempt by Frank to coax a premature lesson, answering the door being a part of his duties.

"Yes, ma'am."

"Oh?" It's a woman, who feigns a surprise. "Is Captain Singleton about?"

"Miss Smallbones." John's eyes needn't veer from his work to recognize that his landlady is on some sort of prowl. "Come inside."

She hurries into the room, clutching a small bundle. "Thank you, Captain." Although she addresses John, her attentions are gathered upon Frank.

"Miss Smallbones. May I introduce my clerk, Private Peevy."

"Oh. How considerate of you to assist one of my many boarders."

"Please to meet you, miss."

"To what do I owe this pleasure, Miss Smallbones? Please, have a seat?"

"No thank you, Captain. My time is brief." Without delay, she submits her excuse. "I thought I might bring you those candles, we discussed." As Miss Smallbones hands over the goods, she maintains her smile upon Frank.

"This is very kind. But you could have given these to me this evening."

"Think nothing of it. But I really must be off. My interests demand so much attention." She pauses, perhaps considering that a brazen proposal might lead to a relief of some of her labors. "Achem. Captain, might you be so kind as to allow Corporal Peevy to attend tea at my house. I will be able to offer something sugary. You do have a sweet tooth, Corporal? Hmm?"

"Yes, miss. Plenty of them."

"Good. Then I will see you soon." Thus Miss Smallbones parts with a skip.

With the door shut safely behind her, Private Peevy's confused head is able to air itself. "Major. Why did Miss Smallbones call you 'Captain' and me 'Corporal'?"

"Well, Frank. That is her manner." Yet the responsibilities of a commanding officer compel him to offer some sage counsel. "Frank, if you wish to avoid the throes of unmerciful matrimony, use caution. Sample her sweets if your teeth may. But stay clear of Miss Smallbones' web."

"Are you talking about marrying, Major? Me and Miss Smallbones?"

Incredibly, the look on Frank's face is one of wonder and not revulsion. And so, suddenly, John realizes he has his work cut out for him, that the process of educating his clerk could be both long and intense. At long last, the B.P.L.A. may have a purpose.

When evening falls, John puts those candles to use, burying himself into more of Mr. Hey's work. Soon, however, he pushes aside the boredom of other people's affairs, although he keeps his pen and paper at the ready. Instead, far from slumber, John's mood nudges him toward the comfort of Henrietta's company, miles away though she may be.

Unfortunately, having posted a lengthy letter yesterday, he's depleted of original sentiment. Joined by the weariness of isolation and the rigors of inactivity, a frustrated John is unable to pen much more than the familiar salutation. Staring at his meager words, he pines over what to him is a lovely name: Henrietta, full of swirls and crossed letters, and flowing from the tongue that it bears repeating.

Suddenly, a draft rushes through the half-open window, blowing out the candles' glow. But the pitch darkness proves brief, when a distant shock of lightning and its trailing boom tell John of an approaching storm. As it happens, while the weather gathers its intensity, it also offers a temptation, that the excitement of a storm might provoke a letter in full bloom.

Closing the door behind him, John is met by the hurling dust of Third Street. Soon it should become mud, the degree of its depth depending upon the strengths of the storm. Guided by the belligerent sky, John's feet carry him northward, headfirst into the brisk wind.

Shreveport seems empty, as if its citizens have hunkered down or evacuated in anticipation of the battle to come. Indeed, in front of John the streaks of lightning are blurred by the clouds, revealing instead, the sudden flashes of faraway artillery. As for the thunder, it's blithe to duplicate those sounds made by the heavy guns of Union ironclads. Although John knows otherwise, he might believe that the war is at Shreveport's doorstep.

After using a wall's lee to light his pipe, he continues his desolate tour. Dark as the streets are, the lightning becomes an aid to navigation, the instances of illumination revealing the straights and narrows of a careful design. Poor Shreveport, wonders John, had it been left to its own devices it would have remained a pleasant, livable place. But war has insisted otherwise, with the town having become a target for friend and, perhaps, foe alike, turning its world asunder.

It doesn't take long before John's walk repeats itself. Still, he's all too willing to continue on, as one can never be so thorough when seeking the unsearchable. Rounding yet another corner, again John takes a gawk of the electric sky. This time he spies something incongruous: a scattering of stars taking its bearings from the town. Apparently, the storm is parting itself, as if to spare Shreveport from the ravages of its greater turbulences. Stirred, John performs an about face.

Anxious to return to the bureau at the opposite end of town, he marches as quickly as he can, occasionally using his cane to probe ahead. Halfway home, the tip of said appendage touches an object. Curiously, John pokes and prods, and when a flash of distant lightning confirms that it's not a dead animal, he picks up his find for a better look.

A child's doll lies limp in his hand, it's sweet, porcelain face highlighted by a carefully tailored dress. How real it seems, yet how sad is its dirty and tattered demise. What was once full of life has become, because of its abandonment, lifeless. Although John knows better, he can't help but feel disturbed by the depiction. Far greater than rumbling thunder, a shudder unsettles his assembled determination, as he considers the possible tragedies and, worse, his helplessness. Anxious to get on his way, John finds a nearby porch so that others may see to the doll's final resting place, and then compels himself to continue to his office, this time keeping his cane close to his gimpy side.

During the night John's correspondence fails to budge an inch, nor is he able to catch much more than a wink of sleep. Unfortunately, the light of dawn brings no relief—only faint stirrings of activity.

All day long Frank comes and goes, more often than not leaving John on his own. Uninterested in Mr. Hey's work and unable to write to Henrietta, on several occasions he tails his clerk and takes to the streets in search of chance encounters—to no avail. His head in a flutter, what John needs most is a stimulating conversation or, better, a skirmish with Miss Smallbones.

But as he stands at the corner of Market and Texas Streets, a sudden renewal of determination strikes John. If the sum of his worries is over his pregnant wife, then Henrietta he must see. Waltzing through his limp, John dispels any notions of guilt about abandoning his post. After all, with the war's emphasis being shifted elsewhere, the Union forces along the Mississippi have relegated themselves into idleness. Still, a furlough could be difficult to justify—even for a major. On the other hand, John is aware that most of the companies of his old brigade have been sent home to round up draft dodgers and to help secure the coast. Perhaps in some manner the B.P.L.A. could lend assistance, especially in the person of its commanding officer.

Upon returning to his desk, John casts a wide net, slowly drawing it tighter to cull those unusable designs. And although at the same moment he's discovering that each wall of his office consists of 48 laths, he knows also that soon he will stumble upon a workable solution.

By afternoon John's thoughts are halfway down the road to Bastrop, so cautiously confident he's become of his perfect scheme. Thus he pays little heed when Frank walks through the door.

"Major. Here's a letter from Houston."

No doubt a bureaucratic annoyance, to which John pays a grudging digression. "Just tell me who sent it, Frank."

"Looks like from some woman. A Mrs. William Shackelford."

Startled at the mention of his sister-in-law's name, John freezes in his chair, his blood running an unexpected cold. He stares straight through his messenger, while that sense of foreboding, which he's managed to allay, returns like an abrupt flood.

"Jewhillikens, Major. You're turning all ashy."

The color of John's face holds every reason for its hasty retreat. A swirl encases his head, rendering him helpless to move his body's strengths to its extremities, while the weight of fear compresses his chest. By no means are these sensations due to a flurry of prospects or suppositions. At this instant the recesses of John's head know of only one thing, that if Georgina has written to him, it's because Henrietta cannot.

There's a dead silence, as if the world has ceased its spin and time emptied of its sands. To be sure, this void could stretch into eternity, for there's little reason to continue differently.

There remains, however, Frank. "Major!" For all practical purposes, he shoves the letter into his officer's face.

Inch by inch John's hand accepts the letter, and tiny tear by tiny tear his fingers pry it open, as somehow his fearful clumsiness steadies itself. Although John's mind has been blurred, his eyes are able to catch the salient words of Georgina's tragic tidings. Indeed, it is the worst of news: one of squelched dreams and realized nightmares, of despondency and prostration, of abject isolation and sudden widowerhood.

Georgina's words become garbled within John's head, merely echoes of a world crashing upon his helpless self. As he gazes passed his clerk, his vision is that of sweet Henrietta, dressed in her finest and gently laid upon her bed, her delicate eyes closed into the deepest of sleeps. How peaceful she seems, forever beautiful and still in possession of her charms. And how lasting is Henrietta's motherhood, as her soft, caring hands cradle her round waste. It's a great silence into which John finds himself cast, a limbo from which he dares not budge.

Yet he does awaken, rudely, from the realization that Henrietta lies not upon a feathery rest, but instead is buried with their unborn child in the cold clay of Fairview Cemetery. The shock is one of finality, with no chance of being avoided or even altered. Never again will John bear witness to Henrietta's pleasant features, nor fall victim to her winning ways.

He looks to Private Peevy, focusing on his terrorized face. "She's dead, Frank. My wife has died."

Duty has no meaning and military formality is but a minor constraint. John has been shaken to the verge of desertion, his panic to flee from Shreveport overwhelming. Nevertheless, he is saved, for although tragedies abound, the powers that be still hold a reserve of compassion. Without entreaty, John is granted a furlough, its duration left to his discretion. In addition, on this mournful journey he's not to travel alone, for the chief of staff of the department has ordered Private Peevy to accompany him.

The preparations are quick and basic. John's gelding is fit for the long trek, but on the other hand Frank must use his wits to procure a mount. A deal is struck with three junior officers, that with the funds provided Private Peevy is to purchase in Texas one suitable horse for each, with the ownership of an old, brown mare passing to him. Unfortunately, the condition of the poor, spavined nag is such that it may never return to Shreveport, let alone survive the trip to Bastrop.

And so the entire command of the B.P.L.A. assembles in front of Miss Smallbones'. It's been less than 24 hours since John learned of his loss and his stupor is still pronounced as he slouches upon his saddle. He and Frank are waiting for Miss Smallbones, who emerges from inside, wielding a bulging muslin sack.

"Major, I baked some bread for your journey. And there's some butter and pickled vegetables." Miss Smallbones cracks a hopeful smile, as she delivers her charity. "Bacon too. And I boiled some hens' eggs."

"We surely are grateful, Miss Smallbones," intercedes Frank.

"Yes. You are too kind."

Always one to appreciate a compliment, nevertheless, she seems nervous with her concern. "Please be careful, Major. You will look after him, Private. Will you not?"

"You can rely on me, Miss Smallbones."

Without further delay, the two begin the arduous procession, which should take John to his belated farewell. It's upon the Texas

Road that soon he and Frank find themselves, heading west out of Shreveport. Slowly, the route takes them passed the cemetery and through the city's line of defenses just beyond Fort Jenkins, until finally, the major and his private face an endless countryside. This is a reversal of John's previous journey from Bastrop, although one of an early spring instead of a late fall. Yet where there is life in the air, there can only be death into the direction he follows. With a shiver embedded in his spine, John has no choice but to meet this destination.

An overnight stay with Francis Simmons' hospitality brings some comfort to the forlorn traveler. Nevertheless, John is fearful of delay, and so rouses Frank well before dawn. As briskly as the private's nag allows, the two continue their push through the East Texas pines.

But as it occurs, a doleful mind couldn't ask for a bleaker setting in which to wallow, the dense forests conspiring to isolate even further a murdered heart. With all despair, three more nights are spent beneath its needles, with the B.P.L.A. rising to three black mornings.

Though dutiful, Frank speaks little, the pall of sadness confusing him into stilling his tongue. However, further down the road the pair come upon a sight which may give John a measurable degree of comfort. After crossing William's Ferry, the first thing catching his eyes are orderly fields. A smile creeps upon John's face when he witnesses a promise being kept, for sitting on a log bench is William Anglin, tending to his accoutrements and readying himself to rejoin his regiment. Soon, the rest of the family welcomes their visitors and shares their meager circumstances.

Although the stay is brief, its impression cannot be lost upon Frank, of how the spirits of his major are bolstered by even those of the leanest means. And so, as the two regain the road, it's apparent when he feels the inspiration, that perhaps he, too, should offer a better conversation.

"Major. I hope you don't think me forward if I ask you to tell me something about Mrs. Singleton. I sure would like to know."

For John, these are unexpected words. But there's no

contemplation required, as Frank's inquiry is taken as a compliment.

"Of course, Frank. It would be my pleasure. Hmm?"

For miles and miles, a delighted Frank is regaled with stories about Henrietta Singleton.

"And when we first moved to San Antonio, she determined the advantages of mastering Spanish." John speaks with boastful pride. "So together, we taught ourselves."

"Sounds like you married an awfully clever woman, Major."

"That I did, Frank. Fact is, her talents were such that I could allow her to prepare some of my briefs, with all confidence and little supervision."

"Jewhillikens, Major. I sure do wish I could find me a wife like yours."

"I am afraid you cannot, Frank. There was only one Mrs. Singleton."

Perhaps it's an unintentional slip, that John speaks of Henrietta as part of anything other than the present. However slight, this mentioning of her passing causes him to pause, his shifting mood becoming noticeable.

"The way I see things, Major, those years you were with Mrs. Singleton makes you the luckiest man in the world. Yessir, as long as you got all your memories, the two of you will always be married."

How can one trip over the truth, as this wisdom strikes a chord?

"Thank you, Frank."

"Jewhillikens, Major. This sure has been a damnable war. All the bad things happening to such nice people. Downright criminal."

John's thoughts gaze toward Frank. What he sees is more than a right-handed man who no longer possesses one, but a sufferer who also never makes mention of it. Whereas Frank has every reason to reserve his concerns for only himself, he instead gives them freely to others.

"That it is, Frank."

It's at Wheelock Prairie where John decides to stay with the Old San Antonio Road. By now Frank's been walking his suffering mount more often than he rides it. But at least the two have left behind the confinements of the pineywoods, that the openness of this rolling land extends all the way to Bastrop's own coniferous tracts. Regardless, it's the old, brown nag which has the final say as to when the B.P.L.A. will reach its destination.

The chance to change this, however, presents itself outside of Wheelock, at a farm in dire need of currency. There Frank retires his old brown in a deal for a splendid mare, the property of a soldier who will never return from the sandy hills of Vicksburg. Considerably, the distance to Bastrop is shortened.

Thus, with the pace bolstered, John makes no excuses for his leg, stopping only for the sake of the horses. Well into the evening, he and Frank ride, their way guided by a mournful moon. But eventually, the force of sheer exhaustion does make John relent, and the two bed down by the side of the road for just a few hours.

It's a late afternoon, and John and Frank have come to the end of their sapping journey. Bastrop's cemetery lies on a hill situated at the town's eastern approach. And although John may feel some reluctance to face this finality, his head doesn't dawdle. Thus, with the spires and roofs of Bastrop clearly visible, he spurs his gelding and guides it toward the cemetery.

Tossing his reins to Frank, John dismounts and struggles up the hill. However, he knows nothing of family plots, only that up to now Henrietta's kin haven't been compelled to lay claim to a particular site. Quickly, John's search becomes frantic, as up and down and across he drags himself, ignoring the pounding pain and creeping exhaustion.

Pushing his misgivings aside, Frank, too, participates in the search. And it's he who first recognizes the futility, that not only is an identifying headstone absent, but there's also too much disturbed ground.

"Major. Why don't we sit down and get ahold of ourselves?"

Hence, the two find the shade of a young live oak. However, John remains flustered and is unable to think clearly.

Meanwhile, the world continues at its own pace. An empty wagon drawn by a team passes along the road below the hill. And although the driver seems to be in a hurry, he spots John and doffs his respectful hat.

"Do you know him, Major?"

"Pardon? Oh. Who can say?"

After only a few minutes of rest, John resumes his chase upon the hallowed ground. Once again, even as the search is prolonged, it proves futile. He's at the point of collapse when he returns to the live oak, with all provocation having run himself ragged. The feeling is of hopelessness, as John finds himself at an utter loss.

Fortunately, a beacon of sanguineness looms, Frank being the first to spot it. "Major. Some people are a-coming. Looks like two ladies and two little ones."

Immediately, John perks from his prone and looks into the distance. "Georgina," he mutters, jumping to his feet with a vigorous wave. "Georgina!"

With newly-found strength, he rushes down the hill, while his loyal private pursues. But John's cane does him good service, it preventing a hard tumble. His sharp eyes are flawless in that they recognize Georgina, who walks toward him with Martha and Mary in hand, along with Mairead and her bouquet of primroses.

"John. It is you," shouts Georgina, all dressed in black.

They meet in an unhesitant embrace, exchanging their trembles. And as Martha and Mary tug at their uncle's trousers, Georgina loosens herself just enough so that she can see her brother-in-law's sullen face.

"Oh, John. Thank God, you have arrived." Her moist eyes speak of her own miseries.

After kissing her cheeks, John leans down to do the same to his receptive nieces. And upon giving Mairead's nervous face a gentle stroke, he returns to Georgina.

"Where is she?"

"Oh John. You poor dear."

Their arms wrapped around each other, Georgina leads John to an almost hidden corner of the cemetery. Without a word the grieved form a circle, as she takes the primroses and places them atop Henrietta's grave. Especially overwhelmed is John, he staring at the bare soil which presses upon Henrietta's coffin, the hardening ground encasing his future and reason for being.

An eternity of silence passes. Mairead's tears have nowhere else to pool, though Frank comes to her aid by producing a handkerchief. It's almost as if this object is a cue, for Georgina suggests that everyone have a seat, and seeing that Frank has become a mourner, himself, manages an introduction. She must know also of the twisted confusion dwelling within John's head, and so takes it upon herself to answer those questions he's unable to pose.

"She made me promise not to tell you. Henrietta did not want to worry you when her condition turned wrongly. But there was nothing you could have done, John. Nothing. It was all so sudden. William was here during her illness. He only returned to Waco three days ago."

John, however, manages to air a terrible fear. "Did she suffer? Please, tell me."

"Yes, John. She did. The doctor performed what he could." The memory forces Georgina to pause. "Henrietta was never left alone. We were always at her side." Her voice begins to falter. "My sister was so brave. So brave. You should be proud of her, John."

His heart sinks even further with this need to know—more for Henrietta's sake than his own. And the harder the reality of her passing sets, the greater the reluctance to leave her side.

Upon learning of John's arrival, Georgina's neighbors trickle forth to pay their respects. And when John Gaunt and Lucie open a family bible—after their fruitless search for a present minister—the impromptu assemblage alters into a fitting service. Once again, Henrietta is led to fields of green and pools of fresh water, and is guided to the right paths. Especially so, with her husband standing over her, she's able to pass through the deepest of darknesses, nevermore to be afraid. Thus and truly, Henrietta Singleton's peace can rise to the heavens, to dwell amongst the angels.

Capped with an "amen," the last of John Gaunt's comforting words sends a signal to this second gathering of mourners, so that soon it's left to Henrietta's dearest to bring up the rear of the procession's return to town.

"Mairead, might you show Private Peevy where to take the horses," asks Georgina, while her daughters cling.

Eagerly, both comply and lead away the mounts.

"He is a good, young man, your private," notes Georgina, as she gazes at the dangling, folded sleeve of his shell jacket. "Henrietta was right when she feared the war. Hated it from the very beginning, and hated those who brought it upon us." She continues with her stare, while Frank and Mairead amble down the hill. "That poor boy. That poor, sweet boy."

It's a message renewed within John, for he, too, from time to time has become enrapt by the absence of Frank's arm.

"John." Georgina breaks her gaze. "Henrietta's headstone awaits your inscription. You do know that this will be our family plot. William wants to erect a fence and plant a shade tree."

"It is a nice site. This hillock upon the hill. Yes, a family plot so that none of us will ever be alone."

"Come John. Let us return home. We shall visit Henrietta, tomorrow. And every day after."

As Georgina takes him by the hand, John looks back, sobered by all which has occurred. Indeed, he thinks, if only he could be so fortunate to be buried at such a pleasant setting, to lie by Henrietta's side.

John's welcome into the Shackelford household is without wear. Indeed, he need only ask and Georgina would be happy to make it permanent. Too ill at ease to remain indoors any longer than he may, John begins his days before dawn, dressing in full uniform, complete with his Colt. However, his leg proves to be confining, its strength limited to only so many steps on a given day. Therefore, John spends his time with Henrietta, sitting upon the ground as he wanders within his mind.

Ever-fretful over her brother-in-law, Georgina orders are for Frank to follow his major, and to keep out of sight to allow for privacy.

It's a sunny day at the cemetery, as a cool, northerly breeze has swept the sky of its clouds. But in spite of this wintry reminder, the bonnets of blue and the brushes of orange are beginning to daub their colors across the open land. Even a robustly red cardinal sings loudly its lilt of renewal. John's attentions, however, remain elsewhere, to that endless azure above and its many emptinesses.

Nevertheless, the Fairview Cemetery isn't for John's griefs and respects alone. He's oblivious to the report of footsteps, until they're almost upon him. Yet when John diverts his eyes to the approaching sounds, he's confronted with cordiality.

"Good afternoon, Major. I hope we are not disturbing you." It's John Gaunt with his niece, both burdened by several bouquets of freshly picked wildflowers. "Lucie and I thought the day too pleasant not to visit my sisters and parents," he explains, pointing his hand.

John responds with a puzzled look. But upon turning his head, he sees a family plot delineated by wrought iron and distinguished by several headstones reading "Gaunt." Gathering himself, he rises to his feet and shakes their relative's hand.

"Lucie, do you think we might spare a few blossoms for the major?"

"Of course, Uncle John." She beams at the opportunity to be of help.

"Thank you, Miss Lucie. Perhaps you should take care of your kin first, and I am sure Mrs. Singleton would be grateful to receive the remainder."

"Very good, Major. Lucie."

She rushes to the task, to bunch posies upon the graves of relatives she never had the chance to know.

"Sisters?" inquires John.

"Lucinda and Electra. Both were taken from us before they were of age."

"Tragic."

"Umm. My parents could never find peace. So they, too, died before their time and were unable to enjoy Lucie." Gaunt looks to the direction of his niece. "She is a delight. I should be thankful that the war has brought her to me."

As John watches Lucie's meticulous arranging, he considers the origins of Gaunt's words. Is he being spontaneous or is there a careful design to what he says? Or should this matter?

Soon, Lucie finishes with her kin and so turns her attentions to John's. Once again, she's fussy as to how she lays her mix of flowers.

John's mind becomes entangled with the process, and when Lucie's work is done, he stands in admiration. Is it possible to fix the charms of nature upon the gloom of man, to make appealing all which is sorrow? Nonetheless, Lucie has done just that, and although John has yet to realize it, so, too, has Henrietta.

"Lucie tells me that she came to think of Mrs. Singleton as her older sister. You know she touched so many with her graces. We shall always carry that."

"Thank you, sir. For your thoughts."

The two men pause for a while, as Lucie joins her uncle's side.

"Come, Lucie. We should return home. Major. Why don't you accompany us, so that we might continue our conversation?"

"I would love that, Mr. Gaunt."

With that, the long walk into Bastrop becomes a brief one, and as the three near the Shackelford home, Gaunt has his final say.

"Major, you must allow me to be of further service."

"There is one matter." John turns about to survey the street upon which already they have strolled. "Frank," he yells. "Come here."

From behind the trunk of a tree, Private Peevy emerges, racing to answer the call.

"My private has been assigned to purchase mounts for my fellow officers."

"How many?"

"Two more, but hopefully an additional one for himself."

"Hmm? I may be able to arrange that, Major. In the morning. Your presence would be an advantage."

"Splendid."

"We will need to ride. So have your private ready your mounts."

At the end of his dash, Frank comes to a sudden halt, out of breath and with a look of failure written upon his face.

"Frank. Tomorrow morning, we purchase the horses."

"Really!" Able to push aside the thoughts of a bungled mission under Georgina's command, the private's mood changes to all smiles

Once again, John awakens before dawn. The scent of Henrietta permeates throughout the room and the empty half of the bed retains a little of her warmth, while upon her pillow his fingers discover a strand of hair. On this morning John is comforted by those essences, the reason why he lingers, though carelessly in that he should be readying himself for a busy day.

As is the norm, it's up to Georgina to rouse the household, she seemingly surprised to find John still in bed. Yet it's even more astounding when later her brother-in-law pays a visit to the breakfast table. Nevertheless, during the meal Georgina finds it futile to pry loose a conversation from John. Indeed, as he excuses himself to return to his room, he seems to be lost in the process of recollection, his tightened cheeks trying to squeeze forth a certain memory or two.

In due time John reemerges from his room, fully dressed and wearing a look of satisfaction, and holding a small rip of scribbled paper.

"Georgina."

"Yes, John," she replies anxiously.

"Has Frank left for the stable?"

"Yes. He should be here shortly with the horses."

"Tell me if you think Henrietta would approve." John hands over his written words. "For her inscription."

"Oh, John." Taking the paper, Georgina reads it aloud. "The autumn winds rushing / Waft the leaves that are searest / But our flower was in flushing / When blighting was nearest." She wilts at the words. "John. Henrietta would love your choice."

"Yes. She did adore it."

"She could recite the verses from heart." Georgina draws a sputtering breath. "Yes, John. I will take this to Mr. Walker, today."

"Splendid." There's a gentle pause. "If you don't mind, I think I shall walk to the stable."

But as he turns toward the front door, it's noticeable that something is amiss, of which Georgina dares not mention. Although dressed in his uniform, today John leaves the house without his Colt.

Frank's second foray into horse-dealing is a whopping success. So much so, that the mare, of which he's become attached, is now his to keep.

As for his major, spending several more days with the Shackleford household is helping to settle his conflicted mind. Even so, John understands that sooner or later he must return Frank and himself to Shreveport, when the impetus arrives.

It's after dinner, and John and Georgina and the girls are enjoying the lengthening day from the comforts of the porch. And upon cleaning the dishes, Mairead and Frank join the assembly.

So far, the tales of Ariadne Smallbones are proving worthy—popular for audience and relaters both.

"Frank used to be sweet on Miss Smallbones," reveals John. "And she on him."

"Miss Smallbones is sweet on just about every two-legged critter she catches wind of. I was lucky this particular failing warned me of her many others," explains Frank, as he holds Martha on one knee.

"Oh what a horrible creature she must be," remarks Georgina. "The poor thing."

Before long, the girls are put to bed by their mother, leaving the others to continue the talk and to hail the occasional passerby. It's only a matter of time before John Gaunt's appearance.

"Major," he harkens, as he stands at the gate. "What pleasant days we have seen."

"Things have been brightening considerably, Mr. Gaunt."

"How are the horses?"

"Behaving quite well, thank you."

"Then I trust you will be leaving us soon.

"Well, I have not considered the actual date."

"Major, I believe word has yet to reach you." There's a bit of confusion in Gaunt's tone.

"Word? What would that be?"

"I have just learned on good authority that Banks is assembling on Berwick Bay. To move up the Teche."

"And to Alexandria, I should wager."

"That stands to reason, Major."

"If that be, then Shreveport also stands to reason."

"A fair assumption."

"Then it seems tomorrow, sir," replies John with a dose of disappointment. "Tomorrow, we will part."

As it happens, the major is not the only one displeased by this sudden turn, the capsized faces of Frank and Mairead attesting such.

In truth, John is surprised by the news, forcing him and Frank to spend half the night in preparation. Mairead pitches in, baking bread and packing root vegetables from the garden for the journey. Georgina, too, is of a thoughtful service, sorting through Henrietta's possessions for items of succor.

By ten o'clock the following morning, the two soldiers gather in front of the Shackelford house to bid their goodbyes. Tethered to one another, each of the unsaddled horses carries two sacks of corn, while John's gelding and Frank's mare are loaded with personal gear and foodstuffs. Indeed, if not for a certain hesitation, the two would be ready to mount.

"Go ahead, Frank. Give Mairead a kiss on the cheek and let's be off."

"Major," she protests, but accepts Frank's tender parting all the same.

"Georgina."

"John. I almost forgot. Something that I came upon this morning." Georgina produces a handkerchief. "This is the last item Henrietta embroidered. These lovely daisies."

"My God."

Eventually, John and Frank manage to tear away, righting themselves in their saddles after an endless succession of goodbye waves. Soon they near the edge of town, where the pair must take the road eastward.

"Major. You think Bastrop might have some prospects after the war. For someone like me?"

"Frank. I believe you may have already found those prospects."

"Jewhillikens, that sure sounds mighty pleasing."

John is amused, even though something else has his mind. "Frank. It would not be a bother if we stop and say goodbye to Mrs. Singleton?"

"Course not, Major. I'd think lowly of you if we didn't."

To John's surprise, Henrietta's headstone is complete and has been set in its proper place. As he kneels next to her grave, he pulls out her handkerchief of embroidered daisies, inhaling from it a whiff of the same air which once had inflated Henrietta's lungs.

And while Frank holds the reins, he reads to himself the epitaph, after which he airs the obvious. "That sure is a sweet sentiment, Major. One that's gonna last forever."

As troublesome as it may be to lead three additional horses, at least they're well-rested for travel, with the corn insuring that they won't have to rely solely upon spring grass. For John, he's never made better time, as the growing days move to a hastened monotony.

Almost without realizing it, John and Frank enter the Sabine country, to the realm of Francis Simmons. Notwithstanding, their imposition upon the planter's open hospitality is one which requires them to bear witness to much upheaval. It seems that Mrs. Simmons has moved into a smaller house in Marshall, the crowded situation compelling her to send a household slave to her husband. Now, Mr. Simmons has under his supervision two cooks, along with the unavoidable turmoil. Since Eugenia is the junior, she's also the most resentful. Yet incredibly, coupled with this transfer of power is a further disruptive complication. Somehow, word has come to Eugenia that her family is not only safe and sound in Vicksburg, but are enjoying a degree of prosperity working for "Massa Lincoln."

"Gentlemen, I don't mind confessing that Eugenia is difficult enough on her own," explains Mr. Simmons over an afternoon libation. "But now that she has been joined by a rival, their antagonisms seem to get piled upon me. Someone must go, and I am sad to say that person cannot be yours truly."

"Sir, you have my sympathies."

"Nonsense, Major. From you of all people. Your fortitude is great and my troubles are trivial. But by chance, would you know of someone who might be interested in acquiring a cook?"

John hesitates with his response.

"Forgive me, Major. I should consider I may be putting a compromise to your convictions."

"Think nothing of it. Your cordiality is your consideration."

Rested and replenished, before long the two riders resume their return journey.

A wall of reluctance greets John, when, eventually, he and Frank approach Shreveport. And it has nothing to do with the likelihood of invasion, rather everything in regards to what he has left behind. Too hasty, believes John, was his departure from Bastrop. However, had he stayed any longer he could have risked remaining there indefinitely, with his shirking of duty bringing shame upon Henrietta's name. Now that they've come so far, John has no choice but to follow the Texas Road as it alters into Texas Street.

"Shreveport sure ain't a Bastrop," notes Frank. "I missed that place a long time back."

"As have I, Frank. I only pray the department has something to busy me. Damn, whatever the hazards."

11 ↝ The Thick Forested Desert

Mile by mile, the Union forces are gaining control over the arteries leading into the body of the South. Those railroads no longer Confederate now receive a proper maintenance, while the wide waters serve both transport steamers and their escorts of iron and "tin." Even the rivers which flow at a trickle can be navigated with a little skill and daring, affording an even greater pliancy of communication. For those in charge, the chances to alter strategy are difficult to resist.

Naturally, the provocations of cotton hold sway, never before receiving such high esteem from the idle mills of New England and the penurious treasuries of the Confederacy. Even as the conflict rages, furtive deals are being struck between enemies to satisfy these demands, unintentionally lengthening the war.

However, with the balances favoring the overwhelming North, thousands of stored bales are there for the taking. Not only would the surge of cotton satisfy New England's mills, but for a few select individuals garner a wealth of prestige. The sad truth seems to be that politics and the ambitions of its practitioners take precedence over sound military judgement—with an utter indifference to the sacrifices and sufferings of the private soldier. Indeed, from its outset, the conflict has never belonged to those who do the actual fighting.

March 10 holds a pleasant surprise for Susha and Sylvie, when they and their regiment embark on the *Duchess of Brownsville.* Although the winter months have left her a little worse for wear, a sturdier sternwheeler there never has been.

Soon, a rumor is confirmed when the armada under Rear Admiral David Porter steers southward, instead of heading north to the railheads pointing toward Georgia. As related by Lieutenant Warner with Vicksburg still in view, it seems that the 42nd and its brigade, along with others from the Army of the Tennessee, are on "loan" to Major General Nathaniel Banks' Army of the Gulf. To the men of Company C's utter disgust, their lives, as well as those of 10,000 additional soldiers under A.J. Smith, are entrusted to a Massachusetts politician, whose powerful connections keep him in uniform contrary to his renown military ineptitude.

Before long, the *Duchess* ascends a few miles up the Old River to where it meets the Red, and a shorter distance down the Atchafalaya to disembark its troops at Simmesport. Thus begins the Red River Expedition, with A.J. Smith, again, leading the way into the heart of enemy country.

Colonel Shaw's 2nd Brigade consists of five regiments. Early in the war, the 24th Missouri was bloodied at Pea Ridge, Arkansas and has tasted nothing but victory ever since. Yet of Shaw's Iowa regiments, only his own, the 14th, has felt the real stings of battle. It was at the Hornet's Nest during the Battle of Shiloh that most of these Iowan's, those who cheated death, were unable to avoid capture, including their colonel. Paroled and then officially exchanged the following November, the regiment completed its reorganization in April of '63 and was assigned garrison duty, where it seethed for retribution

Meanwhile, for the first time Susha catches sight of the 42nd's parson, he having returned from a long furlough. As to why he spent the winter in Iowa, it most likely has something to do with the comforts of home. As it happens, Parson Smith's accepted denomination is unknown to most, he having practiced his profession among the men on too few occasions. However, at least he remains consistent, for at that moment of truth when he might disembark with his flock, he prefers to stay in his cabin aboard the *Duchess*.

As the column takes the road to Marksville, it makes for an impressive sight of blue-clad soldiery. Unlike the Meridian Expedition, the regiments and their brigades are keeping their formations close. Indeed, General Smith's entire command is maintaining good order, if only because at the end of this march lies a known point of resistance—Fort DeRussy. By now the ironclads and the lesser-armored gunboats, trailed by the transports, should have regained the Red River and will be taking its wide loop leading eventually to the Confederate fortification. In effect, General Smith's march to Fort DeRussy is something of a short cut, facilitating a two-pronged attack.

During most of the year the wide lowlands surrounding Louisiana's rivers make for muddy roads. More's the pity, for most of the men of the 42nd are adorned with fresh uniforms courtesy of the quartermaster at Vicksburg. Now these new articles of uniforms are receiving their baptisms of mud, as Company C trudges its way toward Marksville.

"I would like to see those poltrooned marines march through this," quips Proctor. "Wager plenty they would dare not sully their uniforms in this particular river."

"Damn sure of that," agrees Susha, her oath evincing sly smiles from her co-conspirators.

A few miles ahead, a reconnaissance encounters an empty and unfinished fortification. So hasty, in fact, is its abandonment that a few stragglers are captured—strange and wild-looking Texans. Still, the Iowans are not awed as they marched passed Fort Humbug, nor are the men of the 42nd impressed by their first glimpse of Lone Star soldiers, the legendary fierceness of these people receiving an intoxicating deflation.

After a token skirmish at Bayou des Glaises, where the crossing is bridged with the timbers of a cotton gin, the column marches onto a vast elevated ground known as the Prairie des Avoyelles. Well-watered, but well-drained, this land's French-speaking inhabitants have improved Eden with a careful agriculture of bountiful tillage and colorful gardens. Spring is alive on this prairie—more so than any place on earth. Up to now, Iowa's sons have encountered only primitive farming inside the Confederacy, so that they're struck by the Prairie des Avoyelles' keen orderliness and inspired beauty. To be sure, the setting is soothing to those who remain resentful over their separation from "Uncle Billy."

As for the Avoyellites, themselves, the Iowans find humor in their meek defenses. Fluttering above the occasional house is a tricolor, a substitute for the standard of the Confederacy. Be this a show of hasty neutrality, it fools no one, and is judged to be an inept ruse devised by an otherwise clever people.

Regardless, the Prairie des Avoyelles' sheltering groves are ideal for an army's bivouac. Company C has lit its fires beneath two, centurial live oaks, with Captain Pillow imposing himself upon the hospitality of a nearby, tricolored house. And while Ben and Leo are on picket duty, their messmates enjoy their pipes, Susha included. So far, none of Colonel Shaw's soldiers have fired a hostile shot, but the anticipation is that this may change tomorrow at Fort DeRussy. The conversations filling the smoke and air of the camps are of nothing other than the campaign.

"Amos. You know who set that Simmesport house afire?" asks Paps.

Being the orderly sergeant, Amos Ayres functions as the "mother" of the company. "Wasn't one of us. Probably the Fourteenth."

"Makes sense."

"What did you think about those young missies in that town, Amos?" probes Proctor.

"Fair in their features, I would say. Delicate beauties, until they poked their lips with those little cigars." Sergeant Ayres grimaces at the thought.

As he does so, Susha draws a puff and then spews the smoke into the above Spanish moss.

It's all her comrades can do to not betray their secret with a burst of laughter.

"Well now, I find that peculiar, Amos," continues Proctor. "In that there's not one among us who does not fancy the dainty vision of a missy partaking."

"I do accept the queerness of your manner, Proctor. And that you have corrupted the ways of your comrades. The poor devils."

"Amos." Leave it to Paps to return to the serious. "What do you know about this Fort DeRussy? And of Banks and Franklin?"

"Well, if the Rebels don't skeddadle, what I hear is it will be up to our brigade to take it. But don't think the affair will be much trouble. Not with Porter's hundred-pound Parrotts." Sergeant Ayres pauses as he brings an ember to his pipe. "As for Banks, all I know is he's marching up from the Teche Country, and is to join us at Alexandria. We should be in for a wait."

"Those Texans have yet to show much," notes Paps. "Any idea how many are out there?"

"Supposed to be few and far between. George thinks they will fall back to Shreveport and make a stand. It is there capital. And keeping it would bar our way into Texas, were we to get the notion."

"Texas, huh?" Although it's a worthy question, Proctor moves on. "So their general is a president's son?"

"Dick Taylor. Learned to wage a campaign in Virginia under Stonewall. Where he licked Banks."

"Damn sure not a bishop trying to keep us out of Meridian," reminds Bill.

"But this time we have better weather and the navy," joins a more optimistic Susha. Or at least this is what she and her messmates are hoping for—warmer days—since while in Vicksburg they posted home their greatcoats and spare blankets, and even their knapsacks.

Up to now, the conversation is carrying on without Sylvie's assistance, he seemingly in a pensive state. "Amos. Why is this expedition? What is it all for?"

"Hmm?" Ayres seems taken aback by the blunt question. "Because we have orders to keep the French out of Texas, or bring Louisiana back into the Union. Or-r-r." Sergeant Ayres hesitates with the next rationale. "The country needs cotton, and the rebels have hundreds of thousands of bales stored along the Red."

"Why should we care about that cotton?" argues Bill. "I would just assume set it ablaze. Or let the Seceshes do it for us."

"That would be a shame, Bill. Burning it would be like torching money."

"Still don't see how that should bother us."

"Well look, Bill. You know of those dapper rascalites hitching along on the transports? The *Diana*? They're cotton agents from back east. Let us say that you boys on a forage come across a warehouse full of cotton. Should be able to coax a handsome bounty from those agents just for the news of its whereabouts. A fair degree of bother, I would say."

"I will give you that, Amos," concurs Bill.

"Hmm? A bounty, you say?" Sylvie becomes dreamy-eyed over the prospect. "Why, I could come back here after the war and buy up the land. Plant this soil."

"Interesting notion," nods Paps.

"Sergeant Ayres." Suddenly, a shout arrives from the darkest end of the camp.

"Over here!"

"Sergeant Ayres." It's Sergeant Wilkins, delivering a message. "The lieutenant needs you."

"Very well."

As the two sergeants turn toward the company headquarters, Bill asks Wilkins of his opinion. "What do you think, Sergeant? About us forcing Fort DeRussy?"

"Not likely, Stewart. The regiment will be on rear picket, tomorrow." With a slight shake of his head, Sergeant Wilkins parts abruptly.

"Hmm? I don't mind telling," offers Paps. "That is good news."

His remark seems honest. Although the men are brimming with confidence, to have gone into battle so soon would be an uncomfortable concern.

"Amen to that." Bill nods in agreement. "But did Wilkins not seem a little peculiar?"

"I think he might suspect something," confesses Susha.

"Suspect what?" quips Proctor. "Whatever do you mean?"

It's mid-afternoon on the 14th and already the column has marched through Marksville, north to Fort DeRussy. However, the 42nd remains at the town's fringes, keeping watch on the road approaching from the south. With their pickets posted and the companies assigned their ground, the command from Colonel Burness is for the men to stack arms and await further orders. The true meaning is clear: that the messes should build their fires, boil their coffee and harken the events occurring two or so miles beyond.

"Listen. They're throwing out the skirmishers," describes Paps, as he sharpens his ears.

Through the distant air, faint pops can be heard. Quickly, they strengthen, as each side answers the other's challenges. Then, as if on cue, heavier blasts are loosed into the building clamor.

"Porter's guns?"

"Most likely the fort's."

At this point no one dares sips his coffee, lest the slurping would disturb the interpretations of battle.

"Our twelve-pounders have joined." Paps listens more. "Hear that volley? Infantry's at the abatis."

Between the twelve-pounders, the spaces are filled by confusions of small arms. Then, moments later, a steady staccato is heard in its crisp execution.

"Someone's firing by files," notes Proctor. "First-rate."

Several more minutes of steady battle pass, when a sudden, terrible thunder overtakes all, its crushing report rushing through the regiment and continuing well beyond.

"There's the hundred-pounders."

However, almost as quickly as the Navy begins, it ceases its bombardment, as do those twelve-pounders of the Indiana and Iowa batteries. Even the rifle fire's intensity is beginning to wane, it all now having become uncoordinated and at will. For all practical purposes the battle has stopped.

Although they hold their breaths, each man of the 42nd is certain of the outcome. It's not long before their confidence rises to the surface.

"Hurrah for Colonel Shaw! Hurrah for 'Whiskey' Smith!"

Hats are flung, hoops are hollered and Company F choruses its signature dog barks. To a man, there's no sentiment for reserve, even if their role toward victory is short of participation.

With their arms around each other's shoulders, Susha and Sylvie are in no way conspicuous, the comrades they are. Notwithstanding, for the Potters there's more to the celebration of a battle won, this being the relief that each has a spouse who is free from foreseeable peril.

Still, Sylvie's cheers are guarded, mitigated by what may lurk up the Red River. For him, the notion of leaving behind the open beauty of the Prairie des Avoyelles is to foray into a faraway darkness.

"I wish we could stay in this paradise," he confesses to Susha. "I really have no need for all that cotton."

While he sees to the dismantling of Fort DeRussy, A.J. Smith sends most of his troops upriver under the command of Brigadier General Joseph Mower. All in a row the transports follow their gunboat escorts, the *Duchess* tucked between the *Sioux City* and the *Diadem*. With its lazy bends and bows the Red is a tranquil river, its alterable banks crowded with thirsty willows. There's much cultivation, an act of defiance in a broad, flat valley susceptible to unpredictable floods. Currently, however, there exists a troubling lack of flow, forcing the pilots into a constant vigil, as they file their vessels within a narrowed stream. Yet the Red River needs no sirens to make its passionate cries, the wealth of cotton being a more powerful lure.

The crowded *Duchess* is full of anticipation, its passengers excited at the prospects of a comfortable expedition. Richard Taylor's ill-equipped and outnumbered forces have put up only token resistances, the silence of the lead Union gunboats attesting to this lack of enemy targets. By now the Confederate general must know that Banks' army on the Teche is moving north, thus limiting his options to that of retreat. On board the *Duchess* this is the prevailing thought, the soldiers of the 42nd relishing the river journey that will disembark them at Shreveport and an overwhelming victory.

"Porter is sure to be up to Alexandria by now," figures Lieutenant Warner. "Must be around the bend."

"Over there. Smoke," observes Ben. "Johnny's doing more burning."

At the front of the *Duchess'* boiler deck is where Company C is making its "bivouac." As with the other steamboats, she has her bow abutting the bank, waiting for orders to proceed. No doubt another river obstacle has been engineered by Taylor's forces, which up to now are little more than nuisances. Although unlikely, at this position the transports are vulnerable to an ambush, and so a cautious Colonel Burness has ordered Company G ashore as a picket.

"Could be the Navy is reconnoitering the town for a fight," speaks Paps. "Or have come upon torpedoes."

"At least we don't have to fear torpedoes," reminds Lieutenant

Warner. "We being shallow-drafted. One of the ironclads would strike one first."

In close proximity are the Potters, soaking in every valuable word. While Susha finds comfort in the calm atmosphere of her comrades, Sylvie feels otherwise.

"I don't know which is worse," Sylvie tells Susha. "Sunning ourselves like turtles on a log, or rushing headfirst into Secessia."

Suddenly, a distant hundred-pounder roars. However, as no others follow, the noise is given little heed by those on board the *Duchess*.

"Firing at stragglers," surmises Lieutenant Warner.

The latest river obstruction must be one of a special design, its dismantling requiring an excessive effort. But eventually, the orders are relayed, and, with a toot of its whistle, the *Duchess* summons Company G. Relocating their positions mid-channel, soon, the transports return to their upstream journeys.

As it happens, Alexandria is where the obstacle in question lies—although not of man's devious device, but of nature's indifferent creation. Here, the Red River steps down a level into what is a mile-long stretch of rapids, forming with the unusual dearth of water an ideal hazard to navigation at a most inopportune time.

It's below the rapids that Mower's command disembarks to take possession of Alexandria. By now, these river veterans realize that the transports should be able to manage the narrow channel for their runs upriver. However, the deeper-hulled ironclads are a different matter, and since it's known that Confederate gunboats lurk to the north, the Navy must retain the lead. Like lumbering beasts, they lie, anchored below the rapids as if brooding over the decision to risk the chute. Regardless, Adm. Porter will have several days to make up his mind, for the expected rendezvous with the Army of the Gulf is behind schedule. Banks' forces are late, meaning that the Army of the Tennessee will have to bide its time.

To the soldier's dismay, they discover that already Alexandria has been seized by Porter's sailors and the Mississippi Marine Brigade. In addition, Richard Taylor has been expert at evacuating the town of public property, especially cotton, with those bales left behind torched in compliance to Confederate law.

This isn't the first time Alexandria has hosted the bluecoats, its citizens having learned the lessons of occupation. Hence, nearly every house has been boarded shut, even those still inhabited. Also secured are the commercial establishments, their proprietors doing what they can to avoid one-way transactions. Nevertheless, a store empty of its owner is an open invitation to vandals, and "Whiskey" Smith's troops are well-tutored. No barrier's construction is solid enough, as, soon, the merchants' holdings are torn apart for the needs of privationed soldiers and the wants of petty thieves. Before long, even the homes of refugees are broken into, lending promise to disgraceful escalations.

However, there are some among the Army of the Tennessee who take offense. Enough of the company commanders of the 42nd Iowa, and one first lieutenant, have seen to it that their men remain disciplined, thus insuring that Colonel Burness would do the same. Though perhaps he doesn't need to be shamed, his orders are firm in having his regiment form north of town, assuring severe punishments to all stragglers.

Two days later, with the elements of the expedition having not come together still, the 42nd engages in a different sort of pillage. Cotton, regardless of legal ownership, is too important to be treated as anything else but public property, or contraband. There is no guilt to be found with the white fiber, as to its cultivation or how it can be attained. General Banks' stated hopes have been to fill the government's coffers by using confiscated cotton. However, the ambitions of the soldiers may be to assist the cotton agents, which explains why the Iowans have been searching for those warehouses Richard Taylor failed to empty or burn.

The 42nd is getting a little careless in its reconnoiter, for unlike the Meridian Expedition there's little to fear from enemy cavalry. In particular, a portion of Company C finds itself four miles from the Red River.

"George," shouts Proctor, as he stands by a warehouse hidden within a thicket of hackberries.

"Lieutenant! Over here!" join the others.

Proctor, Bill and Ben move to inspect the building's contents and quickly discover what they were hoping not to find.

"Damn," announces Proctor. "Navy has been here too."

Although the warehouse is full of cotton bales, none will be available to make deals.

"This far from the river?" protests Bill.

"Look." Ben points to the lettering on one of the bales.

The message reads "U.S.N." above the letters "C.S.A.," both stenciled in the same blue paint and in several places. After creating Confederate government ownership, Porter's men are free to establish their own claims. And the sailors can afford to be bold, for while the soldiers must act surreptitiously if they are to enrich themselves, sharing the "prize" is a legal naval tradition.

Ben rubs a hand over the blatant deception. "Dry as a bone. They got here long before us."

"Nothing but pure profit for our Navy friends," proclaims Proctor. "The sons-of-bitches. No wonder they cannot uncork the chute with that ironclad of theirs. Damn thing's overloaded with cotton."

Recognizing the futility, Paps shakes his head as he stands outside. "I think it's time we give up this foolish speculating and get back to the war. So we can go home. Perhaps someday."

"Lieutenant!" beckons Sylvie to his officer. "Come see this!"

"Navy cotton!" joins Susha.

"Those people are getting more audacious," replies Lieutenant Warner, as he approaches. "Is it marked 'Navy'?"

"Looks like it, George," is the answer from within. "All of it."

"God, am I sick of cotton." The lieutenant wears the look of disgust. "Better we take those agents upriver as far as we can, and leave them stranded."

"Amen, George," adds a grinning Paps. "Or maybe first thing, we should kill all the lawyers."

Still vexed, Proctor is not shy about airing his suggestion. "I say we set it afire and blame Dick Taylor."

Lieutenant Warner pauses, as if considering the thought. "I might approve. Excepting the Navy could find out it was us. But what Paps said. Maybe we should kill the lawyers."

"George, you think the Navy's still coming upriver?" asks Bill.

"I would say so long as there's the smell of cotton, they will push their boats up wet sand."

"Any word on the *Eastport?* Still stuck in the falls?"

"As far as I know."

Proctor chuckles at what most likely is his pet miscalculation. "You would think his excellency Porter would have the sense not to make his first try at the falls with his biggest boat. By God, I hope all his ironclads make it through and then the falls close up behind. Let him be stranded upriver with his cotton."

"Here, here."

"I commend you for your sentiment, Private Keedy." Lieutenant Warner is as amused as anyone. "By the way, pass the word. Assemble at the chimney in twenty minutes. The regiment is to cover the Bayou Rapides Road."

"Where is Pillow?" asks Paps, as the lieutenant turns to walk away.

"Shilly-shallying at the chimney. Tending to his feet."

"Well, boys. You heard him. Twenty minutes," reminds Proctor. "See to your functions, while you can. Don't want to be caught defiling your breeches before the regiment."

"Or the Seceshes," adds Bill. "Might give them false notions."

And so the messmates seek all directions, Susha and Sylvie finding the densest part of the thicket. Using a downed tree trunk as a suitable prop, the two prepare for what may be another long march.

There are few things a couple can do to while away the time on an ersatz two-seater, squeezing forth a few words about the campaign filling the list. But before all is said and done, Sylvie feels the need to air what has been troubling his head.

"Sure is a much different expedition than Meridian."

"We have been spared most of the marching."

"But the Seceshes put up a fight. I know DeRussy was hardly a long battle, and there has been little skirmishing."

Although of late, Susha has noticed a slight change in her husband's bearing, she hasn't given it much concern. "What are you trying to say, Sylvie?"

"Susha, I get a genuine feeling that things might get terribly thick."

"How do you mean?"

"This expedition is just not being run as smart as Uncle Billy would have it. Banks is supposed to be commanding, but where is he? And you heard what happened at DeRussy after we left. Smith got drunk and let those poor men get mangled by that magazine explosion."

"General Mower is a good soldier." Susha offers a mild protest. "That is the thought."

"That may be. But I wonder what would happen if the Seceshes decide to put up a genuine fight against this confusion."

"Nobody thinks that will happen."

"I have this feeling it will." Sylvie pauses for a moment, gathering himself for an earth-shaking pronouncement. "Susha, it could be best that we tell Lieutenant Warner of our secret. So he can send you home."

To be sure, Sylvie's revelation comes as a shock, tempered only by his recent faint change in demeanor.

"Sylvie, you cannot mean it."

"I believe I do." However, Sylvie's assertion is reluctant.

"But I have yet to earn my bounty, and the war is almost done. It's springtime."

"I know. But that bounty hardly bothers me anymore."

"Sylvie. If I go home now, it will be as a failure."

Now it's Sylvie's chance to sample surprise, that of Susha's pride of a manly sort.

"And it would not be Lieutenant Warner sending me home. That is Colonel Burness' duty. Surely, he would pass out punishments. Not just to you, Sylvie, but to our friends. We both would not want to be blamed for that."

With Sylvie's frangible plea falling upon deaf ears, his only retort is one of silence.

Nevertheless, Susha understands when to offer a bone. "I know if there was to be danger, you would protect me. You always have, Sylvie. Even when we were young. But now we got our comrades to help you, so there is no chance I could come to harm."

Thus overwhelmed, Sylvie has no choice but to relent. Yet at least there is a chance to lay claim to some sort success at the fallen tree. Grimacing, he gives it one last try.

"Seems that compound syrup might be working."

Though Sylvie remains unconvinced, concerning the dangers of the campaign, he is placated.

At last, General Banks' Army of the Gulf trickles into Alexandria in the form of Brigadier General Albert Lee's cavalry. Meanwhile, through driving hail General Mower leads a reconnaissance in force along Bayou Rapides. It's of this action which the 42nd Iowa supports, picketing the roads to Mower's rear, but ready to be called forward should the situation arise. Spending a cold, wet night around pitiful fires, the men regret having sent home their greatcoats.

The following day finds the 42nd posted in the same location. Rumor has it that Mower made contact with the enemy, bringing about some sort of battle. No one in Company C has heard any sounds of musketry or artillery, but as they guard the road to Alexandria, soon they should see evidence of any such fighting.

While they warm themselves, Susha and her messmates gather the nearby hubbub of the 89th Indiana's approach. It's not long after when rattling drums and their accompanying fifes are heard. Led by their colors, the Indianans are a dirty, soaked, tired regiment, though one marching with a dauntless air.

"What happened?" shouts Leo.

"Henderson's Hill! We licked them!"

"Infantry!" joins Proctor.

"No! Louisiana cavalry! Texas artillery!"

"Damn. Lucky Doodles," mutters Ben.

The informal report of battle continues as the regiment marches passed.

"We were amongst them before they could know!"

"They just threw down their guns! We hardly fired a shot!"

Susha turns to Sylvie with the look of both excitement and relief.

As for her husband, he responds with a nervous, even embarrassed, smile.

"How many did you gobble up!" continues Proctor.

"Scores of them!"

"We got their horses and pieces too!"

As they depart from the presence of Company C, the stride of the Indianans is a little more erect, while the girths of their chests inflate to their fullest capacities.

Soon, more regiments follow, their stories the same as the 89th's. And it's in the middle of the column where General Mower has inserted his trophies, that the boasts are not idle.

"Must be two hundred of them," counts Susha, as they trudge by.

"If not more," considers Paps.

Under guard, to be delivered to the provost, are the Louisiana cavalrymen, along with a few Texans. Disorderly and subjugated, not only do they wear the shame of having surrendered after spilling so little blood, also these humbled horsemen are marching afoot.

"No more than a mob of coffee boilers," remarks Proctor.

The individual clothes of the prisoners have an utter disregard for uniformity, with a heavy reliance on civilian apparel.

Susha marvels at the mixtures of patterns, as well as the varying shades of grey and butternut, and even the undyed. "Just how many orders of uniforms you think their army has?"

To which Paps has the answer. "Two hundred, by the looks of it."

Seeing their foes march by within spitting distance is entertaining enough for the men of Company C. At the same moment it dispels any mistaken notions regarding the fighting spirit of Richard Taylor's soldiers. What parades in front of Susha and her comrades can be only a sample of a wretched army.

Even for Sylvie, the sight of the prisoners gives him pause to lessen those ill feelings concerning the campaign. Indeed, he's realizing the Red River Expedition just may be the best situation for Susha and himself to spend the war.

Finally, Porter's sailors have managed to extricate the *Eastport,* with all of the other gunboats and transports making their successful runs up the rapids. However, a greater event occurs when Nathaniel Banks arrives by steamer to take effective command. And although they're marching overland, his infantry under Major General William Franklin is only a day behind.

Concerning its makeup, the Army of the Gulf is an amalgamation of Western and New England troops, with a host of New Yorkers including a strange regiment of fancy red-trousered and tassel-capped Zoaves. There's even a Corps d'Afrique, said to be arriving by river on a later date. Truly, by the sheer numbers of it, this army is absorbing A.J. Smith's smaller command and the initiatives of the campaign.

After marching north to Cotile Landing, Shaw's Brigade relocates its transports. Once again, the soldiers of the 42nd Iowa are on board the *Duchess*, though this time, incredibly, their ranks are expanded by the recent recruitment of two pro-Union sympathizers from Alexandria.

"I find it disagreeable to have them enrolled in the Color Company," complains Proctor, as he empties his pipe into the river. "No doubt a decision commanded by politics."

"Excepting that the Seceshes' attentions would be fixed upon the colors and, hence, those two recruits," consoles Bill.

"I will accept that justice."

As Franklin's infantry and Lee's cavalry march up the river road, A.J. Smith's command remains in its transports. Meanwhile, with the river rising only slightly, the *Eastport* and the other gunboats must scrape along in the difficult channel.

Plumes of smoke guide the *Duchess*' way upstream, as warehoused cotton is flamed by the very planters who own it. As for those who did the actual cultivation, they're turning out along the banks, providing a sort of escort. Much to the amusements of the soldiers, their parades are joyous ones of songs and praises, waving bouquets and fluttering aprons. In the absence of their masters, the scent of liberation is arousing these people into a grand intoxication. Indeed, these spontaneous celebrations of mothers, children and grandparents seem to have the character of an adapted prophesy.

"Did you ever see the likes of such happy folk?" speaks Sylvie, after which he lowers his voice. "Makes our wedding look like a funeral."

Playfully, Susha gives her husband's ribs a poke, glad she is that his bearing has righted itself. "Could be, Sylvie, because their men aren't around to smother things." Which gives her another thought.

"Paps, why do you suppose there are no male darkies?"

"Likely, their masters could not steal away all their slaves. So they took the most valuable."

Regardless, they can find cause for celebration, these families split apart. Because of her own tenuous station, those conflicted gains and losses are not unnoticed by Susha, able she is to see into the gloom this region's ruling heart.

"I don't think the people here have any notion as to how peculiar are their ways. This is why they do what they do."

Cautiously, the armada inches its way upstream to put in at the hamlet of Grand Ecore. Three miles away on the Cane River lies beautiful Natchitoches, Louisiana's oldest town now occupied by Franklin's troops. As for any resistance, the Confederates can offer only a few skirmishes, most coming by chance encounters between their cavalry coming out of Texas and those reconnoitering regiments of the Army of the Gulf.

In the meantime, at Grand Ecore A.J. Smith's command must stretch its patience and again wait for the arrival for the expedition's leader and his headquarters boat, the *Black Hawk*.

Upon settling into their bivouac, Company C is joined by their captain, he having abandoned the comforts of the *Duchess*. This puzzle, however, is solved when it's learned that Colonel Burness has grown weary of Parson Smith's lack of devotion and is sending him home without ceremony. Apparently, Captain Pillow recognizes the example and fears for his own humiliation.

Sitting beneath the glow of the moon and next to the warmth of the fire, Susha and her messmates enjoy their coffee and tobacco. Being discreet, they keep their voices at a softer tone.

"I tell you, Valentine Pillow acting like a soldier does not bode well."

"How do you mean, Proctor?" asks Bill.

Although the subject of Captain Pillow is a vexation to Private Keedy, it also brings him great pleasure. On this evening, however, his rantings take a serious note.

"He's a shamed politician trying to plow back into office through the field of battle. We are his oxen."

"Cannot deny that," agrees Bill. "It is common knowledge

the officer ranks are half-populated by shoddies. But he doesn't command the regiment. And too junior to ever be."

Ben tosses in his worth. "Don't forget that Colonel Burness is keeping a closer eye."

As Susha listens, she wonders to herself if she's the only one present who has put aside their fears? Why should the motivations of Captain Pillow matter under the setting of the Red River Expedition—this campaign of fits and starts, but of little danger.

"George will keep Pillow in step," reminds Paps. "Pull him through, should there come a scrap."

The following day, April 4, finds Captain Pillow in front of his assembled company, conducting yet another inspection. But before he has his men presenting their toilet cloths, he's interrupted by Lieutenant Warner, who brings forth a message from Colonel Burness.

"Complete the inspection, Lieutenant," orders Captain Pillow, as he leaves his men in more capable hands. "Run them through the drill."

"He must think this war cannot continue without his presence," mutters Proctor.

"Company! Rest!" commands Lieutenant Warner. There's a pause. "Listen up and I will tell you what I know."

A hush overtakes the ranks.

"Banks arrived yesterday." Lieutenant Warner shakes his head. "I was told his boat had to assist the *Eastport.*"

"We should hand over that cursed boat to the Seceshes," blurts Proctor. "Let them deal with that Jonah."

There's a brief, concurring round of laughter.

"I will pass that sentiment to Adm. Porter," returns Lieutenant Warner. "But I do suspect we will move on Shreveport in a day or two, aboard the *Duchess,* with Franklin's men marching up the river road. That way the gunboats can offer protection and help reduce the forts at Shreveport. Whether we invade Texas or return to Sherman, I cannot say." He looks to the reaction of his soldiers. "Very well. Sergeant Wilkins. Have the company stack arms and break ranks. I should return in twenty minutes."

"Sir. Company! Order..."

Finally, April 6, and the expedition regains its movement. Albert Lee's cavalry is the first to set out, followed by Franklin's infantry, both overburdened by their extensive supply trains. For the veterans of the Army of the Tennessee, the number of wagons required by the Army of the Gulf pales to the ridiculous. Yet this is the least of their confusion, after A.J. Smith's men learn of Franklin abandoning the relative safety of the river roads for another route.

The following day "Whiskey" Smith's forces put Grand Ecore behind them. With the exception of General Kilby Smith's small command remaining with the transports, the Army of the Tennessee regiments are to follow Franklin. Moving out of the wide valley of the Red River, Shaw's brigade must march up the inclined road unto higher ground. Although it's not much of an angle, for the men of the 42nd Iowa the added exertion is a reminder that they're venturing into a great unknown. Up to now, the land of Louisiana has been flat and well-watered, and not the least bit foreboding.

"Banks missed the river road?" Proctor is amazed at Sergeant Ayres' claim.

"This is what I heard," assures Amos, as he marches alongside the formation.

"Well, if that be the case then Banks' boys deserve to be up front," judges Bill. "Let them be the first to find trouble."

"All Banks had to do was ask us to do a proper scout." Proctor remains incredulous. "We could have sniffed out that goddamm road for him."

"I sure hope 'Whiskey' is keeping in touch with Uncle Billy."

"Well, if he hasn't, Bill, then damn him too."

A few hours later, Shaw's brigade is ordered to fall out for a 30-minute rest, although there's little room in which to spread itself. The narrow road pierces through a land of densely-packed pines, with a tangle of dogwood, catbriar and poison ivy making the soldiers' interval difficult.

"I would hate to bivouac in a place like this," figures Sylvie, as he fans the flames of a fire.

It's at this point that Susha realizes how much she misses her home state. "I don't think I care to be shut in these woods. Not able to see more than ten feet away."

"Sure not Iowa," agrees Ben, while he impales a piece of pork.

"What kind of thinking puts this expedition on one little road?" continues Susha. "We being so stretched, if the front got into a scrape, it would take a full day for us to give help."

It's a sound assessment from a lowly private, which may be lost on those who command.

Because of the undulating land, long ago the road's sandy surface washed away to its red-clay base. Only a small amount of rainfall will turn this compacted path into a slippery way, thus forcing individual soldiers to concentrate on their treacherous footing and the stalled trains. The irony is that the column has entered the dry region between the Red and Sabine Rivers. As the soldiers discover, finding potable water is more of a chore, compounded by the unquenchable thirsts of too many horses and mules, a problem affecting strategy.

The thicker the walls of towering pines are, the greater a desert the forest becomes. There's little in the way of settlement and only sparse signs of cultivation. Indeed, the highest impression upon Susha is that there couldn't be a worse place to wage war. To be sure, she and her comrades would find it impossible to form a line of battle, although there is a less likelihood of sudden flanking attacks.

Evening arrives at the end of another march, the men considering themselves fortunate to have elbowed enough room for a serviceable bivouac. As for the Potters, it's nearly midnight when they return to camp after a stint on the picket. To their surprise they find that their messmates remain awake.

"How come you boys aren't asleep?" asks Sylvie.

"Nearly there," answers Leo. "Just talking over the news."

"I suppose you two haven't heard of the skirmish. The far side of Pleasant Hill," notes Paps.

As they doff their accoutrements, the Potters aren't impressed at what has become almost common news.

Proctor, however, sees to it that they are. "Excepting this time Lee's horses came up against determined cavalry. First-rate Texas."

"Not at all a Henderson's Hill."

"They said the Texans wouldn't skedaddle, until Lee brought up two more brigades."

However, Sylvie's unsure of the significance. "What does that mean?"

"Could be something. Could be nothing," answers Paps.

"Or could be that Dick Taylor wants to keep us from getting some sleep," groans Ben, the only messmate trying to catch a wink. "Wake us to death, all the way to Shreveport."

The following day is a return to the frustrating march at the rear of the Army of the Gulf's trains. Such is the road congestion, that A.J. Smith's regiments fall out as a matter of frequent routine. Understandably so, good soldiers despise a campaign of a slipshod design. For them, the first order would be to find the field of battle and be done with it. Instead, Smith's men must be satisfied to draw out the conclusion and endure the hardships much longer than they should.

As Company C settles for another break in the wilderness, the men sense that the atmosphere around them is changing. From tip to tail the entire column stretches beyond 20 miles: beginning with Albert Lee's cavalry and their cumbersome trains, through Franklin's infantry and their even greater extravagance of wagon and mule, and on to A.J. Smith and his brigades' practical economy, with the artillery batteries scattered throughout. And although specific news may take a while, like the hidden wonders of electricity moving along a current, the sensations of significant events do travel fast. As of late, the campfire perceptions are that something of consequence is happening to the van of this great army of Nathaniel Banks, that the anticipated victory upon Shreveport may have to wait for another time.

Between the Potters' messmates barely a word is uttered, each soldier instead pricking up their ears to attention. As for Susha and Sylvie, they're huddled beneath the privacy of their blankets, having found a peaceful interlude a world away from the troubled pines of western Louisiana. In spite of the odds stacked against them, their calm allows a gentle slumber to descend.

"Fall in." The voice of Sergeant Wilkins barks amidst the company. "Ten minutes."

With their sleep brought to an abrupt end, the Potters try to gather themselves.

"What's happening, Paps?" asks a blurry Sylvie.

"General Smith must have used up his tolerance. Or he has a notion that Banks might be getting into trouble." Paps speaks soberly.

"Ultra-trouble for those paper-collars," vents Proctor of his disgust. "Bully for Dick Taylor."

However, looking up the road as far as her eyes will allow, Susha can see no activity concerning the teamsters. "Just how do we get passed that train?"

As noted by one Private Bob Potter, moving forward under the present circumstances is a daunting task. Most of the drivers are hired civilians, who feel less obligated to cooperate. Along with their Corps d'Afrique escort and the tired draft animals, it makes for an impossibly congested affair. A.J. Smith's solution is to order his toughest regiment, the 14th Iowa, to fix bayonets. Poked and prodded, the drivers have no choice but to force their teams into the entangling forest, with any delay resulting in scattered loads, ruined wagons and dispersed mules. Almost by miracle, it's not long before word shoots up the long supply train that the 14th Iowa means business, thus making the regiment's labors simpler.

Marching immediately behind are their brethren Iowans of the 42nd. The work of the 14th is a sight to behold, though more impressive are the contents of the discarded baggage. Strewn about and ready for a good pillaging are the tailored uniforms of junior officers, shelter tents, campaign furniture such as writing desks, and cast iron cooking gear of excessive weight. Then there are the boxes of comestibles, which do not appear to be of government issue.

Proctor's curiosity can take it no longer. He breaks free from the formation and makes a dash to the nearest wooden crate. Upon securing a bottle, he runs to catch up to his place in the ranks.

"What is it?" asks Bill.

As he continues to march, Proctor turns the bottle to its label side. "Would you believe, walnut catsup? We have been heaving up Jonah on sowbelly and Lincoln pie, while Banks' rascalites dine first-rate."

Securing the bottle in his haversack, Proctor hands his rifle-musket to Bill and makes another foray into the open larder.

"Find some brandy," requests Ben.

Absent for more than a minute, Proctor returns to Company C with a little urging.

"Keep in formation, soldier!"

"Just doing some foraging, Sergeant! Like you taught me!"

In his arms Proctor holds an open box containing an assortment of bottles, of which he divvies.

"I got mustard, Sylvie," notes Susha with a chuckle. "How about you?"

He reads his label. "Ah, damn, Proctor. Mustang liniment?"

"My apologies, Sylvie. Had to grab this on the run, don't you know."

"Keep it," suggests Bill. "So you can rub your legs at the next bivouac."

It's an exhilarating beginning to this stage of their march, one which hides the soldiers' nerves. Still, these Iowans are full of confidence, enough to suppress nearly all fears. For the most part, they're eager to show what they can do, to demonstrate to their foes, and even to the enemies of their foes, just how the soldiers of the Army of the Tennessee can fight.

Before a bivouac can be made, the rumors begin to filter into A.J. Smith's column. To no surprise, near Mansfield, a disaster may have fallen upon Banks and the commands of Lee and Franklin, the hearsay being that Smith's orders are to take him to the open spaces surrounding the summer resort village of Pleasant Hill. There, presumably, he is to join those Army of the Gulf regiments which were not engaged and stop any Confederate advance.

Sylvie is of no mind to use the bottle of mustang liniment, although he sees fit to keep it. The choice for a bivouac, the cemetery near Pleasant Hill, is a practical one made by those in command. Regardless, the irony of stretching among the dead is too apparent to ignore, especially when coupled with the distant sounds of skirmishing. Then again, so is exhaustion, the elixir overcoming the temptation toward the uneasy.

Susha, too, has reached the point of collapse, and upon lying down falls into a simple sleep—little to remember and nothing to forget.

Before dawn, an anxious Colonel Burness has his regiment up and about. Although hurried, there is time to rekindle the fires and boil coffee, and even cook a little salt pork doused with walnut catsup. However, as the men see to their needs, they're confronted by a strange, spectral procession, the likes of which none could have ever imagined.

Dragging themselves passed the cemetery are the bits and pieces of a broken army. They're fugitives from Franklin's injured regiments, exhausted, but desperate to reach the safety of Grand Ecore. As there are no officers among this particular wave, there is no discipline, no marching in formation and maintaining of unit cohesion. Not that these fugitives are of much use as far as soldiering is concerned, for too many of them have discarded their weapons and accoutrements, a shameful exercise to make their flight less of a strain, but also helping to arm their enemy.

The responses from the men of the 42nd are mixed. Some sit in shock, while others shout out questions and listen for the timorous responses. But at least a few of the Iowans react with anger, striking at those who they blame for a campaign going awry.

"You fancy ladies skeddadle back to New Orleans!" provokes Proctor to a couple of unarmed New York Zoaves, still resplendent in their red pantaloons and frilly blouses. "Get back to that cat house of yours and let us men do the fighting!"

On the other hand, there's Sylvie, who having put the situation into an accurate assessment, realizes he as but few options. Reaching into his haversack, he pulls out the bottle of mustang liniment and gives it a toss.

It's a circuitous route Shaw's Brigade must take. Although Pleasant Hill is near, the road leading to it is jammed with remnants of regiments looking to reassemble elsewhere. Colonel Shaw has no choice but to force his command into the pines. But through laborious and time-consuming effort the brigade does manage to regain the Mansfield Road, as they march by Pleasant Hill and Brigadier General William Emory's regiments which bore the lesser brunt at Mansfield. Already, the village is being torn apart for firewood, the soldiers there helping themselves to the un-nailed or otherwise.

The last in line, the 42nd follows Shaw's other regiments to beyond the western edge of town. At a wide, open field on the Mansfield Road, the Iowans and Missourians relieve as ordered a brigade of Emory's. Shifting their position to take advantage of the terrain, Shaw's men, as supported by a light battery of the 25th New York Artillery, are well in front of the Union line, overextended and overexposed before the van of a watchful enemy. However, if the men of the 42nd are feeling any qualms over their predicament, they need only to look to the stoic confidence as displayed by their comrades of the 14th, those hardened veterans who must realize that they, once again, are being thrown into a "Hornet's Nest."

What has been an agonizingly slow campaign for the 42nd has hastened into a succession of movements. Yet by the late morning and into the early afternoon, there is another visit to the stationary interval. Upon posting pickets, Colonel Shaw orders his men to stack arms, but with the companies to remain close to their positions. And so, after modifying a fence row into a light breastwork, it's a return to the burn and boil, the cracker, and the nervous chatter.

Company C's position is at the extreme right of the regiment, which itself is nestled between the 27th Iowa and the 32nd Iowa, the latter unit forming the brigade's left flank. With Sergeant Wilkins at his side, Captain Pillow paces along the fence row, watching the Mansfield Road and the sections of Confederate cavalry blended by the forest at the far end of the open ground.

By contrast, Lieutenant Warner sees fit to mingle.

"George," asks Paps, as he stirs his fire. "Any news when 'Whiskey' is coming up?"

"No. The rest of our corps must still be on the other side of town."

"At least a mile away," figures Bill.

"I don't think Banks expects a battle, today. Emory too."

"Colonel Burness sure begs to differ," notes Bill. "I hope 'Whiskey" does too. Look at our flanks. There's nothing there, and will we be able to count on Emory coming up?"

Earlier, some musicians had traded in their instruments for stretchers, while the surgeons and their assistants prepared their equipment. Thus resigned to an immediate battle, Susha girded herself. But now that this hasn't occurred, she, together with Sylvie, must sit and listen, and feel her fortitude waste away.

"What is General Banks waiting for?" asks Susha.

"So that Taylor can bring up all of his army," speaks a scornful Ben.

"I wouldn't be too bothered about it," offers Lieutenant Warner. "General Smith can come up quickly, and we have New York at our front. Taylor may think we have a whole division in these woods."

A short volley from a few Confederate rifle-muskets interrupts, as if to contradict Lieutenant Warner's assessment. He stands for a better look.

"They're trying to skirmish with our pickets. Draw us out." Yet the lieutenant must realize that someone may need to be calmed. "I better tend to Pillow," he explains, as he rushes away.

Over the next hour, the activity on the Confederate side intensifies. Richard Taylor's infantry is re-enforcing his cavalry to the point where now the foot soldiers outnumber the horse. Even more telling is that his artillery is making a determined appearance, after having forced its way passed what must be the considerable clutter of Albert Lee's abandoned trains.

Already, Colonel Burness has ordered his men to take up their arms, but to keep the formations loose. The wiser ones try not to contemplate their futures, and instead fret over matters such as when the water detail will return from the cisterns. Looking to their right, members of Company C watch the 27th Iowans mimic a practice of the stolid 14th: writing goodbye letters to their loved ones and pinning them to the backs of their sack coats. There's no denying that the clamor about them is only beginning to rise to its crescendo. Nevertheless, little of the noise originates from the men themselves, as if all that needs to be said has.

Still, all the talk in the world can be spoken without muttering a single word. Aside from their own fates, Susha's messmates have additional concerns, that their bargain to harbor a comrade may be taking a consequential turn. The looks on their faces are graver than the others, sketched by their odd responsibilities. Not that Susha's role as a soldier has been a farce, her devotion to duty having shown she's as reliable as any. But at this moment of imminent peril her special gender is burrowing into her comrades' hearts. As they look toward Susha, their shrugging shoulders and pointed brows ask her if she really wants to see this conflict to its end, while their half-smiles and twitching cheeks tell her of no hard feelings.

For Susha the parlance is a familiar one, the thoughtful regards of her comrades heard as if they were aloud. She means to stay where she is, the position next to her husband attained through unrelenting stubbornness. It is a quandary, however, to find a solution in order to ease the apprehensions of Susha's friends, while making her intentions known.

"I say let us start this battle now," she speaks loudly. "And be done with it."

Meanwhile, Sylvie bolsters his hand around Susha's shoulder. The Potters' silent language is a rare one, evolving since their early childhoods at a pace of its choosing. And the message which Sylvie conveys is reassuring, a firm promise that through it all he will protect her.

But while Susha can comprehend Sylvie's silent vow, she also senses the confusion of another, perhaps unintentional, message. His fingers fiddle and scratch about her shoulder, lingering with their touches as if to stay their farewells.

"Sylvie."

Unfortunately, before Susha can say anything further, a shout erupts from another company.

"Taylor's unlimbering his Napoleans."

"Must be a dozen of them!"

Although done on the quick, it is an accurate count, as twelve of the bronze beasts are being readied. In front of the 42nd's position and only half a mile away, the artillery evokes a particular menace. At once, however, it becomes obvious that the direction into which the pieces are being pointed is at a slight oblique.

"They're going after the battery!"

Too soon, the fury is unleashed upon the New Yorkers, who

try their level best to keep up with their overwhelming foe. With all this in front of them, for Shaw's soldiers the exchange of ordnance is a spectacle: roaring flashes from large bore muzzles, arching paths of projectiles as highlighted by their fuses and the eventual bursts of violence it all conveys. At first their marks are off, but the artillerymen are skilled and in short order the intended targets feel their ire. As wondrous as this display may be, however, every man on the line realizes that their little battery of New Yorkers is outnumbered. Before long, the Confederate artillery may grow weary of its diminishing quarry and search for targets anew.

A gulp lodges itself in Susha's throat as Colonel Shaw's skirmishers scamper over the breastworks and rejoin the brigade. This is the final act before the two armies come to a full blow, the opportunity for one or both sides to abandon the field being lost, as is Susha's choice to declare her true gender. Whether she likes it or not, she'll have to behave like the soldier she is and see this battle to its end.

"Fall in," shouts Lieutenant Warner, as do the officers of the other companies.

Formed into two ranks, the entire 42nd Iowa is guided forward to their breastwork. With its hasty reinforcement of the split rail fencing, this instance of military engineering is of a basic design. However, the soldiers behind it can feel the cover afforded by the waist-high breastwork, a crude shield capable of sparing many lives.

Being in the front rank, Susha and Sylvie hunker down on both knees, while each man in the rank behind is stretched a little higher on only one. For the Potters, their seats are at the edge of a bustling center stage of enemy formations. Regiment after regiment of Confederate infantry are poised to the front and to the left of the breastwork, while mounted cavalry stands ready at the right. And all the while, the artillery continues to pound the New Yorkers, whose plight is more and more obscured by smoke. On its own, it makes for an extraordinary exhibition, though the Potters understand fully that the demonstration is for their misbenefit.

Disregarding the guise, Sylvie realizes the moment to take command has arrived. "Make sure you keep your head down, Susha. Let the Seceshes see as little of you as possible." He rearranges a piece of breastwork in front of her. "Just do as I say. When I say it."

"They're limbering up," someone shouts.

"Damn, New York!"

Having endured enough punishment, the 25th New York gathers its surviving horses so that it might secure its endangered pieces to another location. With its flanks unsupported, Shaw's Brigade is now on its own in the face of an overwhelming foe.

While Susha stares at the deadly pageantry, she feels a sudden tap on her left shoulder. It's Lieutenant Warner, leaping over the breastwork and tromping onto the exposed ground. With sword drawn, he dashes ahead a few yards for a better vantage—fearless of the advancing Confederate skirmishers. And upon giving a good survey at what threatens in front of him, the lieutenant turns to face his Company C with some last minute encouragement and instruction.

"Do not show yourselves! Reload quickly, but do not show yourselves!" Walking up and down the line, Lieutenant Warner repeats himself several times. "Listen for the commands!"

With Sylvie's protection and Lieutenant Warner's inspiration, Susha has the confidence that will keep her from turning fugitive, she wanting nothing more than to carry out her duty. Yet to her further amazement, the lieutenant reaches over the breastwork and takes her Enfield. He rushes forward, drops to his right knee, takes a sure aim, and fires. Boom! And then, as if to demonstrate to his company, Lieutenant Warner hunkers down and performs a mock reloading, with the buttplate of the Enfield behind his left side and its muzzle in front of his chest.

"There's one skirmisher who will do us no harm!" he boasts, as he returns the weapon and takes his place behind the ranks.

"Give them hell, Lieutenant!"

As quick as they can, the friends of that skirmisher send some wild shots toward the 42nd, their lead falling both long and short of their marks. Meanwhile, the cavalry which has been biding its time appears eager to hurry along the departing New Yorkers. In neat rows the Confederate horsemen race across the open field, charging in a manner as if they're ignorant of the Union infantry's presence. To what must be their astonishment, the cavalry rides headfirst into the initial volley of Shaw's Brigade, from those regiments comprising the right wing.

Being on the left, the men of the 42nd are mere observers, as the parade of superb horsemanship becomes decidedly ragged. Indeed, the weight of piercing musketry causes the cavalry charge to lose all semblances of formation. Too soon, the ground becomes a horror of tangled mortality, of upended horses failed by their crippled and severed limbs, and of crushed soldiers struggling to free themselves from beneath their lifeless mounts. And it's into this mayhem where the volleys continue to pour.

"Bully for the Twenty-fourth," yells a soldier from Company D. "Bully for the Twenty-seventhh."

"Give it to them, Missouri!"

At last, a distant trumpet blares its mercy through the chaos and clamor, signaling a retreat for the badly mauled cavalry. Shaw's Brigade is repulsing the attack with relatively few casualties of its own, the breastwork and the men's discipline proving their worth. Regardless, Richard Taylor's infantry begins its march forward, this being a more powerful force than their comrades on horseback. Make no doubt, the battle is in its infancy.

By now, the fence row is receiving fire from the skirmishers, though their efforts are little more than a thorn: splintered wood and kicked-up dirt.

Safely pressed against her patch of breastwork, Susha can feel each and every pulse of battle. In that some of its participants are trying to do her injury, suddenly, the war is becoming too well-acquainted with her. She is, after all, the keeper of the weapon which has bloodied one of their own. Glimpsing back at the faces of her comrades, Susha sees that they share the same peril, much in the way that already they have apportioned their identical hardships. Who among them will not answer the roll at the end of the day, she wonders? That's a frighteningly large division bearing down on Shaw's Brigade, whose weight alone should be able to topple the breastwork. In addition, these foes are armed—possibly with the same weapons as hers—and possess every degree of incentives. With all which has occurred since she and Sylvie enlisted, for the first time Susha feels like an invader about to be evicted.

As their march nears, the Confederate officers can be heard barking their commands to the cadence of drums. For the most part, their Texas tongues are indecipherable, but at least one can be understood, his plain and billowy voice carrying itself across the shortening field.

"Guide to the middle," he shouts.

"We will guide you all right! Guide you all the way to hell!" It's the unmistakable voice of Proctor, easing his knotted nerves in the manner he knows best.

Maintaining his mind to details, Lieutenant Warner paces behind the rear rank and shouts more instructions. "Keep your heads down. Follow the commands. Find a butternut and aim at his knees. Do not show yourself while you reload."

Even if Sylvie were to allow it, Susha dares not steal a peek over the breastwork. However, she can all but hear the plodding breaths of her approaching foe, soldiers who must be spent after their long pursuit from Mansfield. To be sure, the passion of triumph is their drive, the likes of which a farm girl from Iowa could never hope to attain.

Suddenly, from behind and to the left, a command from Major Slough bids the entire regiment to readiness. In perfect unison, the captains gather the attentions of their companies.

"Company C," roars Captain Pillow.

"Front rank," blares the chorus.

It's as if all the officers are directing their commands at Susha.

"Ready!"

Reacting much like working machines, Susha and Sylvie cease to think, with their thumbs tickling the hammers and their forefingers ready at the triggers.

"Aim!"

Now the moment of truth, as Susha's eyes greet her foe, who themselves march with their weapons slung high upon their shoulders. In neat rows she's confronted by shell jackets of dull butternuts and greys, of a strange sort of blue and of a soiled, undyed white. Along with overshirts of every known hue, there's a confusion of dis-uniformity and of too many individuals. Be that as it may, when considering the circumstances given of this pageantry any color will do, and it's any color which Susha finds.

"Fire!"

It's been nearly a month since Susha last fired her Enfield, but the kick of the buttplate reminds her of its deadly force. And although the noise of the rifle-muskets is deafening, it also serves to concentrate her senses to the matter at hand. Quickly, the fate of her target becomes none of Susha's concern, her only regard being to ram another cartridge down the barrel of her weapon.

"Load!"

"Keep your head down, Susha," scolds Sylvie.

But as well, the other side has something to say, their officers barking out that familiar succession of commands. The air rumbles with the explosive violence and the breastwork shutters from the impact of too many Minie balls.

With her ramrod midway down the barrel, Susha cringes from the volley's deadly blow. To her surprise, she's survived and is able to relish the calm of the immediate aftermath. Although common as they have become, for Susha the idea to construct this particular breastwork is a work of genius. Nonetheless, a frightful cry from the direction of Company H tells her that some Confederate lead has found its mark.

"Rear rank! Ready! Aim! Fire!"

From the left of the 32nd Iowa to the right of the 24th Missouri, Shaw's Brigade is in full engagement with the advancing enemy. As her right ear rings from the blast of Proctor's Enfield, Susha's left hearkens ahead to the terrible thuds and desperate gasps—the outcome of well-directed musketry. Yet there is no panic, for she and her comrades have become full-fledged implements of war, their movements governed by the drill and coordinated by command.

A Confederate's shout can be heard, attempting to erase the gaps. "Fill in. Guide right."

"Front rank! Ready! Aim! Fire!" is the immediate reply.

With her weapon loaded just in time, Susha joins the volley, thus helping to foil the efforts of that enemy officer. On this turn, however, instead of taking a true aim, it's all she can do to level her Enfield and feel its curse as she squeezes the trigger. Smoke is filling the air and the confusion of sounds begins to meld into one large, indistinguishable din. Tearing open a fresh cartridge, Susha's lips are blackening with the taste of powder. Then, another volley slams into the breastwork, adding more dust and splinters to the clogged air and onto her sweated face.

"Damn! My hat!"

Susha turns to see an agitated Bill, his head uncovered, but otherwise intact. However, he can't afford to consider his good fortune and so, awaits the command.

"Rear rank! Ready! Aim! Fire!"

The battle rages without letup. More and more identical volleys are loosed upon the determined Texans, until the command is given to fire at will. Now it's up to the individual to load, sight and shoot as swiftly as he can.

"Coming over!" warns Proctor, as he positions the middle of his barrel next to Susha's head.

"Boom!"

The barrel of Susha's weapon has become too hot to touch, and to worsen matters, its bore is clogging with the residue of burnt powder. Yet undaunted, she continues to discharge her cartridges in rapid order, oblivious to slaughter's proximity.

And still they come, the unrelenting enemy, so close that Susha can mark individual faces.

"Load," shouts Major Slough, as he races on foot behind the ranks. "Reload and fix bayonets."

"Fix bayonets," echo the junior officers.

In spite of their stalwart performance, unsupported as they are, Shaw's men are in a bad way. The numerical advantage of their foe is telling, deciding for itself the outcome of this phase of the battle. Colonel Shaw has no choice but to extricate his command from this dangerously enveloping situation—a tricky maneuver. Any retreat could panic his men into a skittish flight, and no target is wider than the backside of a soldier. Only a retrograde movement can save his brigade, a march in reverse as Shaw's men continue to face the enemy, firing from within their ranks as they give ground.

With the bayonet in place, loading her increasingly fouled barrel is even more of a challenge for Susha. Glancing at Sylvie to see his progress, she notices that far to his right the other regiments are beginning to peel away from the breastwork. Susha knows the implications, that at this critical point a withdrawal is under way, the hope being that her 42nd hasn't been forgotten.

The officers are at the very backs of the rear rank, while the drummers ready the cadence. Meanwhile, the other musicians and medical orderlies do what they can to carry away the wounded.

"Front rank! Load and come to the ready!"

Susha and Sylvie cap their weapons and cease firing, awaiting the next command.

"Keep your heads down! Heads down!"

"Rear rank! Load and come to the shoulder!"

In a matter of seconds Company C and the rest of the regiment are prepared to move. All the while the Confederates press on, their bullets still impacting and whizzing through the air.

"We ought not be waiting," frets Sylvie.

As well he should, for to the immediate right he spots a force of the enemy rushing to the section of the 27th Iowa's abandoned breastwork.

"Rear rank! Right shoulder shift! Arms!"

"Companies! To the reverse! March!"

As the drums tap out the steps, Susha can feel Proctor's hand upon her back, keeping her in proper alignment as they take their backward strides. In their retrograde, Susha and her comrades are becoming exposed. No longer on their knees behind the protective breastwork, the soldiers stoop in order to make themselves small, a difficult task when marching in reverse.

Regardless, Colonel Burness is of a mind to fight his way out of this imbroglio, to continue doing harm to the enemy while saving his command.

"Companies! Halt!"

"Guide to the middle!"

"Front rank! Ready! Aim! Fire!"

It's a peerless volley, a reminder to those Texans that they're fighting soldiers who belong to William Sherman and not Nathaniel Banks.

"Load and come to the ready!"

The soldiers on the front rank need no further encouragements to speed the process, and in spite of their desires to give way to panic, each holds his small patch of ground.

All the while Sylvie has been keeping his sharp eyes to the right front, watching that enemy regiment as it closes in on the 42nd.

"Right oblique," he shouts, trying to carry his message to the officers. "Watch the right."

However, his cry goes unheeded, lost in the confusion of clamor and haze.

"Rear rank! Ready! Aim! Fire!"

Another volley is loosed in the same direction as before.

With all justification, the ensuing commands are given in a brisk sequence. "Rear rank! Shoulder! Arms! Right shoulder shift! Arms! Companies! To the reverse! March!"

Others in the ranks become aware of the added danger, airing their discoveries as they maintain the retrograde. "On the right! They're coming on the right front! Right oblique!"

"Guide to the middle! Guide to the middle!"

Were Sylvie deaf, his keen eyesight would enable him still to read the lips of the Confederate officers, as they reform their lines. The 42nd's exposed state, coupled with the enemy's proximity, leaves him with no other option, no extra seconds to reconsider. With his sure, left hand, Sylvie grabs a piece of Susha's sack coat and, abandoning Bill's guide from behind, forces himself into her right front while maintaining his reversed steps.

Before Susha can level a protest or wiggle free from Sylvie's grip, the Confederate ranks roar with their flash and din. His timing flawless, Sylvie grunts in reaction, his body reeling backwards into Susha, while the crown of his jolting head delivers a blow to her nose. Then he crumbles, his buckling knees no longer willing to support his wavering frame.

Stunned, as her Enfield plops to the ground, Susha is unaware of the cries from her comrades, who must continue their retrograde. Suddenly, her world becomes silent, bereft of cracking musketry and barking commands. Yet the fog of burnt, sulphurous powder remains, it serving to isolate her from the raging battle. Susha's eyes gaze down upon Sylvie, his face lying against the ground and his limbs spread apart.

"Sylvie," she shrieks.

Coming to his aid, Susha falls upon her husband, rolling him onto his back. But her nervous hands tug at a body offering no resistance. To Susha's horror, the look Sylvie wears is one of shock, his eyes bulging open and his mouth hanging agape. It's as if he's realized all which had happened within its instant. Yet strangely, there is no agony on Sylvie's face, no suffering, for there is no pain.

As stupefied as she may be, Susha, nevertheless, cradles his head under her left arm and feels for what she knows must be a grievous wound. She needn't search far, however, for her right hand becomes coated with blood when it rests upon the middle of Sylvie's chest.

"Sylvie," moans Susha, the sudden reality of her loss evoking an upheaval of shivers.

And as if trying to comfort her husband, she struggles to arrange his arms and straighten his head, unmindful of the deadly Minie balls whizzing about. This done, Susha lies prone, pressing her tearful cheek to Sylvie's and wrapping her arms around his bloodied frame, with all intentions never to leave his side.

12 ↝ Rivers of Red

A battle might be described as a series of momenta. Armies can build strength in movement, then be slowed and halted altogether. Yet, just as sudden, one opposing force can rediscover the impetus and then sweep the field of its adversary. To do so may require pushing through the tiniest of advantages in the terrain, or to wedge a careless gap. Still, there is no greater ally to momentum than that of superior numbers at the right place, and with the gumption to use them.

So it occurs at Pleasant Hill. Before anyone can realize, the initial phase of the battle is over. Upon shifting their positions, the engaged forces leave behind the true progenies of war: those wrecked forms of modern invention and human machinery. But what's next? What is to become of that no longer serving a purpose to the continuing slaughter?

Although she may be oblivious to nearly all which surrounds, Susha can't ignore the blunt object poking at her ribs. She turns her head to reveal a pitiable, begrimed face, upon which from her nose cakes of blood have gathered. It's the buttplate of a rifle-musket gaining the attention of her crusted eyes. Even more so is the brogan next to the weapon, peculiar in that its sole is bound in place with twine, while a bulbous toe of its wearer is exposed to the air. However, quickly Susha gathers the ominous intent, in that the trousers just above this shoe isn't composed of sky blue kersey, but rather is of a crude butternut jean cloth.

"Get on your feet, Yank."

As dazed as she's become, Susha manages to look up, to see a lanky figure dressed in one of the undyed shell jackets.

"Is he alive?" asks the Johnny. "Ehh. Never you mind. He'll be tended to."

Stepping next to Sylvie's idle feet, the Confederate private compares his decaying brogans to that of the Union's. However, the size of Sylvie's is much too small for this tall Texan, and, therefore, is of no use.

Suddenly, a volley explodes nearby. It seems that during the confusion the 32nd Iowa has been left out of the retrograde, and, at the point of being surrounded, is biting back like a cornered cur. Noting the danger, the private carries out his orders with greater haste.

"Gotta get, now. Follow them two, that way." With the muzzle of his weapon, he points at two disarmed Union soldiers, who are shambling toward the Confederate rear.

Incapable of offering any resistance, Susha sits up. Still, before she gets to her feet, she tends to her husband's needs for one final and lasting time. After wiping his brow, gently, Susha sets his eyelids and closes his mouth, giving him the appearance of one in a peaceful sleep. On this field of violence, if Sylvie is to seek his rest he must do so alone, for Susha is being compelled to abandon his side. After all the years behind them and all the years which were ahead, this sudden parting is to be forever.

"Get yourself over that fence," commands Susha's captor. "Help them two out."

With that, the Texan abandons his charges, to look for more captives or, possibly, a sizable pair of brogans.

As she struggles over the breastwork, Susha sees nothing of the battle raging only a hundred yards away, nor does she sense the whirs of flying bullets. Ignoring, too, the horrific debris of Confederacy—the handiwork of her regiment—she directs herself toward the two beacons of blue just ahead. And although Susha drags along, she does catch up, for one of the soldiers is hobbled by a leg wound, while the other is at his side.

Meekly, she tugs at a chevroned sleeve.

"Potter." It's Sergeant Wilkins, trying to seek medical attention on the other side of the field, as ordered by his captor. "Give me your shoulder." Now the sergeant has two crutches, making the going almost bearable. "Are you all right?"

Susha nods her response.

A man of quick assessment, Sergeant Wilkins can see that she's endured too much. With his arm wrapped around Susha, her trembles must be pronounceable, that she's uncalmed and not relieved at having survived.

"Sylvetus is gone, isn't he?"

"Yes." Susha's reply is barely audible.

"Have no frets. I will see to it that you're sent home."

Sergeant Wilkins' long held, but unconfirmed, suspicions won't be much help to the other soldier, who himself belongs to the 27th. However, Susha's clouded mind has a hint that in her greatest moment of need, she's literally in good hands. Thus, as the three plod along, she's able to look back toward the breastwork, to where she knows Sylvie lies and where always he should be.

There must be at least forty of Shaw's men who are now prisoners. As Sergeant Wilkins and the other wounded await treatment, the Confederate sergeant in charge has the fit ones set apart. Their accoutrements confiscated, Susha and her comrades are penned under guard within a roped square. As to what is their future, these Iowans and Missourians can know only of a long confinement at Camp Ford, Texas, the march to said place commencing shortly.

Sitting against a pine tree, Susha stares at the direction where she last saw Sylvie, the resin mixing into her hatless hair. Also in view are the Union walking wounded. And although she's lost all reason for concern, she can't help but notice how Sergeant Wilkins is carrying out a vigorous conversation with his counterpart. Then he points at her, much to the Confederate soldier's demonstrated consternation.

Within a minute the Texan approaches Susha, the look on his face showing both confusion and reluctance. "Is your name Potter?"

"Yes."

"Come along."

Susha follows the soldier to where Sergeant Wilkins rests.

"Potter. Your sergeant tells me he has some peculiar misgivings. And I don't know what to make of it." Amidst the anguish and destruction of battle, the Confederate sergeant can find yet another reason to feel uneasy. "Are you? Are you a woman?"

Drained, weakened and guilt-ridden, Susha looks to the ground. "Yes."

Satisfied, Wilkins speaks up. "I told you, Sergeant."

"Yes. But what am I suppose to do?"

"She cannot remain your captive. Escort her across the lines when this battle is done. Ask your captain."

"My captain is dead," snaps the Texan. "And how am I to know she's not a man posing as a woman, to wiggle out of capture?"

An insurmountable problem perhaps, though Sergeant Wilkins may have a solution. "Sergeant, might I suggest you surrender Potter to the scrutiny of a surgeon. He can take custody. Let him turn her over to the provost and this will no longer be your affair."

Perhaps this is a fitting solution for the Texan. "Very well. Come along, Potter. Let's find us a surgeon."

As they begin to walk away, Sergeant Wilkins offers a final parting, coupled with a question. "Be sure to look after yourself. Potter? Was Sylvie your husband?"

"Yes, Sergeant."

"He was a good soldier. You have my sympathies." Then Sergeant Wilkins adjusts his manners. "Good luck, Mrs. Potter. I hope to see you back in Iowa, some day."

It takes a while to track an amenable surgeon. Happily for the sergeant, he does just that, and so is able to release his burden and rejoin his detail.

Susha, however, will have to wait, for the battle demands its toll and the surgeon is kept busy. Off to the side she sits, alone and unguided, biding her mournful time until she can be assured of her fate. This is how it always has been, others telling her how and what to do. It all changed the day she married Sylvie. Indeed, he was a better husband than all the others Susha had the occasion to observe, with his final act seeing to his wife's continuing welfare. Her face buried in her hands, she weeps without shame, the blood from her nose issuing anew and mingling with her tears.

Darkness falls, and the surgeon and his assistants continue to ply their gory trade by the light of candle lanterns. The moans and groans are given by the frantic paces of probing, cutting and stitching, only to be heightened into curdles of screams by the acts of the surgeon's saw. Without pause, one after another, the stretcher bearers bring in more victims and their varying degrees of damaged flesh and bone.

For a few seconds, the overworked surgeon studies the multiple wounds of the latest unfortunate and unconscious soldier. "That stomach wound looks fatal," he notes aloud. "Though I believe I can heal that leg." But then he thinks the better of it. "Uh-h. Best set him aside."

With her hands covering her ears and her eyes shut tightly, Susha buries herself into a crouch. Nonetheless, she can hear the cries of the wounded left out in the field, begging for a swallow of water or for the unattainable presence of a loved one. Yet even in their distress, there are the practical ones, struggling to be recognized by calling out their regiments: "Forty-second Iowa! Forth-second Iowa!" If only Susha could find sleep to relieve her of this horrible ordeal. If only her head were emptied of the visions and sounds she's encountered during this day. If only she were in that cabin by the coal bank and at Sylvie's side.

Abruptly, a hand taps Susha's shoulder. She looks up to see the surgeon.

"If you are agreeable, we could begin the examination. It ought to be brief."

Slowly, Susha comes to her feet, while behind her the surgeon's assistant turns the other way and unfurls a blanket as a screen.

"If you don't mind, unbutton your coat and pull up your shirt."

At a snail's pace, Susha follows the instructions.

To the surgeon's obvious surprise, his eyes are confronted by the physique of a female. "Yes, ma'am. Please button yourself." He turns to his other assistant. "Ash! Bring over a chair! Achem, George. Soon as we get her comfortable, I want you to find that provost captain. Tell him we have a most peculiar problem." Then the surgeon scratches his head and mutters aside. "Hard to believe, but the terms of the enemy's army have gotten more relaxed than our own. Who would have thought?"

As it happens, that captain of the provost guard is far too occupied with the accumulations of Union prisoners and Confederate fugitives. On the spot he draws up the paperwork and leaves it up to the surgeon to send Susha to Mansfield for a "further review." In reality, the captain is washing his hands of a disagreeable complication, instead, choosing to pass the responsibility onto the bureaucracy of the Department of the Trans-Mississippi.

Thus the morning finds Susha on the front seat of an ambulance, traveling up the same road as did Lee's cavalry and Franklin's infantry two days prior. For most of the trip, the scattered roadside debris of a fleeing army goes unnoticed by the passenger. However, as the ambulance draws closer to the Sabine Crossroads, the site of the Mansfield battle, negotiating the denser wreckage of the Union baggage train alerts Susha's senses. To her horror, the grounds are littered with Union dead, and for almost three miles she's exposed to the reminders of her own personal tragedy. Worse than experiencing a battle itself, this aftermath of neglected corpses in their swollen and contorted states is an unshakeable vision—a beginning of endless nightmares and ceaseless torments of guilt.

The town of Mansfield remains a flurry of activity, what with two battles fought on consecutive days. Public buildings and private homes are now hospitals, amidst streets crowded with captured wagons and supplies. In addition, commands are returning to town, to lick their wounds and await further orders.

Deposited in the middle of this is a female soldier, now a prisoner of a questionable and confused status. To say the least, with problems aplenty in Mansfield, the woes of an enemy soldier matter little. Although Susha's paperwork has been included in a dispatch sent to Shreveport, lacking an escort she must stay put.

How inappropriate, it seems, to lock away a person who has led nothing but a virtuous and industrious life. For three days Susha has endured the lone confinement in a small, empty room within the DeSoto Parish Jail, curled upon the floor with her dirty and bloody face, staring at the emptiness of a wall. And for three days she's hardly touched her boiled beef and corn coosh, taking only occasional sips of water. Lost within herself, her only thoughts are of Sylvie and how he lies unattended at Pleasant Hill. Will he ever receive a ceremony—the due of a brave and kind soul? Surely someone can avail upon himself to prepare a proper grave? However, Susha's continuing recollections of the Sabine Crossroads' open necropolis haunts this hope, her realization being that the dead of a vanquished enemy are given no precedence.

In this horrendous eternity, the nights are more dreadful than the days, in that they prohibit her walled stares. Mercilessly, another blackness overcomes Susha's room, with her drowsy eyes refusing to surrender to sleep—a most hellish of hells. No longer does her dry throat arouse a thirst, and as she shivers from the chill, her blanket remains unused. Although Susha's head may be full of memories both sweet and repeatable, it remains tormented by an overwhelming dilemma, as to how she can continue without Sylvie. The hopelessness of a permanent isolation takes hold, so that somewhere during the long and exaggerated darkness, her wants become narrowed. The only thing Susha desires is to join her husband. Now that Sylvie has left this world, no longer does she have any use for it.

Eventually, another ray of the morning sun slices through the tiny window, touching Susha's face. Though she has succumbed to a moment of sleep, the glare awakens her eyes, putting a halt to a peaceful interlude. Yet before Susha can return to her wall, her weak attentions are stolen by an approaching voice, one she recognizes as belonging to a contemptible specimen.

"For her protection, that's why." It's the jailor, muttering at someone through his perpetual quid of tobacco. "She might become a curiosity, 'round here." His keys jingle as he opens the door. "There she is. Wake up, Potter. You got a visitor."

Susha pays a hazy regard to the stranger entering her prison: a tall, bearded Confederate officer, dressed in an unusually dark frock coat. Wearing no sword, instead the man uses a cane, wounded as he must be.

"I said get yourself up, Potter!"

"That will be enough," speaks the officer firmly. "Leave us be."

Apparently, understanding the impatient tone, the jailor goes about his business elsewhere.

The officer turns around. "Frank. See if you can locate a chair."

Standing at the door is a private, of whom Susha can see is missing an arm.

"Yessir, Major."

The major looks again to Susha, and with considerable effort settles upon a knee. "Ma'am. Is your name Mrs. Sylvetus Potter?"

As to her reply, Susha is lost.

Leaning nearer, again the major attempts to draw a response. "Ma'am. Are you Mrs. Potter?"

Although wrecked and wretched as Susha has become, the major is close enough for her to read every line and curve on his face. She looks into his eyes and recognizes her reflection, her own miseries.

"Yes."

"Mrs. Potter. My name is Major Singleton. You are being remanded to my bureau. Do you understand? You are now in my custody, and I am to handle your case."

Stroking his beard, John's heart sinks as he gazes at the pitiful creature before him, struck as he is by her tragic circumstances. There's a mad rush of pathos being thrusted upon him—uncontrollable in its force and effect. And matched with this is John's dire need to find his sympathy, to give it to a cause and tender its use.

Quickly, Frank returns empty-handed. "Major. That fella won't give up a chair."

Breaking away from Susha, John struggles to his feet as his temper builds. "We shall see. Please excuse me, ma'am. Come along, Frank."

Within seconds a loud commotion emanates from another room—tense, but brief.

John returns, adjusting his revolver's scabbard, while Frank trails with chair in hand.

"Mrs. Potter, might you please have a seat."

Gently, both John and Frank help Susha into the chair.

"Allow me to offer my condolences for your loss."

In no condition to be surprised, nevertheless, Susha is, that the major knows so much of her. "Thank you."

"Would you like a cup of tea? We have the genuine article." Without waiting for a response, John sets that wheel into motion. "Frank, you saw the stove. Brew some tea. And why don't you bring along that saddlebag. Perhaps we might entice Mrs. Potter with some of Miss Smallbones' fare."

"Yessir, Major." Concerning the welfare of their charge, Frank seems as anxious as John.

"As soon as you are fit to travel, Mrs. Potter, we will ride to Shreveport. So you must eat something. I can assign you comfortable quarters and proper clothing there."

Staring at her feet, Susha nods her head in agreement.

"Thank you for understanding, Mrs. Potter. It never should have come to this. You should have been conducted across the lines at first chance. But as to your current situation, I will see to your return to Iowa."

Susha should be cheered by the prospect of someone taking a charitable interest. Yet she remains stunned by her long ordeal, and taken aback from the unexpected care of Major Singleton.

Soon, Frank returns with the saddlebag, and parts to brew the tea.

Like a keeper coaxing a newly captive creature, John manages to get Susha to nibble on one of Miss Smallbones' ginger snaps. Before long she eats three, and even starts on a hard-boiled egg when the jailor enters the room with a candle stand. Without a word he leaves it, only to return with a basin of warm water, soap and a wash cloth.

"Thank you," acknowledges John to the abused jailor. "I thought, Mrs. Potter, you may wish to clean your face. I will leave you to it."

"No." Susha is quick with a mild protest. "Don't go. Please."

"Oh. As you wish."

John's sympathies may have to struggle for space, for now Susha is reminding him that she's accustomed to the company of men. Timid as she may seem, she has, after all, a unique story that would help rebuild his inquisitive nature. However, John knows better than to pry during this delicate introduction.

"It may comfort you to know that I am an attorney. So my inclination is to treat you as my client."

Returning to the room, Frank has a large tin cup in hand. "Ma'am, it has sugar in it."

"Very good, Frank. Why don't you see to our mounts. And when you are done, come back and brew us both a cup. Perhaps, by then, Mrs. Potter would like another. We do have enough, Frank?"

"Yessir, Major."

"Excellent. We may be off in a few hours, yet."

Upon the back of the gelding, Susha's weakened condition compels her to cling to John. However, any misgivings each may harbor about their close familiarity have been cast aside by the practical manner of their travel. Still, it makes for a strange sight: a mounted officer armed with a cane, grasped by a hatless Union captive and escorted by a one-armed private.

Maintaining a slow pace, by the late afternoon they've ridden less than seven miles. During that distance, from time to time, Susha's grip lessens, only to be encouraged by John's strong right hand. Regardless, a weary person's arms can lock into place without regard, while the rhythmic gait of a steady beast and the open air are irresistible calls to slumber.

"Major." Frank beckons John's attention. "I think she's done fallen asleep."

John turns his head. "Mrs. Potter."

"Jewhillikens. She's plum out of it."

With some difficulty, John and Frank slip Susha off the gelding. But as the major cradles her in his arms and places her upon a blanket, her closed eyes acknowledge hardly a twitch.

"She does look like a woman," notes Frank, as the two men stand over. "Don't she, Major?"

"Of course. Still, she must have been a fair stamp of a soldier to have fooled her officers and comrades."

"Hard to believe she's a Yank. That she's the enemy."

"Or that we are her foes. Hmm?" John muses at his own words. "Frank, we should build a fire and remain here while she sleeps. Through the night, I hope."

It's not the sun awakening Susha on the following morning, rather it's the anger of her empty stomach. John and Frank are all too happy to fill it, cooking a stew of jerked beef, turnips and carrots. And it doesn't bother the Texans that their Iowan swallows the last of their tea, Susha's appreciation being worthy of this luxury's procurement.

Resuming their trek, miraculously, Susha finds herself gaining strength. The day is keeping its promise to be a warm one, and soon the three are down to their shirts. And to make work easier on the gelding, Susha spends some of the time atop the mare, while Frank walks alongside. It's a better pace, meaning that Shreveport should be reached around the evening hours.

Along the way John purchases a bonnet, and understanding the advantage of an inconspicuous entry into Shreveport, he deems it necessary to alter the rest of Susha's appearance. Fortunately, he knows just the place to acquire suitable attire, a farm south of town where already he has done considerable bartering.

At first, the Carters show some reluctance at inviting any sort of bluecoat into their home. However, being people of profit, soon, they find amusement with John's flagrant issuing of department promissory notes and his sprinkling of real currency. While Susha bathes away months of dirt and perspiration in her privacy, John secures an array of slightly worn, but clean and untattered garments. His job done, he relaxes on the cutaway porch with Frank and Mr. Carter, each puffing their pipes and awaiting the results.

Suddenly, emerging from the house is a soured Mrs. Carter. "Major. What am I to do with those appalling, infested Yankee clothes of hers?"

"Her soldiering days are done, Mrs. Carter. By all means, please burn them."

"My pleasure," she replies with a look of disgust.

For the most part the wait is a silent one, but when Frank excuses himself to check on the horses, Mr. Carter airs an important issue.

"What do you plan on doing with her, Major?"

"Return her to Iowa. Though there seems to be a rising number of complications."

"Such as?"

"The impossibility of contacting Banks' army. They are in full retreat." John takes a long draw from his pipe. "As to why confuses me. His forces held their own at Pleasant Hill. Routed those two divisions sent down from Arkansas."

"The devil you say."

"Those western troops of Smith's surprised them, while our boys groped toward victory."

"Umm."

"And there is Mrs. Potter's legal status. She cannot be treated as a prisoner, because our laws do not regard her a soldier. Neither can I release her as a civilian, so far away from Union-held territory." John shakes his head at yet another quandary. "I have no idea where the department's intentions lie."

"But I am happy to see you busy, Major. You look more robust."

"Yes. I should be thankful."

The front door swings open, and from it exits an appropriately clad Susha.

"Mrs. Potter. Jewhillikens," responds a returning Frank, though Susha's transformation reminds him of his manners. "Pardon me."

Indeed, it should, even if her attire is a bow to compromise. Susha's brown satinet skirt has been matched to a green, fitted bodice of a similar cloth—a fair reintroduction into civilianship. Still, though her feet are covered with a nice pair of cotton stockings, so too, do her brogans, the only items of government issue Susha is forced to retain.

"You look very becoming, Mrs. Potter," compliments John, as he stands. "Frank, we will have to do our young lady justice with a better pair of shoes."

"I wish you all the luck on that endeavor, Major," reminds Mr. Carter of the shortages.

"How is your nose, Mrs. Potter?"

"I think better, Major. It doesn't hurt as much."

"I doubt if we can avail ourselves upon a physician. They being occupied."

"I understand, Major."

"Very well. Frank, do you suppose the horses are rested?"

"Yessir, Major. I'll fetch them."

"Mrs. Potter. When he returns, I would like for you to ride with me. Sidesaddle if don't mind. And do you think it possible to keep your brogans concealed when we come into town?"

At first the request seems somewhat strange, but quickly Susha grasps the reasoning. "Yes, Major. I believe I can."

"Very good, Mrs. Potter. I know I can rely upon you."

After passing through the sentry on the outskirts of town, the trio dawdle so that they ride into Shreveport proper after dusk. Immediately, Frank takes care of the gelding and mare, leaving John and Susha at Miss Smallbones'. As they enter the front hall of the boarding house, the clanging of dinnerware can be heard from the dining room. John's timing is perfect, for now Miss Smallbones and her remaining boarders are occupied at the table. Quietly ascending the stairs, he deposits Susha into his room, and as he dares not stay alone with her, returns to the parlor.

Soon, with their duties pressing them into the night, the officers part from the dinner table, leaving their landlady unoccupied for John's stealthy approach.

"Miss Smallbones."

"Major! Such a start."

"Forgive me, but I have just returned and have something important to ask of you."

"Major?" Although she must be flattered, Miss Smallbones seems cautious.

"Please, follow me." Abruptly, John grabs a candle from the dinner table, and upon leading his landlady upstairs, knocks at his room. "May I come in, Mrs. Potter."

"Major Singleton!" responds Miss Smallbones.

John gives her a disapproving look and enters to find Susha sitting erect. "Miss Smallbones, allow me to introduce Mrs. Sylvetus Potter. Mrs. Potter has been subjected to a recent tragedy, and as a refugee of war has been placed under the bureau's care."

"Oh. I see."

"My hope is that you will allow her temporary use of my room, while I seek quarters at the bureau. Mrs. Potter kindly has agreed to assist Private Peevy and myself. To occupy her days."

It's the first Susha has heard of this. And although it sounds much like rendering aid to her enemy, she plays along.

"We had an early dinner and Mrs. Potter informed me that she is quite tired."

Her arms folded, Miss Smallbones' pointed eyes assess the situation, piercing through a demure and humbled Susha. "Well, it all seems proper. I suppose it would be fine."

"Thank you, Miss Smallbones. I knew I could rely upon your unwavering charity."

"Mrs. Potter, I hope you enjoy your stay."

"Thank you, Miss Smallbones."

It being prudent not to linger, John decides on a quick goodbye. "Very well, Mrs. Potter. I will return in the morning. Have a good night."

Yet as they leave the room, Miss Smallbones' probing nose may be picking up the scent of something a-foul. Perhaps it's Major Singleton's humbled, albeit abrupt, approach? Then again, there is Mrs. Potter herself, or more precisely, a non-native tongue that her scarce words have managed to reveal.

As for Susha, her mind is crowded by other matters. While the late hours drip away the candles, her tears for Sylvie trickle down her cheeks. Still, the flow is stanched when her thoughts veer towards Major Singleton, Susha being reminded of him by the ambrotype sitting next to the light. Although she knows nothing of Henrietta, she does ascertain the likeness' correct source. What a beautiful lady she is, thinks Susha, possessing a confident bearing, as well as a warm nature. And so it can't be helped, that the feeling evoked within is that she has Mrs. Singleton to thank for inspiring her husband's kind and caring manner.

John's night is a long one, spent reviewing the problem at hand. Then there is the melancholy, when the mere thought of Henrietta pushes him toward an incurable despair, his loneliness highlighted by the stills of the night. Only a busy day of work can bring some relief.

Regardless, with the early morning comes a certain dread, especially when determined knocks rouse John from the floor of his office.

"Major. I know you're in there."

His worst fears realized, John rights himself and dons his frock coat. But at the same moment he's struck by the speed at which the news has traveled, that busy lips are at work.

"Major Singleton. How could you do this to me?" It's Miss Smallbones, who out of respect seems to be struggling to contain her anger.

With little space to maneuver, John has no choice but to take a firm grasp of the situation. "My humble apologies, Miss Smallbones."

"That Yankee woman. Such disrepute she should bring upon my home."

"Please, Miss Smallbones," calms John. "It's not like that. Come in and have a seat."

Not unexpectedly, sitting does little to soothe. "To think she is in my home at this very moment."

"You haven't said anything to her, have you?"

"No, Major. I haven't even seen her. I came here when I first learned."

"Who told you?"

"Never you mind. What matters is that you deceived me, and that she remains in my home."

"Yes, Miss Smallbones. Of course." John takes a deep breath. "Allow me to soothe your fears about Mrs. Potter, and you may read the report sent to me. She is no camp follower. You saw her. She is but a simple farm girl who could not bear to be away from her husband. Who managed to disguise herself as a man and enlist with him." Again, he pauses. "Truth to tell, Mrs. Potter's only guilt is loyalty to her husband, which I find admirable. Do you not feel the same, Miss Smallbones?"

She looks away. "Well, I cannot say."

But although Miss Smallbones seems unswayed, John knows how to shame her. "Did you notice her nose? Swollen, as it is?"

"Yes."

"That happened when the back of her husband's head slammed into her face, the same instant he took his mortal wound. When I first saw Mrs. Potter, she had blood stains covering her uniform. Her husband's blood, for she had remained on the field protecting his corpse, until forced apart by her captors."

"Mercy."

"The poor thing spent several days in a parish jail, taking no sustenance and given no care. I fear that had she not been remanded to my custody, she would have withered away and perished."

Miss Smallbones produces a handkerchief, as a different sort of stress overtakes her brow.

"I apologize for my methods. Please do not allow my clumsiness to be a penalty to Mrs. Potter. Miss Smallbones, I ask not of your charity, but of your tolerance, until I find a way to return her to Iowa." John pauses. "You must forgive me if I have allowed my sympathies for Mrs. Potter to have found a kinship."

Perhaps more than anything, it's the last portion of his plea that moves the most.

As her pinched face opens, Miss Smallbones lets out a gentle sigh. "Very well, Major. I accept your apology. I am sure we can come to an arrangement. But I warn you, my rules must be strictly obeyed."

"Of course. And I thank you, immensely." Without shame, John seals his victory. "I should have heeded Private Peevy. He had confidence in your understanding. That your heart is too tender to have done otherwise."

"He said that?" Suddenly, Miss Smallbones' demeanor attains a little glow

"Yes."

"Really?"

The B.P.L.A. is where Susha takes her meals and bides her time. Nourished and rested, her head is clearer and better able to take in the surroundings. From Susha's standpoint, this office seems too insignificant to be a part of departmental bureaucracy—or an Iowa justice of the peace for that matter. So small are the dimensions, that in spite of sitting at opposite ends, she and John are only a few feet apart. As well, the B.P.L.A. is a place of few words, what with Frank elsewhere and the major busy with papers. Not that Susha is in need of conversation, but the awkward silence is making this day much too long when she would prefer to have them all shortened. And so Susha asks herself if she should take the risk of becoming a nuisance?

"Your wife is so pretty, Major." Softly, Susha breaks the silence.

John's response is a look of confusion. "I beg your pardon?"

"The likeness of her in your room. Is that not your wife?"

"Oh. Indeed, it is."

"Please forgive me, Major. I ought not be taking you away from your work."

"Oh, but you're not, Mrs. Potter. This really is not my business." John drops the document from his hands. "And I am finding it quite tedious."

"May I ask your wife's name?" inquires Susha with a timid smile.

"Henrietta," returns John with a grin of his own.

"I knew she would have a pretty name. It fits her, don't you think?"

"Very much. Indeed." Susha's need to be inquisitive enlivens John, providing the inspiration to seek a diversion. "Mrs. Potter, is there anything you need? Any item I might acquire for you?"

"Oh? I don't know, Major."

Up to now, John's inclination has been to shelter Susha, to keep her out of view for obvious reasons. Nonetheless, the benefits of the sun and a mild breeze might outweigh the risks of a hostile encounter.

"Then perhaps I might interest you in a stroll."

"I should like that."

Pleased, John rises to his feet. However, before he takes his cane in hand, he makes certain that his Colt is displayed prominently at his side.

As they step onto Third Street, it's Susha who continues the conversation. "Major. Could you tell me more about your wife?"

Without hesitation John replies, "Of course, Mrs. Potter. I would be delighted."

He proceeds to lead Susha through what he recognizes as the least active neighborhoods of Shreveport. And all the while, John regales a surprisingly interested Susha with his tales of Henrietta.

"My Henrietta can recite Scott from heart, she a devoted admirer. Are you familiar, Mrs. Potter?"

"Only just, Major. I never have had the time to read him."

"Well, if you would like, I might locate something of his for you."

"I would, Major. Thank you. But I don't think I can read those French books like Mrs. Singleton."

"Neither can I, Mrs. Potter. Walter Scott it is."

Before long, their meander takes them to the riverfront, an idle place when compared to normal times.

"Still the same as when I last saw it," observes John. "A week ago."

Susha gazes at the waters. "My regiment came up the river, Major. All the way passed Alexandria. We had to wait there for the gunboat *Eastport*. It got wedged into the falls there. Was not nearly as much water down there as here." She shakes her at that particular ineptitude. "I don't see how they possibly could get that Goliath across those falls again. It might cork up the river for good, I fear."

John smiles at Susha's summation, that the culmination of this ill-conceived campaign could come down to too little water and too much boat. He also finds himself intrigued, curious as to why this modest young lady would be so willing to enter into such a hellish conflict.

"Mrs. Potter, would I be too forward to ask you to tell me something about yourself?"

'Oh no, Major." Susha is surprised that a man of such stature would be interested. "What do you want to know?"

"Well, for instance, your given name."

"Elizabeth. But everyone calls me Susha. And everyone calls my husband Sylvie." She pauses, her eyes returning to the river's flow. "We grew up together. Known each other most of our lives. Sylvie knows everything there is about farming. More clever than farmers twice his age. And he's always eager to learn more. Sylvie's never afraid of hard work. Never."

"I admire men of such caliber."

"He would like you too, Major." As Susha takes a breath, her lungs sputter and her eyes begin to pool.

Ever-resourceful, John produces Henrietta's daisy handkerchief and takes it upon himself to apply it to Susha's moistened cheeks.

"What is to become of my poor Sylvie?"

Again, John is quick with his response. "Mrs. Potter, there now. Your husband has been looked after. You may not know that your army regained its lost ground. That they fought the battle to a draw. It is a certainty your husband was given a decent burial before they withdrew. Without a doubt, he now lies at peace alongside his comrades."

"You think so, Major?"

"Yes, I do, Mrs. Potter. And I believe that his last wish would be to see to your safety. That you return to your family."

Once more, Susha gazes upon the water, as John continues to blot away the odd tear.

"It looks redder now than when we first came up it. The river."

"You could be correct, Mrs. Potter. It can change overnight."

Into this river of red Susha's attentions become fixed, as slowly she composes herself.

"Mrs. Potter." Understanding that they've had enough of a stroll, John makes a proposal to help bolster her spirits—at least medicinally. "Why don't we return to the bureau, so that I may offer a drop of brandy."

"Thank you, Major. That would be nice."

With that John extends his left arm, accepted by Susha's hands, as the two reverse their stroll.

Soon, they return to the office, and John wastes no time to pour a small brandy into a teacup.

"Morning, Mrs. Potter." It's Private Peevy, returning from an errand.

"Frank, may I speak with you." John's insistence is abrupt. "Outside."

"Major?"

Seemingly worried that he may have done something wrong, Frank is reassured as soon as they are out of Susha's earshot.

"Frank. Listen. Do not mention Mrs. Singleton's passing to Mrs. Potter. I wish not to upset her any further. Speak of my wife only with the living."

"I understand, Major."

But just as suddenly, John's memory is stirred, and he pokes his head through the doorway. "Mrs. Potter. Private Peevy will remain here with you, while I attend to that matter of which we spoke. I believe I just recalled where I might locate some of those books."

Thus Susha enters upon a routine of an unknown duration. And although it may not be of her making, there certainly is a benevolence to it, her two keepers too willing to see to her comfort.

While Shreveport is a prolific manufactory of rumor, it also serves as a magnet for news of the genuine article. John has learned that his old cavalry unit, Parson's Brigade, has returned from Texas, and even engaged the enemy. Disbelieved until confirmed, it seems his former comrades not only participated in a battle against Adm. Porter's armored fleet on the Red River, but also won the field, as well as the water.

Shortly thereafter, there occurs the appearance of Richard Taylor's infantry, the anxiety for the people of Shreveport being that Banks is hot on their tail. In reality, these soldiers are being sent to Arkansas, to what John figures is an overwhelming response to a minor threat. For the time being, Taylor pursues Banks' larger force, but with little more than cavalry.

Notwithstanding, there is some disconcerting information of which John keeps from Susha. In his great rush to retreat to the Red River after Pleasant Hill, Banks not only abandoned his wounded to the mercy of his enemy, but his dead as well. For Sylvie, there would not have been an honorable burial, the likelihood being that his body was tossed into a mass grave at the expediency of a Confederate detail.

With this news, John's determination to accommodate Susha strengthens, to make the B.P.L.A. as recuperative a setting as possible. To be sure, while Iowa beckons, she needs to be kept busy and cheerful, her active stay being his greatest concern.

Before a new dawn, John stands alone at Miss Smallbones' front entry. But his wait doesn't last when the door swings open to reveal his charge.

"Good morning, Mrs. Potter."

"Morning, Major."

"I trust your night went well?"

"Yes. I believe so, Major. I think I slept nicely."

"Splendid, Mrs. Potter. And I trust your husband was watching over you. Proud that you are keeping up his good name."

"Thank you."

Susha closes the door behind her and the two begin their stroll to the B.P.L.A.

"Mrs. Singleton would be delighted too. I only wish I could send for her to offer more suitable company."

"No, Major. Not in her condition. Besides, you and Frank are the best company I could ever hope for."

"That is nice of you to say so. Clumsy and inept as we can be."

"This is not truthful at all, Major."

"Well, I am happy you feel that way, Mrs. Potter. But I do apologize that I cannot be more precise concerning the length of your stay."

"Major, that hardly bothers me. I am in good hands. This much I know."

"But my fear is that your days will repeat themselves, Mrs. Potter."

"They ought not."

John agrees with a nod. "By the way. I have discovered a path for you to post a letter home. Though you yourself may likely outrace any letter you send to Iowa."

"Almost surely."

The sun begins to break as John's thoughts find a pause.

"Mrs. Potter, are you familiar with the game of chess?"

"A little."

"Frank and I play it often. Perhaps we can teach you?"

"I would love that."

"Splendid. But I must warn you. Frank can be a cunning devil. As for me, a weaker commander there cannot be. I really only see chess as a centerpiece for good conversation."

"That sounds first-rate."

"Honestly, I am looking forward to learn more about Iowa farming. The variety of what you raise. It is astounding. But somehow, I find myself even more curious about that friend of yours. From Arkansas. That snaggletooth fellow you mentioned."

"Oh, yes. Private Hill." Susha smiles her enthusiasm. "What I know and what I heard."

"Precisely. Tell me more, if you please."

"Certainly. Hmm? Let me see..."

And so it's on to a discussion of Union infantry and Confederate cavalry tactics, which may lead to mutual lessons of German, with a chance to reflect on Bible studies and medieval history and, of course, to compare the incompetence and shortcomings of army officialdoms.

Ten days have passed and, still, Susha resides in Shreveport, her status remaining unresolved. But at least her nose has healed, although the small bump on its bridge looks to be permanent. Meanwhile, Susha bides her time nicely, with John being successful at keeping her occupied, as well out of public fascination

"These here socks are the best I've ever had, Miss Susha. Why, those fingers of yours must be the most cleverest that ever took to knitting."

"Thank you, Frank."

"Thank you, Miss Susha."

"If you can find me some cloth, I could sew for you. Possibly a uniform."

"Landsakes, Miss Susha! You would do that for me!"

"Of course, Frank."

"Miss Susha, you are the best."

There are reliable reports that Banks' forces have been able to fight their way back to Alexandria, where they must wait for Porter's fleet and its navigational difficulties. Whereas recently the fears among the citizens of Shreveport had been for their personal safeties, now they've shifted to the real danger of Banks' army slipping away from its destruction.

Aware of this frustration, John's growing anxiety is that this community's voice will turn against his efforts. Because of his rank within officialdom, he's privy to certain information not boding well for his client. It seems that during their retreat, "Whiskey" Smith's men have been careless with the torch, taking out their thwartations upon the innocent countryside. To what degree, it's hard for John to ascertain, except that he has learned of the timely arrival of Texas cavalry rescuing Natchitoches from a sinister conflagration. He knows all too well that his ears are only a day or two ahead of the general public's, and that, soon, the need for retribution may clamor upon the convenient.

The following day moves quietly for the bureau, with a busy John reading a set of fresh orders, trying to digest the unwritten vagueness and implications.

Meanwhile, Susha begins stitching together a pair of trousers, cut from a piece of butternut wool procured by a resourceful Frank.

It's the beneficiary of her skills who breaks the hush, rushing through the door. "Major!"

"What is it, Frank?"

"It's the *Eastport*! It's done struck a torpedo and has sunk fast!"

Be this true, the news for the people of the Trans-Mississippi is celebratory. However, before John can share the joy, he must consider the implications concerning Banks' exit from the Red River country.

On the other hand, there's Susha, who shakes her head at the *Eastport's* rumored fate. "Tsk, tsk, tsk," she remarks, before resuming her sewing.

Returning to the work at hand, over and over John reads his orders, ringing out every letter of content, which does little to soothe the confusion. There remains but one option, that being to consult a trusted and occasional associate.

Leaving Susha under Frank's supervision, soon John finds himself at the home of Mr. Hey, who himself is doing the greater portion of listening.

"As you can see, my orders are implicit in that I am to ride south and gather evidence of the enemy's deprivations concerning private property. But as to what I am to do with Mrs. Potter during my absence, they remain vague.

"I concur."

"My fear is of those in the department who wish to make use of her predicament. Or I should say, the matter pertaining to her sex. Perhaps display her as a sample of Union vulgarity. Something of the sort."

"It may be that your efforts, thus far, have delayed such."

“These are the third set of confused orders I have received. And the most incontrovertible.”

“Hmm?” Mr. Hey then looks through his desk. “Major, you look as if you could use a sip.”

“I have no doubts that I do. Thank you.” As Mr. Hey pours the whiskey, John continues. “My tolerance for this shilly-shally is spent. All I know is that Mrs. Potter needs to be home, among her family.” He takes a breath. “She is a pleasant and virtuous girl, you know. Kind and resourceful. At this very moment she’s tailoring a uniform for my private.”

“The devil you say.”

“I don’t mind confessing that I have a special interest concerning her welfare.”

“I’ve sensed that, Major. And I commend you. But you most definitely are at an impasse.”

“I was afraid your conclusion would be the same as mine.”

“Well-l-l? A conclusion?” Hey’s eyes turn sly. “I should not be so hasty.”

“I don’t understand.”

“Come now, Major. Do you believe justice is exclusive within the boundaries of our profession? Does the law blanket every right and expose every wrong?”

“Hardly.”

“Then why should you allow the law and its entanglements to impose this particular injustice?”

John is shocked to hear these words from such a respected attorney. Yet at the same instant, his esteem for Mr. Hey reaches new heights.

“Major, I have come to estimate you as a man of action. If so, then I urge you to take it. Besides, your reputation is such that it should withstand the blow.”

“Yes.” With a resolved look, John makes up his mind. “But damn my reputation. And damn the law.”

A crucial letter John has composed, entrusting it to Frank for delivery to Francis Simmons. Within it is an offer, which should come as a shock to the refugee planter. Just as important, John has included a brief outline to his scheme and of what he believes is sufficient funds. Also vital, to see to Frank's security John has given him a functional, short-barreled shotgun, a weapon made surplus by the recent largesse of Banks' fleeing army. Allowing for Mr. Simmons' cooperation, John calculates that Frank's trip should require three days, meaning that his return is imminent.

"I sure hope these trousers and jacket fit him," airs Susha, yet again, as she finishes her touch.

Still, she knows that something is afoot—certainly to her benefit. Since on this afternoon the major is spending more time at the door than behind his desk, Susha realizes that the hour is near.

Unable to enjoy his pipe and brew, John feels the need to seek a more calming diversion. "Mrs. Potter, I have become offended by this poor excuse for coffee. Might a brandy interest your cup?"

"Please do, Major."

Upon emptying the vile contents of both cups onto the street, John replenishes them with a more refined libation.

"Thank you, Major."

With his pipe and intoxicant in hand, John lingers over Susha while she works. "Frank will be thrilled when he sees his new uniform."

The wafts of tobacco smoke descend upon Susha, bringing about another craving. But although she's witnessed several local women partake, themselves, she deems it unwise to beg the major's indulgence, as surely he's accustomed to Henrietta's better habits. Susha's sip of brandy will have to suffice.

"Please tell me more about Buena Vista, Mrs. Potter."

However, before Susha can boast again of the virtues of Iowa soil, John becomes distracted by the recognizable clip-clops of a particular mare.

"Rather, might you contain that thought, Mrs. Potter. I believe you may be on your way home, shortly."

"Landsakes. Whatever do you mean, Major?" Because her sewing rests upon her lap, Susha must strain to peek.

"You shall see in a minute's time," smiles John, as he steps beyond the door. "Frank! Come inside and bring her with you!"

Susha expects Frank. But that she hears of a woman in his

company brings a shock, especially since this relates to her freedom. Then there's the bray of a mule, thus adding more to Susha's confusion.

"How was your trip, Frank?"

"It went just like you hoped, Major." Frank enters the office. "Evening, Miss Susha. How you been?"

"Fine, thank you." Although Susha may be happy of Frank's safe return, her attention stays fixed to the door, and upon whomever is about to follow.

"Never mind about that, Eugenia. Tend to that later and come inside."

"Yes, Massa Major. Don't need to be fussing. I's a-coming."

Yet another surprise for Susha, that the major's worries of late seem to be over a slave.

"Mrs. Potter. This is your servant, Eugenia," introduces John, as Francis Simmons' former cook enters the room. "Eugenia. This is your new mistress. Miss Susha."

Even understanding that "servant" is often used as the less harsh of terms, the word "mistress" leaves no ambiguity. What's unnerving is that Susha finds it being applied to herself.

But before John can explain, Eugenia has her own protest. "Lordy, she don't look like no mistress to me."

"Never mind, Eugenia. Take that chair and sit next to Miss Susha. Frank, shut the windows and door, while I light some candles."

"Yessir."

As they shuffle about the room, Susha sits astonished at her conscription into peculiar institutionalism.

Eugenia seats herself by her new mistress, after which John begins to address them. But aware of the cook's stubborn nature, he decides to make his sentiments plain.

"Eugenia. I want you to understand that your freedom depends on helping Mrs. Potter reach Vicksburg. Do not mind me and I will send you back to Master Simmons. And he will put you to work in the fields."

Eugenia looks away, as she considers the affront. "I be doing your biddin', Massa Major. But I does so out of the goodness of my heart. For Miss Susha here."

Although bewildered, at least Susha knows something about

gratitude, as she smiles her thanks at her "servant."

"Very well, Eugenia. Then I commend you."

With a mighty nod she crowns her triumph, and then turns to Susha with a smile of her own.

"I take it, Frank, that Eugenia knows something about our plot."

"As much as me, Major."

"Then, Mrs. Potter, perhaps I should bring you to light. First, let me apologize for taking the liberty of securing Eugenia on your behalf. You should not be offended, this being a formality. Eugenia knows the road to Vicksburg and upon reaching the safety of Union forces, you will grant her freedom. And she may join her family there."

"Oh. I see." Susha's enthusiasm is subdued, if only because of the stunning news.

"This is also why I had Frank purchase a mule, to carry the two of you to Vicksburg. I have papers to prepare. A passport. A letter of introduction to be given to the first Union officer you encounter. There are other preparations. But I believe in two or three days' time, you and Eugenia should be ready to part."

"This is all so sudden."

"Yes, Mrs. Potter. But I did not want to lift your hopes only to have them dashed. Perhaps it was wrong of me not to have kept you informed."

"Of course not, Major. You were very considerate."

"Excellent. Eugenia, do you think you can lead Miss Susha to Master Simmons' old home?"

"You knows I can, Massa Major. With my eyes shut and my ears full of cotton."

"Frank. Take care of the mounts. When you return, I have to approach Miss Smallbones on a matter, and then we can have dinner." John lets out a sigh of relief. "Mrs. Potter, I believe this affair is about to be resolved."

Thus the instructions begin, as the B.P.L.A. alters into a classroom of sorts. As well, it's to become a warehouse of accumulated foodstuffs, documents, funds and gear, enough for a trip John figures will last six to seven days. But as Susha is a veteran of two campaigns, he has all the confidence that she can complete the journey. As for Eugenia, John suspects that a march of manumission and reunion is incentive enough for her to conquer greater navigations, much less a trip across a small state.

13 ⥲ "Broken-Hearted, I'll Wander, Broken-Hearted, I'll Remain"

Citing blame and excuse-making are frequent occupations for those commanders in retreat. The truth is, a campaign gone awry becomes fertile ground for pointing fingers—the last, desperate defense of failed ambitions and tainted reputations.

Incredibly, even their pursuers will play at the same sort of contest. Whereas a single, resolute mind could annihilate the invading enemy, and with the shock create political havoc throughout the North, instead the native force is dividing unto itself.

At least Shreveport can breathe easy, the threat of harm having turned to the opposite direction, upon Alexandria, where Banks lingers for Porter's fleet's downstream struggle. But as anxious as the Union forces are to evacuate the Red River country, and as keen as their foe is to bury them in it, events are at a standstill. Strange as it may seem, Richard Taylor's stripped army is for all practical purposes laying siege to Nathaniel Banks' "campaigning garrison."

With the preparations behind them, the dash for the freedoms of two begins in earnest. The first leg of the journey is to Minden, thirty miles east of Shreveport—under the escort of John and Frank. It's here that proper accommodations have been secured, as well as up to date intelligence concerning the road ahead. But Minden is also where Susha will have to part from her patrons, for John and Frank's orders demand already their presence far to the south.

Morning has arrived and things are moving with haste. After an informal and rushed breakfast, John goes through his final instructions, as he and Susha sit upon the hotel porch.

"Your papers should satisfy all persons. I cannot stress enough that you should guard them with your life."

"I will, Major."

"And do not rely solely upon Eugenia's bearings. Use the map and information I wrote. Remember, you own Eugenia. Treat her as such in front of strangers. And do not forget, I altered your age to twenty-five."

"Yes, Major."

"Speak as little to others as possible. Your talk has no flaws, while those you may encounter have little but. Oh, and if you were to display a tobacco habit, you certainly would be mistaken for a native." John is a bit embarrassed at this suggestion. "Take no offense."

"Of course not. Perhaps I should give it a try."

Upon reaching into his frock coat, John's demeanor turns more somber when he reveals John Gaunt's pepperbox. "Mrs. Potter, I believe you capable. This was loaned to me by a friend. But I doubt he would mind if I transferred its care to you."

For Susha, the offer of a weapon is a surprise.

"Remember, there is a degree of lawlessness out there. Producing this pistol, you might prevent such."

"I see."

"Always keep it on your person. In your haversack with your papers. You only need to point and pull the trigger. But use both hands, as it may chain-fire. Several barrels may fire at once."

She nods her understanding.

"It is loaded, but the hammer rests on an empty barrel."

"Thank you, Major. I will feel safer."

"Then I believe I have said all I can. Except that you should sell the mule when you reach Vicksburg. To pay for your passage."

Scratching his head, John searches for an item or two that he may have neglected. But while he can find little else to say, there remains much which needs to be aired. Although at one time utter strangers, if not sworn foes, three weeks of constant company have altered formality into friendship. Now, Susha and John are facing an end this.

"I do wish I could have met your wife, and her family."

"And I yours. Perhaps, some day, I may have reason to ascend the Mississippi."

Although Susha knows better, she allows herself to relish the prospect. "Oh, Major. That would be wonderful. And please bring your Henrietta."

John smiles at her enthusiasm. "Frank should be here soon with the mounts." He pauses. "Mrs. Potter?"

"Yes, Major."

"May I ask if you decided on your plans for Iowa?"

"I cannot say as yet."

"If I may be so bold, might I suggest that you not return to your parents. Mrs. Potter, your recovery has been remarkable, but I fear their home would be a difficult transition. They may lack the proper sympathy for one who has experienced as much as you."

"Yes," sighs Susha, at what she's come to dread.

"Perhaps you might impose yourself upon your brother-in-law and his wife. From what you have related, he holds a portion of responsibility."

"Yes. I ought to do that, Major. Eliza and I are chums, don't you know."

"It should make for a comforting setting. For all of you."

"It will," agrees a smiling Susha, who then pauses. "Major? Will you return to Bastrop?"

John ponders the question, his thoughts diverted to his profoundly lost future. Yet also he considers Susha, of how she's surviving her ordeal, finding hope on the unforeseeable horizon.

"Yes. Bastrop is where I always should be."

"I hope, Major, that you will be careful. Promise me to stay away from the fighting, and return to Henrietta as soon as possible." There's a genuine trepidation in Susha's voice.

"Yes, Mrs. Potter. I will return to Henrietta. That you can be assured."

"And take care of Frank too. Please, Major?"

At that moment, Private Peevy approaches in his new shell jacket and trousers, walking with the saddled mounts, and accompanied by Eugenia atop the mule.

"Seeing to Frank's safe future will be my utmost pledge."

The exodus continues, but instead of parting from Susha and

Eugenia, John and a puzzled Frank tag along—unexpectedly as travelers four, rather than two and a mule. Nothing is made mention of this, even after a couple of miles, until at last, Frank seeks to clarify.

"Major, when are we turning back? We are suppose to?"

With a pained grin, Susha looks to John. "Major, I would feel guilty if I caused you to derelict your duty."

John brings his mount to a halt, as do the others.

"Maybe the time has come for us to say goodbye," continues Susha.

"You may be correct, Mrs. Potter." Of course, it's the inescapable behind John's reluctance.

Susha's pulls come from two directions, as well. "You're such a kind man, Major. You and Frank, both."

"You're a fine person, too, Miss Susha," speaks Frank. "We surely will miss you."

"It was such fortune to fall into the hands of two kindly gentlemen. I shall always think of you fondly."

A sad silence takes command, as if trying to lengthen the moment. Nevertheless, John is the officer present, as opposed to a senseless interlude.

"Eugenia. You need not run away from Miss Susha. Your freedom is coming, soon enough. All legal."

"You know I won't, Massa Major," she answers from the back of the mule.

"The two of you will need one another."

"Eugenia and I have been getting along very fine, Major. There should be no problems."

"Very well." John doffs his hat and backs his gelding a couple of steps. "It has been my pleasure, Elizabeth Potter. Susha. I wish you nothing but safe travel and future prosperity." With that, John encourages the mule with a slap to its rump.

"Give my regards to Mrs. Singleton," bids Susha, as the mule scampers beneath her.

"That I will," replies John, only to whisper to himself. "That I will."

While Susha and Eugenia ride eastward, the two Texans slowly turn their mounts to the opposite direction. His body twisted on his saddle, John keeps his eyes toward his former charges, up to the moment when, eventually, they become a speck upon the distance.

"God, I pray she comes to no harm," he mutters, as he rights himself forward and kicks his gelding into a trot. "God, I pray."

Not a word is spoken on the return to Shreveport, and not a wink is slept when, finally, John reclaims his room and bed. Although he's given his best to one cause, there do remain others.

The morning finds John at Mr. Hey's.

"I must congratulate you on your fine bluster, Major."

"Thank you."

"Before those who stood in your way learn of your flank, you shall be well south. You need not worry, Major. The young lady's absence soon will become a forgotten concern."

"That scarcely bothers me, Mr. Hey. My only concerns lie with her."

"Then I say your client did well to retain your services."

John shrugs away the compliment.

"When will you depart?"

"Almost within the hour. Which is the main reason for my visit."

"What can I do, Major?"

Producing a scribbled paper, John explains himself. "My intentions are plain. But I should say I am asking you to execute my property. Should I not return."

"Major. I see no likelihood in that."

"As do I, Mr. Hey. But one can never dispel the chance."

"Of course."

"I believe all my creditors have been satisfied. But were there any claims, my property here in Shreveport will suffice. Any items remaining should be given to Private Peevy. And as far as what I own in Texas, that would belong to my sister-in-law and her husband, Captain and Mrs. William Shackelford of Bastrop."

"This all seems straightforward," accepts Mr. Hey.

"Thank you, Mr. Hey. Thank you for being a good friend."

Since the B.P.L.A. will travel onto a scorched earth with

supply from a commissary speculative, it needs to procure more provisions. Now, as the two Texans are packed and ready to depart from Shreveport, John is in no mood for delay. Still, there is a source where he might be able to attain foodstuffs on quick notice, though one he would just assume avoid.

"Miss Smallbones. Before I leave, once again I would like to thank you for your understanding," approaches John.

Sitting upon her rocker on the kitchen porch, Miss Smallbones plucks away at a young rooster. "I cannot say I am unhappy she left us. And that servant of hers. I will never understand that, Major."

"But did you not at least find Mrs. Potter charming?"

"We never exchanged words."

Although John may be appalled, he's not surprised by Miss Smallbones' obstinacy. "I see."

"What can I do for you, Major?" Her tone is impatient.

Pressed for time, John has no choice but to prey upon his landlady's weaknesses. "Miss Smallbones. Private Peevy and I are within minutes of departing southward. To what hazards I cannot say, except that we are certain to run short of rations."

"That is a shame," she notes, while continuing her de-feathering.

"Indeed."

"How then do you propose to remedy your situation, Major?"

Shamelessly, with a look of submission, John offers his entreaty. "Miss Smallbones? May I interest you?"

No doubt, it's worth a consideration on her part, requiring only a small investment. "Very well." As Miss Smallbones rises to her feet, the feathers upon her apron sprinkle to the porch. "Here, Major." She hands over the rooster. "Finish this, while I see what I can spare."

Moments later, at the front of the house, Frank awaits upon his mare with his shotgun slung at his left side. "Jewhillikens, Major," he remarks, as he spots John with a sack in hand. "How'd you get all this?"

"I had to work for it," he answers, with a look of disgust. "Simple as that."

A burning sun beats down upon the road to Monroe. Said town is a lofty goal, for not only is it east of a definable halfway point, beyond it the chances of encountering a Union force will increase with each mile. Nevertheless, Monroe remains many miles away, and Susha understands that the mule must be spared. For at least a couple of hours, she and Eugenia are afoot.

"You means to say, Miss Susha, they ain't got no negro peoples in Iowa?"

"Never have I seen one."

"Lordy. Don't tell me your peoples don't like us negroes?"

"Yes. But don't feel slighted. There are plenty of Iowans you would not like, yourself."

Eugenia giggles. "There sure be plenty of us negroes, too, that always grinds my gizzard."

There aren't too many miles before Eugenia's bare feet give out, so accustomed they are to the kitchen floor. Soon, the two remount the mule, both comfortably astride with Susha at the reins.

"Landsakes. How can a day in May be so hot?"

"Gets more painful hot than this, Miss Susha."

"All the more reason to return to Iowa. And for you to get in the shade of your loved ones."

"That Iowa of yours sure must be all paradise. They wanting to keeps us negroes from pleasuring in it."

"It all seems selfish, doesn't it?"

"You ain't that way, Miss Susha. I can hardly tell you even being a married woman. Most of them acting all huffy-like."

Concerning the compliment, Susha is at a loss.

"You be getting you a new husband in Iowa, Miss Susha?"

Although innocent enough, for Susha it's a shuttering question.

Her hands grasping her mistress' waste, Eugenia can sense her ache. "Miss Susha. Something wrong?"

"No Eugenia. No. There's not much sense in getting a new husband. I would be unable to find one as first-rate as my Sylvie. Another marriage would likely be a lifetime of letdowns."

"Umm. I see what you mean. But I's thinking, since I's about to be free, I want to get me a husband first thing. Miss Susha, you think you can tell me how I can get me a good man?"

"Of course, Eugenia. Hmm? Let me see..."

The same sun has been blistering elsewhere. After three days' travel, John and Frank find themselves south of Natchitoches in a land known as Rigolet Du Bon Dieu. As the two Texans discover, what was once a region of plantations and prosperous farms is now one of charred ruins and unsupported chimneys, and of bloated livestock. Hardly a family has been spared, for even the freemen of mixed blood and the slaves of less complicated lineages have had their houses and cabins destroyed. To John's growing dismay, he's learning that a defeated and retreating army knows no limits to its capabilities.

It's up to the B.P.L.A. to help document these wanton depredations. Everywhere John and Frank go, the hated name of A.J. Smith is exposed as the principle culprit, with his soldiers of the Army of the Tennessee having performed their baneful deeds with a certain fervor. The best they are able to do is record eyewitness accounts, evidence as it is: of a red-headed sergeant from the 58th Illinois, who led a detail of pillage and arson, of a tall, black-bearded corporal from the 14th Iowa, who robbed the pockets and purses of individuals, of two German-speaking brothers from the 89th Indiana, who bayonetted every pig and cow at hand, and of many more similar incidents.

The B.P.L.A.'s task is daunting, with John's personal loss vanishing among the tragedies before him. Now, other disquieted feelings do their bidding, and the more he chronicles their sources, the greater the outrages fuel his requisite for justice. A.J. Smith and his men, along with the rest of Banks' army and Porter's stranded fleet, remain at Alexandria. And as that town is only a day's march away, John is anxious to finish his work on Rigolet Du Bon Dieu.

In splendid partnership, Susha and Eugenia continue their journey. As it happens, a mistress and her servant riding upon a mule make for an inconspicuous sight in these parts, especially after Susha acquires a couple of pipes. Fortunately, the going has been without incident, and now that Monroe is to the rear, it should be very much downhill.

The routine is to make an evening bivouac away from the towns and settlements, a practice of which Susha is expert and Eugenia is adopting. On this particular morning, a distant rooster awakens the former private, though she waits for the second round of craws before she rouses herself. It's still pitch dark and the air remains cool as Susha replenishes the remnant embers of the campfire. Breakfast will be the last of the bacon and some related corn coosh, prepared by the time Eugenia welcomes the day.

Quickly, the meal is devoured and the fire smothered, with Susha tending to the dirty pan, scouring it clean with sandy soil and a magnolia leaf. The sun is barely up, and she's satisfied that they'll be off to an early start. In fact, so eager is Susha, that already she has her haversack of documents strapped upon her shoulder.

Thorough as she is, Susha's eyes are fixed to the task at hand as she calls aloud. "Eugenia, bring up the mule. I am about ready." There's no reply. "Eugenia?"

Susha turns her head to face what she believes is some sort of confusion. Instead, what confronts her is much worse, stomach-churning in that her greatest fear materializes.

Standing at the edge of camp are two men of military age, their morning call having been muffled by the dew and lacking a social tone. The tall, straw-hatted man nearest to Susha has a muzzle-loading carbine dangling from his side, indicating that he's an unhorsed former cavalryman, while the other wears nothing atop his balding head, and as well, seems to be unarmed. In addition, sitting in submission behind, as if guarding the rear, is their short, miserable cur. Shoddy and indifferent in their clothing, and covered with cakes of greasy dirt, these two, long ago, must have discarded any unit affiliation in trade for a freer, if not lawless, way of life.

In a flash, Susha abandons her crouch, while Eugenia stands by the mule in a frozen silence.

"Looky what we got here, Wilburn," declares the straw-hatted one.

"Don't know what to make of it, Sid," replies his high-nasally accomplice, as he stares at the mule and the possessions it carries. "Got no menfolk with them, but got a fine-looking animal."

"My words to the letter," agrees Sid, his open smile revealing great gaps between his dark, greedy teeth. "Yessiree, Wilburn. It sure ain't wise to be traveling this road without no escort." He motions with his hand for his cohort to look over the mule, while he steps toward Susha.

Regardless, she's quick to recognize the danger, and with her haversack at her side, she's able to do something about it. Holding her ground in the face of this menace, Susha pulls free the pepperbox pistol and points it, thus reversing the threat in one fail swoop.

"Take another step and suffer a chain-fire!" she warns.

Taken aback by the sudden abuse, Sid stops in his tracks, his head appearing to race through its options. The unintended tendencies of a pepperbox are well-known, that several shots from its barrels can discharge at once. Yet although Sid may understand the perils at such close range, he should know nothing of the woman behind the weapon. Is she, in fact, too afraid and is all bluff?

"Let that sling slip over your head! I want to see that carbine on the ground, you goddam son-of-a-bitch! That cartridge box too!"

Susha's forefinger begins its slow but decisive tug, negating any want for Sid to hesitate.

"Simmer down, missy," he declares, as, cautiously, he disarms himself. "Me and Wilburn's just funnin' with you, is all."

"Back away from your carbine!" Then Susha turns to her other adversary. "You! Join him!"

"Do as she says, Wilburn," begs an increasingly nervous Sid. "She's got no sense of humor."

Soon, both of Susha hands hold forth a deadly firearm, with the two careless bushwackers forced face down upon the ground. Try as they might, no cajoling or conniving can sway her from an uncompromising stance. Her blood up, now that Susha has gained the upper hand, she's in no hurry to lose it.

"Eugenia. Find something to bind their hands and feet." So that at least Sid understands she means business, Susha touches the top of his skull with the muzzle of the cocked carbine. "You so much as twitch and I will scatter your goddam brains. Understand?"

"Yes, ma'am."

Although she may be fidgety, Eugenia manages to bind the bushwackers' hands to feet, topping the process by losing their boots into the thick woods.

All the while the captives plead with their captors, bemoaning their fears of leaving behind loved ones and those who are dependent.

Notwithstanding, Susha sees fit to silence further protests, gagging the two without mercy. "How many widows and orphans have you two made?" she sneers.

Curiously, the bushwackers' mongrel has taken a passive stance, as if contemplating its prospects.

"What you gonna do with them, Miss Susha?"

"I can hardly say, as yet," she replies, the carbine pointed at Sid's wincing face. Then she addresses her sheepish quarry. "In case you are wondering, Sid. I have killed. And they were better men than you."

A stillness ensues, as if that moment of a final decision is mired in hesitancy. However, the mood to tarry dissolves, as Susha finds the urge to speed a goodbye. Laid open for this is Sid's vulnerable side, which is about to feel the brutal brunt of Susha's sharp brogan.

"Uhh!" he reacts from the loss of wind and the crack of a rib.

"I don't want to risk going to hell over these two," explains Susha of her mercy. "We should leave, Eugenia." Before she steps away, however, she delivers a final warning. "Understand my words. If I ever see your ugly faces again, I will take that risk."

Without wasting another minute, the young ladies mount and kick their mule into a swift withdrawal, followed by the mongrel.

It's nearly thirty minutes before Susha slows the mule, with Eugenia retaining most of her shock.

"Lordy, Miss Susha! You sure was a wildcat back there! I never would have thunk it! And so cool in front of them bushwackers!"

"The army taught me that," she replies, relieved that her fury has subsided

"Whew. You had me thinking you was getting even for them Secesh killing your husband."

"Oh no, Eugenia." Susha pauses for just a bit. "No, the Seceshes that shot my husband were brave soldiers doing their duty. But the major told me all about the bushwackers and the things they do. I suppose I just have the same rage in me that he has for those people."

"I see what you mean. But Miss Susha? You think the major, hisself, would've shot them bushwackers, iffin' he had the chance?"

"Oh no, Eugenia. The major is a man of justice. He would have hanged them, instead."

At Bayou Rapides, John and Frank follow a series of skirmishes and slow advances. And upon attaching themselves to the periphery of the headquarters camp of Colonel William Parsons' Brigade, the two become privy to a bevy of information, including that of the encirclement of Alexandria.

What a bold siege, indeed, where Banks' army of more than thirty thousand strong, along with Porter's fleet, is being invested by Taylor's force of six thousand men. Yet the urge to tighten the vise increases by the day, as the Union forces have entered upon a grand enterprise of engineering ingenuity. In order to allow the trapped gunboats to descend the depleted rapids at Alexandria, a dam is under construction downstream, the hope being that the Red River will rise to a level above the obstructions. There's not a man in Taylor's army who doesn't realize the ramifications of destroying those boats, as well as ensnaring Banks' forces.

In the meantime, there are some spoils to enjoy, as Union pickets have been overrun and a few of their outward camps consumed.

"Jewhillikens. So this is genuine coffee."

During the late afternoon John and Frank sit at their camp, savoring a gift from a 19th Texas captain.

"Easy now, Frank. Sip and enjoy. Those beans are like nuggets of gold."

"They surely are. Think of what we could wrangle from Miss Smallbones."

"That would be up to you, Frank. Personally, I am finished bargaining with that woman."

Suddenly, the sharp, assorted cracks of horse weapons erupt from a distant skirmish, answered by bursts of an infantry's rifle-muskets. There must be a specific objective to this particular fight, as its intensity sounds consistent and its duration stubborn.

"Could be some of the Twelfth's, Major," reckons Frank. "They sure seem close. Jewhillikens!"

Understandably, Frank's enthusiasm is affecting his ability to measure distance. But that still he possesses a zeal perplexes

John. While his private takes careful note of the vibrated air, Major Singleton stares at the young man's folded right sleeve. How could there be any fight left in him, after such an alteration which will leave him forever at a disadvantage? Yet John knows firsthand that the "call to arms" is often too terrible a lure to resist, that were he to cut loose Private Peevy, he'd be mounted with his shotgun within minutes. Although Frank is the last person who needs to see another battle, to keep him away from such may require a great deal of fortitude.

The road to Vicksburg flattens considerably, as it slices through a land of much de-population. Only a handful of the villages can be described as being half-occupied, while several are devoid of people entirely. Few of the fields are planted, with many farm dwellings and plantation homes having been turned into ruins. Nevertheless, as eerie as this emptiness may be, at least it holds some advantages for Susha and Eugenia. No longer do they deem it necessary to avoid the citizenry and their potential inquisitions. Even the threat from bushwackers is sure to be lessened in this region sparse of prey. Although their supply of food is almost depleted, for the pair seeking their freedoms eastward, there's little standing in their way.

With reins in hand and trailing behind over her shoulder, a plodding Susha urges the mule. In spite of the perspiration stinging her eyes and her aching muscles pleading their case, she's determined to push on for two more miles before taking a rest. As for Eugenia, half-asleep she rides atop with the dog upon her lap, they both having succumbed to their worn feet.

They're a blur, those figures in the distance who seem to be milling about the road. As to what they could be up to, Susha squints and searches for a clue, she coming to a stop. Before her stomach churns, however, she spies the hint of a color which might bring a little comfort. Nevertheless, Susha needs a confirmation from another set of eyes.

"Eugenia? Eugenia!"

"What's that?"

"Look up the road and tell me what you see."

It takes a moment for Eugenia to sharpen her sight. "Them men's all wearing blue. They belong to Massa Lincoln?"

Indeed, they do, as Susha and Eugenia soon learn. However, it wasn't long ago when these men were under a different sort of bondage. Be it coincidence or providence, the two young women have stumbled upon an outpost of a negro regiment.

"What you think you be doing, missy?" asks the corporal of an approaching Susha.

Meanwhile, one of his privates spots the carbine and sling secured around the mule's neck. "Where'd you get that gun?"

Susha can only smile, not so much with relief, but at the reaction she knows her tale is about to evince. Soon enough, this picket of soldiers, her comrades, should hear the fanciful worth of several earfuls.

It takes some doing for Susha to convince the pickets of the truth to her story. Eugenia's verification, however, does little for the cause, so that Susha's last resort is to rely upon a demonstration. To be precise, with the aid of a borrowed Enfield, she shows her skeptical comrades her flawless grasp of the army drill, crisply applied and carefully noted. The result is that an officer is summoned, to conduct the first of what should be several interviews up the chain of command.

"Mrs. Potter. You expect me to believe you fought at Pleasant Hill?" inquires the doubting lieutenant, one of many former enlisted men given a commission in a negro regiment.

"Yessir, Lieutenant Greene."

"Then tell me. Who was on your right at the battle?" he asks, while clutching Major Singleton's letter.

"My husband."

"Mrs. Potter, I refer to your regiment's."

"Oh. The Tweny-seven Iowa was on our right and the Thirty-second on our left."

"She being right, Lieutenant?"

"I don't know, Corporal Strang." The reply is snappish. "Mrs. Potter. Who commanded your brigade?"

"Colonel Shaw."

"Your regiment?"

"Colonel Burness."

"Your company?"

"Captain Pillow. Company C."

"I believe her," judges Corporal Strang. "Why she knows the drill better than anybody."

His privates nod in agreement.

"Put a uniform on her and give her a musket, and I bet she makes a fine-looking soldier."

Susha gives a bashful grin at what she takes as a compliment.

"Very well," deems Lieutenant Greene. "I suppose the captain needs to hear of this. And the colonel, and every general he can find. Mrs. Potter, I believe I should even write a letter to my parents." Then he shakes his head. "A peculiar war this has been, Corporal. Just what do you think we might see next?"

To which Corporal Strang can offer only a shrug.

In that Cloutierville is saved from destruction, John nurtures hope of a similar fate for much larger Alexandria. Unfortunately, when lazy wafts of rampant smoke are witnessed from distant Bayou Rapides, the promise of a rescued city is dashed. Soon thereafter, news comes into camp that Porter's fleet has completed its navigation over the rapids, meaning that Banks' army is free to abandon Alexandria, and do to it as it pleases. And because the Union numbers are overwhelming, any withdrawal toward the Mississippi should not be difficult to cover. As for the aggressive moves of Richard Taylor, these can be taken only from the perspective of an underlying weakness.

When John and Frank ride onto the streets of Alexandria, the day after its occupiers have fled, they discover that little mercy has been shown to the former capital. Dark and spindly are its smoldering remains, as if the town has been caught petrified by the horror of its own cremation. The vestiges of a busy riverport are being picked and scratched at by some of its shadowy inhabitants, their need being to find recognizable tokens of their lives. Indeed, the conflict has come to its worst, realizes a disgusted John, when he sees that the pasts, presents and futures of the innocent no longer hold any account. To be sure, the humiliation and degradation of civilians are becoming just another element of modern warfare.

Recovering from their initial shock, John and Frank set about their work. At least one structure is left intact, the Catholic church, whose priest confronted the Union conflagrationalists at his doorstep, shaming them away from the holy sanctuary. For the time being, however, it's not a place of worship, but a house for the many homeless.

The testimonies given to the B.P.L.A. prove to be vivid: tales of rampant abuse and rabid theft, of systematic and haphazard destruction, and of abundant applications of camphene and turpentine. Given no opportunity to gather any possessions, families were forced from their homes, only to have their dwellings looted and torched before their terrified eyes. So contagious was the arson that even the property of known Union sympathizers was burned, indifferent had been the liberators to the protests of their like-minded confederates. As with Rigolet Du Bon Dieu, the common thread to Alexandria's incineration is A.J. Smith. From several sources the general had been witnessed riding through the streets, encouraging his troops to make liberal use of fire, thus performing a definable criminal act. Yet incredibly, as best as John can ascertain, the conflagration of Alexandria ran counter to General Banks' orders, whose officers of the Army of the Gulf were seen trying to prevent the purposeless destruction.

With their interviews nearly completed, John and Frank reach the front pews of the sanctuary. There they come upon a woman in an advanced state of pregnancy, stretched out with her two small children sitting at her side, but with no husband in sight. Immediately, John is stunned by what he sees, but also by that recurring vision born from the arrival of Georgina's tragic letter. That he's powerless to reverse this destitute woman's situation drives a sharp pain into his chest, unable to right just one of the multitude of wrongs. As she opens her eyes with a moan, John kneels to her side, taking her hand and pressing it against his heart.

"Ma'am. My name is Major Singleton. Is there anything I can do for you?" There's an urgency in his voice. "Should I summon a doctor?"

The poor woman manages a smile. "That is kind of you, sir. But I am only exhausted."

"Ma'am, are you certain?"

Again, she smiles.

However, an idea strikes John, as he motions to Frank. "Fetch the coffee."

"Yessir."

"And bring something for them to eat, Frank. All the boiled beef and the Yankee hardtack," continues John, as he pats the heads of the two, little girls with his free hand.

After surrendering their small fortune of coffee beans, John and Frank proceed elsewhere to survey the ruins. Eventually, before dusk, they find themselves at the banks of the river, overlooking the newly built and partially destroyed dam. Predictably, its hasty construction is of filled material consisting of brick, lumber and timber. It seems that not all of Alexandria has been destroyed by fire, and because the dam is the result of genuine military expediency, John's legal opinion tells him that it is no crime. Nevertheless, his mind remains dazed as he stares at the mass of calculated ruin, at the lives and livelihoods which will take too many years to rebuild.

"Jewhillikens, Major. Look at the cotton there," points Frank, to several saturated bales protruding above the water's surface.

That Porter's men have been ravenous for cotton is widely known in Shreveport. Now to see the culmination of their efforts going to waste only adds to the weight of Union outrages.

"It looks as if the gunboats needed to lighten their loads to make certain they could get over the falls. They must have been in a rush." John's eyes give a quick estimate of the numbers. "Or could it be that they were frustrated with their failures? The reason behind all of this."

"I believe you're right, Major." Uncharacteristically, Frank's face sharpens. "Damn, how it gives me an awful itch to get some retribution."

"It would seem that justice demands that, Frank. But I have doubts about our means."

While the B.P.L.A. documents evidence in Alexandria, Parsons' Brigade pushes on, helping to keep the pressure on Banks' retreating forces. Later in the day, John postpones his chronicling of victims' accounts for the more pressing pursuit of their tormentors. Before midnight, he rediscovers the brigade headquarters, and Frank is able to spread his blanket. By contrast, however, John spends his night next to a candle, busily weakening his reserve of paper and ink.

When dawn arrives, he strips down to his vest. Already there's a flurry of activity, intensifying from a night's worth of scattered skirmishes. Yet in spite of the building excitement, John remains somber, the result of a decision-made combined with the losses incurred—both personal and as witnessed.

"Frank."

"Yessir."

"I want you to saddle your mount and report back to me."

"What about yours, Major?"

"Leave it be. I have a pressing duty for you alone."

In a matter of minutes, Frank returns to camp, leading his mount and wearing a keen look.

"Very good. Do you think you are prepared for a long ride, Frank?"

"As long as you want, Major," he replies, as he secures his gear.

"All the way to Shreveport?"

"Sir?" Suddenly, Frank's excitement sags.

With saddlebag in hand, John offers his explanation. "Frank, these vital papers need to be put into safekeeping. Do you understand? Secure this with your life."

"Of course, Major." Perhaps the word "vital" is mitigating Frank's disappointment.

"Wait in Shreveport for my return. But should I fail in this, the finished report may become your responsibility. Consult Mr. Hey about the papers. Trust his judgement."

Understandably, Frank is contracting the same somber mood as John. "Major?"

"Don't worry, Frank. Simple caution." John pauses before he begins the most essential portion of his instruction. "Among these papers is a letter to Mrs. Shackelford. Frank, what I am about to ask of you is not as your officer, but as a friend."

Clearly, for Private Peevy these are flattering words.

"Should my demise occur, I would like you to deliver that letter in person. That is after the war and after you have been mustered out." John pauses. "Is my request unreasonable? Will you do this for me?"

Frank's response is without rumination. "You know I will, Major. You can count on me."

"Of course I can, Frank. I always have."

"But I don't think it's gonna come to that."

"Not likely." John places the saddlebag over the mare's neck. "If you wish, you might stop at Alexandria or Cloutierville. To come upon some additional intelligence."

"Yessir, Major. I might do that."

"My regrets about the coffee."

"I have none, Major."

Appreciating his private's endorsement, John nods with a smile. "Perhaps you should be off." Out of sheer thoughtfulness, he extends his left hand. "I want to thank you for being the best comrade I ever had. Just remember to keep cultivating an independent mind. You're a whip smarter than most, Frank. Too much so to become a follower or leader."

Although showing some perplexity, Frank gives a vigorous shake, after which he mounts his mare.

"You be sure to look out for yourself, Major. I'll be seeing you in Shreveport."

"Don't worry, Frank. You taught me well."

While Private Peevy rides away, John is relieved that he's keeping a promise given to Susha Potter. As for that other vow made at the same moment, he understands now that it may have to be amended.

Since John has let it be known that the work of his bureau is at a hiatus, he's been kept busy. Dashing between the regiments and maintaining contact with the division and the baggage trains, for the most part the major is helping to moderate the shortage of officers

From the day of Alexandria's liberation, Taylor's army has been fighting a campaign of stalling tactics: harassing the Union column, attacking their trains and burning the bridges in front of their retreat. The hope has been that Banks' forces will be slowed enough to allow for the Confederate infantry's return from their

Arkansas adventure. A battle even looms on the Prairie des Avoyelles near Mansura, the opposing forces forming their lines and letting loose with their dueling artillery batteries. In one aspect the allure of the surroundings is matched by the beauty of this particular confrontation, for little blood is spilled to despoil the land. When Banks orders his overwhelming infantry to advance, his adversary is left with no other choice but to back down, thus bringing the battle to an abrupt end. For the Armies of the Gulf and of the Tennessee, the safety of Simmesport, and the Atchafalaya and the Mississippi just beyond, is but an easy march away.

As frantic and desperate as the chase has become, at least this one night affords a brief lull between John's duties. After seeing to his gelding, he curls upon his blanket amidst a grove of black walnut, alone although surrounded by hosts other cavalrymen.

Exhausted as he may be, John's eyes refuse to stay shut for more than a minute. Not only is his head agitated by the surrounding activities, but as well, it's haunted by those visions which cannot be laid to rest. There is, of course, the woman at the Catholic church, who has been driven destitute by calloused individuals in spite of her helpless condition. Who will champion her cause and that of her children, when there are but a capable few in a scorched land of the many needy? John knows full well that his attempt to come to that poor woman's assistance is unlikely to have a lasting effect, that her family's fortune will be years of misery and hardship at best. Like that one particular victim, John, too, has been rendered helpless by indifferent forces, his limitations made severe.

A gentle breeze whispers through the leaves of the walnut trees, giving a sort of motion to the stationary stars twinkling above. Cheerful they are in spite of the abounding despairs, their constant light being a reminder of where eventually all outcomes find themselves.

In time, John does manage to drift away, back to Texas where he belongs and where he should have remained. It's there, from his deepest recesses, that those mirages of memory are evoked of Henrietta McKie and Mrs. John Singleton, of courtship and marriage. Over and over, John's surrendered mind reminisces through the past, from his initial recollections of Henrietta, through all of her impressions which helped to forge the character he carries. Though their years together were few, that span held a concentration of moments, each and all treasurable, even when John suffered as an invalid.

With all certainty, there is an eternity to this, as are the shining stars. At perfect rest Henrietta waits for John—peaceful and calm, and carrying their child as always she will. And so a conclusion arrives, that it matters little to how and when the two of them will reunite, if only because this fate is as true as the heavens.

"Nineteenth! Saddle up!"

Out of nowhere, John's tranquility comes to a sharp end by the call to arms.

"Henrietta," he mutters, as he gathers himself. "Henrietta."

While most of Banks' forces are huddled in what is left of Simmesport to await their transport across the Atchafalaya, A.J. Smith's regiments retrace a few miles in order to secure the rear. And because a pressed-upon Richard Taylor and his generals recognize this as a last opportunity to punish their malefactoring enemy, an ensuing battle becomes a forgone conclusion.

Dry to a state of dustiness and bordered by combustible scrub lies the open ground west of Yellow Bayou. It's into this arena that the combatants are being thrown. The want for Taylor's troops to thwart A.J. Smith's men and push on to destroy those exposed forces at Simmesport is sobered from the very beginning when they're ordered to leave their saddles and form their lines afoot. Although well-armed, courtesy of the debacle at Mansfield, these men understand that dismounted cavalry can suffer a deadly futility when attacking the hardened infantry and artillery of the Army of the Tennessee. Throughout the afternoon, the grumblings and hesitancies run rampant among the ranks and as well from some of the commanders.

For the most part, however, the orders are being obeyed, as regiment after regiment continue to rush into the fray, trying to claw their way into a slim advantage and, perhaps, greater exploitations. All the while, a skillful General Mower, commanding under A.J.

Smith's absence, shifts his confident forces to meet these multiple threats, accepting his share of casualties, but delivering more. With the sere conditions, unintentional fires give rise, adding to the smoke and confusion which always seem to prevail with these affairs. Indisputably, Yellow Bayou is proving itself to be a bloody, if not regrettable, fight.

Just to the edge of all this remains John, carrying out his duties as messenger, adviser and keeper of sanguinary accounts. Through the dense clouds of war, he's been able to discern little on his own, though there are the reports of the direct participants, who enter and return from the opaqueness of battle in ever-decreasing numbers. John's senses tell him that the end is near, that the perpetrators of misery and destruction are escaping punishment. The artillery fire has all but ceased, the musketry becoming sporadic, while an air of relief concerning the campaign's close is blowing in among the survivors.

His shoulders sag at this realization, for John's attentions remain keen for the battle which faintly breathes. It's been a long, hot day, what with the sun beating at a broil and the frenzy occurring beneath it. Having been mounted during the majority of this period, John is worn, with his leg agonizing to the point of losing its feeling. Regardless, others have suffered much worse, compelling him to keep his discomfort to himself. Even John's parched mouth must remain so, for as he tugs at his canteen, he feels no weight.

With his bare arm, he wipes the stinging perspiration from his eyes. However, such a flood requires more assistance, and from a vest pocket John locates Henrietta's daisy handkerchief. What a beautiful spring it could have been, he's reminded, as he gazes at his wife's delicate embroidery, its flowers and leaves bursting forth a renewal. That never came to be, as a winter of much despair has altered into a withering and wilted pre-summer. Ignoring his irritated eyes, John bunches the handkerchief against his nose. For fear of losing her scent, he's never washed it, and now, as he takes deep whiffs, he's able to touch Henrietta's very being. How intoxicating is the fragrance, it blotting out the abundant violence and its vulgar sounds. For all intents and purposes, John becomes lost, wandering miles and miles away from the spilled hatreds of Yellow Bayou.

But there's another scent in the handkerchief, that being of Susha Potter and her tears of mourning, for she, too, left behind a tiny portion of her vivid self. What a blend it all makes, discernable in its individual traits to John's sensitive nose, yet with an undeniable compatibility of its elements. Again, he buries himself into the handkerchief, seizing upon a shortened past whose sands fell full, yet thankful for a future saved. For John, the feeling evinced is one of comfort as opposed to sadness, of a modest measure of success instead of abject failure. Thus the message is received, striking John beyond ambiguity that, for the first time in his life, his obligations are satisfied.

"Major Singleton!"

The sudden call forces John to regain himself, as he spots three approaching riders. Immediately, he recognizes the foremost of the officers as being Colonel Parsons, himself, with his right arm stretched out and pointing southward.

"Major!" With each wearing a look of urgency, the colonel and his entourage pull on their reins. "Assist the captain, over there. His squadron needs encouragement."

Looking to the noted direction, John squints to see a distant chaos of milling cavalrymen, all mounted at the extreme perimeter of the battlefield. Immediately, he's able to comprehend the meaning behind Colonel Parsons' seemingly vague order.

"Sir," acknowledges John.

He spurs his obedient beast, leaving the colonel to his last gasp at coordinating the brigade. However, John is less interested in what could come up from behind than he is of the uncertainty lurking ahead. It's an irresistible lure into which he dashes, his recovering vision staying focused upon the assembling group of Texas cavalry, while his gelding chops at the ground to further cloud the air. Scarcely does either man or mount breathe during their sprint, the tension of the moment having usurped all of the usual faculties.

Soon, John brings about a halt and finds himself in the midst of confusion, to where the captain in question is struggling to maintain control.

"Captain. May I be of service?"

"Thank God, sir." Like the segment of the regiment he's

inherited, the captain is harried and exhausted, attempting to muster some composure for a final charge. "We're trying to bring an attack on what just might be an exposed flank. Over there. Somewhere."

John's eyes are unable to penetrate the smoke and dust. "I see."

"Would you lead my left wing?"

"Of course."

"Form a single rank and keep them up with me in the middle. And we'll see what happens."

"Very well. Good luck, Captain."

In his excited state, John neglects to reconsider the sketchiness of the captain's plan of attack. Nor does he care to give a second thought to the junior officer's suspect ability to command. Instead, John does as he has been asked, and rushes toward that leaderless left wing.

"Where is your officer?" shouts John, as he reaches the far end of the squadron.

The answer is slow in coming, but at least one Texan manages to emerge with an opinion. "I done guess it must be Doboy, sir. That is Sergeant Church. Over there."

"Sergeant Church," hails John.

"Doboy," comes additional shouts.

He could be hardly twenty years-old, the sergeant who has been bestowed the command of his company. "What do you need, Major?" Wearing no insignia, he's accompanied by what must be his corporal.

"Sergeant. Have them form one rank. Guide to the middle of the squadron. I will ride in front, so that they should all keep behind."

The sergeant seems surprised at the command, as is the corporal. "What do you mean, sir?"

"Form a line of attack, Sergeant! Guide to the right and I will be to the front. Wait for the captain's command," repeats John, who rides to his position, ignoring the possibility of any protests.

"Doboy," objects the corporal. "You ain't gonna listen to him. Singleton's not with the regiment anymore. Look at that cane!"

"Shut your mouth, Buck!" Burdened by the suddenness of his additional responsibility, the sergeant hesitates to consider his options, which are few if he sees the other companies forming the line. "Company B! Fall in on my mark! One rank, behind the major! Guide right!"

As the gelding faces forward, John looks over his shoulder to observe the progress of the squadron's formation. It's come down to this, he notes, that the conceivable fate of a nation is in the hands a hundred or so ragged and disinterested soldiers, led by one officer who isn't up to the task and another who always has doubted the cause. The chances of a breakthrough—with a follow up of the destruction of Banks' army and a hierarchy of political futures—are thinner than a hair. Yet at the fore sits John upon his saddle, keen for retribution, while recognizing the futility of it all. Such is an acceptable fate.

By now, the captain is gaining control and has drawn his sword in anticipation.

John would do the same, were he similarly armed. Then again, he does possess an implement which could help point the way, and pulling his cane from his belt, he begins to wield it. However, the ridiculousness of such a scene compels John to think otherwise, his shreds of dignity requiring a different track. With no sentiment other than one of relief, he drops his now useless orangewood cane, to add to someone's collection or take root if it may. Instead, grasping his Colt, John displays it high above his head, readying it to lead the charge and perhaps level its own sense of equilibrium.

The span it takes for the troops to fall in is remarkably brief, and somewhat of a shock to John. Before he knows it, the captain points forward his sword and looks to his superior officer for a confirmation that all is at the ready. Tilting his revolver toward the enemy, John gives it a vigorous wave to signal that, indeed, the moment to give the command has arrived.

"Squadron. Forward. March," shouts the captain.

"Forward. March," echoes John.

The movement is slow at first, as men and horseflesh struggle to maintain the single rank. As it gains momentum, the line becomes jagged, until, when the squadron enters into the smoke of the battlefield, the charge alters into a mad dash.

The maddest of them all is John, out-distancing the rest of the troops, as he closes in on the enemy. A loud volley is heard, but not felt, as Mower's infantry misses its mark. Nevertheless, it's a volley all the same, discouraging to rampaging cavalrymen, who must realize the flank it is attacking is not so exposed, after all. As quickly as it had formed, the attack begins to fade on its own accord.

Not so for John, who can see directly ahead the ranks of two ominous shades of blue. His gelding froths at its mouth, its tongue hanging from exhaustion and its eyes gaped open in fright. Yet nearer and nearer to their enemy do they continue their charge, with the rider hunkering over instinctively so as to make himself as small as possible.

Within seconds those Union uniforms become Union faces, thus reminding John that his Colt is within its range. Without thought, he cocks the hammer of his weapon and points its muzzle toward a target of many, all the while keeping his balance and commanding his mount.

Who would dare care for this place, for to do so would call to question one's ability to reason? Yet John's concerns are overwhelming, all-consuming. This insignificant squat of land has become a treasured field, a splendorous ground worthy enough to make a reckless charge.

Boom! It's the combined flash and noise from dozens of rifle-muskets, fired from a distance which for these weapons is a mere close quarter.

As the gelding collapses from the impact of so much lead, John tumbles from his saddle, flung like a feather in a wind. When he strikes the ground, however, it's with an uncontrollable thud and a helpless roll upon the dust. Coming to a stop with his face to the sky, John lies motionless, as he struggles to regain his senses. But he's unable to clear his stunned, clouded head, or move muscle and bone. Even the commotion and calamity about him carry on unheard. It's all that John can do to draw open his eyes, to see the bleary haze of smoke and the tranquil heavens above. His blood rushes to make fertile the soil, leaving behind that which has been both sharp and vital, fair and charitable. Now those attributes must find service elsewhere, away from a deprived land, to one of peace and plenty. The excruciating pain to be imposed by the Minie balls is too late in arriving, for John's suffering is coming to an abrupt close. Finally, a heart beats no more, thus enrolling with its brethren of many thousands, good people who have stumbled through the darkness.

"Hold your fire!" resonates the command.

"Company. Hold your fire," shouts Captain Pillow.

"Reload and come to order!" continues Lieutenant Warner.

The men of Company C breathe a sigh of relief, realizing that the cavalry charge to their front has fizzled into little more than a feint.

"Damn. What came over that fool?" mumbles Proctor Keedy, as he tears open a cartridge.

"Some chivalry looking for glory," considers Bill Stewart.

"No glory in that," offers Paps. "He doesn't look like chivalry to me." He squints for a keener view. "No. Makes no sense. 'Less he wanted to see us dead more than he wanted to be alive."

"Damn," replies Proctor. "I hope he forgives us for not obliging. Private Stewart?"

"I concur, Private Keedy. I concur."

To the rear of the *East Pike Run's* boiler deck leans Susha against the railing, dressed as she is in a black poplin befitting her passage. With some fascination, she watches as the boat's lines are cast free from its Vicksburg wharf. Suddenly, there's a mild uproar, as the *East Pike Run's* sidewheels begin to churn the murky waters, thus initiating the way upstream. Yet this is a weak distraction, as Susha's attentions return to the Louisiana side of the river, to the land where the greater portion of her life lies abandoned.

Gone is that last semblance of Susha's army past, her issued brogans having been replaced by a pair of newly-purchased lady's bootees. Still, she has retained a trace, the injury to her nose forever to be a reminder. In addition, clinging to Susha's side is the cloth haversack given to her by Major Singleton, still containing her papers, funds and pepperbox.

For nearly a week Susha's story has fallen upon sympathetic ears—from the lowest sack coat of Vicksburg's ranks, to its highest double-rowed frocks. And the unsolicited contributions have been generous, so much so that now Eugenia's middle brother owns the mule and the former kitchen slave, herself, no longer walks barefooted.

Susha had been placed under the care of a colonel's wife, who had extended her previous visit from Davenport into a posting of her own. And what a fine "mustering out" it has come to be, for under the thoughtful and gracious tutelage of Mrs. Swartout, the former Private Potter has reacquainted herself with the wondrous ways of Iowan womanry.

Nonetheless, at this moment of departure, Susha feels the trepidation. Although she longs for Iowa, she fears the guilt of leaving behind Sylvie. As the two of them have trodden upon every square foot of Buena Vista together, the entire landscape shall carry forever his memory. Each patch of ground will remind Susha that Sylvie is no longer a part of it, that their dreams have become unredeemable. Alone she must contend, for Sylvie's soil is in the heart of Louisiana, shared with many strangers, though comrades they may be.

The water below is discordant, its flow disturbed as the *East Pike Run* pushes away from the wharf. Into this busy Mississippi drips a trickle of Susha's gentle tears, lost forever as it's overwhelmed by those mightily apathetic waters. The whistle of the steamboat attempts to drown the noise of its machinery, bidding another farewell to Vicksburg. But when the pilot releases the lanyard, his toot is answered by an identical call, originating from the near-distance.

With her misted eyes Susha looks to the middle of the river and sees a sternwheeler steaming fast upstream. Its agents having located a rich cache, the boat is loaded to a clever excess with bales of cotton, and likely is destined for a railhead on the Ohio River. Although this scene warrants little attention, Susha can't help herself, in that the sternwheeler possesses an as yet definable attraction. Then she spies the name, *Duchess of Brownsville,* the same vessel which had transported Sylvie and herself from Iowa to St. Louis many months ago, and up the Red so recently. Now, it seems the *Duchess* has altered itself from an implement of war into one of its principle causes, as it plies upon the conflict's chief artery with the country's most treasured commodity. Her cheeks still dewy, Susha gazes in resignation, her acquired perceptions shaking her head at what is nothing less than a shameless pity.

14 ↝ A Different Spring

Although prosperity waits for no man, all too often it is delayed by the conflicts of war. It's been a year since the Confederacy's final collapse, and during that span Iowa's finest are returning to their homes and occupations—first at a trickle and then by great floods. Because of the hazards of their service some need time to recover, while others must be resigned to sit aside for the rest of their lives. However, for the most part Iowa's former soldiers have been reacquainting themselves with their civilianships to a remarkable order. Virgin lands are being broken by the plough, creating the need for more mills, with new communities founded and existing ones expanding. Even Des Moines is losing its isolation, as its long-awaited railroad connection regains some of its lost impetus. Then there's Buena Vista, growing by population as its volunteers have come home to create or expand their families.

And volunteers they were, each and every one of them within all the districts of the state. Whatever their reasons may have been for enlisting, the young men of Iowa filled the prescribed quotas and negated the need for a draft. In the end, not a single Iowan had been compelled by law to serve.

Several times a week Eliza Potter takes a short jaunt into Buena Vista proper for social purposes, as well as to make a purchase or two, and to fetch the mail. Since it's too much trouble to hitch a wagon, she usually walks, and as Ethan's legs have grown considerably, he always tags along. Green abounds and even a few blossoms are springing forth. With an open sky and the road a little less muddy, mother and son have opted for a perfect day to take their stroll.

But by the time the two reach Buena Vista, Eliza has to drag herself into Siler's Mercantile, for the burden of carrying Ethan's future sibling is beginning to tell. Instead of lingering for the latest tittle-tattle, she decides to collect the mail and then proceed with her visit to Anna Cox's. At least there Eliza can catch her breath for the walk home.

The letter addressed to Mrs. Sylvetus Potter fails to raise Eliza's brow, yet a glance at the return gives her reason to pause. "Mrs. William Shackelford," it reads, the letter having been sent all the way from Bastrop, Texas. For Eliza, the town is familiar, since Susha had sent there a letter addressed to Major John Singleton only two months prior. However, Mrs. Shackelford's name is a strange one, and Susha isn't one to carry on a secret correspondence. Suddenly, the thoughts of Anna Cox or tired feet are escaping from Eliza's concerns. An urgency sets in, to which she takes Ethan by the hand and rushes toward home.

By kind coincidence, Hezekiah Harber and his sons overtake Eliza with their lumber-laden wagon. Cyrus and Cecil mind not a bit that they've surrendered their seat to an expectant lady, happier they are to walk alongside and take turns mounting a ticklish Ethan upon their shoulders.

"So tell me, Eliza," asks Mr. Harber, a longtime Buena Vistan. "Was Susha able to get all of those bounties and bonuses owed to her?"

"No, I am afraid not, Mr. Harber. Only those that were Sylvie's."

"That is a shame." He shakes his head. "Right or wrong, Susha did play the soldier. She did fight for her country. A country where able men stayed home."

"Oh, Mr. Harber. I only wish more of your sentiment were in positions of power."

"It boils my blood when I see our government ruled by petty parsimony. If only those scoundrels would ever take the chance to meet Susha, they would sink in their shame. Such a fine girl."

"Yes, she is, Mr. Harber. Very fine."

Breaking away from his stable-expansion ambitions, it's

Granger who lifts his wife from the wagon and takes charge of Ethan. But because of her urgency, Eliza leaves her husband behind with the Harbers, making a beeline for the house.

"Susha," she shouts, as she opens the front door.

The response is at best muted, the reason made clear when Eliza enters the kitchen.

"Susha," she whispers.

There she sits upon her rocker, the former Private Potter, applying her toes for a gentle motion. And cradled upon her lap rests eighteen month-old Robert Sylvetus Potter, his heavy eyes succumbing to his daily, afternoon nap, unbothered that his mother's hands are busy with knitting.

"You're back so early."

"Susha. I have a letter from Bastrop, Texas."

"From Major Singleton?" Susha's face opens wide with the news of her long-awaited reply.

"No. It's from a woman. A Mrs. Shackelford. See."

"His wife's sister?"

"Susha. Open it." As Eliza seats herself, she takes the knitting into her own hands and places the letter atop an increasingly restless Robert.

The hands that had been knitting take hold of the letter. However, where once they were so deft at patterning Susha's own yarn, now they are clumsy and unsure. It requires a full moment for her to pry open the letter and even more time to unravel its fold. Still, there lingers the reluctance, brought on by this sudden intrusion of an unexpected pen.

As for Eliza, she's an angel of patience, as well as an adept interpreter of circumstances, who knows an ill harbinger when she sees it.

"Susha. Why don't you read it so that all can be given its peace?"

As she focuses upon the letter, Susha is coaxed by the inviting eloquence of penmanship—such a flaring and fluting of the alphabet. Then there are the words themselves: graceful, yet firm in their flow, ornate, yet simple with their content. But as captivated as Susha may be, the true intent of the letter begins to sink. And so an awful rush of foreboding chills her blood, as the margin about her head becomes dim and opaque.

All the while Eliza resists the temptation to peer over her sister-in-law's shoulder, allowing for both privacy and reassurance.

Still, as Susha continues, she feels as if she's beginning to suffocate with distress. Shifting Robert to her shoulder, somehow her eyes remain fixed upon the letter. With her silent lips keeping pace, the longer Susha reads the more hostile the kitchen becomes, its atmosphere altering to one of constriction. A gasp breaks free, accompanied by a wet, shaky brow.

"Are you all right, Susha?" Eliza can stay silent no longer. "What does it say?"

Never mind that the real damage was done two years prior. What Susha needs at this moment is some sort of remedy—fresh air and sunlight, and wide open spaces for a start.

"Susha."

As she stares sullenly at Eliza, Susha's mouth falls agape. Not a word spills forth, only a faint gesture of "no" pivoting from her head. Suddenly, Susha stands from her rocker, and the letter drifts to the floor, as she makes certain her grip on Robert. With the missive from faraway performing its crux, its neglect gathers no concern, allowing Susha to bolt for the outside kitchen door and the absence of confinements beyond.

At a steady trot she flees, mother and son securing their mutual holds upon one another. Although Robert is a healthy, robust child, for the arms that carry him he weighs but a feather. As well he should, for his mother has endured much: from dirty, back-breaking drudgery, through a cold, wet march of living off the land and a dry campaign ending with her blood-splattered widowhood. Indeed, Susha Potter has outlasted her foes, so that now she can revel upon the miraculously fertile fields of Iowa. For her, the rearing of a child under the pleasant conditions of her brother-in-law's farm requires only a fraction of her strengths.

The air is fresh and familiar, and the sun kind and bolstering. Susha has come to rest beneath the spread of a large, solitary Osage orange, one which has been spared the ravages of Granger's axe at Eliza's urging. Now its twisted bark serves as a backrest, its overhanging limbs being a ceiling of sorts. Thankfully, the tree lacks walls, and the open spaces of Iowa are free to circulate and cast their influences.

In the warmth of his mother's cradle, Robert continues his nap. As his head is huddled against Susha's cheek, his curly, blonde hair bears the streams of her tears. In spite of her dolor, she, as well as Robert, take solace with their joint intimacy—one equally dependent as the other. Then there is the vastness of the prairie itself, it having nothing in common with the crowded, unpleasant hills of the Deep South. At last, with her loved one safe in her arms, Mrs. Sylvetus Potter is returning home.

A gentle wind brings a chill, followed by the sounds of approaching, delicate footsteps. With every care, a shawl is draped around Susha and Robert, and a handkerchief applied to her cheeks.

"Sweet Susha."

Ever discreet, as well as thoughtful, Eliza has allowed for just enough space before pursuing her sister-in-law. Although Susha's letter to Texas may seem to have been an inquiry concerning the return of the pepperbox pistol, which she still possesses, certainly Eliza has sensed the true intent. Now it's being made obvious to her, that, in fact, Susha is attempting to settle the past.

Not that the former Private Potter has been disconnected from her soldiering days. Quite the contrary, for on two occasions George Warner has paid a call, he remaining considerate as to the welfare of his privates. Also, it was only six months prior that Susha attended Paps Hutchinson's wedding in Newton, he having succumbed finally to the conformities of matrimony. Then there was the time that Granger sold two teams of horses to Proctor Keedy and Bill Stewart's growing freight business. In addition, only last November, Susha's dutiful brother-in-law crossed party lines in order to vote for the candidate who was opposing Valentine Pillow. Along with other, smaller encounters, Susha visits her past almost as a matter of routine.

Now the upsetting news, unexpected with its pronouncement of a tragedy times two. And because Susha had anticipated happy tidings, as opposed to an obituary, the shock is multiplied even further.

"Oh, Susha. The poor major."

At first, there's a reluctance to speak. Instead, Susha remains turned away, her soggy cheek buried into Robert's hair, as she continues her soothing, rocking motion.

With letter in hand, Eliza doesn't seem sure as to what to say, to utter the appropriate words and bring about a response. Whatever rests upon the top of her head may have to suffice.

"Mrs. Shackelford wrote that you need not bother about returning the pistol. That its rightful owner thinks you should keep it. What with it having brought you good luck and all."

Of all things, the mentioning of the pepperbox jars Susha's attention. Slowly, her puffy, wet eyes look toward those of Eliza.

"Such a kind man," mutters Susha. "But so forceful on my behalf. Me, a stranger who meant nothing to him. Me, a foe who took up arms against him."

"We can never be too grateful for his deeds," speaks Eliza, as she continues to blot the tears.

"He did not tell me his wife had passed away. He talked of her as if she was still alive."

Eliza continues to console, stroking Susha's mussed hair into its proper arrangement.

"I think the last words I said to him was that I hoped he and his wife were together as soon as possible." The guilt etching itself upon Susha's face is as readable as Georgina's letter. "Oh, Eliza. Had I known."

"How could you have?" Eliza takes a breath. "But at least now they are together, lying at each other's side. And Mrs. Shackelford believes her sister and the major are happy. Happy in their eternity."

"Yes, they are."

"Is that not the best each of us can hope for?"

But Susha's face remains sorrowed and chilled, as if one trouble solved is another gained.

"What is it, Susha?"

"I will never be with Sylvie, again. He's lost from me, forever."

"Oh, Susha. You should not say that." Eliza musters all of her loving logic. "Who is in your arms? Is Robert not the very image of his father? Another Sylvie. Yours to care for. Yours to guide. Will he not become the perfect Sylvie? There may be nothing left in this world of the poor major, but our Sylvie lives on. And for the rest of our lives."

Indeed, it is a reality difficult to deny. And so Susha's face begins to gladden, her tears slowly altering their chemistry to that of joy.

Drawing an exaggerated yawn, Robert begins to awaken from his nap. But his head appears hazy, as if he's not quite sure of his setting. Before the child cries out in fright, however, his hand draws across Susha's face, and his little fingers stroke the familiar bump on the bridge of her nose.

"Mama," mutters Robert, who yawns once more and returns to his nap.

Readers Guide

1. Obviously, sisters Henrietta and Georgina's given names have similar origins. What could this be?

2. What would be the most logical reason for John and Henrietta Singleton to have resided in San Antonio prior to the war?

3. In spite of his wife's apprehensions, why does he feel the urge to hurry his recuperation, so that he can return to his regiment?

4. What are the financial circumstances of John and Henrietta?

5. Surmise, if you may, the actual site where John's brothers were slain.

6. Is there any symbolism behind the carved, orange wood cane?

7. Ultimately, will Henrietta Singleton have her way, and is she acting selfishly?

8. How does a community in Iowa acquire a name like Buena Vista?

9. Is it unrealistic, during an era when men dominated, that Susha Potter can be an equal in her marriage with Sylvie?

10. Do Sylvetus Potter and Emma Pye behave like typical second-born offspring?

11. Is Eliza Potter too worldly for the period setting? She is, after all, a farmer's wife.

12. On the other hand, is Susha's brother-in-law and Eliza's husband's enlistment too sudden? Explain?

13. Have family gatherings changed so much over the decades?

14. Is Mr. Potter—Susha's father-in-law—a bit too familiar? And just what is a "Copperhead"?

15. Can you blame Sylvie for his anger against his father?

16. And what are the motivations behind Susha's own enlistment scheme? Are they realistic? Just how does she manage to get Sylvie to acquiesce?

17. How can Henrietta Singleton's fears of releasing John back to the Confederate umbrella be soothed so easily—this in spite of her pregnancy?

18. Have you ever witnessed the antics of grey foxes? Discuss what the author is trying to pose, and assume that he's had some experience with these creatures.

19. Can slaveholders such as John Gaunt and Francis Simmons be sympathetic characters?

20. Compare Mairead and Eugenia. How similar and how opposite are these two characters, who will never cross paths?

21. Is it really possible for Susha Potter to carry on as a man? And what of her physical examination, and of how she must bunk with so many men? But most importantly, how can she attend to her private functions?

22. Have you ever been put into a situation where you form solid friendships on such quick notice, as do Susha and Sylvie with their messmates? And would you become alarmed if a Pleasent Hill moved into your neighborhood? What about that Lieutenant Warner?

23. And then there is the surname for Captain Valentine Pillow? Was the author being a smart-aleck or is he making an inference?

24. Gentlemen, could you ever fall in love with a war profiteer like Ariadne Smallbones? And ladies, would you ever allow your innocent brother to do the same?

25. During her foray into Mississippi with her regiment, Susha Potter's personal conflicts are exposed—some of which she's had no clue of harboring. Are there any sympathies for this, or, perhaps of more interest, parallels from the reader?

26. Is it far-fetched to think that upon learning of Susha's secret, her messmates agree to keep it as such, even during the invasion of central and northwestern Louisiana?

27. Why does Major Singleton show so much compassion for a captured Susha, as does Private Peavy?

28. What is the greatest irony of Susha's stay with John and Frank's bureau and her eventual return to the safety to Union lines?

29. Other than the news of Henrietta's passing, what incident made it obvious that John Singleton would not see the end of the novel?

30. Will Susha Potter find her peace, and live a life of contentment?

31. Do a count of the solicitous characters verses those who display their otherwise baneful traits. What is your ratio? And what sort of reader prefers this?

32. Finally, are there any genuinely historic figures who make appearances in *A Private and Her Foes*? Name them? Or at least speculate? This is not an easy task. Good luck!

33. Okay, okay, there's one more "finally." In *A Private and Her Foes* appear two, minor characters who wind up in one of the author's unpublished manuscripts, the pair making significant contributions to that unread narrative. Who can they be? Perhaps the eventual answer rests in the hands of the publisher? On the other hand, that the author is shameless, there can be no doubt.

www.ingramcontent.com/pod-product-compliance
Lightning Source LLC
Chambersburg PA
CBHW010747310726
48980CB00004B/391

* 9 7 8 1 6 3 2 9 3 5 1 7 5 *